Tegen Punishment

Inge-Lise Goss

Published by Olivebranch Press

DEDICATED TO PETER

CONTENTS

Acknowledgments   i

Tegen Definition   ii

Prologue   1

1   A New Encounter   4

2   The Hearing   8

3   The Decision   16

4   First Sighting   20

5   Job Begins   30

6   Verifying Identity   37

7   Compound Visit   45

8   A Truth Revealed   52

9   New Problem Arises   57

10   A Missing Tegen   66

11   Gun Range   72

12   Threats Surface   81

13   The Wrong Man?   87

14   An Unexpected Visitor   93

15   Worthington's Niece   101

16	Late Night Plans	109
17	Diversion	116
18	Lies Fade	126
19	A New Player	131
20	Unforeseen Demand	138
21	Quid Pro Quo Agreement	144
22	The List	150
23	Wandering Arachnids	156
24	Informative Date	168
25	Assignment	175
26	Captives	187
27	Gunshot Victim	195
28	The Meeting	203
29	Storage Shed	215
30	Enemies Within	228
31	The Suspect	237
32	Captured Tegens	242
33	False Accusations	257
34	No Traces Left	265
	About the Author	275

ACKNOWLEDGMENTS

My gratitude goes out to my outstanding editors, Jeff LaFerney and Nancy Buford. Their suggestions, comments and detailed edits greatly enhanced my story. As always, I am especially grateful to my husband, Peter, for all of his encouraging words. I wish to extend a thank you to Ernest Walwyn and Debbie Prince, members of the Border's Writers Group, for their professional critiques of my work. I want to give a special thanks to C. Michelle McCarty for generously giving her time to help me polish my story. Last, but not least, I'd like to thank Ashley Fontainne for designing such a unique and exciting book cover.

WHAT IS A TEGEN?

A Tegen is a mutant hybrid species with combined human and spider DNA. Immortal, Tegens possess unique skills: radar-like night vision, retractable climbing claws, venom-ejecting deadly poison needles, the capacity to spin spider-silk, and an innate self-healing mechanism. All Tegen offspring are born to human mothers. Those with the right DNA face a choice upon reaching their twenty-fifth birthday—transform to a full-fledged Tegen in The Tegen Cave or die. Tegens stop aging after the transformation process. To remain in a human-like form, Tegens must consume *venotrolia*, human blood tainted by Tegen mutant spiders, and periodically devour tainted human flesh. A Tegen's only enemy is fire.

The scratch from a Tegen's needles or a bite from one of their spiders results in paralysis and death to any human. No antidote exists.

.

PROLOGUE

Running through the moonlit woods, Fran giggled. "You'll never catch me."

"But I will," shouted her pursuer while he darted between the trees.

She maneuvered through the heavy foliage and ducked behind an overgrown brush. Breathless and eager for the game to last longer, she covered her mouth to muffle her heavy breathing and listened intently for his footsteps.

Not hearing any noise for several minutes, she wondered where he was and leaned around the bush.

"Gotcha!" He grabbed her hand and pulled her closer.

"How long have you been there?"

"A while." He lowered her to the ground and kissed her perfect lips. "Now will you give back my keys?"

"Well…" She planted soft kisses on his neck. "What will you give me for them?"

"A night you won't forget."

She laughed. "I think you've already given me one of those—several times. But never in this spot."

He grinned and started to unbutton her blouse. "That can be arranged."

She gave him a sensuous smile. "Wait a minute. Let me get out of these pants." She stood and unhooked her belt.

He rested his elbow on the ground and gazed at the pretty blonde.

She sprinted away between the trees as she shouted, "You didn't expect me to be that easy did you?"

"Oh, come on, Fran." He leapt to his feet.

She hid behind a tree and waited.

Moving after her, his foot landed in a trap. "What the heck?" In an instant, the rope tightened around his ankle and yanked him into the air, leaving him hanging upside down.

Smirking, Fran stepped out of her hiding place. "I made it just like you taught us yesterday. I did a good job, don't you think?"

"Fran, let me down."

"You look pretty cute swinging like that. I think I'll leave you there for a while."

"I can get out of this."

"Okay, if you can do it in less than ten minutes, you can have your way with me." She giggled again.

"And if I do it in five minutes?"

"Then I'll have my way with you." Fran laughed and dashed away.

Ever since she joined the religious group, she had been curious about the old barn that no one was allowed to enter. She ran to it and stopped to catch her breath. Pulling his keys out of her pocket, Fran succeeded in opening the padlock with the fourth one. She edged the door open and peeked inside. The deserted barn held hay bales stacked along one side. An unusual grouping in one corner attracted her attention. She stepped closer to get a better look.

Brushing some strands of straw from the stack, she felt a cobweb and drew her hand away. A pile of bodies was covered with spider webs. A crush of confusion and fear swept through her. She covered her mouth to prevent a scream from escaping.

"What are you doing in here?" Her pursuer, now free, stood by the door.

She ran to him, threw her arms around his waist, and buried her face in his chest. With trembling lips, she pointed to the stack. "Look...look...bodies...dead people."

"I sure wish you hadn't come in here." He removed her arms from around him.

Horror gripped her features. "You know about this?"

He went to the door, shut it, and lowered a piece of wood into the brackets, locking it. "Yes."

She sucked in a ragged breath. "But...but...why? Did you murder them?"

"No." He moved closer to her.

Her eyes darted around the space, searching for another way to get out. Nothing. She was trapped. "Then…who are you protecting?"

Wearing a crooked smile, he tilted his head. "Let me show you." He strode to the end of the bales of hay, pulled out a box, and carried it to her.

Her mouth became bone dry. Her blouse, now soaked with sweat, clung to her.

He raised the lid on the box and took out a mesh-like container. "The killers are in here."

Staring at the spiders crawling inside, terror closed her throat, and she couldn't utter a word.

Looking at her, he undid the latch that secured the spiders and lifted out two. "You should have given back my keys when I asked for them." He dropped the spiders on her chest.

She opened her mouth to scream, but no sound escaped.

1

A NEW ENCOUNTER

Two hours before dawn, I managed to ease out of Conner's arms without waking him. Tiptoeing around the hotel room, I slipped on my clothes, put my backpack over my shoulder, and eased the patio door open. I glanced over the railing to make sure the balconies below were empty before ejecting my climbing claws, an ability I acquired when I became a full-fledged Tegen. Crawling down the wall, my feet landed on the concrete surrounding the swimming pool.

Moving at a brisk pace, I maneuvered through a seedy part of town with trash littered sidewalks and boarded windows, and then stopped under the awning of a closed pawn shop. Not a soul was in sight. I inhaled deeply, swung around, and decided to go a few more blocks before calling a taxi.

"Hey, baby," a harsh male voice called out behind me.

Not wanting a confrontation, I picked up my pace.

The stranger yelled, "Hey, baby, slow down."

I looked over my shoulder and saw an unkempt man hurrying toward me with a paper bag clutched in his hand.

"How's about a drink?" He held up the bag as an offering.

"Not tonight." I continued walking.

And then to my horror, a black Cadillac Escalade, like the one driven by Conner's men, came barreling down the street.

I ducked between two buildings, followed by the stranger.

The car's tires screeched as the vehicle stopped at the curb.

To my surprise, Kendall, a cold-hearted Tegen enforcer, climbed out of the car. At the same time, the stranger grabbed my arm. The stench of booze on his breath and the smell of pungent body odor reeked from him, almost causing me to lose everything in my stomach.

Kendall gripped the man's neck.

The stranger's eyes closed, and he sank to the ground.

"Sara, get in the car," Kendall ordered.

Not wanting to argue with the man who sent chills up my spine whenever I saw him, I followed his demand.

On the way to the airport, neither one of us spoke. Since Kendall had showed up so conveniently, I figured he had been waiting for me all night. Did he think when I went off with Conner I'd forget my Tegen duty and not leave Baton Rouge to face my impending punishment?

Kendall dropped me off at the terminal and left. I hoped he wouldn't be accompanying me on any of the flights, but that hope quickly vanished when he appeared at my gate. I felt relieved when he sank down in a first class seat while I continued back to the coach section of the airplane.

As a Tegen, I was required to keep my home a secret from Conner. After spending all day traveling in order to evade his possible tails before reaching Bismarck, I felt exhausted when I walked into my bedroom. Two hours later, I found myself wide awake and worrying about the unknown punishment in store for me. I had harbored Wendy, a fugitive Tegen who had broken the prime rule—no killing for revenge or sport. With poisonous venom running through our Tegen veins, killing mortals was easy, and Wendy couldn't control that ability. Her anger unleashed death and, by protecting her, I had placed others in jeopardy.

Unable to fall back to sleep, I dressed and drove to the Tegen administration building, the place set for my hearing in seven hours.

I slid out of my car and sat down on a low stone wall that surrounded the gothic-style complex. Everything seemed serene and peaceful, hardly a place where rulings were deliberated and handed down.

Suddenly, a gunshot rang out.

My eyes opened wider. I looked around but didn't spot any movement.

Another gunshot echoed through the trees behind me, followed by the sound of twigs snapping, leaves rustling, and feet pounding against the hard ground. I jumped up and swung around. An average-sized man, brandishing a pistol, came charging toward me. Kendall was twenty feet behind him. The stranger leapt over the stone wall. Figuring he had committed an offense against Tegens, I tackled him to the ground and the weapon tumbled out of his hand.

As the shooter attempted to retrieve the gun, Kendall grasped the man's wrist.

"Ow," he moaned as I rose to my feet.

Kendall yanked him up. "Blake, a gun? Really?"

"Thought the bullets would slow you down," Blake said. "At least long enough for me to clear out."

From the way they were talking, I assumed Blake was a Tegen and he knew bullets were worthless against our species. They could cause some injury, but those wounds would quickly heal.

Kendall pinned Blake's hands behind his back and slapped handcuffs on them. "Where did you get the weapon?"

"Promised I wouldn't tell."

Kendall's huge frame towered over Blake. His hard, black eyes bore into his captive. "Guess we'll have a little fun tonight after I take care of another matter. Let's see how long you can keep that promise."

"Oh, come on, Kendall, I only have two weeks left in the brig."

"You only *had* two weeks left. That's changed."

"But…"

They continued talking, neither one of them had acknowledged my presence. I slowly backed away. Before I reached the stone wall, Blake turned toward me and smiled.

"Sara Alston." He eyed me up and down. "Oh, yeah, he'll go for you."

"Who?"

Kendall clutched Blake's arm and hauled him across the grass.

Attempting to look over his shoulder, Blake yelled, "Be careful in the compound. Don't cross the line, and stay away from the Baa…"

Behind the administration building, the door to a structure that looked like a Midwestern tornado shelter flew open. Kendall pushed

Blake inside, and the door slammed shut behind them.

Easing down onto the stone wall, I wondered how Blake knew my name, not Sara Jones as I'd grown up, but Sara Alston, the name I'd used since moving into the house of Dr. Lance Alston, my biological father. Had Blake been at one of the gatherings I had attended? And what did he mean by, "He'll go for you?" Who is *he*? A new boyfriend wasn't anything I wanted. Did someone plan to set me up? Blake was a Tegen, so why did he tell me to be careful in the compound? Maybe blowtorches were kept there. Since I had no intention of visiting any compounds, I decided it wouldn't be a problem.

An acrid smell of smoke drifted toward me. I raised my head and saw gray clouds billowing out the chimney of a small, drab concrete building about a hundred feet away, polluting the air.

A door creaked open and Kendall stepped out. There must have been an underground tunnel because I didn't see him entering that building. I knew he'd be the one to carry out Wendy's punishment, a penalty that left only ashes, before my hearing. Could flames devouring her body be causing the smoke? I shuddered.

Tears flowed down my cheeks. Wendy had stayed with me in Baton Rouge, and when she wasn't acting up, I had liked her. I chewed my bottom lip. Maybe if she had received help in managing her mood swings, I wouldn't be sitting here, watching the smoke floating from the building's chimney and fearing what the punishment would be for my crime of harboring her.

2

THE HEARING

After pleading my case, I walked out of the council chamber and sat on a chair while the members deliberated the verdict.

I replayed the hearing in my mind. One council member, Albert Eisner, seemed to have a grudge against me by the way he kept hammering me with intimate questions. Did he think Wendy and I had that type of relationship? Father, who was also a council member, put a stop to Eisner's badgering. I wondered if that would have a negative impact on my sentence.

Earlier, Father told me I didn't need to stick around after my testimony. I could go home and wait to be summoned, but I feared that someone might construe that I was receiving special treatment. Given what went on with Albert Eisner, I decided it was a good decision not to leave the administration building.

Kendall strolled past me and went into a room down the hall. A few minutes later, he came back. I cringed when he sat down on the bench on the opposite side of the hallway. Why was he hanging around? Would he somehow be involved in my punishment? Or did he think I would make a run for it? If that was my plan, I'd have been long gone by now.

"Hey, sorry I'm late." A familiar voice snapped me out of my speculation.

I gazed up at Brett, a Tegen who still believed I was his girlfriend.

He bent down and wrapped his arms around me. "My plane was

late and my cell phone's not working." He sank down in the chair next to me. "Have I missed you." Brett tucked a loose strand of my hair behind my ear and brushed his lips against mine. "How are you doing?"

"The council's questions were grueling, but I think it went okay." Based on the way Brett was acting, I doubted he had been told that I spent my last night in Baton Rouge with Conner. I had expected Kendall to inform him, but Brett didn't show any signs he knew, and I wasn't about to enlighten him.

Suddenly, Father's angry voice erupted from the other side of the closed door, "She won't survive there."

My eyes snapped wide open and panic welled up inside me. I had never heard Father yell before. I swallowed hard. I could feel my stomach churn while my hands trembled. On the way to the administration building, I had convinced myself that my punishment wouldn't be severe since it was my first offense. In that moment, my naïve expectation vanished.

Brett and I looked at each other but didn't speak as harsh voices spilled out of the chamber. The words melded together, making it impossible for me to discern what they were saying. I glanced at Kendall. He remained stoic, not showing the slightest sign that the loud voices disturbed him. Maybe council members often got into heated discussions; with only five members, it sounded like they were all voicing their opinions at the same time. The noise grew louder.

Every muscle in my body tensed. Brett caressed my arm. I wished I had listened to Father. Sitting at home waiting for the phone to ring would definitely have been better than listening to the angry voices spewing into the hallway.

Silence descended. Had they reached an impasse? The air remained hauntingly quiet.

My eyes met Kendall's. I sensed he already knew, or suspected, what my punishment would be.

"Miss Alston?" A black-haired woman moved toward me with a cell phone pinned to her ear.

"Yes."

"They're ready for you now." The woman opened the door to the council chamber.

Trying not to show any fear, I straightened my shoulders and held my head up high as I walked into the chamber. Heavy footsteps echoed behind me. I glanced over my shoulder and saw Kendall entering the room. Was it customary to have a Tegen enforcer present for verdicts?

Then I noticed two vacant seats at the council table. Terror crept up my spine when I realized one was Father's chair. No one had left the council chamber while I sat in the hall. Looking for him, my eyes swept around the room. He sat on a bench against the wall, and Albert Eisner sat about fifteen feet from him. Had they both recused themselves from my case? Or wasn't it by choice?

"Miss Alston," said Gary Willis, the council member who occupied the center seat in front of me.

"Yes, sir."

"You have been found guilty of harboring a fugitive Tegen. The council has not been able to reach a consensus on your punishment for breaking that rule since there has been a special request regarding your sentence."

I took a deep breath, guessing Kendall was behind the "special request." What had I ever done to him?

Willis went on. "Due to the nature of that request, we have decided to allow you some input into your sentence. If you do not wish to consider this special request, we will determine another punishment. Any questions?"

"No," I said, wondering if the "special request" played a role in Father's outburst.

"Please have a seat, Miss Alston." Willis gestured toward the front row. After I was settled, he opened a folder and continued. "Kendall Vickrey would like you to work with him to apprehend Theodore Snyder, a Tegen who has broken several rules and has been on the run for over two years. Most of that time, he managed to evade our radar. We obtained a lead to his whereabouts six months ago when a person ended up dead in North Carolina from a spider bite. The victim had a few broken bones and his body had significant bruising, causing his family to question the cause of death." He nodded toward Father. "Your father was called in to verify the cause of death. In the process, he ran some tests and determined the man had died from poisonous venom, but it came from a Tegen, not a spider. Of course, the victim's death certificate shows spider bite as the cause of death.

"John Darwin, a Tegen enforcer, tracked Snyder to Florida a few weeks later. Unfortunately, Snyder was on to him. Darwin's ashes were returned to us along with a warning note: 'Any Tegen who comes after me will end up like John Darwin.'" Willis flipped to another page, and then looked at me. "Miss Alston, if you have any questions while I'm briefing you, feel free to ask them as we go along."

"Well, I already have several. First, why me? I've met a woman who works with Kendall. Wouldn't she be better qualified for this assignment?"

Willis leaned forward and motioned toward the back of the chamber. "Mr. Vickrey, would you answer Miss Alston's question?"

Kendall strode to the council table, turned, and gazed at me. "Miss Alston, you are very skilled with manmade weapons, and you are proficient in being able to defend yourself without having to rely on your Tegen abilities, which helps keep our existence a secret. My female colleague also possesses those abilities; however, she doesn't possess your physical attributes and tends to stand out, but not in a positive way that would draw Snyder's attention. Does that answer your question?"

Kendall's female associate I had seen certainly would stand out—tall with a muscular build like a football player. "Why is it important to *draw* his attention?"

"We need to get him away from a religious compound in order to capture him without casualties. Naturally, we don't want to broadcast the existence of Tegens in the process. Any more questions, Miss Alston?"

I eyed Kendall, a freakishly tall, sinister-looking man. "And how about you? Won't you stand out?"

"Yes, and Snyder would recognize me. I will remain in the shadows. "

"Then wouldn't it be better if another Tegen enforcer went?" I knew there were six enforcers.

"The other enforcers already have pressing matters that need to be handled."

My eyes moved to Willis. "Since Snyder has been rather evasive, why didn't Darwin have any associates with him?"

"He did. Two. We haven't heard from them since they left here." He thumbed through some documents in the folder. "Calls to North Dakota might not have gone unnoticed. Their instructions were not to contact us unless it was an emergency."

"Using their disks?" I asked, referring to the small round device with dual buttons, carried by all Tegens. The button on the black side was used to call our spiders within a thirty-foot radius. The button on the white side was used to signal for help and sent GPS coordinates to designated Tegens' cell phones.

"No. Snyder is very savvy and has one. Not wanting him to detect they were Tegen, they traveled without their disks and their Tegen rings were well-hidden in garments they wore."

"How about *venotrolia*?"

"Darwin handled that through a third party. To ease your mind, that third party was checked out and didn't play a role in Darwin's demise. As far as Snyder, he takes care of his own needs by obtaining *venotrolia* and tainted flesh outside our sanctioned gatherings."

"How do you know that?"

"From a Tegen who traveled with Snyder and is currently behind bars in our complex."

I figured he was talking about Blake, the man I tackled the night before. "Are there other Tegens with Snyder?"

"No. Everyone else at the compound is a mortal." He glanced at a document. "It's a religious compound, Fellowship of the Good Earth. They use a symbol with the initials FGE embedded in it and believe in getting back to the basics—harvesting a large portion of their food, raising livestock and chickens, weaving baskets, staying off the grid. Their members are carefully screened, and they seldom associate with outsiders. Snyder has been a member for only three months. We don't know how he managed to infiltrate. Our prisoner was captured before Snyder joined the religious group."

"Who's keeping track of Snyder in Florida?"

"Snyder is no longer in Florida. He left shortly after he killed Darwin, and we suspect that Darwin's associates met the same fate. We lost track of Snyder for four months. Six weeks ago, a death certificate issued in Arizona showed the cause of death was the result of a spider bite. Two days later, the cause of death was changed to influenza. We sent a couple of people, Tegens whom Snyder didn't know, to Arizona to check it out. They had state credentials so nothing indicated we were involved. They learned that was only one of five death certificates issued in Sedona during the past few months showing influenza as the cause of death. All of the people who succumbed to that illness were under forty years old. They lived at the compound. All the bodies were cremated."

"Sedona? The tourist town?"

Willis nodded. "Yes. Creating an additional problem. The compound is in the mountains north of Sedona. While our Tegens were checking out the local medical center, three men came in, two sporting beards. The clean shaven man's left leg was wrapped in a bloody towel, and he immediately got attention. One of the bearded men kept looking around and seemed nervous. That caught the attention of our disguised Tegens, and both bearded men appeared to be in their mid-twenties and Snyder's size. They managed to lift fingerprints. Sure enough, one was Snyder. From there, our Tegens did more research—found out about the religious compound, the length of time Snyder had been there, and his alias, Alex Newark. Previously, when we managed to locate him, he used names that maintained his initials T.S. but not this time."

"And my earlier question—who is keeping track of him now?"

"We've hired a private investigation company, mortals, to follow his moves when he leaves the compound, which happens about once a week. They've been given a cover story that Alex Newark's father is concerned about his wayward son and wants them to keep tabs on Newark's whereabouts until the father gets back to the States, which will be in a couple months. Per the father's instructions, the company stationed three investigators in Sedona. They have been directed not to make contact with the subject. Two weeks ago, one of the investigators had an accident. He was climbing with a group when he slipped and fell nearly a hundred feet and landed on a rocky terrain. In addition to broken bones, he sustained a severe head injury and has been in a coma. He is in a hospital in Phoenix. His fall might have been accidental, but we haven't ruled out foul play. His colleagues believe it was an accident and are continuing to keep track of Newark. In case it wasn't unintentional, we don't want to leave them in harm's way any longer than necessary. Miss Alston, that brings you up to date on everything we know about Snyder. Do you have any more questions?"

"Yes. Why did he run in the first place?"

Willis tapped his knuckle on his forehead. "Sorry, I should have started with that. He harbored his girlfriend, a Tegen, who had broken the prime rule. While we were in the process of bringing her in, he took off and killed two people during his escape. Mr. Vickrey will leave for Arizona tomorrow afternoon. Since you lack the training our enforcement teams receive about how to capture a fugitive Tegen, if you take on this assignment and then decide in Arizona it is too dangerous for you to handle, you are free to abandon it and return home. We don't want any more Tegens to suffer at the hands of Snyder."

"If I should take it on and then return home before he's captured, will I be faced with another sentence?"

"No. Your slate would be clean." Willis put the documents back in the folder and held it toward me. "Take this so you can study the case before you make a decision. Your father can answer any questions you might have when you get home."

I stood and took the folder.

"You're free to go now."

Father came over to me and, without saying a word, put a protective arm around my shoulders and led me out of the council chamber.

Outside the building, Brett sat on a bench, checking his phone. He stood when he saw me and headed in our direction with a hostile, furious expression on his face.

"Why didn't you tell me?" he snapped.

"Please, not now." My head was swimming with thoughts of Snyder's crimes.

He grabbed my arm. "Now."

Father stepped between us. "Brett, Sara's had a rough morning. Whatever you want to discuss with her, can't it wait until later?"

Brett's nostrils flared and his lips twitched. "No!"

"Father, it'll be okay. Can you wait for me in the car?"

Father stared at Brett and then trudged away.

"Okay, what is it?"

"Why didn't you tell me you spent your last night in Baton Rouge in Conner's hotel room?"

"Brett, the first time I saw you after I arrived in Bismarck was when you showed up in the administration building. I was waiting for my sentence. You expected me to blurt that out the second I laid eyes on you?"

"I dropped everything in Colorado so I could be here for you.

And you…you've been with Conner. How could you, Sara?"

"I never asked you to drop everything and come home. You did that on your own. Also, we've never had any kind of understanding that we're committed to each other."

"We certainly have."

"No, we haven't."

"So where does this leave us?"

"I don't know." I rubbed my temple. "But I can't think about it now. I need to make a decision about my punishment."

"Your punishment? Don't you know what it is going to be?"

"No. I've been given a proposal but haven't decided yet."

"Your father must really have control over the council. I've never heard of any Tegen having a choice in what the punishment should be. It must be tough." Sarcasm dripped from his lips.

"It's not like that."

"Sure it is." His brow deeply creased and his eyes bored into mine. "Let me know when you have time to think about *us*. Boy, did I have you wrong. I thought we had something special going."

I reached out to touch him. He backed away. "Come on, Brett, don't be like that. I care about you."

"And you're doing a bang-up job showing it." He stormed off.

Feeling dejected, I worried that Brett would never get over my night with Conner. At the same time, I didn't want an exclusive relationship with Brett, but I did want him in my life. I glanced at the folder clutched in my hand, sighed, and went to Father's car.

3

THE DECISION

"Sara, I'd rather you didn't go with Kendall," Father said, driving home.

"I've tracked down criminals and been in precarious situations before. I'd prefer to accept that assignment than sit in a prison cell or have some kind of physical punishment."

"Under normal circumstances, I'd agree with you, but Theodore Snyder is a Tegen. If he suspects your true nature, you'll end up like John Darwin. The stakes are too high."

The gate to Father's house, an impressive mansion built in the southern colonial style, swung open. We drove down the long, curved, tree-lined driveway until we reached the front door.

"Isn't there some way I could disguise my being a Tegen?"

"Yes," he said as we climbed out of the car. "Earlier, before I learned Snyder was living in a guarded compound, I wasn't totally against you assisting Kendall." Father opened the front door. "I had a special garment made for you to cover your upper arms. The material will prevent a Tegen from sensing the pheromones being secreted from your body when rubbing against your arm. Snyder wouldn't be able to detect you're a Tegen unless that garment is removed. There's also a compartment in another garment for your ring to remain well hidden."

"If the garment covering my upper arms will keep me safe and he won't be able to see my ring, then why are you worried now?" I sat down on the couch.

"As long as that garment stays concealed under your clothing, you are protected. But if Snyder suspects you're not a mortal, he might probe more deeply and insist on touching your bare arm." He sat next to me. "There is nothing I can give you to consume that would stop the pheromones from being released when your arm is rubbed by a Tegen."

I placed my hand on his. "Father, I do have a sense of self-preservation. If I believe I might be in danger I can't handle, I'll come home."

"So you've already made up your mind?"

I nodded. "I'm not crazy about going with Kendall, but I don't like hearing about innocent people dying at the hands of a Tegen. Snyder uses his venom freely for his convenience. If someone doesn't stop him, investigations could lead back to us—and threaten all Tegens."

A hint of a smile crossed his face. "I knew you'd feel that way, and like your mother, once you've made up your mind, there's no way to change it." He rose to his feet and took my hand. "Come on. We have work to do."

"Huh?"

"You need a cover story. The only outsiders allowed into the compound are Dr. Worthington and his nurse. He signed the questionable death certificate. You're going to become his nurse."

"And why would he hire me?" I followed him into the den.

"His current nurse has just won an all expense paid, month-long cruise in the Mediterranean. In order to claim her prize, she has to leave on Wednesday."

I smiled at him. "What a coincidence? You never doubted I'd accept Kendall's 'special request.' Then why were you so angry during the council's deliberations?"

"You heard that?"

I bobbed my head.

"It wasn't about the assignment. It was about the possibility that Blake Eisner might accompany you and Kendall. He's the man Gary Willis referred to in the briefing—the one who travelled with Snyder."

"But he's behind bars because of that. Why would anyone consider letting him come? He might aid the fugitive."

"Exactly. But he happens to be Albert Eisner's son, and Albert thinks Blake could help admit you into the compound. He's wrong. Blake would get you killed. He's smart in some ways but completely foolish in others." Father chuckled. "He tried to escape from Kendall using a gun."

"Not too swift."

Father opened a drawer in his credenza, took out a box, and placed it on his desk. "You need to have some nursing skills. I'm going to teach you how to give shots, use a stethoscope, take blood pressure, apply tourniquets, and anything else I can cover before you leave with Kendall."

After sticking the hypodermic needle dozens of times into oranges, Father insisted I use his arm for practice. I cringed, plunging in the needle. He didn't even flinch. Following his instructions, I did it nearly two dozen times. His arms would've been black-and-blue if he hadn't been a Tegen. When I got the hang of it, he moved on to having me find a vein in his arm and slowly inserting the needle. Even though I heal quickly, I still feel pain when I'm shot, stabbed, or slugged. I couldn't help but think being continuously poked must hurt him.

Finally, five hours later, Father put the needles away, and spread out other medical equipment.

At midnight, Father and I called it a day and headed upstairs. In my room, I found four nurse's uniforms, two pairs of white, comfortable-looking walking shoes, and undergarments on my bed. I lifted up a well-padded bra and saw a note attached to a small compartment inside the cup. It read: "Put your ring in here. It'll be close to you, but no one will be able to feel it." I ran my hands over the padding. I'd look two sizes bigger, as if I'd had a boob job. Next, I checked out the unusual sleeved camisole. The soft, white fabric on the sleeves was thicker than the rest of the garment. To make sure everything fit, I stripped, put on the padded bra, and tugged the camisole over my head and down my arms. The sleeves ended right above my elbows. On top of it, I slipped on one of the uniforms. It had three-quarter-length sleeves to cover the protective camisole. I turned around in front of the mirror and thought I looked pretty good in the uniform. It seemed to amplify every curve of my body, which I assumed was by design since my task was to attract Snyder. My eyes moved to the other clothing lying on the bed. There wasn't another padded bra or camisole. "Mmmh," I mumbled, and then figured it was to prevent anyone from discovering my true identity if they rummaged through my things—nothing in the drawers or closet would be unusual. But I needed to bring some regular bras and camisoles just in case someone searched my room; lacking bras could raise an alarm. Then I removed my Tegen ring, knowing it would be tucked away in my bra during the assignment but still close enough to touch. My hand looked so bare. I opened my jewelry box and took out the ruby ring Conner had given me and slipped it on my finger. Admiring the crimson stone, I decided to wear his gift until it was safe to show off my beautiful, black ring again.

Before going to bed, I packed the uniforms and a few other things. Climbing underneath the blanket, I felt a tinge of excitement about my mission. It would help protect Tegens. Then Brett popped into my head. I considered calling him since it wouldn't be possible during my assignment.

My cell phone rang. I glanced at the clock—1:39 a.m. Picking up the phone, I looked at the caller ID. No name appeared, and I didn't recognize the number, but it had a Bismarck area code. I answered, "Hello?"

"Have you decided to go?" The deep, gruff voice put me on edge.

"Kendall?"

"Yes. I'm scheduling an 8:15 a.m. flight. Need to know if I should get you a ticket."

"But you weren't going to leave until the afternoon. Has something come up?"

"The hospitalized investigator died an hour ago. He was found on the floor. I want to visit the Phoenix hospital before going to Sedona."

"Okay, I'm in."

"Meet me at the airport at 7:00 a.m. Do you need a ride to get there?"

"No. I'll manage," I said, not anxious to spend any more time with Kendall than absolutely necessary.

4

FIRST SIGHTING

During breakfast, I gulped down a big glass of *venotrolia*, figuring it might be a while before I could enjoy it again. Then Father and I headed to the airport. On the way, I asked, "Can you call Brett, and let him know about my assignment? He's already mad. I don't want him to think I'm ignoring him on purpose."

"He left last night for Colorado."

"Huh? When did he call you?"

"He didn't. Gary Willis called after dinner. Gary wanted to know what decision you'd made. I filled him in. Then he mentioned Brett had gone back to his job. I didn't ask him how he knew."

A wave of disappointment washed over me. Slumping in my seat, I stared out the window, wondering how I could salvage our relationship—maybe not the way we had once been, but perhaps regain our friendship.

Father stopped at the curb in front of the terminal, and we both got out. "Now remember, if you feel you are in danger, come home." He wrapped his arms around me. "I'll miss your daily calls. But if you should have an opportunity to use a pay phone without being noticed, I'd like to hear your voice." He kissed my forehead.

"Bye, Father. Don't worry. I'll be careful." I pulled up the handle on my suitcase. Entering the terminal, I bumped into Kendall. "I know I can't call home, but will you be able to?"

"I'll keep the council informed as to our progress." He took a large envelope out of his briefcase side pocket and handed it to me. "Your name is Susan Anderson. Everything you need is in here."

"Thanks." I rifled through the envelope's contents, searching for a driver's license. Lifting it out, my picture and a New Mexico address surprised me. "How did you get this so quickly?"

"I made it."

My new name used Sara Alston's initials. "And what's your name?"

"Kade Vance."

Checking in for the flight, I was surprised to learn that Kendall had reserved first class tickets. Maybe that was a luxury afforded to all Tegen enforcers because they had such tough jobs. Keeping Tegen existence a secret while apprehending wayward Tegens required ingenuity, skills, and taking risks. Some of the fugitives might be their friends. I couldn't imagine having to haul off a friend to be punished, or worse, to carry out the punishment myself. No wonder Kendall presented such a cold façade.

On the flight to Phoenix, Kendall explained the game plan. We'd each rent a car. I'd drive to the Red Hills Motel in Sedona. He'd go to the Phoenix hospital to find out what he could about the investigator's death. Then he'd head to Sedona. He'd be staying at the Edgewood Inn, a place close to the targeted compound, which was located in Oak Creek Canyon.

"Dr. Worthington is looking for a temporary nurse," Kendall said. "His nurse is going to be gone for a month. Did your father teach you some medical procedures?"

"Yes. He had me practice giving shots for over four hours. I even know how to give one in the butt. Would you like a demonstration, so you'll know I'm up to snuff?"

A faint smile crossed his lips, which was the first time I had ever seen a pleasant expression on his face. "That won't be necessary. You have a 4:00 p.m. appointment with Dr. Worthington to interview for the temporary position. Information about his office is in the envelope. Read over Susan Anderson's background before that."

"What happens if he doesn't hire me?"

"He will," Kendall said without a hint of doubt in his tone. I wondered how he was so certain since Dr. Worthington had a connection to the compound, not to Tegens.

"Before eight, leave a note face up on your car's dashboard with your room number on it, written backwards—room 311 becomes 113. I'll come to your room and we can discuss how things went at the hospital and Dr. Worthington's office along with how we'll contact each other."

He reached into his briefcase, pulled out a picture, and showed it to me. "That's a blurry photo of Theodore Snyder."

I studied the image of a clean-shaven man with blue eyes and wearing a hat. He appeared to be good looking, but I couldn't clearly make out his features. Below the rim of the hat, I saw blond hair. Under the photo was written "height 6-feet 1-inch." I held up the picture. "You don't have a better focused picture of him?"

"No. Numerous pictures of Snyder were on a CD and also in a computer file. Darwin took the CD with him when he left to capture Snyder. The computer file has been erased. The responsible Tegen is being held in the brig and will be dealt with after this mission."

"What type of punishment will he get for erasing that file?"

"Based on the description the Tegens gave us about Alex Newark, the alias used by Snyder, his hair is now medium brown and he has a beard, which conceals a large portion of his face," Kendall said, ignoring my question. "His eyes are blue, indicating he isn't wearing colored contact lenses. At least, he wasn't when they spotted him. That could change."

"This picture still gives me an idea what he looks like, even if it's blurry." I handed it back to Kendall.

"The investigators keeping track of Newark have taken quite a few pictures of him. We didn't want to establish any type of connection between the investigators and North Dakota. I'll be picking up the photos tomorrow."

Exhausted from sleeping only a few hours the night before, I leaned my head against the window, gazed at the fluffy white clouds below, and closed my eyes.

"Can I get you anything before we land?" I heard a woman's voice say as I began waking up. To my shock and horror, I found myself snuggled against Kendall.

"Oh." I sat straight up. "Sorry," I said to the man who sent chills up my spine.

The flight attendant looked at me. "Would you like something to drink?"

"Water, please."

Embarrassed to look at Kendall, I stared out the window and drank the water.

A half an hour later, the plane touched down in Phoenix. We gathered our luggage and headed to the car rental counter. Glancing at the local time, I felt relieved that I had acquired two additional hours due to the time zone change, plenty of time to drive to Sedona and easily make my appointment.

At 3:55 p.m., I walked into the foyer of the medical center that housed Dr. Worthington's office. At the reception desk, a woman with a warm smile told me to take a seat until I was called.

I picked up a magazine and sat down among a few patients waiting for their appointments. By the time I was thumbing through the third magazine, a tall, casually dressed man with a nicely trimmed beard strode toward the reception desk. While the receptionist pounded on her keyboard, the man turned around. His eyes seemed to fix on me, but he could've been looking at something behind me. Then he said something to the receptionist, walked away, and took a seat on a row that faced me.

Flipping pages without really reading them, I sensed the man staring at me. As I wondered if it was because he found me attractive or if he was eyeing me for another reason, a middle-aged woman wearing a nurse's uniform appeared in a doorway near the reception desk.

"Alex Newark," the nurse called out.

Holding the magazine up higher and forcing myself not to show any emotion, out of the corner of my eye I saw the bearded man vacate his chair and head to the doorway where the nurse stood. I had been told Snyder hardly ever left the compound, and the doctor went there if medical needs arose. What was he doing here? Tegens didn't need to see doctors. At least I knew firsthand what my target looked like, sporting a beard and dyed hair.

Fifteen minutes later, he walked through the foyer and briefly glanced at me on his way to the exit.

I waited another twenty minutes before the nurse opened the door and called, "Susan Anderson."

I followed her into an inner office with a name plate on the door—"Dr. Worthington."

"The doctor will be with you shortly," the nurse said and turned on her heel.

Sitting down in a chair facing his desk, I had the urge to look through the stack of papers on it. I stood up and went toward the framed credentials hanging on the wall behind his desk. Looking over my shoulder, I noticed a note stuck to a folder. From my angle, I couldn't read all of it, but I did see "FGE" written on it, which I knew from the documents I had read stood for "Fellowship of the Good Earth." Straining my neck, I picked up the word "body" with "Thursday" underneath it.

Footsteps pounded on the tile floor, and the sound kept getting louder.

I swung my head around and stared at the framed credentials hanging on the walls.

"Sorry, to keep you waiting, Miss Anderson," a raspy voice said behind me.

I turned around and saw a gray-haired man who appeared to be in his sixties, wearing a white lab coat. "Very impressive credentials, Dr. Worthington. I've worked with a couple of doctors who graduated from the University of California Medical School in San Francisco. They speak highly of it."

"Probably wouldn't know them. I've only kept in contact with a few of my fellow students, and they're practicing back East. Please take a seat, Miss Anderson." He gestured toward the chairs on the other side of his desk.

I circled around him and sat down.

"It's been one of those crazy days that happen so often on Mondays," he said, easing down in his chair. "Too many emergencies." He gazed at me. "Have you been in Sedona long?"

Susan Anderson's résumé stated she had been working in a hospital in Albuquerque. "No. I just arrived a few hours ago."

He sifted through a stack of folders on his credenza and pulled one out. He opened it and took out a document. "According to your application," he said—and I wondered who had completed it—"you held your prior job for four years, and you want to relocate to Sedona permanently."

"Yes."

"You more than meet the qualifications I'm looking for. You do realize this is only a temporary position? My nurse will be out of the country for a month." He smiled. "She won a fabulous trip."

"I know it isn't a permanent position, but I'm hoping that something else might open up during the month. Of course, if you hire me, I won't leave your employment until your nurse returns."

"I'm glad to hear you say that. It's confusing to patients—and me—when new nurses keep appearing. How soon can you start?"

"Right away."

"Good. Janice, my nurse, can show you around tomorrow, her last day before she takes off. Be here at 8:00 a.m. Our first patient appointment is at 8:30."

I rose from my chair. "Thank you, Dr. Worthington."

He walked around the desk and shook my hand. "And thank you, Miss Anderson. I hope you like it in Sedona. I certainly do."

"Please call me Susan."

"Okay, Susan. See you tomorrow."

With that task accomplished and feeling pleased I had seen the fugitive Tegen, alias Alex Newark, I went to the store to pick up a few things before returning to the motel.

Since I had been told to leave a note on my dashboard before 8:00 p.m., I had assumed Kendall would show up around that time. Instead, I was still waiting for him two hours later as my stomach growled for *venotrolia*. I had gulped a glass of it at breakfast and normally wouldn't need it this soon again, but nothing about the day had been normal.

Leaning back in my chair, I thought about Snyder, alias Newark, eyeing me and hoped he didn't already suspect I was a Tegen. Blake Eisner, a former and maybe still a buddy of Snyder's, knew my name. Had someone circulated my picture? But why?

A tapping sound drifted from the bathroom.

I went to check it out and saw the shadow of a person outside the bathroom window, something unusual for a second story. Figuring it had to be Kendall, I slid the window open. "There is no way you can fit through this window."

"Open your door. I'm going over the roof."

"Okay." I closed the window, hurried to the front door, and

swung it open.

Within a minute, Kendall stepped into my room and shut the door behind him. "The stairwell is next to the office. Didn't want to go by there."

Seeing his backpack, I asked, "Did you bring any *venotrolia*?"

"Thirsty already?"

I nodded, anxious to taste the energizing liquid.

He moved to the table in the corner, dropped his backpack on it, and pulled out a thermos. "Here." He handed it to me.

I unscrewed the top and took a sip. "Thanks. Do you want any?"

"No. It's all yours." He strode around the motel room. "Fridge, a little kitchenette, but not a safe place to keep *venotrolia*."

"Did you bring any spiders?"

"Yes. Like I said earlier, Snyder—I guess it's Newark now—knows I'm a Tegen. No reason to pretend otherwise." He sank down in a chair by the table. "How did it go?"

"Want a beer or anything before we get started?"

"A beer."

I got one from the fridge and gave it to him. "It went well. I start tomorrow. While I was there, Alex Newark came in to see the doctor."

Kendall tilted his head. "How do you know that?"

"A nurse called his name, and he marched through the door leading to the examination rooms and the doctor's office. Any idea why he paid the doctor a visit?"

Kendall shook his head. "You sure it was him?"

"Do you think there's more than one bearded guy named Alex Newark in town?"

"The hired investigators claim Newark hasn't left the compound for two days."

"Well, then, there are either two Alex Newarks or he's getting away from the compound without being noticed or the investigators aren't very good. Does the place only have one entry and exit spot?"

"To reach the compound, you have to cross a private bridge that stretches over a river gorge. A guard gate is on the other side. It's surrounded by two six-foot chain-link fences with barbed wire running along the top. The inside fence has signs on it that say, 'Warning: Electrified Fence.' The fences run between trees and foliage. From a distance, they're not very noticeable."

"That sounds like a prison. Are they trying to keep the people in or uninvited guests out? Is it possible to climb up one tree and move to the branch of another one that's outside the fences?"

"Most of the trees near the fences are on the outside. None are situated so that would work. But a Tegen could climb up a tree, eject webbing, swing over the fences, and land on the ground. It would be difficult to avoid touching the fence when leaving, but not impossible. The worst that could happen to a Tegen is getting shocked. Most likely, it would short out the electrified fence and draw attention."

"He might've gotten out that way."

"Yes, but I doubt he could do it without being noticed. Inside the fences are several large buildings, a green house, a small chapel, a chicken coop, a barn, and three or four other structures. People were milling around. Didn't see anyone trying to escape. Blowtorches were leaning against some of the buildings."

"Prepared for unwelcome Tegens?"

"Looks like it."

"That place doesn't sound all that holy. Is it possible something else is going on there besides pursuing religious freedom?"

Kendall shrugged and gulped his beer.

I took another sip of *venotrolia*. "What did you learn at the hospital?"

"The hospital staff has concluded that the man became disoriented as a result of his head injury and tried to get out of bed, slipped, smacked his head on the floor, and died. The scene had been cleaned up. Nothing to find. No one has requested an autopsy to confirm cause of death. Dead end." He dug into his backpack and pulled out a cell phone and a small laptop computer. "These are for you. I have the phone number, but I'll only call in case of an emergency."

"Emergency—like he's onto me, and I have to get out fast?"

He nodded. "Not out of town, but head to a public place. There could also be other types of emergencies."

"Like you're in danger," I said, doubting Kendall could ever be in danger.

"That's always a possibility. Remember what happened to Darwin. He was also an enforcer. No one is indestructible." Kendall took a small piece of paper out of his pocket and put it on the table. "My number and the number of a Tegen in Flagstaff are on this. Memorize the numbers, and then burn the paper. Don't call unless it's an emergency. Your phone could fall into the wrong hands. Only put in numbers that won't cause any concern if they were seen. Any number with a Bismarck area code would raise a red flag."

"Are we going to meet daily for updates?"

"Often. Maybe not daily. If you need to talk to me, leave a blue sheet of paper on your dashboard."

Blake popped into my head. "How did Blake know my name?"

"When I found him, he was snooping around in the administration building and had a folder in his hand. Your picture was in it."

"Did the folder contain your 'special request'?"

"Yes."

"Any possibility he faxed it to someone, or somehow distributed it before you caught him?"

He studied my face. "No. Why?"

"Newark, or his namesake, kept staring at me at the medical center while he waited to be called."

"Blake wouldn't have had enough time to do that. It's doubtful he even knows how to work a fax machine, and he had no idea how to reach Snyder, alias Newark. They split company when Snyder left Florida. As far as Newark staring at you, it fits right into the plan. He'd be attracted to you and want to get acquainted. Then when the opportunity arises, you can draw him away from the compound. We need to take this slowly. We don't want innocent bystanders killed in the process. Newark has to believe you're a mortal and not have an inkling he's in danger when we move in to capture him."

"The morning I tackled Blake, he yelled at me to stay away from the compound. Maybe when he was captured, he didn't know where Snyder was, but he would've learned that when he saw your 'special request.' Any possibility Blake could find a way to contact Snyder?"

"No. His movements are very restricted in the brig." Kendall briefly lowered his head and stared at the floor. "Moving on, every morning there'll be a covered Styrofoam coffee cup in your car. It will contain *venotrolia*. Daily could be more often than you want, but you might need the extra energy. Drink it while your car is still in the parking lot. Discard the container in the garbage can situated at the end of the first level of motel rooms."

"Do you want me to get you a key to my rental?"

He shook his head. "Not having a key isn't a problem. Have you got any questions?"

"I can't think of any more right now."

Kendall grabbed his backpack and headed out the door without saying another word. Gazing at the closed door, I said, "Goodnight," to no one.

5

JOB BEGINS

I arrived at the medical center ten minutes early. The front entrance was locked. I peered through the glass pane. A few people milled about inside. I knocked on the glass. A heavyset, short man wearing green medical scrubs came to the door. He said something I couldn't make out through the closed door and motioned toward the side of the building. Guessing the building had another entrance for the staff, I walked around the structure and saw a woman open a door in the far corner. Moving that direction, I noticed a white van with its side door standing wide open. No one climbed out or in the van as I reached the back entrance and went inside the medical center.

I headed to Dr. Worthington's office and found his door locked. Turning around, I missed bumping into him by a few inches. He carried a paper sack, which I assumed held personal items. "Good morning, Dr. Worthington," I said as he stepped around me. He unlocked his door, hurried inside, and stuck the bag in the bottom drawer of his desk.

"Good morning, Susan." He sounded out of breath. "Janice should be at the nurse's station down the hall." He motioned that way. "She'll help you get started."

His behavior piqued my curiosity about the sack. Walking away from him, I made a mental note to check it out later.

"Hello, hello," said the middle-aged nurse with short, brown hair who had escorted me into Dr. Worthington's office the prior day.

"Oh, Susan, I'm so glad he hired you for my job. I was getting really worried he wouldn't find anyone before I left." A big grin curved her lips. "Did he tell you about my prize—a month-long cruise in the Mediterranean for two…all expenses paid. It's a dream come true! To tell you the truth, I can't even remember entering the contest." She chuckled. "But I enter so many of them that's not a surprise."

"Congratulations. I've entered a lot of contests and never won anything." I held up my purse. "Is there any place I can put this?"

"Sure, honey." Janice opened a bottom cabinet that already had one purse in it which I figured belonged to her. "Just put it in here. It'll be safe."

I pushed my purse into the cabinet.

"We share this nurse's station with Dr. Wilson's nurse, Mary Ann. She sits on that side." Janice pointed to the area behind her. "Mary Ann just had extensive foot surgery. She isn't scheduled to be at work for another five weeks. Dr. Wilson only works part-time in Sedona— Wednesdays and Fridays—and he's made arrangements with another nurse here to help him out when he's in Sedona. So you'll be the only one in this nurse's station while I'm away.

"I want things to go smoothly for Dr. Worthington when I'm gone and made some notes to help out whoever filled in. He's such a wonderful man." She picked up a small binder and handed it to me. "It's all in here. I've written down where you can find various supplies, how to handle emergency calls, stuff about the patient files, and some things about the computer system. You can't get computer access until you've been set up as an employee. Patients will start coming soon. The human resource department is on the second floor, Room 220. They're expecting you. Just come back here when you're finished."

A half an hour later, I left HR, sporting my name tag on my uniform and carrying a folder that contained information to get on their computer system, a health insurance application, and a brochure about their retirement fund. The latter two items seemed unnecessary to give a temporary employee, but it was protocol.

"Now you're an official employee." Janice touched my name tag. "Before the next patient arrives, let's get you set up on the computer."

Following her instructions, I punched in the ID listed on a sheet in my personnel folder and created my password. The system only gave me access to Dr. Worthington's patients' files. I felt anxious to search for the one belonging to Newark, but with Janice hovering over me, that would have to wait.

All morning I shadowed Janice and anticipated having some free time during lunch to do a little snooping around. That wasn't to be. A few of the nurses were taking Janice out to lunch for her last day before the big trip, and she insisted I come along. Since I needed to blend in, I didn't refuse.

Shortly after we returned to the clinic, Dr. Worthington came to the nurse's station. "I'll be back in twenty minutes. Just have the next patient wait in the lobby until I return."

"Will do," Janice said as he rushed off. "He has a new puppy. His wife calls whenever the little thing misbehaves. It probably got into something again." She picked up a folder. "Can you put this on his desk? He needs to write up some prescriptions."

"Sure." I took the folder, thinking this was my opportunity to search his desk. After laying down the folder, I tried opening his bottom desk drawer, the drawer he had stuffed a sack in earlier. It was locked. Using a paperclip, I picked the lock. Staying alert for the sound of footsteps heading my direction, I slid the drawer open and looked in the sack. It contained a plastic bag filled with a white powdery substance. It reminded me of cocaine, but I couldn't imagine the doctor being involved with illegal drugs. Wanting to know what it was, I carefully opened the bag, scooped a little in my palm, and quickly sealed it up again. Using the paperclip again, I locked his desk. Leaving his office with the substance secured in my fist, I ran into Janice.

"You've been gone for a while. Is everything okay?"

"Yes. I bumped into the desk and the folder fell out of my hand. I've been picking up all the documents."

"A couple of out-of-state lab reports we received for a patient haven't been entered yet. I wanted to show you how we do that."

"I need to make a quick visit to the restroom first."

"Hurry," Janice said.

I walked at a brisk pace to the ladies' restroom, went into a stall, took a wad of toilet paper, and put the substance in it. I wrapped extra paper around it and eased it into my pocket.

Returning to the nurse's station, I sat down next to Janice and asked, "Do I enter the lab reports before Dr. Worthington sees them?"

"Oh, no. All lab reports go to him first. After he's reviewed them, he drops them in that basket." She pointed to one that had the name "Janice" on it. Then she proceeded to explain the process of entering the reports into the patient's file.

"I'm back," Dr. Worthington said, going by the nurse's station.

"I'll go get your next patient," Janice said, walking toward the lobby door with me right behind her.

When that patient was situated in Room #3 and ready to see the doctor, Janice and I stepped into the hallway.

"Let's reverse roles," she said. "You go get the patients and take care of them based on the reason for their appointment, like you've observed me doing all morning. You'll learn more that way."

The afternoon went by quickly as I dealt with the patients while Janice watched.

When the last patient left, she said, "You did great. You were so sweet with little Jack when he ran to the door because he didn't want a shot. I feel like I'm leaving Dr. Worthington in good hands." She opened the cabinet and took out her purse. "Do you want me to get your purse, too?"

"No. I think I'll sit here for a while and read over the binder you gave me."

"See you in a month."

"Have a good trip."

"Thanks. I want to say bye to Dr. Worthington." Janice headed down the hall.

Finally, I got on the computer without anyone nearby and quickly pulled up Alex Newark. My eyes widened as I read that his latest visit to the doctor was a follow-up to a laceration on his shoulder that he received a week prior. "Huh," I mumbled. He couldn't be Snyder; Tegens heal quickly. Then I noticed Dr. Worthington had entered the information about the laceration. Was it just a cover-up to see the doctor?

"How was your first day, Susan?" Dr. Worthington asked from somewhere behind me. I minimized the file on the screen, turned around, and saw him walking toward me.

"Good…good. Janice got me off to a good start."

"Glad to hear that." He came closer and glanced at the patient chart lying next to the computer. "Oh, you're updating the patient files with today's visits. You can do that tomorrow. No need to stay late."

"I'm almost finished. I want to start fresh tomorrow."

"Suit yourself, but don't stay long. The back entrance will be locked at six-thirty. After that, the security guard will have to let you out. Have a nice evening," he said, walking away.

"See you in the morning."

As soon as the doctor was out of sight, I maximized Newark's file and continued reading through it. He recently had a flu shot. He had been given prescriptions and had an x-ray for a sprained ankle. Then I saw his completed new patient form, dated two years earlier. I shook my head. Newark can't be the right guy. Why did the prior Tegens who had been to Sedona believe he was Snyder? Fingerprints. Two bearded guys had come in with the injured man. Snyder must have been the other guy.

With my mind racing over how to track down the fugitive Tegen, I shut down the computer, grabbed my purse, and left the medical center.

I pulled into a slot at the motel parking lot, reached in my shopping bag, and took out a pad of blue paper. I tore out a sheet, folded it in half, and placed it on the dashboard and then went to my room.

After warming up leftovers from the night before, I sat at the table and ate while I skimmed through my newly acquired pocket-sized book on medical terms. Then I heard a tapping on the bathroom window. I hurried to it and slid it open.

"Open your door," Kendall said.

Within a few minutes, he was sitting at the table, drinking a beer while I finished off my pizza. "Sure you don't want a piece?"

"Yes." He watched me devour the last bite. "What do you need to talk to me about?" He dug in without even asking how my first day of being a nurse went.

I stood, got the small bundle of toilet paper out of my purse, and laid it on the table. "What's in this?"

He touched it. "Ah, is something wrong with the toilet paper at the medical center?"

"No...no." Trying to prevent the substance from falling out, I carefully spread open the toilet paper and pointed to the white powder. "That."

Kendall tilted his head, tapped his index finger on his tongue, and pushed it into the substance. He raised it and licked the powder. "Cocaine." He gave me a puzzled looked. "Does this have anything to do with Newark?"

"I don't know." I told him where and how I had obtained it.

"Dr. Worthington is into drugs?"

I shook my head. "He doesn't seem like the type…but what is the type? I have no idea how he got it or what he intends to do with it. And I don't know if it has anything at all to do with this mission. But I did learn today that Newark is *not* Snyder. Newark has been Dr. Worthington's patient for over two years. He's had a sprained ankle and a cut on his neck that required medical attention. He's *not* a Tegen."

He reached in his backpack, pulled out several pictures, and handed them to me. "Is this the man you saw at the clinic?"

I looked at the image of the bearded man. "Yes. That's the Alex Newark who's one of Dr. Worthington's patients."

"The documents you saw there might be part of his cover-up."

Wondering if Kendall could be right, I said, "I guess it's possible, but they sure look authentic. The Tegens that were here earlier—when they got his fingerprints—could they have been mistaken they were his and not the other bearded guy with him?"

Kendall sat quietly, staring at the table, like pondering the possibility. "They did get two sets of fingerprints. I'll have someone find the name of the man who belongs to the other set."

"Did you discover anything more about the compound? I'm still having a hard time believing it's a religious group that lives there. With the secure fencing and guards, I just don't buy it."

"If something else is going on there, Snyder didn't set it up. That compound was around before he joined the group." He took a long swig of his beer. "One building is loaded with weapons and ammunition," he said casually.

I narrowed my eyes and wrinkled my nose. "Huh? Are they some kind of militia group?"

He shrugged his shoulders.

"Did you swing over the fence to see that?"

"Yes."

"Did you have a problem leaving?" I asked, wanting to know in case I decided to do a little exploring.

"Saw a stepladder leaning against a building. Stood it close to the fence. Used it to help me avoid the electrified fence on my departure."

"Won't someone wonder why a ladder is near the fence?"

"Given the distance between the two fences and the tree, I doubt anyone will suspect someone used it to escape."

"How about the Tegen inside?"

"If it is brought to his attention, he might be concerned, but more than likely he would just shrug it off."

"Do you think it would be possible for a mortal to use the same method?"

"If they could swing a rope over the closest branch, which is at least ten feet above the fence and about four feet away, they could manage to leave. But there are sensors on the outer fence and cameras placed inside the compound pointing toward the fences."

"Then how did you manage to get in and out without being detected?"

"Found a blind spot."

"And where is this blind spot?" I asked, trying to pry as much information out of him as possible.

His dark eyes bore into me. "Sara, you're not going in that way."

"What if I needed to get out?"

Kendall's eyes dropped to the floor for a minute. Then he raised head and said, "It's behind a shack near the back of the compound." He rose to his feet. "I need to check something out," he said, going to the door. "Unless you leave a slip of blue paper on the dashboard, I won't be seeing you tomorrow."

"Okay." I watched him leave.

Lying in bed, I thought about Newark's medical file. I doubted it wasn't legitimate, but somehow I had to find out the truth.

6

VERIFYING IDENTITY

The next day at work, I placed my medical terminology book in the drawer underneath the computer and put my purse in the cabinet. Checking over the list of appointments, I had some questions. I went to Worthington's office and tapped on his door. No answer. I gripped the door handle and slowly eased it open as I said, "Dr. Worthington?" He wasn't there, but his medical bag sat prominently on his desk.

Figuring he was somewhere in the building, I wandered around and found him in the break room drinking coffee with another doctor. "Good morning, Susan. This is Dr. Wilson. You share a nurse's station with his nurse, Mary Ann, but she's out on sick leave. You probably won't get a chance to meet her."

Dr. Wilson, a middle-aged, bald man, stood up and extended his hand toward me. "Happy to meet you, Susan."

"Glad to make your acquaintance," I said, shaking his hand. My attention moved to Dr. Worthington. "I have a couple of questions about two of this morning's patients I'd like to discuss with you."

"You can talk in front of Dr. Wilson." Worthington sipped his coffee.

"They're coming in for vaccinations. Do you want to see them, or should I just handle it?"

"I don't need to see anyone that just needs a shot. I'm sure you can take good care of those patients."

"Then I'll get ready for them," I said and headed back to the nurse's station.

The morning seemed to fly by, but I often had to pretend I understood what Dr. Worthington was talking about, even though I didn't have a clue. He didn't show any sign that he had picked up on my inexperience.

I ate lunch at the nurse's station while I tapped on the keyboard, looking for other patients who lived at the compound. I attempted to search by address. Nothing came up. Then I began clicking on each of Worthington's patient's files. They were in alphabetic order. No one with a last name beginning with an A or B had the same address as Newark. Starting the C's, I sensed someone near the nurse's station and looked that direction. There stood Newark himself, wearing a smile on his face. With an uneasy feeling vibrating through my body, I asked, "May I help you with something?"

"Yes. I'm desperately in need of company while I drink a cup of coffee."

I returned his smile. "And the doctor sent you to me?"

"No. I heard you were working here and snuck in."

"Well, Mr...?"

"Alex Newark, and you're Dr. Worthington's new nurse, Susan Anderson."

"And how do you know that?"

His smile widened. "I saw you in the lobby and asked Janice. She figured you'd get hired for the job." His eyes dropped to my chest. "And that's the name on your name tag."

I glanced at his hands. No Tegen ring, but that didn't necessarily mean he wasn't one. He could have been hiding his ring just like I was. "Newark? You're one of Dr. Worthington's patients?" He nodded, and I went on, "And he's been seeing you for a cut on your shoulder?"

"How do you know that?"

"I sat next to Janice while she updated your medical file."

"Now that we know each other, how about that cup of coffee?"

I checked my watch. "Can't. The two o'clock patient will be here soon."

"How about after work?"

"Sure. Why not?"

"Five-thirty?"

"That works."

"I'll pick you up in the parking lot," Newark said and then strolled toward the back exit.

Dr. Worthington approached the nurse's station. "Does he have an appointment today?" he asked, fidgeting with his watch and looking at Newark walk away.

"No."

"What was he doing here?"

"He came to see me."

Worthington cocked his brow. "You know him?"

Shaking my head, I noticed a grim expression on Worthington's face and wondered why. "No, but we were both waiting in the lobby at the same time on Monday," I said, hoping that would end his questions.

Without saying another word, he spun around on his heels and hurried back to his office.

Before I left to meet Newark, I put on a lightweight sweater to cover part of my uniform so it didn't stand out. Walking out the back exit, I saw my date leaning against a white pickup truck.

Newark strode toward me. "How about a beer instead of coffee?"

"Sounds good. I'll follow you there," I said, remembering what happened to the other Tegens that crossed Snyder's path, and I could be mistaken that Newark wasn't him.

He tilted his head. "I thought we'd drive together."

"I don't want to leave my car here."

"Okay, have it your way."

He drove to a bar in the middle of town and parked. I pulled into a slot a few cars away. Newark escorted me into a busy establishment. He knew the hostess and scored us a private table near the back.

After we placed our orders, his cell phone buzzed. He yanked it out of his pocket and looked at it. "Sorry, business." Newark stood, and while he moved toward the restrooms, he said into his phone, "Don't leave the compound. The problem…."

The barmaid placed two glasses and a pitcher of beer on the table.

"Thanks," I said as she hurried off to another table.

For a minute I wondered if I should pour or wait for Newark and decided to pick up the pitcher and fill both glasses."

Sitting back down at the table, he said, "You'd think I could have one night without being bugged."

"You must be in high demand." I sipped my beer.

"No. Just work with a lot of dumb asses."

"Sorry to hear that."

"So am I...so am I." He took a big swig on his beer. "So tell me, Susan, what brings you to Sedona?"

"I needed a change. I've vacationed in Sedona. The red mountains are magnificent. What better place could I have picked?"

"You got that right. You planning on making this your permanent home?"

"Yes. If I can find another job when Janice returns."

"We sure could use a full-time nurse at the compound."

"Compound? Where's that?"

"North of town. In Oak Creek Canyon."

"Are you hiring now?"

"It doesn't exactly work that way," he said and gulped the rest of his beer.

"How does it work?"

"Well, you..."

A tall, muscular man with a full head of brown hair and a rugged beard slapped Newark on the back with one hand and held a bottle of beer in the other. "Yeah, buddy. Mind if I join you?"

"Yep, I mind."

"Glad it's not a problem," the tall man said, pulling up a chair next to me. His arm rubbed against mine as he sat down.

Could this man be a Tegen? My eyes moved to his hands. No Tegen ring.

"Susan, this guy who can't take no for an answer is Sean Lange."

"Hello, Sean," I said.

Lange winked at me. "What do you see in this guy?"

I smiled, not knowing what to say.

"Come on, Sean. Sit and drink your beer and be quiet."

Lange took a long pull on his beer. "You know you're needed back at the compound."

"Sure do. An hour or so won't make any difference."

"Why don't you take off now? I can take care of this pretty lady."

"You'll scare her off like you did Fran."

An angry expression crossed Lange's face. "She had family obligations. Didn't have anything to do with that."

My eyes drifted back and forth between the two men. They were both about the same size. Newark had blue eyes and Lange's were brown, but he could be wearing colored contact-lenses. With both of them by my side, I wondered how I could determine if either one was the sought-after Tegen.

While they continued talking about Fran's departure, I drank the rest of my beer and picked up the pitcher. *Accidentally*, I slightly swung it, smashing it into my empty glass. The glass tipped over, landing on the hard surfaced table with a crashing sound and shards going everywhere, including on my lap. "Aaaah. Sorry…sorry." I jumped out of my seat, wiping the broken glass off my uniform. Then I bumped into the back of Lange's chair, tipping it forward. He splayed his hands on the table to prevent smacking into it.

"Sorry."

He picked up a napkin and brushed the glass away from his hands. A few drops of blood came from small cuts. The napkin soaked it up.

"Oh, I'm so sorry about this. Let me help." I raised the edge of my sweater, prepared to wipe away the remaining blood.

"Don't worry, Susan," Lange said. "I got this. I don't want you to ruin your sweater." He stood. "I'm going to go wash my hands." He left the bloodstained napkin on the table and headed to the restroom.

"Are you okay?" Newark asked. "You didn't cut yourself?"

I looked at my hands and flipped them over. "No cuts."

The barmaid came with a brush and pan. As she began sweeping the glass shards from the table top, I managed to push the napkin into my lap and carefully stick it in my pocket.

"Is everyone okay?" she asked, clearing off the table.

"Yep, no injuries." Newark looked at the barmaid. "Hey, don't take away the beer."

"I'll bring you another pitcher." She walked away and motioned toward a guy who held a broom and dustpan.

We stepped away from the table while the man took care of the glass on the floor.

When we sat back down, Lange returned to the table as the barmaid brought two glasses and a pitcher.

She asked Lange, "Do you want another Heineken?"

"Just bring another glass."

Newark filled our glasses. He probably didn't think I could handle the task after the mess I had made the previous time.

"So, Susan," Lange said, "are you the new nurse Worthington hired?"

"Yes. Are you also one of his patients?"

"Sean doesn't like doctors," Newark said. "Probably hasn't seen one for years." His eyes moved to Lange. "When was the last time?"

Lange tapped his chin. "Let me think. Most have been when I broke my arm. Gotta be nine...ten years ago."

Playing my nurse's role, I said, "You really should go in and get your cholesterol and blood pressure checked every year. An annual flu shot would also be a good idea."

"You sure sound like Worthington," Lange said.

"So you have seen him?"

"Can't avoid it. He comes a couple of times a month to the compound to see patients."

"Why can't they go to the clinic? Are they disabled?"

"No. They want home visits."

I looked at Newark. "You mentioned the compound earlier. You thought they could use a full-time nurse. Any possibility I could get a job there after Janice comes back?"

Lange gazed at Newark with a stern expression on his face. I took it to be a warning.

"Possibly," Newark said.

"Let's see how well you like Sedona after a week or so," Lange said. "People don't always stick around once the newness of the place wears off."

"I can't imagine wanting to leave." I felt anxious to give the blood-stained napkin to Kendall to have it analyzed.

"This is a great place for hiking and rock climbing. Do you do either of those?" Lange asked.

"I love hiking, and I've done a little rock climbing. Are you skilled at that?"

"Sean doesn't even know how the ropes work."

Lange frowned. "Oh come on, Alex. I'm not that bad. And don't you think you ought to be getting back to the compound?"

Newark checked his watch. "Yeah, it's probably that time."

"I need to get going too." I stood up.

"You don't need to leave just because Alex is."

"Sean." Newark sounded irritated.

"No. I can't stay," I said and then left with Newark.

In the parking lot, Newark said, "There's a local band playing here on Friday night. Care to go with me?"

"Sure. Should I wear my dancing shoes?"

"Definitely. Pick you up at eight?" After I nodded, he asked, "Where are you staying?

"Red Hills Motel, Room 214."

He opened my car door. "See you then," he said as I scooted behind the steering wheel."

When I reached the motel, I placed a blue sheet on the dashboard, wishing I could've also obtained a sample of Newark's blood. That was on my to do list for Friday night. Tipping over a glass wouldn't work again. I needed to come up with a more creative way besides poking him with a knife.

I kept checking the time as I watched YouTube videos about how to deal with handling injured people, how to clean wounds and properly apply dressings, and how to shave hair around a cut. At 11:00 p.m., I figured Kendall wasn't going to show and turned off my computer.

While I brushed my teeth in the bathroom, he tapped on the window.

I wiped my mouth and then slid the window open.

"I'm not coming in," Kendall said. "There's a navy blue Ford truck in the parking lot with a guy inside. It hasn't moved all evening. Did you stir up anything today?"

"Well, I went and had a beer with Newark, and a guy by the name of Sean, Sean Lange, joined us. He also lives at the compound. Neither one of them wore a Tegen ring."

"Probably by design. If one is Snyder, he knows he's being hunted. He wouldn't want to broadcast his identity. Did you learn anything?"

"I got a sample of Lange's blood. Let me get you the napkin." I hurried into the bedroom and grabbed it. "It's stained with his blood. Could you get it analyzed?"

"Yes." He took it from me. "How did you manage to get that?"

"Broke a glass and finagled around so Lange ended up putting his hands on some of the broken pieces."

"Is he suspicious?"

"I don't think so."

"That could be why the truck's out there." He reached in and raised my hand. "Good, you're not wearing it," he said, looking at my fingers.

"Before I left Bismarck, I hid my black ring in my bra and that's still where it is."

"Keep it there. A problem has come up that I need to deal with. I won't be in town tomorrow. Stay in public places. In case of an emergency, call the second number you memorized."

"Oh, I have a date Friday night with Newark."

"I'll be back before then."

After he left, I went to the front window and carefully adjusted the drape so a small open slit appeared at the edge. I peered through it and saw the blue truck with someone inside, but I couldn't make out any features. The truck was situated even with my room. Maybe I had screwed up getting Lange's blood. Or could it be because I was interested in the compound? Questions continued buzzing around in my head as I climbed in bed.

7

COMPOUND VISIT

Checking over the patient appointment list, I noticed eight people had the same appointment time—1:00 p.m., and then there weren't any other appointments listed after that. Thinking it could be a whole family, my eyes drifted over the names. None of them had the same last name. Then I headed to Worthington's office to ask him about it.

I stepped through his doorway. "Dr. Worthington, there seems to be a problem with today's patient appointments. Eight are scheduled for 1:00 p.m." I showed him the list.

"Not a problem. They live at the Fellowship compound. We're going there after lunch for our bi-weekly visit." He looked over the list. "Go through their files and put together the supplies we'll need to take."

Between patients, I gathered the supplies needed for each patient and placed a check mark next to the name. I reached the bottom of the list and studied patient eight's information—Frances Michaels, twenty-three, six weeks pregnant. I wondered if she was the Fran that Newark and Lange had talked about the day before. Did she go home to her family when she discovered she was pregnant? Gazing at her file, I hoped the father wasn't Snyder. Would she leave without telling him? I sighed, thinking I might have it all wrong—Frances might not be the Fran who left.

* * *

Shortly after lunch, I climbed into Worthington's passenger seat, and he drove out of the clinic's parking lot.

"The folks that live at the compound stay to themselves," Worthington said. "They're a religious group and don't allow strangers to come on the compound. The place has guards to keep outsiders away. Only talk to the residents about their medical issues. Don't ask any questions about anything else, and don't wander around. Stay only in the patient area."

"How many people live there?"

"It used to be somewhere between 150 and 170, including children. Their numbers have been dwindling. My guess would be around 130. When we're there, wash your hands often. They've had some bad cases of influenza—four deaths."

"Four? Were they senior citizens or infants?"

He shook his head. "No. I wanted them to be taken to the hospital, but Sheldon Barton, the Fellowship leader, wouldn't allow it."

"How come Alex Newark goes to the clinic, instead of waiting for you to come to the compound?"

"A few of the people who live at the compound come to the clinic for their appointments. Some are allowed to do as they please, and others are restricted. Maybe it has something to do with their position in the hierarchy of the religious order."

Since Worthington had signed the death certificates, I, along with Father and other council members, had assumed he had a special relationship with the religious group. Based on what he had just said, that might've been a faulty assumption. Worthington only mentioned four had died from the flu. What about number five? The cause of death had been changed from spider bite to influenza. "When you go on vacation, does Sheldon Barton allow another doctor on the compound to see the people who need medical attention?"

"He did about a month ago. A patient died. And that doctor wrote the wrong cause of death. It caused quite a problem and had to be changed. I doubt Barton will allow someone to fill in for me again."

"The doctor wasn't competent?"

"Dr. Collins was an excellent doctor. Worked at the medical center. The patient was unable to speak when Dr. Collins saw him. He misread some of the symptoms and the blood draw results but insisted on sticking with his diagnosis."

The fact that Worthington talked about him in the past tense did not go unnoticed by me. "Then why did he change the death certificate?"

"An autopsy was planned, but then Dr. Collins had a climbing accident."

"He died?" I asked, recalling one of the investigators on the case had a climbing accident before Kendall and I arrived.

"Yes. It was such a tragedy. Left a wife and two sons."

"Then how did the death certificate get changed?"

"The autopsy was no longer necessary, and Dr. Barton thought the 'spider bite' cause of death could turn away future people that might want to join the Fellowship. I subsequently changed it to the correct cause of death—influenza."

Worthington stopped at the guard gate and lowered his window.

"Good afternoon, Dr. Worthington," said a man with a holstered pistol slung over his shoulder." He leaned down and looked through the window at me. "Is this your new nurse, Susan Anderson?"

"Yes."

The guard opened the gate.

As Worthington drove into the compound, my eyes swept around the area. A few children played on a playground not far away while a group of women looked on. Off to one side, I saw a man tilling some ground. A few women walked along a dirt road carrying baskets. I couldn't make out the contents.

Worthington stopped in front of a large, white brick house. Its grandeur was nothing like I had expected. Since a large group lived there, and based on Kendall's brief description, I figured the buildings would look like dorms, warehouses, or office buildings.

Worthington and I each took a box of medical supplies from the back seat, went to the front door, and rang the bell. The door flew open. In front of us stood a short, stocky woman with curly, gray hair.

"Hello, Dr. Worthington," she said.

"Hello, Mrs. Hoffman." He tilted his head toward me. "This is Susan Anderson. She's taking Janice's place for a month."

"Oh, yes, I heard Janice won a vacation. Welcome, Miss Anderson."

"Please call me Susan," I said, stepping over the threshold.

She smiled. "Dr. Worthington and Susan, everything is set up for you in the back two bedrooms." Hoffman looked at Worthington. "They're the same rooms you've used for years."

While she escorted us down the hall, I noticed we only passed closed doors. The first room we entered had a regular doctor's examination table, two stools, and a side table with a box of tissues on it. We placed our boxes on the table.

Worthington turned to Hoffman. "Give us ten minutes to lay out our supplies, and then send in the first patient."

The supplies were spread between the two rooms according to the patients Worthington planned to see in each room. The rooms appeared similar to normal medical examination rooms, except bleaker. No pictures hung on the untouched, gray walls. The rooms seemed exceptionally clean and sterile. Not homey in any way.

Two hours later, seven patients had been seen. Then Worthington said to Hoffman, "You can bring in Fran Michaels now."

"Oh, I'm afraid she's not here," Hoffman said in a sad tone. "She had a family emergency. We're hoping she'll be back."

Worthington flipped through her folder. "Do you have a number or an address where I could reach her?"

"If you want that information, you'll have to talk to Dr. Barton. Would you like me to give him a call?"

"Yes, please."

Hoffman headed down the hall.

"Doctor?" I asked. "Is Dr. Barton a medical doctor?"

"No…no. He has a degree in theology. Let's get everything packed up."

While we gathered our supplies, urine samples, and blood draws, I hoped I'd have an opportunity to see more of the compound. "Will we be going to another building, or will he come here?"

"He'll probably want me to go to the administration building."

"Can I go with you?"

"No."

The clicking of Hoffman's shoes on the hallway wooden floor ended my possibility of asking questions about that building.

"He wants you to go to the administration building," she said, standing in the doorway.

After we put the boxes in Worthington's car, he picked up his medical bag. "You can either sit in the car or stand nearby to wait for me, just don't wander out of this parking lot."

"Okay." Wondering why he took his medical bag, I watched him go to a plain looking, light gray, wooden structure with very few windows. A man dressed in coveralls stood on the front stoop and escorted him inside.

Off in the distance, I heard children singing. With all the security, that was an unexpected sound. My eyes drifted around the parking lot, and I saw a blue Ford truck parked between two white trucks. One was a Dodge Ram which probably belonged to Newark. Was that the same blue truck parked at the Red Hills Motel the night before? Wanting to get a better look at it, I walked toward the truck at a slow pace in case someone in the house was keeping track of me.

I casually went past the blue truck, memorizing its license plate number. At the end of the row of vehicles, I turned around and began strolling back to Worthington's car. When I went passed the white Dodge truck, feet pounded on the ground behind me. Guessing I might've gone farther than the compound police approved, I looked over my shoulder and saw Newark jogging toward me.

"Hey." He stopped next to me. "So what do you think of the compound?"

"I haven't seen very much of it."

"Maybe someday."

I noticed Worthington approaching his car and looking around. Seeing me, he motioned for me to join him.

"Dr. Worthington's ready to leave. I don't want to keep him waiting."

Walking by my side, he said, "Just wanted to say hi. Need to get back."

"See you tomorrow."

He hurried off.

When Worthington and I were settled in his car, I asked, "Did Dr. Barton have some kind of medical problem?"

"No. Why?"

"You took your medical bag."

"Just habit." His voice sounded jittery.

I sensed that wasn't the reason but couldn't think of a way to get him to divulge more. "Any success in getting Fran Michaels's information from Dr. Barton?"

"Dr. Barton says he'll locate her family and contact them," Worthington said in a doubtful tone. "Fran is a real beauty and always cheerful. You couldn't meet a sweeter girl. She's an elementary school teacher and wonderful with the kids. It would be such a shame if she's not told that she needs to seek medical attention."

"There's a school at the compound?"

"Not a school, but classrooms. There are sixteen school-aged children. None of them attend public schools."

From what I had gathered about the compound, I figured Dr. Barton was probably irritated that Fran had left. Locating her family to alert them about her medical issue most likely wouldn't end up on his agenda. "Any idea what part of the country she's from?"

"Oklahoma."

"Will she be okay if she doesn't get her medical problem taken care of?" I asked though I didn't have a clue what the urgency was.

"She is pregnant, so she'll have to see a doctor within the next six months. Given her blood analysis, she might be rushed to an emergency room before then."

Since I supposedly was an experienced nurse and had seen her medical file, I could be revealing my lack of knowledge by asking more questions about her medical condition.

After we drove away from the security gate, Worthington glanced at me and asked, "Are you seeing Alex Newark?"

I felt like that was none of his business but was curious why he would inquire. "I'm going out with him tomorrow night. Is there something I should be concerned about?"

"The folks that live at the compound tend to be a little secretive and not necessarily truthful." He reached over and patted my hand. "Be careful."

"Truthful? What have they lied about?"

"How certain injuries occurred."

"You think they're violent?"

"I don't have any proof, but a black eye and a bruised face doesn't happen when you *accidently* slash your hand with a steak knife."

"Oh, I see what you mean. Anything else I should know about?"

"No...no. And that only happened once," he said and then pressed his lips together into a thin line.

I sensed he wanted to strengthen his warning but he feared he might've already said too much. Wondering if someone at the compound had something on Worthington, my mind flashed to the white powder, the cocaine, I found in his drawer. Could there be a connection?

8

A TRUTH REVEALED

After Worthington mentioned the day before that Fran's blood analysis indicated a medical problem, I wondered if that condition happened when a woman became pregnant by a Tegen. Father would know, but I couldn't risk calling him from the conspicuous public phone near the restrooms.

I decided to check the patient charts taken to the compound. When I opened the box, it was empty. I thought Worthington might be looking them over prior to having the records updated in the computer system.

Before I had a chance to ask him, the first patient showed up. She was early but only needed a flu shot. I went to the foyer and ushered her into an examination room.

As soon as she left, the next patient arrived. It was almost lunchtime before I had a chance to go to Worthington's office. He sat at his desk, writing a prescription.

"Do you have the files we took to the compound yesterday? I want to update the patients' information."

"They're right there." He pointed to a stack on his desk.

"Are you finished with them?"

"Yes. You can update the records on the computer now."

Back at the nurse's station, I flipped through the files, looking for the one belonging to Frances Michaels. It was gone. Since Worthington never saw her, there wasn't anything to update, but why had he removed her chart?

An emergency patient arrived, her husband yelling for help. She was quickly taken to one of Worthington's examination rooms. The woman had cut her arm with an electric bush trimmer. Based on what I had learned watching a YouTube video, I put a tourniquet on her upper arm to slow down the bleeding. To my relief, Worthington rushed in and took over. I helped as much as possible, but was definitely out of my comfort zone. After he stitched up her arm, he left while I bandaged it.

I picked up the prescriptions Worthington had written for her as I walked with her back to the waiting room.

Her husband rose to his feet. "How are you doing, sweetie?"

"Better," she said in a weak voice.

I gave him the prescriptions to be filled. After they left, I went back to that examination room to straighten it up for the next patient.

Worthington walked in and shut the door behind him. "Who are you?" he asked in a stern tone.

"Susan Anderson," I said, knowing I had blown my cover.

"What do you really do, Susan? Are you FBI?"

His line of thinking surprised me. "Have I done something wrong?"

"I suspected the first day after Janice left that you weren't a registered nurse. Your performance this last hour verified that. You have some nursing skills, but your abilities don't match your résumé. What are you doing here?"

"Well…"

"Tell me if I'm right. You're here about the compound. I figured someday the law would be looking into their illegal activities."

Letting him believe his theory was certainly better than the truth. "How would you feel about that?"

He sighed. "Good. I hate going to that place every other week. I hope you can shut it down."

"Why do you go?"

"Can't get out of it."

"Care to elaborate?"

"Not now." A brief smile flickered across his lips. "We have patients waiting. They like you. You can stay, but don't attempt anything you can't handle. Understood?"

"Yes." I returned his smile. It was a minor miracle that he was allowing me to continue my nursing role even though I had been hired under false pretenses and lacked the required nursing abilities.

During the rest of the afternoon, each time I had a patient ready for Worthington, he stepped into the examination room.

Shortly before 6:00 p.m., the last patient left and I had an opportunity to look for Frances Michaels's digital file. Nothing came up. I opened the list of Worthington's patients. No Frances Michaels appeared. Thinking it was a computer glitch, I searched for Alex Newark. His file popped right up. Then I checked for Frances Michaels again. Nothing.

I went to Worthington's office. "I can't seem to find the file for Frances Michaels on the computer."

"I know. I looked for it earlier."

"Has this happened before—a file missing for a person who has lived at the compound?"

He nodded.

"Do the clinic computer whizzes know about that?"

"Well, we really don't have any "computer whizzes" here, but that problem has never been reported to the company who provides us with technical support."

"Why not?"

He fidgeted with his watch. "I guess I'd better tell you. Shut the door."

I closed it and sat down in a chair facing his desk.

"It's my niece. She's twenty-four and lives at the compound." A sad expression crept across his face. "My wife and I raised her since she was four years old. Her parents died in a car crash."

"She's being held there against her will?"

His brow creased. "She's been there for almost two years. The first year she was happy. Now she looks well but seems withdrawn. The Fellowship of the Good Earth used to have a wonderful leader, Father Cerane. Ashley, my niece, had just graduated with a degree in chemistry. Her boyfriend, Kyle, was teaching high school math. Before she started graduate school, they thought it would be fun to live there for a couple of years—help work the land, tend chickens, gather eggs, make baskets, sing and dance, and worship God. Father Cerane welcomed all denominations.

"Then everything changed almost a year ago when Sheldon

Barton became the leader. The security fences were erected, a gate installed, and guards hired to prevent visitors from entering the premises. Ashley can only come home for a few hours on holidays, and she comes with an escort, not her boyfriend. We probably wouldn't even be able to see her that much if I didn't take care of the compound's medical needs."

"That's why you believe something illegal is going on there?"

"Partly. Once when I attended to a patient who had fallen off a roof at the compound—they didn't dare move him because they thought he had broken his back—they wouldn't call an ambulance. After I determined he didn't have a broken back, they allowed a couple of their guys to bring him to the clinic for x-rays. As we headed back to my parking spot, an open door to one of their buildings offered a clear view of stacked crates. A few tops were open, and I saw all types of weapons inside. The Fellowship owns some land south of town, which I've gathered is a gun range. The organization having some weapons didn't alarm me until I realized they maintained an arsenal.

"And now they have seven, if not more, scientists working on something in one of the buildings." He sighed. "I don't know why I'm telling you all this. You're FBI. I'm sure you know all that."

"Your niece told you about the scientists?"

He shook his head. "No. The guy I told you about in the car—the one with the gouged hand—told me when he as under the influence of pain medication. I was the only one in the room with him."

"Have they threatened to hurt your niece if you don't provide them with medical services?"

"Barton has inferred it."

"Why haven't you called the police about it?"

"If they stormed in there to get her out, who knows how many lives would be lost? And her boyfriend is the guy whose hand I took care of. I doubt she'd leave without him. Can the FBI close it down?"

"These things take time," I said, not knowing how to answer his question and not wanting to give him false hope. Shutting down the compound was not part of my assignment. Whatever was going on there started before Snyder arrived, and Kendall already knew about the weapons from his first visit inside the compound fences.

"Okay…okay, I'll have to leave it to you and the FBI."

"What happened to Father Cerane?"

He shrugged. "I was told he went to a commune in Oregon. I can't get anything more specific out of Barton."

Since he was opening up to me, I also wanted to ask him about the falsified death certificates but feared that might spook him into thinking his medical practice was under investigation. I glanced at the clock on the wall and saw it was 7:20 p.m. "Sorry, I need to go. Don't worry. Things will work out," I said even though I had no idea how I could help his niece.

9

NEW PROBLEM ARISES

Reaching my motel room, I quickly showered and put on a pair of designer jeans and a light blue blouse with three-quarter sleeves that covered my special camisole.

Newark arrived right on time, dressed in jeans set off with a big brass belt buckle, a plaid shirt, alligator cowboy boots, and a Stetson hat.

I eyed him up and down. "I take it the band plays country music?"

He smiled. "What other type is there?"

When we were settled in his truck, he pulled out of the parking lot, and turned in the opposite direction at the corner than I had expected. "Aren't we going to the same bar we went to on Wednesday?"

"No. The band switched venues. This place has a bigger dance floor."

As we drove in the direction of the compound, I wondered if I had underestimated Newark. Could he be Snyder? I replayed all my movements the day before at the compound in my head. Nothing came to mind that would've raised anyone's suspicions. Also, I doubted any of its residents knew they had a Tegen in their midst. Then I recalled the scientists Worthington mentioned. Could there be a connection to Snyder?

To my relief, Newark turned into a packed parking lot next to a large cabin-looking structure. People milled about outside the door.

"Looks like they've got a good crowd."

He pulled into the only vacant spot on the back row. "Always do on weekends."

Once inside, we looked for an empty table. Not seeing any, Newark suggested we sit at the bar. "Something will open up. Happy Hour ended at seven. Some folks will clear out after they finish their pitchers of beer. The band doesn't start until nine."

While we waited for a table, Newark ordered us beers.

"I'm curious," I said. "What do you do at the compound?"

"Well…the compound is the home of Fellowship of the Good Earth. We're a religious group and try to live off the land. We can't grow all our food, but we do manage to produce a large portion of it. Besides the vegetable garden and fruit trees, we have a chicken coop with around a hundred chickens, a woodworking shop, a quilting room, and a basket weaving area. Even if it's a small operation, there's always work to be done."

That description certainly didn't explain why it was so heavily guarded. Nor why it appeared they couldn't get by without him for an evening, but now was not the time to pry deeper. Then I saw Lange, holding a cute redhead's hand, approaching us.

"Hey, buddy," Lange greeted Newark.

"Didn't know you were going to be here," Newark said. "Hi, Beth." Then he introduced her to me.

"Joe's saving us a table by the dance floor. Care to join us?" Lange asked.

"Sure." We picked up our beers and followed Lange.

When we reached the table, the man sitting there, who I assumed was Joe, rose to his feet. "I'd better be heading back," he said, leaving.

Lange waved over the barmaid and ordered a pitcher of beer.

"Still liking Sedona?" Lange asked.

"So far, so good," I said.

"Susan was at the compound yesterday," Newark said.

"Oh." Lange cocked his brow.

"She came with the doc."

With both of them living there, I had expected they would've already discussed my visit.

"It's beautiful there, don't you think?" Beth said.

"You live there, too?"

"Sure do. I love the scenery and getting back to the basics."

"Have you been there long?"

Before she could answer, the barmaid brought the order. Lange poured as static came through the speakers. I looked toward the stage and saw the band all set up.

"Good evening, folks!" The band leader jumped around to rev up the crowd. "Ready to whip up your heels and have a good time?"

Cheers and hollering, "Yep," came from the crowd.

"Okay. Let's get started." The leader signaled the other band members, and the music began with "Seein' Red."

"Care to?" Newark said, stretching his hand out toward me.

I took his hand, and we stepped onto the dance floor. He was a good dancer, and a few times I had a hard time keeping up. I made a mental note to take an advanced dance class.

A slow and romantic song started. Newark held me close to him. His cologne had a nice, pleasant, sexy smell. I had to admit his body felt good next to mine. How could I feel that way when I knew he might be a killer?

When that song ended, we headed back to our empty table since Lange and Beth were still on the dance floor. Newark picked up his beer glass and took a big swig. "Did you leave a boyfriend behind in Albuquerque?"

I never told him where I supposedly lived before coming to Sedona. Did he somehow get a hold of my résumé? "No. That all ended before I left."

"There's probably a heartbroken guy wandering the streets of Albuquerque right now."

"Doubt that, and if there is one, it has nothing to do with me." I picked up my beer and sipped it.

Lange and Beth came back to the table. Lange looked at me. "How about the next dance?"

"Okay," I replied and glanced at Beth. She didn't seem fazed that her date had asked me to dance. Lange took my hand. I felt a scab and gently touched the sore on his hand. "Oh, I'm so sorry I caused that." Then I knew Lange couldn't be Snyder. Tegens heal quickly.

"That wasn't from the broken glass. I scraped it on some barbed wire." He pulled me into his arms and swung me around the dance floor. He was also a good dancer but not in Newark's league.

After that tune, I danced again with Newark. As we were heading back to the table, he dug his cell phone out of his pocket and glanced at it. I figured it must've been on vibrate.

"What a way to ruin an evening," he said. "Sorry, I need to get back to the compound."

"I didn't realize farms needed to be attended to at this hour."

"Sometimes they do," he said, not elaborating. "Hey, can I have your phone number?"

I rattled it off and watched him enter it into his cell, and then he pushed his phone back into his pocket.

"Oh, can I have your number?"

"Thought you'd never ask." Newark smiled and then proceeded to give it to me.

Leaving the establishment, I spotted a man with a lean build and blond hair staring at me. Something about him seemed familiar, but I couldn't place the face and hoped he wasn't someone from my past who knew my true identity.

At the motel, Newark walked me up the stairs to my motel room and then wrapped his arms around me. Expecting him to try to kiss me, I said, "Alex, I really enjoy your company, but I like taking things slow."

He dropped his hands to his side. "Slow it is then. You free on Sunday evening?"

"Yes."

"How about dinner?"

"Okay."

"Seven-thirty?"

"See you then. Good night." I opened my door.

"Good night, Susan. Sorry, I had to cut our date short."

"No problem."

As soon as I closed the door behind me, Kendall strolled out of the bathroom. "Don't tell me you climbed through the window?"

"Nope. That would never work. I got here about a half an hour ago."

"What would you have done if I had invited Newark in?"

"I doubted you'd want to get that friendly with him," he said without answering my question. "I didn't expect your date to end this early."

"Newark received a call needing him back at the compound."

Kendall sat down at the table and pulled a thermos out of his backpack. "Thought you might want this since I couldn't drop any off in your car this morning."

Smiling, I quickly unscrewed the lid. "Thanks." I drank a large gulp of *venotrolia*, put down the thermos, and said, "Lange isn't a Tegen. He has a scab on his hand."

"The blood on the napkin verified that. Do you now agree that Newark is the fugitive Tegen?"

"The fingerprints our Tegens lifted…did you find out who the other set belonged to?"

"A guy by the name of Gil Tunell. His prints were in the system because of a burglary in Florida. Served a day in jail. Then got bailed out. He took off before he had his day in court. There's a warrant out for his arrest."

"Florida? Do you think he came here with Snyder?"

"Tunell left Florida almost a year ago. Since he was with Snyder at the clinic, we're assuming he lives at the compound, but that hasn't been verified."

"Yesterday I went with Worthington to the compound—his bi-weekly visit."

"See anything?"

I proceeded to tell him everything I'd observed and what I'd learned from Worthington.

Kendall leaned his elbow on the table and rubbed his chin. "Interesting," he said, staring at the floor. "Any thoughts about what the scientists are working on?"

"With all the weapons, I originally thought germ warfare, but wouldn't that be a job for chemists not scientists?"

He shrugged his shoulders.

"I don't know either. Anyway, do you think there's any possibility Snyder told someone about himself in order to become a member of the Fellowship—so he could live in a guarded place?"

"Don't see that. Too dangerous. People wouldn't want to be around him if they knew he was lethal."

"Yeah. If he wanted something, all he'd have to do is snap his fingers."

"Your first thought is probably right…some type of germ warfare." His dark, piercing eyes focused on my face, sending an uneasy sensation running through me. "You never answered my earlier question. Do you agree Newark is Snyder?"

"His two years of medical records still bug me. They look so authentic, but someone connected to the compound is a skilled computer hacker. Records on Frances Michaels disappeared completely. Oh… do you know if a mortal becomes pregnant by a Tegen, does her blood develop some abnormalities?"

"You suspect this Frances was impregnated by Snyder?"

"I don't have anything concrete to go on. Her blood analysis showed a problem. Then the idea just hit me. I think we should try and track her down if there's a possibility."

"Is she attractive?"

"According to Worthington, she's a real beauty."

"Snyder has an eye for good-looking women. That's why I have no doubt that Newark is our man."

"Not everyone at the compound has seen me."

"Word gets around. For a while, you almost had me believing we had the wrong guy. Lange seemed to be homing in on you."

"I still haven't ruled out Newark might not be our target. I'm going out with him on Sunday night. Maybe I can find something to confirm it one way or another. If you are so convinced he's the right guy, why not capture him then?"

"A few things need to be checked out first."

"Like what?"

"Where he keeps his spiders. If he has any hidden, preserved bodies at the compound."

"You never answered my question. Do mortals impregnated by a Tegen have abnormalities in their blood?"

"Yes."

"What does it show?"

He pulled out his cell phone. "Call your father."

As I punched in the number, Kendall stood and looked out a small opening between the drawn drapes.

"Hello, Kendall," Father answered.

"It's me," I said. "Kendall's letting me use his phone."

"It's good to hear your voice. Are you okay?"

"Yes. One of Dr. Worthington's patients, Frances Michaels, is pregnant. There's something abnormal about her blood that concerns him. She's taken off and Worthington doesn't know how to reach her."

"Can't he get that information from the religious leader?"

"Sheldon Barton, the leader of the compound, wouldn't give it to him. Barton told Worthington he'd contact her family, but Worthington is doubtful."

"I know where this is going. You suspect Miss Michaels was impregnated by Snyder."

"Yes."

"I'll have someone look into her whereabouts. What do you know about her?"

"She's twenty-three. A teacher who comes from someplace in Oklahoma. They say she's a real beauty."

"That will give us a good start. How's the assignment coming along?"

"It's…" I began and stopped when I noticed Kendall staring at me. "Fine."

"Is Kendall watching you?"

"Yes."

"I'd better let you go. I love you, Sara."

"I love you too." I disconnected and handed Kendall his phone.

"Your father is going to have someone look for her?"

I nodded.

He peeked out the window again and then sat at the table. "When you were chatting with Worthington, did you ask him about the cocaine?"

"No. He seems to be on my side. Since I want to maintain my cover, I don't want to say anything that might get him upset, and it's unlikely that info about the cocaine will help us in any way to capture Snyder."

"We have an unexpected problem."

"What?"

"Blake Eisner."

"Blake? Isn't he still in the Tegen prison?"

"Albert Eisner arranged for his son's release under the premise that Blake would live with him for a year and report to an enforcement officer every day. Considering Blake had been with Snyder for almost eighteen months and knew we were looking for him, his sentence was pretty light."

"What was his sentence?"

"Six months—one week each month he went without *venotrolia* and his ring. He didn't do well during that time.

"Father said I couldn't go without my ring for more than five days. How did he survive?"

"In bad shape. He recovered in time for his next session."

I fidgeted with my hands, thinking that wasn't a light sentence. Kendall must've seen worse since he viewed it differently.

"I presume Blake has taken off. He knows Snyder is in Sedona. Do you think he'll show up here?"

"Yes. I had a crew tracking him down. Yesterday, the trail ended in Flagstaff. Blake doesn't have a car—no rental or purchase—and he hasn't taken any form of public transportation from there. He left his cell phone in Bismarck. Three Tegens are in Sedona looking for him."

"Maybe he's at the compound."

"Possibly. One of the Tegens is checking that out."

"Checking it out. Is he—a he or a she Tegen?

"He."

"Is he at the compound?"

Kendall nodded. "Blake has seen our travel arrangements. Most likely he's hanging around here."

"You were in my room expecting him to show up?"

"The folder he saw didn't contain our aliases or where we would be staying. Blake arrived in Flagstaff at 11:15 p.m. last night. We're assuming he hitchhiked to Sedona."

"Maybe that has something to do with why Newark received the call to return to the compound."

"That crossed my mind. But it's unlikely a mortal could've caught Todd, the Tegen who's looking for Blake, and it would be difficult for a Tegen to catch him unless they were prepared. Todd is aware of what happened to the prior enforcement team that went after Snyder. He'll get out of there if he senses danger."

"I can see you being able to capture someone smaller than you just by using your brute strength. If the target is relaxed around the Tegen and not expecting a problem, he could easily be drugged. But otherwise, how would one Tegen capture a larger Tegen, assuming they both were equally skilled at physical combat?"

"Like you would capture a wild beast—shooting them with a tranquilizer dart, a net from a tree triggered when the target steps in a certain spot, or a disguised hole in the ground. The latter two would still require that the target be tranquilized in order to keep the captive

Tegen secure while being moved."

After I considered those methods for a few minutes, I said, "At the bar tonight, a man stared at me and his face seemed familiar. Could he have been one of the Tegens in town?"

"Was the bar in the busy part of town?"

"No. North of town."

"Then he wasn't a Tegen. You haven't called your boyfriend have you?"

"Boyfriend?"

"You know who I'm talking about."

"Conner is not my boyfriend," I said adamantly though wishing otherwise in my heart. "And he doesn't have a clue where I am."

"Keep it that way." He stood, slightly moved the drape, and looked out. "The cab of the blue truck looks empty. The driver might be watching from another location. Don't want anyone to see me leaving. Go to the office. Ask about anything. If someone is stationed outside to keep track of your moves, that'll draw their attention away from your room."

I waited for Kendall to put the empty thermos in his backpack, and then I headed toward the office. Before opening the plate glass door, I cringed. The blond-haired, familiar-looking man from the western bar was checking in.

10

A MISSING TEGEN

Standing near the stairwell, I scanned the parking lot. The dark blue Ford truck was prominently parked as usual in a space where the driver could easily observe my room. From my vantage point, I couldn't make out the license plate to determine if it was the same truck I noticed at the compound.

As I entered my room, I recalled previously seeing the blond-haired man at the bar where Newark and I went on Wednesday for a beer. That guy probably drove the blue truck. Why was he checking in? I figured someone, Newark or whoever was Snyder, either knew or suspected I was a Tegen. Blake could've alerted him. Maybe Blake had known all along where Snyder had gone after he left Florida and somehow he deceived Kendall into believing he had no idea. From what I had heard earlier, I thought Kendall's methods for extracting information were infallible.

But if Snyder knew my true identity, I couldn't understand why he hadn't made any move to capture me like what happened to the Tegens in Florida. Newark had an opportunity earlier. Then it occurred to me, he probably wanted me to lead him to my colleagues. Three Tegens had gone after him in Florida. The council wouldn't send out only one Tegen to handle the task, especially one who wasn't a Tegen Enforcer.

With Blake on the loose and possibly my identity blown, I bolted the door and secured a chair under the handle. That wouldn't prevent him from getting in, but it would give me a warning. I went to examine the bathroom window. A smile crept across my face, realizing I could squeeze through the opening, but it would be impossible for an average-sized man. Blake fit that category.

A loud tapping sound awakened me and I groggily lay quietly listening. The tapping continued. I glanced at the nightstand clock—3:14 a.m. Forcing my feet to the floor, I staggered into the bathroom and slid the window open. "What's wrong?"

"Open your door. I'll explain inside," Kendall said.

A minute later, he walked through the doorway, closing the door behind him. "The blue truck is still in the parking lot, but no one is in it."

"Well, that's probably because the owner's checked into the motel." I told him about the guy with the blond hair.

"Most likely he's a member of the Fellowship of the Good Earth. We've learned how Snyder moved up in the religious order ranks. However, that isn't the reason for my late visit. Todd is missing."

I gasped. "He never got back from the compound?"

Kendall shook his head. "His last communication was at 12:32 a.m."

"You don't think he's already…"

"No. No sign of smoke has come from the compound. We believe he's being held, thinking a rescue attempt will be made. That's how we suspect the two Tegens with Darwin were captured. They had been waiting for Darwin to bring Snyder out of a secluded homestead."

"Before Todd was captured, did he find Blake?"

"No. He discovered what the scientists were working on in the lab. He even sent pictures. Then his phone went dead."

"Is it some type of germ warfare stuff?"

"It's our spiders."

"Huh? Snyder gave them some of our spiders? I thought all Tegens cherished them."

"Obviously not Snyder. He still needs to have a private stash someplace. He'd deteriorate without them."

"What are they doing with our spiders?"

"Trying to create more by splicing their DNA into common

spiders. Todd snatched a white lab coat. He claimed he was a new member and recorded a conversation with one of the scientists. He streamed that through to one of the other Tegens. The scientists know if someone is bitten by one of our spiders it means death—no antidote. They also know that our spiders will come to a specific sound."

"Snyder gave them his disk?"

"I doubt he'd give it up. They probably replicated it. That wouldn't be very difficult with the right equipment."

"So Snyder gave them an almost invisible weapon. Unless someone has been told about our spiders, no one would be terrified of them. I'm guessing their plan is to set them free. Let the spiders take care of some targeted person or group and then retrieve them for their next mission."

"The plan is to make money at it. Do a few demonstrations and then threaten in order to achieve the pay off they want."

I shook my head. "No wonder Snyder was able to infiltrate the religious group and call some shots. He's probably told the mortals we are a danger to their money making venture."

Kendall nodded.

"How are we going to rescue Todd, get our spiders out of there, and capture Snyder?"

"I'm working on a scheme now."

"Care to share?"

"Not yet." From his backpack, Kendall pulled out a small, ovoid case, a disk, a small box, a plastic bag, an odd-shaped black bag, and four milk bottles. He placed each item on the table.

I smiled, knowing the ovoid case had Tegen spiders inside, and the plastic bag contained their food.

"You can have some spiders." He handed the case to me.

I couldn't wait to see them and slowly raised the lid. I stuck a finger inside just to feel them. With my other hand, I picked up the disk and looked at the edge of it. My initials—S.A. for Sara Alston—were inscribed on it.

"You brought mine with you!"

"Your father sent the disk to me."

I closed the lid to my spiders. "I'm going to keep them with me. Leaving them here would be too dangerous. Also, Snyder probably already knows I'm a Tegen."

"Not necessarily. I don't doubt he is suspicious of you, but he doesn't have any confirmation. He, or someone helping him, contacted the hospital, the one on your résumé. They confirmed you had worked there. Your degree was also checked."

"Maybe he thinks I'm an investigator, working for law enforcement, like Worthington believes. I'm sure the FBI can set up an airtight résumé, just like we can."

Kendall took a tube of lipstick and a small, travel-sized perfume bottle out of the small box. All I could think of was that he didn't like the shade I wore or the perfume I used.

He held up the lipstick and removed the cap. "Tranquilizer darts are in it." He pointed to the top of it. "This part is a lipstick. It's safe to put on. See this small lever on the side?" He gestured toward it. "Snap it down and a small dart, about the size of a toothpick, is ejected out of the bottom. It's been loaded with three darts."

"So I could pretend to be putting on lipstick when I release one."

"That's the idea. Each one will render a Tegen unconscious for about ten minutes. That'll give you an opportunity to restrain the Tegen or get away, depending on the situation." He raised the perfume bottle. "The bottom of this contains a knockout drug. Just turn this," he said, touching a band near the bottom of the bottle. "And drops will be dispensed. Two drops in a beverage will put anyone to sleep—a Tegen will be out for approximately fifteen minutes, a mortal longer—but it takes around five minutes to kick in."

Then he pulled a dart gun and darts with small cylinders attached out of the black bag. "A dart from this will put a Tegen out for about an hour." Kendall's eyes drifted around the room. "Leave it loaded on your nightstand at night. There doesn't seem to be a good place to hide it during the day. See what you can figure out, but remember, if the dart gun falls into the wrong hands, it could be used on you."

I examined the dart gun. The number twelve was stamped in bold letters on its side. "Are they all numbered?"

"Yes, if handled by Tegen enforcers."

"Do you think Todd was hit by a dart?"

"Snyder knows how to sedate a Tegen, but he doesn't know about the lipstick."

"How did he learn about the tranquilizing darts?"

"He used to occasionally work with a Tegen enforcer."

"You've got to be kidding?"

"No."

"No wonder he can capture one—setting traps, darts, drugging. Is he also an accomplished fighter?"

"Yes."

I gestured toward the milk bottles. "I can buy those at the store. You didn't need to bring me milk."

"They don't contain milk. With the white plastic wrap that these milk bottles have, it's easy to hide *venotrolia* inside. The caps have been sealed. If you don't break the seal when you open one, you'll know it's been tampered with. The driver of the blue truck in your parking lot might make it difficult to be able to leave *venotrolia* in your car. Drink these bottles sparingly, and I'll deliver a new supply every three or four days."

"Is there anything I can do to help rescue Todd?"

"He wasn't captured until after your date ended last night. Is there any way you could lure Newark away from the compound today?"

"I have his cell phone number. Let me think about it. If I manage, how can I reach you?"

"A Tegen will be watching your place and another one watching the compound entrance. If he leaves and heads to the motel, we'll know you succeeded."

"What about Blake? He could be at the compound guarding Todd."

"I can handle him." Kendall slightly moved the curtain and peered out. "The blue truck is gone." He left without saying another word.

After sleeping for a few more hours, I climbed out of bed and browsed the brochures in the room and then called Newark.

"Hey," he answered. "What a nice surprise. Do you miss me already?"

"Well, of course."

"I don't mean to brush you off, but I'm kind of busy. Were you calling just to chat, or did you have something else in mind?"

"I'm thinking about going on a Pink Jeep Tour today, and I wondered if you wanted to join me."

"Sounds like fun, but I'm not going to be able to get away from the compound today. Too much work to do."

"Okay, I'll let you get back to it. See you tomorrow."

"Looking forward to it."

"Bye." I hung up and opened the drapes. The blue truck was nowhere in sight. Instead of staying cooped up in a motel when I might possibly help free Todd, I figured I'd drive around town and see if anyone tailed me. At least that would keep one member of the Fellowship away from the compound while Kendall and the other Tegens searched for Todd.

Before I left the room, I put the dart gun and a black jogging outfit into my backpack. I was itching to explore the compound and look for Todd, but Kendall was calling the shots and my assigned punishment required me to follow his orders.

11

GUN RANGE

While I waited at the stop sign to turn left onto the main road running through Sedona, a white Dodge Ram truck like Newark's drove past me, heading south out of town. I recalled Worthington telling me the Fellowship owned some land south of town. In case Newark was behind the steering wheel, instead of turning left, I went right and followed the Dodge truck.

I kept checking the mirrors to see if I had a tail. A long line of cars behind me made it impossible to detect if any were following. About five miles out of town, the white truck made a left turn. A minute later, I executed the same turn along with two other cars. Then I noticed the truck making another turn. As I got closer, I saw he was traveling on a gravel road. Knowing I'd stir up dust and easily be spotted behind the truck, I continued along the paved road for a couple of miles and then stopped on the shoulder. After several cars went by me, I made a U-turn and headed to town to buy binoculars and a ski mask.

Unable to quickly find a ski mask, I settled for a cap and large sunglasses. Then I headed to another store and bought binoculars. As I drove toward the gravel road, a white Dodge Ram zoomed past me going the opposite direction. Though I didn't know if it was the same truck I saw earlier or if it belonged to Newark, I still wanted to check if there was a gun range at the end of that gravel road. Maybe I'd find something interesting there.

I parked at the edge of the pavement shortly past the gravel road. I tucked my hair into the cap, put on the sunglasses, and slid the binocular strap around my neck. The area around the gravel road was covered with sagebrush and a few cedars. After hurrying across the street, I stretched out on the ground between some sagebrush and watched for a possible tail. Not seeing anything suspicious, I climbed over a field fence and camouflaged myself in the sagebrush as I moved forward. Up ahead, the gravel road forked. A gate was on one side. I ducked down and looked through the binoculars and saw a gun range. Bingo! Shooting benches, gun rests, and target stands lined part of the area. Beyond that, something reflected the sun. As I continued toward the gun range, I heard music. I looked through the binoculars again. An Air Stream trailer with its door wide open, a small metal building, and a Jeep were on the other side of the main shooting area.

Staying low to the ground, I crept closer and dropped down behind a gun range bench when the music stopped. Then I heard a male voice say, "...not until then. Yeah." An average-sized man with spiked, copper-colored hair appeared in the doorway with a cell phone pressed against his ear and a holster slung over his shoulder. He stepped down to the ground. "No. Don't see anything. Pretty quiet….Okay, I'll look." As he strode around, he swung his head back and forth. Instead of a pistol in his holster, I saw a dart gun like the one Kendall had given me. He circled the trailer. "No. Nothing. See you in an hour." He headed back into the trailer. Music started again.

Based on the man being armed with a weapon capable of tranquilizing a Tegen, I guessed that Todd was being held captive inside. For a minute, I debated going back to the car to get my dart gun but knew I wouldn't be able to do that and free Todd before whoever was on the other end of the call showed up. I reached in my pocket for my phone to call Kendall before remembering I had left it in the car.

I had no manmade weapons on me, and the guy in the trailer was armed with a dart gun. While I mulled over my options, I stealthily moved to the metal building and hunkered down behind it. Thinking something useful could be stored inside, I edged to the door. It was padlocked. Not having anything on me to pick the lock, I inched toward the Jeep and cautiously gripped the back handle and pushed it down. A soft click came from the mechanism.

Suddenly, I sensed someone behind me and jerked around, ready to pounce. Seeing the pistol in his hand, I grabbed his arm, twisted it, and flipped him to the ground. The gun landed a few feet from him. I swung my foot out to kick the pistol farther away from him. He gripped my ankle and yanked. Maintaining my spider-like balance, I leapt into the air and pounded my other foot hard into his groin. He moaned and released my ankle.

"Hey," a loud angry voice yelled from the direction of the trailer.

Fearing that any second a dart would drill into my back, I rushed to the far side of the Jeep, out of reach from a potential shooter.

A gunshot rang out.

I dropped to the ground. Lying a few feet from me, I saw a man, face down with his arms splayed out and a pistol clutched in his hand.

A loud rattling noise and banging erupted from inside the trailer. Then the barrel of the dart gun stuck out through the trailer door.

Another gunshot pierced the air.

The barrel no longer protruded from the doorway. Silence descended. Slowly I rose to my feet and, wondering where the shooter was, swept my eyes over the terrain. Then it struck me. The shooter must be a Tegen whom Kendall assigned to watch my motel room.

I made my way to the trailer, expecting the Tegen to join me any minute. The spike haired man's body lay in a puddle of blood near the door. I pushed him aside and stepped in. A short man wearing a lab coat was slumped in the corner seemingly unconscious Todd.

I went outside to look around but didn't see signs of anyone coming toward the trailer. Knowing time was ticking and there was no way I could carry Todd to my car parked on the road, I searched the dead man's pockets for keys to the Jeep. I dug out a key ring. On it were two small keys, not the size of a car key. I rushed out to check the pockets of the other dead man.

As I began going through his pockets, the guy on the ground twitched. Pulling out his keys, I wondered as I tugged him away from the Jeep's tires if he would be found before it was too late. The first key I tried turned in the ignition. The engine roared to life. I backed the car next to the trailer, lining the passenger door up to the step.

Going back into the trailer, I saw the unconscious man was

handcuffed to a pole and wore a Tegen ring. For certain,Todd. I took the small keys retrieved from the spiked-haired man. Neither key unlocked the handcuffs. I rummaged through the drawers next to the trailer's sink and found a roll of wire. With the end of it, I managed to pick the lock.

After freeing Todd's hand, I used all the strength I could muster and dragged him toward the entrance. Yanking him through the doorway, his white lab coat soaked up the blood on the floor. His head smacked against the step as I attempted to get him into the Jeep's back seat. Realizing I couldn't get him in the car that way, I removed the binoculars around my neck and laid them on the front passenger seat. Then I wrapped my arms around his body and hauled him into the back seat. When I had succeeded, I found myself in the back seat under him. I gripped the other handle of the back seat and pushed the door open. I squirmed out and hit the ground with a thump. I stood and slammed the door shut. Hurrying around to the other side of the car, I noticed my clothing was covered from head to foot with blood. I pushed Todd's legs in and closed that door.

Seeing all the blood smeared on the side of the car, I went back into the trailer to grab something to wipe it off. While inside, in addition to getting a towel, I gathered up the dart gun and darts. I placed them on the passenger seat and then went to work cleaning off the blood on the Jeep. Satisfied, I climbed into the front seat and drove toward the locked gate. Seeing it was field fencing on a wood frame and concerned someone could be coming along the gravel road soon, I backed up, gunned the engine and smashed through it. Splitters of wood sprayed over the front of the hood. Driving toward the paved road, I felt irritated that the other Tegen hadn't come to help me.

I stopped in front of my car, looked over my shoulder and stared at Todd in the back seat. According to Kendall, a tranquilizing dart would only knock a Tegen out for an hour. With vehicles going in both directions on the road, I couldn't move him unnoticed to my car. I decided to drive around until Todd became alert.

Ten minutes later, I heard him stirring and glanced at him in the rear view mirror. Suspecting he was coming to, I parked on the shoulder of the road, leaned against the door, and watched him.

His eyelids fluttered, and his lips twitched. His breath came in loud gasps, and then his eyes slowly opened and met mine. He cracked a smile and said, "Sara Alston. What are we doing here?"

"Well, what's the last thing you remember?"

"Talking to a guy in a lab coat." He bent his head and looked at his clothing. "Like the one I'm wearing but without the blood." Todd ran a finger over some of it. "Is this my blood?"

"No. It belongs to one of your captors."

He squinted. "Now, I do remember feeling a poke in my neck. A dart?"

I lifted up the dart gun retrieved from the trailer. "Might've been shot from this."

Todd glanced out the car windows. "Where's Kendall?"

I shrugged. "Maybe he's still at the compound searching for you."

He patted his chest and hips. "They took my cell phone. Kendall doesn't know I'm with you?"

I shook my head. "I didn't have my cell phone with me when I found you. I'm only supposed to call him in case of an emergency, and now that's not the case. You feeling okay?"

"Rummy. How did you find me? And how did you manage to get me away from Snyder?"

"I followed a white Dodge Ram truck," I began and then filled him in.

"Amazing. Who was the shooter?"

"I figured it was the Tegen who had been watching my motel room. And I might add, I'm not happy that she or he didn't come to help me get you out of there."

"I think you've got it wrong. Kendall is a marksman. The other two Tegens are well-trained in combat and know how to handle weapons but not marksmen from such a long distance that you couldn't spot them.

"You think the shooter was Kendall?"

He shook his head. "He wouldn't leave you there to fend for yourself after shooting them. He'd want to know why you were there….No, it wasn't him. Have you acquired an admirer among the compound residents, so they would kill their own to defend you?"

"I doubt it, but then who was the shooter?"

He shrugged. "Maybe Kendall got someone else to watch out for you after I was captured."

"Possibly," I said, thinking Todd could be right. "This car might've been reported as stolen. We better get going back to my car.

How do your clothes look under the lab coat?"

Todd peeled off the coat. The blood had soaked through to his shirt; only a few spots were blood free. His jeans were also stained, but the stains appeared almost black, not a dark red like his shirt. "What do you think?"

"Not good. How would you feel about just taking off your shirt?"

"Not a problem." He unbuttoned his shirt and slipped out of it.

Todd had a firm, muscular body. I understood why he didn't mind showing it off.

"Better," I said with a smile and then gestured toward my clothing. "Can't go to the motel looking like this. When we reach my car, I'll need you to get a bag out of the trunk."

"You come prepared."

Parked in front of my car, I stayed inside the Jeep and changed into the jogging outfit. Todd kept a look out for activity on the gravel road behind us while he used the towel to wipe of fingerprints on the inside and exterior doorknobs.

I stuck all of our bloody clothing in a bag and handed it to Todd. Then I took the towel and rubbed it over the front seat and steering wheel. I gathered up everything on the passenger seat and exited on that side of the car. Crouching low, I made my way to my car and climbed into the passenger seat. Todd had the engine running. As soon as I closed the door, he drove away.

"Where to?" I asked.

"A phone booth. Need to call Kendall."

It took about fifteen minutes before we spotted a convenience store with a pay phone on the front wall. He stopped next to it. I moved the binoculars, dart gun, and darts to the trunk and then went to the restroom to wash the blood stains from my hands while shirtless Todd placed the call.

Todd sat in the driver's seat when I returned. "How did it go?" I asked, climbing into the car.

"Well…well…you know you never can tell with Kendall."

"What does that mean? He isn't glad you're okay?"

He stared out the window and said, "I think he is, but I got the impression he wasn't happy that you were involved."

"Huh? He's happy you're free, but mad that I helped?"

"Kendall doesn't ever sound happy or mad, more like stern all the time."

"You got that right. You weren't on the phone long. Did you tell him everything?"

"No. Just told him I was free and you rescued me. Then he wanted to know where we were. I'm supposed to drive down the road for a mile, and then we'll wait for him there." He started the engine and pulled out of the parking lot. "Guess I'd better get us there."

Worrying that Kendall might send me home before Snyder was captured since I didn't get his approval to rescue Todd, I said, "When I went to the gun range, I didn't know you were there. I mean it worked out well, but I didn't disobey Kendall's order on purpose. Actually, he never gave me an order not to rescue you. He did say I couldn't go to the compound, but that was it." The minute I followed that white truck though, I knew that was against Kendall's implied orders. He wanted me to arrange some kind of date with Newark to get him away from the compound, not to chase him down and go exploring property owned by the Fellowship on my own.

"No need to explain it to me. Just Kendall."

"Have you been with him before when he's gone after a fugitive Tegen?"

"Often." He slowed down and cut to the curb.

"Has he sent Tegens home if they go against his implied orders?"

"Depends if that puts the mission in danger."

"Any idea how long it'll take him to get here?"

"Nope."

"Oh, did you see any sign of Blake when you were at the compound?"

He shook his head.

I wanted to see this assignment through to the end. Todd could've very easily gone up in smoke if he had remained in Snyder's custody. Who knows how many other Tegens and mortals might die at the hands of the fugitive? I hoped Kendall would still view me as a valuable asset to his team.

"Todd, did you have any trouble entering the lab where the scientists are trying to replicate our spiders."

"Not really. Climbed up and went through a second story window. The lab's on the first floor, no windows. I noticed a woman entering a room and coming out wearing a lab coat. Went in there and got my own lab coat." He grinned. "It fit pretty good. Too bad you ruined it with all that blood."

"Couldn't be helped. Maybe you can swipe another one. Was it a supply closet?"

"No. The room had a rack with lab coats hanging on it. Most had name tags on them. It was late. Only a couple of people were working in the lab."

"Any idea how many of our spiders are there?"

"I saw three mesh-like cages. I'd guess a couple hundred in each cage."

"Kendall figures Snyder has some stashed away for himself. He couldn't have taken very many when he escaped. The spiders have been multiplying."

"And, unlike us, Tegen spiders aren't immortal; otherwise, there'd be thousands."

A car's tires crunched on the shoulder of the road.

I looked out the rear window and saw a Chevy Tahoe and a Ford coupe stopping behind us. Kendall climbed out of the Tahoe and strode toward my car. He opened the back door and slid in. "Todd, Marge will drive you back to your hotel."

I had expected Kendall to say something positive about Todd being free, but he sat quietly in the back seat with his hard, steely eyes fixed on me while Todd got out of the driver's seat and headed to the coupe, two cars away.

Kendall's jaw tightened. "Do you not understand how to maintain a cover?"

"Kendall, I didn't know Todd was being held at the gun range. When I figured he was there, I overheard part of a conversation and knew someone would be showing up in an hour. I didn't have time to go back to my car and call you."

"Where was your car?"

"Let me start from the beginning," I said and filled him in on my visit to the gun range.

"Who was the shooter?"

I squinted. "It wasn't someone you had watching me?"

"No. Had that been the case, I would've known about your exploit earlier."

"Well then, who do you think it was?"

His eyes remained focused on my face. "Besides Newark and Lange, have you had any interaction with anyone else at the compound?"

"The patients I saw when I was there with Worthington. Two were guys. One had an arm in a cast. Not very likely that he could be the shooter. The other guy was older and had arthritic hands. It couldn't be him. Maybe the shooter wasn't even trying to help. Maybe the person knew what was going on. Killing those guys while I was there would make me the prime suspect. Oh, and one of the guys wasn't dead when I left. Granted he was in bad shape…but still breathing. If someone showed up there right after I left, he could've been taken to a hospital."

"Did he see you?"

I nodded.

"An ambulance would've been called. I'll have it checked out."

"What should I do with the bloody clothing?"

"Is it all in your trunk?"

"Yes." Since Kendall wasn't giving me any indication as to whether or not I was in trouble with him, I asked, "Am I still okay on the assignment?"

"Yes. In the future use your cell phone to contact me if you run into another problem."

"So I can call you even if it's not an emergency?"

"No. Discovering where a Tegen is held captive would fall in the category of an emergency," he said, enunciating each word very slowly, like he wasn't sure I could grasp it.

Then I wondered if it was his way of giving me a warning not to do anything without his approval. "Is Blake at the compound?"

"Yes. Stay in your room this evening. If Newark should call and want to take you someplace, make up an excuse why you can't go." Stepping out of the car, he said, "Open your trunk."

Driving to the motel, I felt relieved that Kendall hadn't booted me from the assignment until I noticed a white Ram truck in the parking lot.

12

THREATS SURFACE

Climbing out of my car, I saw Newark standing by his truck.

"Hey, Susan," he said, walking toward me. "How was the Pink Jeep Tour?"

"Oh, I didn't want to go alone, so I went jogging."

"Go on any interesting trails?" he asked, sporting a pleasant smile.

"With this scenery, all the trails are interesting." Not wanting to dwell on places I couldn't describe, I asked, "Did you get all your work done at the compound?"

"Yeah, it didn't take as long as I thought it would. Got plans for this evening?"

"Yes," I said without elaborating. Then behind Newark, I spotted the man with blond hair near the stairs. My eyes drifted over the parking lot, searching for the blue Ford truck. There wasn't one. Had Newark dropped off the guy?

"Looking for someone?" Newark asked.

"A friend. I thought she might be here by now, but I don't see her car."

"How about letting me take you and your friend to dinner?"

I plastered a fake smile on my face. "That sounds good, but I'd better ask her first. I'll call you."

"Okay. I'll wait for your call." He went to his truck.

Walking toward the stairwell, I sensed Newark's eyes on me. I passed the blond-haired guy, and it appeared his attention was focused on Newark, not me. Was he planning to chat with him when I was out of sight?

As I finished showering, my cell phone rang. Thinking it was Newark, I ignored it while I dressed and blow dried my hair. Then I picked up my phone and saw the caller had left a message. I didn't recognize the phone number. The message said, "Hello, Sara. Need to tell you a few things. Call me. Blake."

A crush of confusion and fear swept through me. How did he get my number? Had Kendall somehow swayed Blake into working with us to apprehend Snyder?

I sat on the edge of the bed and wondered if I should return his call or if it was some kind of trick. Had Newark given Blake Susan's number? And had Blake called to verify Susan and Sara were the same person? Questions kept bouncing around in my head.

Someone knocked on my door.

I picked up the dart gun, pushed a dart into it, and peered through the peephole. A tall, broad-shouldered woman stood in front of my door. I inched it open. "Yes?"

"Kendall sent me," she whispered, holding up her hand to show me her Tegen ring.

Not convinced, I held the dart gun firmly in my hand and opened the door wider. "Come in."

As she entered, her eyes drifted to the dart gun. "Hey…hey. No need for that. Call Kendall." She handed me her phone.

While I kept a watchful eye on her, I punched in his number.

"Marge," he said.

"No."

"Sara, the woman with you is a Tegen. We have a problem. She'll explain." He disconnected.

I gave her back her phone. "Kendall says there's a problem, and you'll explain it to me. Have a seat."

"A problem is putting it mildly," she said, sitting down. "I'd say we have three."

"Three?"

She nodded. "We suspect Isaac has been terminated."

"Who's Isaac?"

"A Tegen who came with Todd and me when Blake took off."

"Snyder burnt him?"

"That's what we think happened in the scorched trailer at the gun range."

"Scorched trailer? The one Todd was held in?"

"Yes. You told Kendall two guys were watching Todd. Both were shot. One's in a hospital in Phoenix. He's in surgery with only a slim chance he'll pull through. The other one's in the morgue. There are charred remains—actually just a couple of small bones and ashes—in the trailer. Isaac reported in shortly after I returned from dropping off Todd, and that was the last time we heard from him. Snyder, in a disguised voice, called Kendall on Isaac's phone. He confessed to killing Isaac. Told Kendall where he could find the ashes. He also said that would happen to every Tegen hanging around Sedona."

"Are the local police searching for the perpetrator—the person who shot the two guys? And the arsonist who started the fire?"

"Nope. As far as we know, the crimes haven't been reported to the police. We haven't figured out how they got around that yet."

"You mentioned three problems. Are you counting that as three since three guys were killed...well, one is still alive."

"No, that's all one problem. We had planned to capture Newark tomorrow when he picked you up for your date. That plan is no longer on the table."

"Why?"

"When Snyder called Kendall, he also said that all the spiders at the compound would be released if anything happened to him. We don't know if that was an idle threat or if he had some means of getting it done. Until we can figure that out, capturing him is on hold."

"Third problem."

"Blake. He's at the compound and knows you're a Tegen. In Isaac's last communication, he had Blake secured and prepared to take him out of there. Blake insisted he was on our side and wanted to help capture Snyder—saying something like 'It'll help redeem me in the eyes of the Tegen Council.'" She pursed her lips into a thoughtful expression. "That makes sense. We're immortal, unless we meet Isaac's fate. Who wants to live a life constantly on the run? Eventually, he'd be caught. Most Tegens who take off because they've broken a rule are captured within thirty to sixty days. Snyder is the exception...probably because he knows how Tegen enforcement teams do their jobs."

"Then why is Blake a problem?"

"Timing. From Isaac's communication to Snyder's call to Kendall, Newark wasn't at the compound. Who captured Isaac? Was Blake the culprit?"

"Maybe Newark sneaked back into the compound."

"No. I was patrolling the exterior fence perimeter, and a hired investigator was watching the entrance. No white truck entered and only a blue truck and a maroon coupe left."

"Did Isaac let Blake go based on what he said?"

She shrugged. "We don't know."

"Maybe Snyder has recruited another Tegen."

"Possibly, but besides the six of us here, including Snyder and Blake, the closest one is in Flagstaff. We don't have microchips though, so we can't rule out that another Tegen is here. Word gets around, and most Tegens know Snyder has been on the run for two years. It's a Tegen's duty to report him if they see him, providing they can recognize him. He's disguised himself well here. I doubt any of us would voluntarily join forces with him."

"Tell me is there any possibility that Newark isn't Snyder?"

"I heard you questioned that before. When we were searching the compound earlier for Blake, we went through Newark's bedroom. He had a couple of bottles of *venotrolia* in a drawer."

"I guess that confirms it…but they could've been planted to lead us away from the real Snyder. Any spiders in Newark's room?"

"No. Besides the ones in the lab, there are probably some hidden in another building. With people wandering around, we haven't been able to check all of them."

"Yeah, he'd keep them well hidden. Oh, I need to call him. Earlier, he wanted me to go out with him tonight. I told him a friend was coming over. Then he said he'd take me and my friend to dinner. I told him I'd ask her and then give him a call."

"Boy, he is persistent." She smiled. "Going out with him tonight is out of question."

"I know, but I still need to call him." I tapped on his number in my cell phone.

"Hey, can you make it?" Newark asked.

"Sorry. My friend just wants to hang out here."

"Any possibility I could change her mind?"

"Doubt it."

"Okay. See you tomorrow night."

I hung up and walked to the fridge. "Do you want something to drink?"

"A beer if you've got it."

I took out two, opened them, and handed one to Marge. Settling back down in my seat, I said, "Blake called and left a message."

"Blake? When?"

"About an hour and a half ago." I picked up my phone, clicked on voice messages, and handed her the phone. After she listened to it, I said, "It could be some kind of a trick. Can you tell Kendall about it?"

"I'm calling him now," she said, pulling out her cell phone. "Yeah, it's me....Blake called Sara. He wants her to give him a call....Okay, I'll do that." She hung up. "From the documents Blake saw in Bismarck, he knows you're pretending to be a nurse in Sedona. He doesn't know you're using the name Susan."

"Since Susan is a new nurse in town, he's probably figured it out."

"As far as we know, he hasn't seen you since he arrived in town. There's still room for doubt even if it is slim. Newark could've given him your number to confirm Susan is Sara. Don't call him. Ignore all his calls." She finished off her beer. "That brings you up to speed. I need to get going."

An idea snapped into my head. "Is Blake by any chance a skilled marksman?"

"You thinking he might be the shooter?"

"Well, it wasn't a random shooting."

"I'll check with Kendall." She headed toward the door.

"How can I help?"

"Kendall never gave me any instructions for you. You'll have to ask him."

"Will he be here later?"

Marge shrugged. "Watch out for Blake. He might show up since Sara never called him." She opened the door and left.

After locking and bolting the door, I stretched out on the bed, feeling disappointed I wasn't asked to do more toward capturing Snyder. When I accepted this assignment, I had assumed Kendall wanted me to play an active role in the mission because of my skills, not just pretend to be a nurse and attract Newark's attention. Based on the two dates with him, not once did I sense the slightest inclination I was in danger. With the exception of driving to and from the bar the night before, we were never alone.

Earlier, I had worried about being sent home for exploring the gun range without Kendall's permission. Not obtaining his approval no longer concerned me. I had no intension of sticking with the passive role he had laid out for me. I got out my laptop computer, and with a few deft keystrokes, the Fellowship of the Good Earth's website appeared. The home page was a collage of pictures. The one in the center featured a bridge leading to a metal archway displaying "FGE" prominently on top of it—no gate prevented anyone from entering. That picture was circled with smaller ones of people harvesting crops, clearing land, and singing around an open fire pit. I went to the "About Us" tab. There I read about their religious beliefs—worshipping God, enjoying all His abundance, and extending kindness to all. I moved to the next tab. It featured their religious leader, an elderly man with gray hair and a matching beard. The name under it wasn't Sheldon Barton. I briefly wondered if it could be his picture and someone screwed up on the name. Then I recalled Worthington saying that Barton had only been the leader for less than a year. Before that, the leader was Father Cerane, the man in the picture. After Barton took over, drastic changes were made at the compound, like increasing security and restricting some members from coming and going freely. Probably nothing on the website had been updated since Father Cerane left. I wondered if Barton had crossed paths with Snyder before he arrived. Otherwise, why would Snyder seek out the compound? And why would Barton permit such nefarious goings on if he weren't in partnership with Snyder?

My cell phone rang. I jumped off the bed, grabbed it from the table, and glanced at the caller ID. No name displayed, only the number Blake had used earlier. I had the urge to answer it. Instead, I laid it down and listened to the continuing rings, hoping he'd leave a message. Within a minute, my phone chirped, indicating a new message. After clicking on it, Blake's voice came through. "Sara, Ted suspects Susan is a Tegen. We need to talk. Call me."

Figuring Ted was Theodore Snyder's nickname, I stared at the phone and wanted to return Blake's call, but since he said "Ted suspects," some doubt remained. Even if Blake was on the up and up, calling him could erase Snyder's doubt. My number would be in Blake's phone. Since I didn't talk to him, it would only show that he had left messages—messages that weren't answered.

13

THE WRONG MAN?

After eating a bagel, drinking a cup of coffee, and downing a bottle of *venotrolia*, I went shopping for items I needed to become more active in the apprehension of Snyder.

I scored a black ski mask, oversized purse, latex gloves, and a knife without delay, but it took an hour to find a sleek sheath undetectable enough to wear on my calf or thigh. A knife was useless against Snyder, but could come in handy against mortals doing some of his bidding, like those assigned to guard Todd.

Before returning to my motel room, I headed back inside another store where I had seen a pay phone earlier. Keeping a watchful eye on the entrance, I placed a call to Father's private number.

"Hello," he answered.

"It's me."

"Sara, are you okay?"

"Yes. I'm using a pay phone. Were you able to locate Frances Michaels?"

"No. She hasn't gone home. Her parents were told that she went to a commune in Oregon. They weren't able to obtain any additional information from the compound leader. They're worried. They haven't heard from their daughter for several weeks, and she used to call them two or three times a week."

"Maybe she somehow crossed Snyder."

"If she was pregnant with his child and he poisoned her and then preserved her body with the intent to drink her blood, he'll become ill devouring any of it as if he had consumed a Tegen's blood."

"Would he be incapacitated if he drank her blood?"

"Definitely. He'd be deathly sick and might even wish he were dead for two or three days. After that, he wouldn't be able to keep *venotrolia* down for seven to ten days. He'd be very weak."

"Is there anything he could do to improve his condition?"

"Rest in the cave. But since that won't be an option, he could find a little comfort by constantly touching some of our spiders and keeping them next to his skin."

"Would he know to do that?"

"Only if he realizes that Miss Michaels was pregnant with his child. Otherwise, he'll have no idea what's causing his problem. Remember, this is all speculation. We don't know if Snyder was responsible for her condition or if he killed her. An investigator is looking for her in Oregon."

The entrance door opened. As a woman and man, each carrying a child, entered, I caught a glimpse of another man standing outside the doorway and peering in.

"In case I'm being followed, I'd better get out of this store before someone comes in here looking for me. If you find out anything else about Frances, will you contact Kendall?"

"Yes. Sara, are you safe?"

"Yes, Father. No attack has been made against me. Kendall gave me a couple of weapons I can use to fend off Snyder. I'm hoping we can capture him before he does more harm."

"Don't forget you can come home if you feel you're in danger."

The man who had been standing outside walked through the doorway.

"I need to go."

"I love you, Sara."

"I love you too, Father." I disconnected, gathered my purchases, and headed to my car with the stranger not far behind me.

Shortly after 7:30 p.m., Newark, holding my hand, escorted me to his truck in the motel parking lot. As he drove to a restaurant south of town, he asked, "Did you go sightseeing today with your friend?"

"No. She left early this morning." Thinking he might already know how I spent the day, I added, "And I went shopping. How was your day?"

"A couple of chickens got out of the coop. Besides chasing them down and calling the doc, nothing eventful happened."

"Dr. Worthington?"

"Yeah. A guy was pretty sick, and we wanted to make sure it wasn't anything contagious. It turned out to be a bad case of the flu."

"Flu?" I said, recalling that was the cause of death listed on five recently issued death certificates. One had been changed from a spider bite. Maybe that's what they all succumbed to. "Dr. Worthington went to the compound?"

"Yes. He wanted to take Clyde—that's the guy—to the hospital, but Clyde didn't want to go."

Since Clyde could talk, whatever was wrong with him, it hadn't been caused by our spiders. Spider victims couldn't utter a word and were unresponsive with their unmoving, wide open eyes. "How is Clyde doing now?"

"Not good," Newark said, parking next to a steakhouse. "They've got the best steaks in town here." He looked at me. "You're not a vegetarian or anything like that, are you?"

"No. I'm a meat eater."

We were seated in a booth next to a packed, noisy table. It sounded like they were celebrating a birthday. I wanted to suggest that we be moved to a quieter location, but the noise didn't seem to bother Newark.

After we placed our orders and were working on our second glass of wine, the noisy party began breaking up, and the participants streamed out of the restaurant.

Newark's cell phone rang. He pulled it out and glanced at the number. "Sorry, I better take this."

I had expected him to leave the table, but instead he stayed and answered it. "No, that won't work.…Have the guards walk the fence line…Yeah…No." He hung up and put his phone down. "We're having problems with our security system. No one can figure it out."

"When I went to the compound with Dr. Worthington, it looked like everything was pretty secure. Have you had any break ins?"

"The fences are really to keep out deer. Protect our crops. They'd eat all of it if they managed to get in…and wolves. A few years ago, one got in the chicken coop and killed almost all the chickens. We had to do something."

"How long have you been with the Fellowship?"

His jaw twitched, "Oh…aah…little over three years," he said, but I figured he was lying.

I still doubted he was Snyder. At the same time, Snyder had been on the run from Tegens for over two years. He obviously was clever and knew how to blend in. My eyes dropped to his phone, lying face down on the table, and I saw his initials—A. N.—in silver on it. I gestured toward his cell phone. "I've never seen initials look that good on a cell phone."

Newark picked up his phone. "They're in the plastic cover. A fellowship member engraved and then inlayed the initials in silver." He handed me his cell. "Here. Get a better look."

Admiring the engraving, I ran my fingers over it. "Very nice." I gave him back his phone.

As Newark put it in his pocket, he nodded toward someone behind me. "Sean. Seems like whenever I take you out, he manages to show up."

"Did you tell him we were coming here?"

"Nope. Must be a coincidence."

This was the third time I had been out with Newark, and each time Lange had appeared. Coincidence? Probably not. Why was Lange following us?

When Newark finished his main course, he excused himself to talk to Lange. As he stood up, I noticed a scar on his neck and recalled reading his medical records. Within the last year, he had a sprained ankle and a cut on his neck from a car crash. Kendall had to be wrong—Newark couldn't be a Tegen.

While he was gone, the waiter cleared the table. Seeing Newark's wine glass was empty and wanting to prove to Kendall that Newark wasn't Snyder, I picked up my napkin and quickly wrapped it around the glass and carefully slipped it into my purse. Then I saw a small boy staring at me. Did he see me snatch the glass? As I wondered if he was going to squeal on me, he gave me a big mischievous smile. I smiled back. Then I quickly downed my wine, and put my glass in the spot where Newark's glass had been.

Newark strolled back to the table. "Sean wants us to have a drink with him and Beth after dinner. Are you game?"

"Sure," I said, but I didn't want to go there with the wine glass in my purse. "Could we swing by my room first? I need to change shoes. I broke a strap." I bent down, gripped a shoe strap, and yanked, tearing it in half. I raised my leg. "See."

"Not a problem. Can't have you tripping around town with a broken shoe."

Lange and Beth stopped by our table. "We're heading out," Lange said. "See you in a few."

Within a half an hour, I had dropped off the wine glass in my room and changed shoes. On the way to the bar where we were meeting them, I spotted Kendall behind the wheel of a car heading in our direction. Since I had never noticed him following me before, I guessed something was up.

Kendall verified it when he parked in a slot close to us. Newark and I headed toward the entrance. Newark didn't like the meeting place. He chatted about the poor service and didn't seem to pay any attention to the large man not far behind us.

As we entered the establishment, I glanced over my shoulder and couldn't see Kendall anywhere. "There, at the table over there," Newark said, gesturing toward a table on the other side of the room.

After we all greeted each other, I excused myself to go to the restroom. Unfortunately, Beth decided to join me. With her by my side, I couldn't sneak outside to find out what Kendall wanted. There was a possibility he had followed me often, but this was the first time he didn't conceal himself. Something definitely was amiss.

Figuring it might be a while before I could talk to Kendall and wondering if Beth thought anything unusual was going on at the compound, I began by asking, "Have you been dating Lange long?"

"No. We're not dating. Sean's girlfriend, Fran, had to go home because of a family emergency, and my boyfriend is working on a big project at the compound. We're just hanging out together until Fran returns or until Josh, my boyfriend, finishes the project." She stepped into a stall.

Since Fran was Lange's girlfriend, and he wasn't a Tegen, I must've jumped to the wrong conclusion when I heard about Fran's unusual blood problem, but why wasn't she at home? Waiting for the next available stall, I looked for windows. There was only a narrow, long one. Not big enough for me to climb out of if I managed to return to the restroom later.

Washing my hands, I asked her, "Josh never has time to take you out on weekends?"

"No. Work. Work. Work. He's worn out when he comes to bed, and he's gone before I wake up."

"Oh, that's got to be tough. What's the project?"

"Secret. He won't tell me. Josh did say it would change our lives for the better. It's probably something to do with food—either preserving it longer or finding a way to produce more. Josh always wants to help feed the poor."

"Before joining the Fellowship, what did Josh do?"

"He's a chemist. He has a couple of patents. He needed a break and heard about the Fellowship, but it sure doesn't seem like he's getting any break at all."

As we headed back to the table, I asked, "Are you also a chemist, Beth?"

"No...no. I'm not that smart. Never went to college. I work at the daycare center at the compound. Love those little kids."

When we reached the table, both Newark and Lange were standing up. "Susan, there's a problem at the compound. Sean and I have to get back."

"What kind of problem?" Beth asked.

"A fire. It's under control now, but a few people are hurt."

Beth's eyes popped wide open. "Josh? Is Josh okay?"

"Yes. The fire wasn't in that building."

She sighed. "Oh, thank goodness. But the kids...are they all okay?"

"We don't know, Beth." Lange ushered us all toward the door.

"I'll come with you. Do you want me to call Dr. Worthington?" I asked, playing my nurse's role.

"No. We need to assess the damage first." Lange's tone sounded harsh. "Dr. Barton would've already called if Dr. Worthington is needed. Those hurt might just have minor burns."

Sliding into Newark's truck, I looked around for Kendall. He was nowhere in sight, but the car he had driven to the bar hadn't budged.

14

AN UNEXPECTED VISITOR

As I sat on the edge of my bed and wondered what was going on, a loud tap came from the bathroom. I hurried to it and slid the window open. "Do you want me to open the door?" I asked Kendall.

"No. There was a problem at the compound."

"I know. Newark and Lange took off to check out the damage from a fire."

"I had anticipated they'd leave during dinner."

"They left as soon as they heard. Before that, Newark mentioned something was wrong with their security system. Maybe that's why they weren't told earlier. What happened?"

"We don't have all the details."

"What do you know?"

"It appears someone was moving spiders in a small cage between buildings, somehow tripped, and the cage flew open. The guy started screaming that the spiders were loose. Marge managed to catch some of them before that guy grabbed a blowtorch. Flames shot up everywhere. One building was badly singed. We don't know if there were casualties."

"Is that why you followed me to the bar—to tell me about the mishap at the compound?"

"No. One of our mortal investigators has been found dead in his hotel room."

"From our spiders?"

"No. Overdosed. The police were called in. They've ruled out foul play."

"You think Snyder had something to do with it?"

"The timing seems suspicious. I haven't reached any conclusion yet."

"The fences and heightened security at the compound happened before Snyder showed up. Assuming the investigator's death wasn't an accident, whatever the reason behind the added security might be why he was silenced, and it has nothing to do with Snyder. Has the remaining investigator been questioned about it?"

"That investigator is a woman. She seems nervous. Doesn't want to talk about anything."

The woman's problem could be Kendall. "Did you question her?"

"Yes."

"Can I talk to her?"

His eyes fixed on me for a few seconds. "No. Our mission is to capture Snyder. If something else is going on at the compound, it isn't our concern. The contract with that private investigation company has been terminated. The woman might already be on her way home."

"Some of the spiders that were accidently freed at the compound could still be alive. People there might be in danger. Do you want me to help retrieve them?"

"No. Marge and Todd are searching for potential stragglers. The guy in the hospital, the gunshot victim who survived at the gun range, is starting to come around. He could be talking in a few days. If Newark doesn't already know you're a Tegen, he will soon."

"Newark isn't a Tegen. He has a scar on his neck from an injury he received during this past year."

"It's probably a phony."

"Well, I have his fingerprints. I'll get them." I went into the other room, picked up the bag, and returned. "They're on the wine glass in this plastic container."

"I'll have it checked." He took it from me.

"If Snyder isn't Newark and he's not Lange, any idea who he could be?"

"No. Blake might need a little persuasion to obtain that information."

"Well. That's your specialty. Is Blake still at the compound?"

"Yes." Kendall's phone beeped, indicating a text message. He glimpsed at it. "Problems." He abruptly left.

As I closed the window, someone knocked on my door. Thinking Kendall had decided to come in after all, I went toward the door. In case it wasn't him, I picked up the dart gun and looked through the peephole.

A big smile crossed my face. I laid down the dart gun and flung open the door. Grasping my late visitor's tie, I pulled him into my room and slammed the door shut. I felt his warm breath on my face and flushed with pleasure as I wrapped my arms around his neck and passionately kissed him. Seeing his glowing, seductive light brown eyes and inhaling his unique masculine scent, a rush of excitement swept through me.

He planted kisses down my chest while he slowly unzipped my dress. We undressed each other without saying a word. He swept me up in his arms. My skin tingled with anticipation. He carried me to the bed while our lustful desires rose. His lush lips curved against mine. Our breath and flesh intertwined as we made love.

We snuggled in sated bliss. He trailed his finger along my cheek, brushing away my hair. "How are you coming along on your new mission?" Conner asked.

Ignoring his question, I asked, "How did you find me?"

He kissed my forehead. "I have ways but expected you to try to infiltrate one of my customers. Gun smuggling…not part of the family business."

I rolled on top of his chest and gazed at his handsome face. "Huh?"

"Sheldon Barton."

"Sheldon Barton? Gun smuggling? That's not the reason I'm here."

He smiled. "And here I intended to offer you some assistance."

"Like a sharpshooter?"

"Interesting you should bring that up. A woman, who bears a remarkable resemblance to you, was seen at a gun range owned by the Fellowship of the Good Earth, Barton's current cover. Apparently she was there to rescue a man in his custody. It appeared she could use a little help."

"You don't think that woman could take care of herself?"

"The man observing her was not aware of her exceptional skills."

"So how long have you had me followed?"

"Since you were first spotted at a bar with Gil Tunell, alias Alex Newark, who is right hand man to Rodney Kalstein, alias Sheldon Barton." He stroked my cheek. "Seems everyone is using aliases, Susan Anderson."

"Rodney Kalstein. I've seen pictures of him on the news."

"Wanted for running a gun smuggling ring. Due to his legal problems, he handed his business over to a competitor for a percentage of the profits, but Susan Anderson already knows that. You're probably trying to figure out who took over his reins. I must admit, I'm impressed you were able to locate Rodney Kalstein when the feds don't have a clue where he is."

"Was Rodney Kalstein ever one of your colleagues?"

He shook his head. "No."

"Then how do you know all that about him?"

"Until you showed up in Sedona, I only knew what I had read in news articles. You're here for a reason, and based on your moves, it has something to do with the Fellowship of the Good Earth. It didn't take my investigating team long to put it together. Had you just been here to locate Rodney Kalstein, you would've already called in the authorities. You must be after a bigger fish. But since you claim Kalstein isn't the reason you're in Sedona, is it to improve your medical skills? Move up the ladder in the medical profession, Nurse Anderson?"

I grinned while trying to come up with a reasonable explanation. "No. I'm here because of spiders."

Conner's eyes narrowed. "Spiders? The deadly kind?"

"Yes."

"Does someone at the compound have them?"

"Yes." Then attempting to steer Conner away from the truth and wanting to keep him away from the compound, I added, "Sheldon Barton."

"How did...how did Kalstein acquire them?"

I shrugged.

"How do you know he has deadly spiders?"

"A few compound residents have died from spider bites after he took over the compound."

"Since you're immune to the venom, did one of your parents'

colleagues contact you about the situation?"

Conner knew my deceased, adoptive parents were arachnologists. "Yes," I lied. "They feared the spiders might be set free if the police were contacted. We want them retrieved without any more fatalities."

"Spiders? Is that why the trailer at the gun range went up in flames and the reason for the fire a few hours ago at the compound?"

"I don't know."

"The ogre-sized guy, the man you rescued at the gun range, and your woman visitor, who all recently arrived in Sedona…are they immune to the venom and part of the team to either retrieve or destroy the spiders?"

"Yes," I replied. "But you are not immune. Conner, you have to stay away from me until this problem is taken care of. You might have sharpshooters, bodyguards, skilled fighters—none of them are equipped to fend off poisonous spiders. There isn't an antidote against the venom. Anyone bitten will die, including you. Please, go someplace where you will be safe."

"Sara…is it okay if I call you Sara?"

"While I'm here, call me Susan."

He gave me a sensuous smile and enveloped me in his arms. "Susan, sharpshooters don't need to be close in order to be of value. I've heard Rodney Kalstein has a terrible temper and doesn't hesitate eliminating anyone that gets in his way. An investigator who was keeping track of someone at the compound died earlier this evening." He glanced at the clock on the night stand. "Let me rephrase. Died last night from an overdose—not self induced. Most likely, he learned Sheldon Barton's true identity. Even if your goal is not to obtain information from Kalstein," he said, and I saw doubt behind his shining eyes, "with him in the picture, I will not leave you unprotected."

Conner always seemed to have a wealth of knowledge about various things not available to the general public. I wondered if there was some way I could use him to help identify Snyder. "According to my resources, most members of the Fellowship of the Good Earth are devoted to the organization's religious goals. It appears they have nothing to do with the corruption that Kalstein brought when he took over the Fellowship. By the way, do you know what happened to the prior Fellowship leader, Father Cerane?"

"He was booted out when Kalstein decided the compound would

be a good hiding spot. He never leaves the fenced in area. Since Father Cerane had followers, Kalstein couldn't eliminate him without drawing attention. Father Cerane along with a few of his devout followers went to a commune in Oregon."

"Why would he just up and leave like that?"

"I suspect leverage. Kalstein probably has something he holds over the religious leader's head," Conner said.

I knew from personal experience that using leverage was how the Crussetts, Conner's organized crime family, kept certain associates in line. "The spiders arrived at the compound around four months ago. We haven't been able to determine if Kalstein recruited a new member in order to obtain the spiders or if one of his faithful members acquired them from an outside source. To stop further spreading of those deadly spiders, my team needs to find the source. Do you have any information about new recruits?"

"Any idea how Kalstein plans to use them?"

I figured he might be more helpful if I revealed part of the truth. "Extortion. He has a group working on trying to replicate the spiders. Then he'll demonstrate his deadly weapon. Lives will be lost. He'll demand a certain amount of money from a company, organization, or maybe even a government and threaten to set some spiders loose if his demands aren't met."

"Spiders can't be controlled. Does he plan to burn down places once the victims are dead?"

"No. These spiders can be called." I climbed off Conner and took my disk from my purse. Knowing several people at the compound already had one, the disks were no longer a secret. "With something like this."

Conner examined it. "You've had this for a long time. I first noticed it after my brother died. How did you get it?"

"My parents," I said, referring to the Joneses and continuing the lie, "discovered a particular species of spiders were drawn to a specific high-pitched sound. They had one of these made. But something went wrong in the lab, and those spiders died. I kept this as a remembrance. I didn't know it even worked until one of my parents' colleagues contacted me. I *do* have to be within thirty feet of the spiders." I climbed in bed next to him.

"So you push the button on it and they come?" he asked, pointing at the button on the white side of the disk.

"Yes, but it's the button on the black side. Since I'm immune, I don't need to worry about the spiders biting me in the process. I don't know how or if Kalstein has resolved that problem. Getting back to my earlier question, do you have any information on Kalstein's recruits or new members to the Fellowship?"

"I'll check into it." He pulled me tightly against his body and smothered my lips with his. Our bodies melded together once more. Afterwards, he held me in his arms. I drifted off and dreamt about the man lying next to me.

The alarm clock buzzed.

I awoke with a start and then met Conner's eyes and smiled, happy he was near me. Last night had not been a dream, although I often dreamed of him.

"Good morning," he said and brushed his lips against mine.

"I need to get ready for work."

"Really?"

"Yes."

"Can't you call in sick?"

I trailed my finger over his perfect lips. "I need to maintain my cover if I hope to retrieve the spiders without any more casualties."

He took my hand and stared at the ring, the ruby ring he had given me. "I like your ring," he said with a smile. "What happened to your black ring?"

"I keep it close."

"Where?"

"Close."

"When can I see you again?"

"Not here, but don't leave my room until I'm gone."

"Mmmh. I'm going to enjoy watching you get dressed."

Since I only had twenty minutes left to get ready, I quickly showered and put on my underwear. As I began to slip on my special camisole, Conner said, "Do you really want to wear that padded bra? Sweetheart, you don't need it."

"Before I arrived, I was told that Sheldon Barton and his close associates liked women who were well endowed."

"You can turn their heads without that."

"Well, now it's too late. Alex might think something is strange if all of a sudden I become a size or two smaller."

Conner rose and pulled me into his arms. "That extra padding

doesn't allow any of those guys to get very close to you. I like that."
He looked behind me. "Why the dart gun?"

"I need information about the location of the spiders. Dead men can't talk. Now, back to bed," I said, pointing toward it. "I have to finish getting ready."

He sat on the edge of it and watched me while I dressed. "I'm staying at the Amara under the name Max Heller."

"Another alias?"

"Yes."

"Is someone looking for you?"

"No. But it's better to stay under the radar."

Since I was responsible for his brother's death and his family believed I was dead, I guessed he didn't want his family to know his whereabouts and possibly have a member show up in town.

"With all these aliases, I'm going to have to make a list so I can figure out who is who."

He grinned. "Could you share that list with me?"

"Certainly. Oh, and don't drink from any of the milk containers in the fridge."

"You don't want to share it?"

"It isn't milk in the containers. It's poison."

"For the spiders."

"Yes," I said, though I had no intention of killing a single one.

He leaned back and rested on his elbows. "I'll look into Kalstein's new recruits."

I tilted my head. "Do you have someone on the inside?"

"The compound has been having problems with their security system. They've hired some new guards."

I smiled, knowing one of them, if not more, worked for Conner.

15

WORTHINGTON'S NIECE

While I looked over the list of scheduled patients, Libby, the receptionist, approached my nurse's station. She carried a box. "Susan, Dr. Worthington wants you to go to the compound."

"Is he there?" I asked, wondering if it could be one of Snyder's tricks to get me there.

"Yes. He's been there since around eight last night. A fire broke out and some people were injured. He'd like you to bring these supplies." She placed the box down on the counter.

"Are any of the injured in a hospital?"

"Not that I know."

"What about today's patients?"

"I've already started calling to reschedule them."

Driving along the curvy road toward the compound, I spotted a silver Chevy coupe behind me that kept passing cars whenever possible. I thought it might be one of Conner's employees, trying to catch up to me. In case that meant there was a problem, I pulled over to the shoulder of the road, but the coupe zoomed past me.

When I reached the turn off to the compound, the silver coupe, or its twin, was parked on the other side of the street with the driver in the car. At the compound entrance, the guard gave me a nod and then opened the gate. Another guard inside the fenced area directed me to park in front of the house, the same house where Dr. Worthington and I met with patients the prior week.

Stepping onto the pavement, I glanced around for Worthington's car and couldn't see it anywhere. A pang of doubt hit me—Was the doctor safe? Loaded down with the box, I went and rang the doorbell.

Hoffman opened the door. "Hello, Susan. Dr. Worthington is attending to those injured in the fire in another building." A heavyset man appeared next to Hoffman. "Dan will escort you there."

"Let me take that," Dan said, reaching for the box.

After taking it from me, he led me to a large building with rows of windows running along the sides. Dr. Worthington's car was parked by it, so I was relieved. A building nearby was charred on one side from the fire. Burnt wooden slates and timbers were crumbled beneath it. Across the dirt lane stood a tall structure that only had windows on the second floor. I guessed the lab was located inside since Kendall mentioned someone had been carrying a spider cage and tripped. That problem would've occurred close to the burnt building. Blowtorches must've been employed to destroy the poisonous spiders on the loose. With the noxious odor of pesticide floating around me, the cleanup crew probably wasn't certain that the flames had taken care of the spiders. I doubted any of the residents had been warned to watch out for dangerous arachnids crawling around.

"Miss Anderson," Dan said, drawing me out of my speculation.

I followed him into the building and down a long hallway lined with closed doors that had name tags hanging by each one and assumed the structure housed residents. Then I noticed "Alex Newark" on one of them and recalled his room had already been searched by either Marge or another member of Kendall's team. They found two bottles of *venotrolia* in one of his drawers.

Dan stopped at the end of the hall by three opened doors. Dr. Worthington was wrapping a man's arm inside one of the rooms. The man's face and clothing were smeared with soot. Dan walked in and placed the box on the floor.

"Thank you," Worthington said to Dan. "Susan, I've checked all the burn victims. I didn't have enough supplies to wrap all of the wounds. Find the pain pills in the box and begin administering two to each of the nine patients. Their doors will be open. Most are upstairs. If they're sleeping, don't wake them. When you finish, come back here."

I rummaged through the box and found three pill containers. Holding them up, I asked, "Are all these pain pills?"

"No. Only the white pills."

I slipped on a pair of latex gloves, opened a container of white pills and took out two. "Is it okay if I begin with this man?" I said, referring to the patient next to Worthington.

"Yes."

The man popped the two pills in his mouth and downed them with a glass of water.

I distributed the medication to the patients in the other two rooms while Dan stood guard in the hallway. Then I went by an open exterior door and up the back stairwell with Dan not far behind me. He probably had orders to keep an eye on me.

The first room I peeked in on the second floor housed a patient, sound asleep. The next two patients had burns on their hands and were eager for the pain pills, but they couldn't manage to take them without a little help. I ended up putting the pills in their mouths and holding their glasses of water to their lips while they drank.

In the next room, a twenty-something, crying woman sat on the bed.

"This should help," I said, gently touching her shoulder and looking at her soiled clothing and the bandage on her forearm. I stretched out my hand to give her two pills.

"I don't want any medicine," she said as tears continued streaming down her face.

"This will help with the pain."

"I'm...not in pain. I wasn't...burned. My uncle just...wanted me to leave my door open."

"You're Ashley?"

She nodded.

"Ashley, what's wrong?"

"They're blaming... Kyle, my boyfriend, for the fire. It...it wasn't him. He doesn't have...anything to do with...the spiders."

"Where is Kyle?"

"Locked up somewhere." She sniffled. "We should...we should've left when Father Cerane did." She cradled her head. "Why...why did I think...it would be the same?"

Then I noticed Dan standing right outside the door and went to it. "This patient needs some privacy." I closed the door.

"Ashley, if I can get you out of here, will you leave?"

"Not without Kyle…They'd kill…kill him for sure…if I took off."

"If I managed to get Kyle out first, would you be safe?"

"Maybe. I'm…I'm still useful. But…but you can't…get him. They'll…kill you…like the others."

"Others? How many?"

"Don't know… People keep disappearing."

"Are you allowed to lock your door at night?"

"Yes."

I surveyed the area out her window and saw the side of the burnt building. "Can you leave your window ajar?"

"Yes…but how…"

"Don't worry about that. Just leave it slightly open."

A loud knock reverberated through the room, and then the door flew open. There stood Newark with a hostile, furious expression on his face. "What are you doing, Susan?"

"This woman is having some serious cramping—female problems. She has a small lump on her right side and said she sustained a fall. It might not be anything that we need to be concerned about, but I'm going to have Dr. Worthington check her out to make sure. I didn't want to examine her in front of Dan. Did I do something wrong?"

"We don't allow residents to shut their doors if they have a visitor."

"How about couples and families?"

"Couples share a room. Families are in another building."

"Then how should I have handled this?"

"We *do* make exceptions for medical situations."

I walked toward him and gave him my best worried expression. "You're not mad at me, are you?"

His hard face softened. "No, but please try to follow the rules when you're here."

"I didn't know I was breaking a rule. Do you have a list or something you could give me?"

"I'll get you a list. Can I give it to you at dinner tomorrow night?"

"Are you asking me out, Alex Newark?"

"Yes, Susan Anderson."

"Okay, Mr. Newark."

"Seven, Miss Anderson?"

"Yes. I'd better finish distributing these pills," I said, holding up the container. "Oh, can Dr. Worthington close the door when he checks this woman?"

"Only if you are in the room with him."

"That can be arranged. See you tomorrow." I smiled at him and headed toward the next open door.

After I finished handing out pills, I noted Ashley's room was the third one from the back of the building. Going down the stairs, I ran into Worthington. Since Dan was within earshot, I said, "Dr. Worthington, there's a woman upstairs who is having serious cramping. She has a small lump on her left side. Could you check it out?"

His forehead creased. "Susan, remember…"

I put my index finger against my lips and softly said, "Shhh." Then I raised my voice and went on. "Alex Newark knows about her condition and doesn't want you to examine her behind closed doors unless I'm there. Do you want to examine her now or after you've finished with the other patients?"

"Let's do it now."

I led him to Ashley's room and closed the door behind us.

"Ashley," he whispered. "Where does it hurt?"

"Nowhere. Your nurse just said that since she closed the door. Mr. Newark wasn't pleased, but she handled him well."

Worthington turned to me. "Closing doors with a visitor in your room is forbidden."

I mouthed, "I know."

Ashley looked at me. "Can I tell him what we talked about?"

"I'll fill him in later. Just enjoy each other's company for a few minutes."

"Dear, are they treating you okay here?"

"Not bad, but Kyle." She began sobbing again.

"Where is he?"

"Locked up…Probably beaten again. They say…he started the fire."

Worthington enveloped her in his arms. "Shhh…shhh." He looked at me. "I think his prison days are numbered."

"Really?" Ashley asked, sounding a little uplifted.

"Yes, dear. No time frame, but the problem is being worked on."

Ashley and Worthington talked about how good it would be when she came home while I wondered how Beth seemed so happy to be at the compound and Ashley couldn't be more miserable. Were the residents divided? From what I had seen and heard, more shared Beth's point of view than Ashley's. How long could Kalstein continue to hide the truth about what goes on within the compound from all the residents? Maybe he's having a hard time. Ashley had noticed people were disappearing. Kalstein probably killed them off if they questioned too much.

A soft tap came on the door.

"I think that's our signal. Time's up." I inched the door open. "The patient is getting dressed. Give us just another minute," I said to Dan.

Worthington kissed Ashley's cheek. "Stay strong and be careful."

"I love you, Uncle."

Worthington caressed her arm. "Bye, dear."

I went with Worthington to check on the next patient.

Two hours later, I drove back to the medical center while trying to figure out how I could find and free Kyle. I decided a commotion of some sort within the compound could distract the guards while I searched for Kyle. I knew just the person to handle that job.

Walking toward the nurse's station, the scent of lilacs, my favorite flower, wafted through the air. On top of my desk stood a bouquet of lilacs with red roses scattered throughout, an arrangement Conner had sent me often. I bent down and sniffed the fragrant aroma as I lifted up the card: "To Susan, the woman who invades my dreams. Love always, Max." I smiled, thinking I had better get busy on that alias list.

"Someone has an admirer," Libby said, dropping off an x-ray for Worthington. "New boyfriend or an old one who appreciates you?"

"Neither. I don't know anyone named Max," I said, not wanting to take the chance of Alex Newark hearing about a boyfriend.

Libby squinted as she stared at the bouquet. "Really? You have no idea who sent them?"

I shook my head. "Maybe a patient? But I don't recall anyone with that first name. I'm going to check Dr. Worthington's patients listed in the system."

"Well, you're the only Susan here. They have to be for you, or somehow the florist screwed up and delivered them to the wrong place. Anyway, enjoy!" She walked away.

While I was busy admiring the flowers, Worthington came to the nurse's station. "From Alex Newark?" he asked, disgust evident in his tone.

"No. From someone named Max. Do you have any patients by that first name?"

"Not that I recall offhand. Let's talk about the compound. Come to my office."

I took another sniff of the lilacs and then headed down the hallway to his office. "You must be beat. You should've gone home."

"I intend to do that after our discussion. Can you close the door?"

I eased it shut and took a seat, facing his desk.

"What did you and Ashley talk about?"

"Kyle. She's really worried about him. I told her I'd get him out."

"And how about Ashley?"

"She won't go without him, so I plan to get him out first. Don't worry. She'll be out soon."

He rubbed the bridge of his nose. "How are you planning to manage that?"

"It's better if you don't know the details," I said since they hadn't been formulated yet. "However, neither one of them will be safe in Sedona while Sheldon Barton runs the compound."

"But aren't the feds going to shut it down?"

"That takes time, and time is not on Kyle's or Ashley's side."

"So they'll be in something like witness protection?"

"Something like that," I said, though I didn't have a foggiest idea how to make that happen.

"Will I know when she's out?"

"I'll tell you, but you'll have to proceed as if you weren't aware that she no longer resided at the compound."

"I understand." He stood and took my hands. "Thank you. I'd love to rush home and give the news to my wife, but she doesn't handle secrets well. Now at least I'll be able to sleep peacefully soon when I know Ashley is safe."

Worthington walked me back to the nurse's station on his way to the back door. When he was out of sight, I headed to the payphone by the restroom and called Conner's cell phone.

"Hello," he answered.

"It's me."

"I didn't expect to hear from you until after your work day ended. How did it go at the compound?"

"That's what I want to talk to you about. Are you at the hotel?"

"Yes. Room 226."

"Is it okay if I come now?"

"I was just about to suggest that."

"See you in a few."

16

LATE NIGHT PLANS

Walking out of the elevator on the second floor, I saw two men, clad in suits, pacing in the hallway. I immediately knew they were there for one purpose—to guard Conner's room. He never stayed anywhere without at least two bodyguards nearby. I almost expected to be frisked when I stopped and tapped on his door.

Conner opened it. My heart lurched when he guided me through the doorway and to a Jacuzzi, ready to be occupied. "I thought we'd enjoy soaking in the tub while we discussed business."

"Business? I didn't think you liked to mix business and pleasure."

He caressed my cheek, softly kissed my lips, and started unbuttoning my blouse. "I guess business will have to wait." He put his face close to my neck and inhaled. "You smell delicious."

Seeing the glow of excitement in his eyes, my mind went blank. All I wanted was for him to keep touching me.

Within a few minutes, we both were lying on the bed naked. "How about the Jacuzzi?"

"It can wait." His lips slowly moved down my body, adding fuel to the desire roaring inside me. My breathing became ragged. My fingers knotted in his hair as his kisses continued downward.

In the warm afterglow, he pulled me close. I moved my leg on top of his and enjoyed the feel of his masculine body. Suddenly, Ashley popped into my head. I trailed a finger across his chest. "Are you up to talking business?"

"The Jacuzzi is probably cold. How about a shower first?"

After sharing an intimate, steamy shower, we sat on the couch, ready to talk business.

Conner opened a bottle of champagne and filled two flutes. It didn't seem like the proper beverage to be consuming while discussing the compound problem, but since I wanted his help, I didn't voice any objection.

I took a sip and caressed his hand. "Will you promise that you won't go anywhere near the compound?"

"Until I know more, I can't make any promises."

"Conner, there are poisonous spiders there, and I think some might be loose."

"What makes you think that?"

"I was there today and smelled pesticide near a charred structure."

He studied my face, and his eyes locked on mine. "I promise."

I sighed with relief.

"But you can't sway me into not helping you."

"Good. Besides retrieving the spiders, I want to free two of the compound's residents."

"Two?" he asked in a puzzled tone.

"Do you already know about the one prisoner?"

"Yes. The man who started the fire. He would've been eliminated, but Kalstein wants to keep him alive for some reason."

"Because of his girlfriend. She's part of the team working on the spider project. According to her, he didn't start the fire. On a prior occasion, he was badly beaten and his hand gouged. Worthington attended to him."

"He must be a rebel—doesn't want to follow the boss's orders."

"Do you have problems like that?"

"No one is ever forced to work for me. It's always by choice." He tucked a loose strand of hair behind my ear. "I pay well if you're ever thinking about crossing the line."

Then what Blake had said the first time I saw him flashed into my head—don't cross the line. I wondered what he meant by that. Working for Snyder?

Conner wrapped his arm around me. "Sara, it's okay. I know that would go against your nature. You're one of the good guys...or in your case, good gals."

I kissed his cheek. Even though he wasn't a law-abiding citizen, he was still the man I loved and wanted in my life. "Do you know in which building he's being held?"

"Yes." Conner stood, opened the top desk drawer, took out a folded sheet, and spread it out on the table.

I walked to him and looked at the document. "You have a map of the compound? How did you get it?"

The corners of his mouth slightly curved up. "The prisoner is being held in this building," he said, pointing to a small structure.

"I need to get oriented to this map. Where is the building that was exposed to the fire?"

Conner tapped on it with his index finger.

"The prisoner is in the building next to the one I think houses a lab where spiders are kept. Do you know if I'm right?" I pointed to the two-story structure with no first floor windows.

"That building is off limits to everyone except a select group of ten or twelve people. Something is going on, but I have zero information about it."

"Could you create some kind of diversion by the gate to draw Kalstein's men there to give me some time to free the prisoner and his girlfriend?"

"Yes," he said without hesitation. "But from what I've heard, the guy is in really bad shape. He might need to be carried out of there. You can't do that alone."

"Any suggestions?"

"Well." He scratched his forehead. "I can have someone help you. Andy. He's a guard."

"Andy? That name sounds familiar. Was he with you in Baton Rouge?"

"Yes. Your rescue victim will have to be driven out. Andy will park a black Expedition here," he said, indicating a spot near the burnt building. "That car is bulletproofed and has a section of the flooring that can be raised. There's enough room in that compartment for one person, not two."

"His girlfriend is petite. I can get her out another way."

"Kalstein will send someone after them. Where do you intend to hide them?"

"Got any ideas?" I knew this was one of his specialties, but in most cases, he was dealing with corpses.

"I can handle it."

"Where should I deliver her?"

"Will you be able to call me?"

"I have a cell phone, but I doubt it's secure."

"Andy will give you a phone. When do you intend to make this heroic rescue?"

"Tonight, around 1:00 a.m. Most of the residents should be asleep at that hour. Is there a way you could disable the electrical fence?"

"Already part of the plan. You'd have to come and go that way."

I put my arms around his neck. "Thank you."

"Does your spider retrieving team know about this exploit?"

"No. It deviates from our mission. Doubt they'd approve."

"I'll have the list of the new residents living at the compound tomorrow."

"List. I have something for you." I plucked a sheet out of my purse and handed it to Conner.

He looked at the list of aliases and smiled. "I'll pin this on the wall."

"I'm sure the cleaning people would appreciate it."

"Yes, it's always nice to know who's staying or visiting their establishment." He pulled me into his arms and kissed me passionately. "Now that business is out of the way. Can we get back to more pleasurable activities?"

I raised my head and kissed his chin. "And what do you have in mind, Mr. Crussett? Oh, sorry, I should have looked at the list. I mean Mr. Heller."

Leaving Conner's hotel, I walked two blocks to my car. Earlier, I hadn't wanted to park in the hotel's parking lot in case I was being followed.

Before going to my motel, I went shopping for a rope, a black jogging suit in what I figured was Ashley's size, and another ski mask. Thinking about purchasing a gun, I walked into a store retailing that type of merchandise but didn't see any silencers. A loud gunshot would bring people running. On that thought, I headed back to my car. I drove toward my motel and thought about my assignment—capturing Snyder. Kendall would not be pleased that I planned to enter the compound without his approval, but I doubted his approval would be forthcoming under any circumstances. If he should find out about my evening outing, I'd have to beg for forgiveness.

Pulling into the motel parking lot, I saw a dark blue Ford Pickup and assumed it was the same one that had been there almost each night. The cab appeared empty again. I wondered if the driver was in his room or if he was lurking around someplace as I headed up the stairs.

I pushed the key into the doorknob and discovered the door was already unlocked. Slowly, I inched it open.

"Sara. Marge here. You don't need to worry about coming in."

I stepped into the room and closed the door. "What are you doing here?"

"Where have you been? Kendall's been looking for you."

"Earlier today, I went to the compound. Worthington was there treating patients and wanted me to help him. After that, I returned to the medical center for a while, and then Worthington gave me the rest of the day off. I decided to do some shopping." I held up my packages. "And then drove around, checking out the scenery. Gorgeous. Have you had a chance to appreciate it?"

"Sara, you should've called. Left a note or something." She picked up her cell phone. "I need to call him."

"You know, I had my phone on. He could've called me."

Marge gave me a disgusted look like I had done something terrible. Well, maybe if she knew the truth about my afternoon, she'd give me the same look.

"She's here....Went sightseeing...Yeah." Marge disconnected.

"Kendall's coming over. Don't leave."

I glanced at the clock, 7:23 p.m.—plenty of time for a chitchat with Kendall before I took off. "When will he be here?"

"He didn't say."

"Has something happened?"

"He'll tell you about it." Marge stood and left.

While I waited for Kendall, I watched the news, ate a bowl of soup, and drank a bottle of *venotrolia*. Then I gathered the items needed for my late night exploit and stuffed them into my backpack.

Time was ticking away. The nightstand clock said 10:38 p.m. Feeling irritated that Kendall hadn't shown up yet, I changed into my black jogging pants and a light blue sweater. I slummed down in a chair and stared at the television.

Shortly after 11:00 p.m., he tapped on the bathroom window. I quickly went and opened it. "You know, I go to work," I barked. "I need sleep!"

Ignoring my outburst, he said, "We have a problem. Newark is not a Tegen."

"I've told you a few times I doubted he was. I guess it took his fingerprints to prove it."

"Alex Newark isn't his real name. It's Gil Tunell. The medical records you've so heavily relied on are not completely accurate. He's been at the compound for a year, not two."

"Do you want to come in?" I asked, hoping he'd refuse.

"No. The blue truck is in the parking lot. It doesn't appear anyone is in it, but the driver could be lying down or close by."

"So who is Snyder?"

"Need to find Blake to obtain that information."

"He's not at the compound?"

"We're not sure. He hasn't been spotted leaving. We haven't been able to search all the buildings. They've increased security. At least twenty guards patrol the grounds."

"Since you were concerned about my whereabouts, did something happen today?"

"I received a message from someone claiming to be Snyder. Untraceable. Burner phone. He claimed he had captured and terminated another Tegen, one of my team. Marge and Todd were accounted for. You were missing."

"Why didn't you call me? I had my phone on."

"I suspect Snyder has tapped my phone. How he managed it, I don't know."

"Why do you think that?"

"He knew about Tunell's fingerprints. Mentioned it in the message. This evening, I purchased another phone. Here's the number." He handed me a small slip of paper. "Memorize it. Then destroy this note."

"I have a date with Newark tomorrow night. It seems like he's pretty high up in the religious organization. Today, when I was at the compound with a female patient, I closed the door to give her some privacy. A guard had been following me around, but he wasn't the one who pounded on the door....It was Newark."

"They don't allow residents to shut their doors when they have a visitor."

"It would've been nice if someone had told me the rules. Newark is giving me a list tomorrow. Could Snyder's victim be Blake? He told Todd he wanted to help us."

"Possibly. Two residents were bitten last night. Cause of death indicated the flu. Worthington tell you about that?"

"No. He never mentioned it. There was a strong smell of pesticide near the burnt buildings. Some spiders could still be crawling around."

"We've retrieved eight. Probably more are loose."

"From what I've gathered, most of the residents don't know about the spider project. They'd have no idea they could be in danger."

"Keep your dart gun handy, and don't trust anyone." Kendall pushed the window shut, and then he was gone.

I glanced at my watch—11:49 p.m. After slipping off my sweater and putting on the black top to my jogging suit, I peeked out the front window. The blue truck hadn't budged. I took my special lipstick with darts inside and stuck it into my bra. I flung the strap of my backpack over my shoulder and walked out the door.

17

DIVERSION

I kept checking my mirrors, looking for a tail, as I drove along the winding road. About a mile from the compound, I passed a bridge that extended over the gulley, flipped a U-ey, and parked on the shoulder.

With my backpack secured in place, I stealthily moved across the bridge, went around some homes, and headed through the foliage.

Somewhere behind me, a dog barked and growled. I scurried up the closest tree and looked around. Not seeing any sign of the hound, I scooted down the tree's trunk and proceeded toward the compound fence. When I spotted it, I slipped on my ski mask and saw small red lights on the fence posts, indicating electricity ran through the chain link.

Staying hidden in the trees and bushes, I crept along the back of the compound until I reached a tree near the center of the fence and a shack on the other side of the interior fence—the blind spot Kendall had mentioned. The red lights on the interior fence still glowed.

My eyes dropped to my watch, 12:54 a.m. I climbed up the tree to a branch approximately ten feet above the fences, opened my palm, and spun a long strand of spider webbing, stronger than most ropes. While securing it to the end of the branch, I felt remnants of a similar web material. That reassured me it was the tree used by Kendall to enter and exit the compound. Gripping the webbed strand, I swung over the two fences and dropped to the hard ground.

Standing up, I brushed off my bottom and looked for the rope-like strand. It had swung back and clung to the tree, almost unnoticeable against the trunk. I moved into the dark shadows of the shack, edged to the other side, and cautiously moved toward the next building.

A loud explosion erupted. Shouting and the sound of running feet followed. Then a burst of gunfire rang out. Conner had come through.

I stayed on full alert and charged toward the building where Kyle was imprisoned. Going around the last structure before reaching my destination, I saw a guard pacing and wondered if it could be Andy. In case it wasn't him, I pulled my knife out of my sheath and inched toward the man.

Another burst of gunfire and the sound of voices yelling came from the front of the compound.

The guard unholstered his weapon, walked to the dirt lane, and turned in the direction of the commotion. I leapt on his back, knocking his gun from his hand and slamming him to the ground. Holding my blade against his throat, I said, "What's your name?"

"Huh?" he mumbled.

"Name," I demanded.

"Martin."

Since some Tegen spiders could still be on the loose, they'd be blamed for any poisoned victims. So without any hesitation, I ejected my poisonous venom filled needles on my fingers. "Sorry, Martin," I said, scratching his neck. I would've preferred to handle him in another way, but leaving witnesses wasn't an option.

He swung around, scrapping his arm against my knife in the process. To avoid the blood seeping from his wound, I jumped to my feet and backed away. He rose, grabbed his pistol and came charging toward me. I ran to another building. He made it halfway there before collapsing in a heap. I wiped my knife on his pants, slipped it back into the sheath, and picked up his gun. Then I yanked the guard behind a stack of lumber probably intended to be used for repairing the burnt buildings and took a few pieces of wood to cover the trail of blood. In order to help confirm he had been poisoned by a spider, I didn't want to leave any sign that he had been trying to defend himself and stuck his gun back in the holster.

The fusillade of gunshots continued. Another explosion went off. It probably wouldn't be long before the authorities showed up.

I went to Kyle's prison and picked the lock. Within a minute, I was bending down by a badly beaten man, stroking his bruised face. "Kyle?"

He opened his puffy eyes and looked at my head covered with the ski mask. "Please...no more."

"Don't worry about the mask. I'm here to help you get away."

"I can't leave Ashley," he mumbled.

"She'll be joining you once you're out of here. Can you stand?"

He pressed his hand against the wall and attempted to rise. I wrapped my arm around his waist and tugged him up as he moaned. With his weight resting on me, I staggered toward the door.

A tall, heavyset, muscular-looking man, dressed in a guard uniform, entered. "Sara?"

I recognized him and knew he worked for Conner, but after I nodded, I still asked, "Andy?"

"Yes." He picked up Kyle as if he weighed nothing. "This way."

I followed Andy to a black Expedition and opened the vehicle's back door.

"Pull up the small silver lever. It looks like part of a seatbelt."

As I lifted it, the floor rose, revealing a compartment. A blanket covered the bottom of it, and I briefly wondered if it hid blood stains from bodies that might've occupied the space.

Andy eased Kyle into it.

"Wha...where are..." Kyle murmured.

"Shhh," I said. "You'll only be in there long enough to get you out of the compound and to a safe place. Try not to make any noise. Don't worry about anything."

Andy closed the compartment. "Here." He handed me a cell phone.

"Thanks, Andy," I said and then took off for Ashley's building.

Mayhem and loud noises continued from the front of the compound.

When I reached the exterior wall of her building, the smell of pesticide still hung heavily in the air. I slipped off my shoes and put them along with the cell phone in my backpack. I scampered up the side of the structure to Ashley's window. Just like I had requested, it was ajar. In order not to scare her, I took off the ski mask and then slid my hand through the opening and raised the window.

Ashley hurried toward me. "This is dangerous. You could fall." She held onto my arm.

I lifted my leg over the ledge and stood up in her room.

"Your feet? Where are your shoes? There's a lot of debris out there, especially from the fire. Any cuts?"

"No problem." I took my shoes and a jogging outfit out of my backpack. "It's easier for me to climb with bare feet."

"I heard explosions, gunshots, and all kinds of noises. Did you do all that?"

"No. I don't have any idea what's going on." I handed her the black jogging suit. "Put this on."

"Is Kyle out?" she asked, taking off her pajamas.

"Yes."

Without asking any more questions, she tugged on the outfit while I unlocked her door and peeked out. A man was lying face down in an awkward position in the hallway near the stairwell. I stared at the body and didn't detect any sign of movement. I looked at Ashley. "Stay here."

I edged the door open wider and cautiously went to the man. I rolled him over to see his face. He was the guy who had escorted Worthington to Kalstein's, alias Barton's, office. His eyes were fixed wide open, but he couldn't see me or anything. He had either been bitten by a Tegen spider or scratched by a Tegen. Noticing Ashley peering out her door, I hurried back into her room. I closed the door and began rummaging through my backpack.

"Does he need help?" she asked.

"No," I said, pulling out my disk. "He's beyond help." I pushed the button on the black side to call Tegen spiders.

She pointed at the device. "Where did you get that?"

"A friend gave it to me."

"You have a friend who works in the lab?"

Not wanting her to dwell on it, I said, "I don't know where he got it."

"It's cool how those things work." She squinted and briefly covered her mouth. "Oh…oh, are spiders loose in here? Were the man's eyes wide open?"

"Yes."

"He's been bitten. He'll be dead soon." Her eyes drifted over the floor and then came to rest on me. "You're not wearing any protective gear. You might get bitten if a spider shows up."

"I'm immune."

"You are?"

I nodded.

"A guy here is too. I don't know who, but he's given us samples of his blood. I'm working with that to try to develop an antidote."

Satisfied no spiders were in her room, I slipped the disk back into my backpack. "Are all of the rooms up here occupied?"

"No."

"To avoid the burnt debris below your window, we'll use another escape route. Where is the closest unoccupied room on the other side of the building?"

"Four down."

"We'll go there in a minute." I put her pillows under the covers and tucked the blanket around them so it would appear she was in bed. "Ready?"

"Yes." She grabbed a small handbag.

I gestured toward it. "Let me take that."

She handed it to me.

After tucking it into my backpack, I inched her door open and scanned the hallway. "Follow me. Close the door behind you."

We crept toward the unoccupied room.

I slowly opened the door. Peering inside, I spotted a spider cage, similar to ones owned by some Tegens, on the bed. The lid had been removed. A woman's body, face down, was on the floor. Wondering what was going on, I turned to Ashley. "There's a spider cage in there. Go back to your room."

Rushing toward her room, she made no attempt to be quiet.

I wanted to search for the spiders, but time was ticking away. I couldn't do that and get Ashley safely out of the compound.

Back in her room, I looked out the window and checked the area below. No one was in sight. I handed her a ski mask. "Put this on."

"But we need to warn everyone about the spiders."

"Maybe the cage was secure. I didn't get a good look," I lied, trying to put her mind at ease.

As she yanked on the ski mask, I put mine back on. I took a rope out of my backpack and tied the end of it around Ashley's waist. "I'm going to lower you slowly. If possible, try not to land on the charred wood," I said, removing my shoes.

The throbbing sound of sirens came from off in the distance as shouting and gunfire continued near the entrance.

"But I'm too heavy for you."

"I can manage. We need to hurry." Then I instructed her to climb out the window as I held firmly onto the rope. Within a minute, she was on the ground and I was climbing down.

"Wow, can you move fast!"

"No more talking. Just follow me." Leading the way, I moved stealthily around the nearby building.

"Aaah," Ashley said.

"Shhh."

"Ba…"

I looked over my shoulder and saw Blake holding onto her arm.

"Sara?" Blake asked.

I pulled Ashley away from him. Since he didn't seem to put up any resistance, I asked her, "Did he scratch you?"

"Really? Sara?" Blake said.

I glared at him.

She checked her arm. "No."

"Why didn't you return my calls?" Blake asked.

"What calls?"

"I called you twice…Susan Anderson."

"Who?" I said, feigning ignorance.

"Your alias—Susan Anderson."

"Blake, I'm not using that name."

"You're not?"

I shook my head. "No. I'll call you later. What's your number?"

He rattled it off.

"Lena, we need to get going," Ashley said, and I thought, *She catches on quickly.*

"Okay, *Lena*," Blake said. "I'll wait for your call."

Ashley and I hurried away. I kept glancing behind us, expecting Blake to be nearby, but I couldn't see him anywhere.

Reaching the fence behind the shack, I felt relieved when I saw the small red lights were off. I took a grappling hook out of my backpack and tied it to the rope. Keeping my hand out of Ashley's view, I ejected a small amount of webbing and spread it over the end of the rope so it would cling to something in case the hook didn't find its mark. I flung it toward the branch, and then tugged. The rope was taunt.

"The fence next to you is electrified," Ashley whispered. "We could die if we touch it."

"No red lights. The electricity is off." I ran my hand over the fence and then moved the backpack to my chest. "I want you to get on my back. I'll climb up the fence, and then we'll swing to the other side."

"I know how to climb ropes."

"You do?"

She nodded.

"Go first. I'll hold onto this end. Be careful around the barbed wire."

Ashley climbed up the fence, reached as high as she could, and grasped onto the rope. She swung her feet over the rows of barbed wire and continued climbing, easily avoiding the barbs on the exterior fence. When she reached the branch, I followed suit.

Sitting next to her in the tree, I began pulling up the rope. The end of it caught on the spikes. "Stay here." I crawled down the tree trunk, scaled the fence, and freed the rope. After I put it in my backpack, the red lights on the interior fence flashed and beeped. The timing seemed too perfect. Conner probably had someone keeping track of me. I scanned the area and caught a glimpse of some movement near a building in the compound but nothing on my side of the fence. I recalled the other times he had me followed and I never saw his men. They were experts at avoiding detection.

I gazed up at Ashley. "Can you get down okay, or do you want my help?"

"I can do it," she said as she descended. Standing on the ground, she splayed her fingers and wiped them on the bark. "Something really sticky is in that tree. Cobwebs. Look." She gestured toward her sleeve. "It's all over me."

I slipped my shoes back on and pulled the silky, soft fibers off my clothing. "Oh, it's on me too. It'll wash out."

"Could any of the lab spiders be out here?"

"I'll check," I said, thinking there was a possibility a spider or more had latched onto our clothing. I fished out the disk, pushed the button, and ran the device over Ashley and along the ground around us. "No spiders. We need to get away from here." I stuck the gadget in my backpack.

Trudging through the foliage, Ashley asked, "How did Kyle look?"

I wanted to tell her he looked good, but it wouldn't be long before she saw him. "Not good."

Tears drizzled down her eyes. "Any broken bones?"

I put my arm around her shoulder. "I don't know. He's probably getting medical care right now."

She sniffled. "How did you get him out?"

"A friend. Kyle was concealed in a car. You'll be with him soon. The people at the compound are going to be searching for you soon if not already. We need to pick up the pace."

About ten minutes later, I saw the bridge we needed to cross.

Blinking red and blue strobe lights shone through the trees. A police cruiser was parked behind my car.

"Take off the ski mask," I said, tugging mine off. I put them in my backpack, pulled out two colorful t-shirts, and handed her one.

Wearing the t-shirts, we headed over the bridge.

An officer climbed out of the patrol car. "Good evening, ladies," he said, moving toward us. "Does this car belong to one of you?" He gestured toward it.

"It's mine. Is there a problem, officer?" I asked as Ashley grabbed my hand.

"Up the road, there's been a…" he began.

A black sedan with its horn blaring zoomed past us.

Without saying another word, he rushed to the cruiser and sped after the black sedan.

"I was so afraid he was going to take me back." Ashley released my hand.

I felt relieved that I didn't need to deliver a string of lies to the policeman in order to justify where Ashley and I had been and why we were out at that hour. "You don't need to worry about that. You're safe with me." I'd feel safe with me, too, if Snyder wasn't roaming around someplace.

After we were settled in my car, I pulled out the phone Andy had given me and called Conner. "Where to?"

"Head south on the highway. When you see a silver van behind you, stop at the side of the road."

"Got it." I disconnected. "We're looking for a silver van."

Then I thought about the woman on the floor. "Who used to occupy the room near yours, the one with the spider cage in it?"

"Doris. She works in the mess hall and used to bring meals to the lab."

"Used to? Did she quit?"

"No. She started asking questions about our project. We're not even supposed to talk about it outside the lab. Someone higher up heard about her, and then she wasn't allowed to bring over the meals anymore."

"Why did she move out of your building?"

"Doris wanted to live in the dorm closer to the mess hall. She only moved out yesterday."

I figured she never left. Instead, she met her fate with a spider because she said too much about what was going on in the lab.

Ashley pointed at the rear window. "There's a silver van behind us. Is Kyle in it?"

"I don't know." I stopped on the shoulder of the highway. "Stay here while I verify that's the right van." Strolling toward it, something odd struck me about the vehicle's paint job—almost like it had just been sprayed. Patches of a dark color appeared around the windshield. Doubting Conner would use a van with that appearance, but curious about the occupants and not wanting the wrong people to know Ashley's whereabouts, I continued walking to the vehicle.

A frumpy-looking, stocky man, wearing paint stained coveralls climbed out of the driver's seat. At the same time, an average-sized man with a muscular build got out on the passenger side.

One man ready to escort Ashley would've been enough. Seeing two men prepared to handle that task, confirmed it wasn't the right van. I wondered how they knew about Conner's arrangement to pick up Ashley. Avoiding saying too much, I asked, "Is there something I can help you with?"

"We're here for the delivery," the stocky man said.

Behind me, a car door creaked open. I looked over my shoulder. "Stay in the car."

"Larry, the girl." The stocky man tilted his head toward my car.

Larry started moving toward her.

As I blocked Larry, the stocky man drew his pistol and pointed it at me.

"Get over here," he said, brandishing the gun and motioning for me to move out of Larry's way.

"No."

"Not afraid of guns, huh?" He stared at me. "I'd put a bullet through your dumb head right now, but the boss wants you alive."

"What do you want with my passenger?"

"She's needed at the compound," he said, keeping his weapon fixed on me.

Based on what I knew about Snyder, neither man fit his description. I slowly moved toward him as if I intended to get in the poorly painted van. He grabbed my arm. Pushing his hand away, my poisonous needles scrapped his skin.

His eyes narrowed, and he pressed the barrel of the gun into my chest. "Get into the van," he said through gritted teeth.

I gave him a sinister smile but didn't budge.

"Let go of me," Ashley yelled.

I glanced behind me and saw Larry yanking Ashley toward the van.

A silver van drove past us. The sound of screeching brakes, tires crunching on the loose gravel along the shoulder of the road, and a cloud of dust followed.

A second later, a gunshot rang out.

Ashley screamed as the man who had been tugging her landed on the ground with a bullet wound in the center of his forehead.

I turned to the stocky man. My poison had taken care of him. To hide the cause of his death, I picked up his weapon, pointed it at his chest and pulled the trigger.

The dust behind the van subsided. With his gun secured in a gloved hand, the man staying at my motel strode toward the poorly painted van.

18

LIES FADE

Ashley appeared to be in a daze. I pushed her behind me and stared at the blond-haired man. "What do you want?"

He motioned for me to be quiet. Doubting he intended to harm us, I didn't say a word as he pulled a gadget out of his pocket—a device I knew was used to search for bugs. Since the man came from a nicely painted silver van, I figured my conversation with Conner had either been overheard or he had a disloyal employee working for him. I put my arm around Ashley and remained motionless while he moved the gadget over us. Nothing. Then he went to my car and began the process there.

Keeping Ashley next to me and guessing the bug had been planted in her purse, I grabbed my backpack, unzipped it, and pulled out her purse. I handed it to the man. He ran the gadget over it. Nothing. I gave Ashley her purse as he went back to searching. He found one attached to the back of the driver's seat and destroyed it.

"A bug," Ashley said to my surprise. "Who put it there?"

The man continued going over my car. Nothing. "All clear," he announced.

"Ashley, probably someone at the compound put it there, but I have no idea how they managed to get into my car to do it."

"Miss," the man said, looking at Ashley. "Come with me. Sara, Mr. Crussett wants you to go to his hotel room."

"You work for Conner?"

"Yes."

"Then you won't mind if I give him a call."

"That's what I would expect."

As I kept a watchful eye on him, I retrieved the cell phone out of my car and tapped in Conner's number.

He answered after the first ring. "Sara, did everything go okay?"

"Well…a couple of complications. I'm with a man who claims he works for you. Can you describe your employee who was assigned to drive the silver van?"

"Thale. He's around six feet, blond hair. No visible scars. Let me talk to him."

I handed the man the phone. "He wants to talk to you."

"Hey, boss….the pink one…" He gave me back the phone.

"So," I said into it.

"That's Thale. You can let Ashley go with him. Are you coming here?"

"Can't. I need to make sure my cover is still intact. I'll call you tomorrow on this phone."

"Any problems, call me or open your door and yell help."

"Will do." I disconnected and took Ashley's hand. "This man's name is Thale. He'll take you to Kyle."

She hugged me. "Thank you, thank you."

Watching Ashley leave with Thale, I realized I had been mistaken about the man who checked into my motel. Thale worked for Conner. He wasn't the driver of the blue truck. Conner's employees would attempt to stay hidden from my sight. Not park in such a conspicuous location.

I climbed into the Corolla and drove to my motel, dreading what Kendall might say to me. Since neither Newark nor Lange was Snyder and I hadn't befriended anyone else at the compound, he might send me home for not following his orders.

I didn't need to wait long to hear from Kendall. He was sitting in my room when I walked in.

"Where have you been?" he asked without showing any emotion.

Then I began the lie. "Newark called after you left and wanted to meet for a drink. He sounded upset. We need the names of the new residents at the compound—those that have been there four months or less—so we can find Snyder. I had hoped I could somehow get him to talk about that. I waited and waited at the bar, but he never showed."

"Your car was parked on the road not far from the compound. How did it get there?"

"Well…I thought something might be wrong since Newark sounded upset. So after waiting for him for almost an hour, I drove to the compound. But as I got closer, I heard an explosion and gunfire and pulled off the road."

"You weren't in your car."

"Okay, I was curious about what was going on, so I crept toward the compound. Were you responsible for all the mayhem?"

His dark eyes fixed on me. "No."

"Do you know what it was about?"

"No."

"Since you saw my car, you must've been there. Did you find Blake?" I asked, wondering if he already heard about my escapade from him.

"No."

"Do you think Blake is the terminated Tegen Snyder mentioned?"

"No. And neither do you."

How does he know that? "Kendall, why are you here?"

"Marge found Blake. He said you had been there helping a compound resident escape. He believes you are using the alias Lena. Now tell me again how you spent the last few hours."

"You already know," I said, relieved I didn't run into Blake until after helping Kyle escape.

"Why did you sacrifice our mission for that girl?"

"She's Worthington's niece. She's been held prisoner there. That's what Barton is holding over Worthington's head. Worthington will do whatever Barton says to keep his niece unharmed."

"How does freeing her help our cause?"

"She's a chemist and has been forced to work on the spider project. She pointed out the building where the lab is held."

"Barton will look for her."

"She's gone someplace safe. I haven't a clue where."

"Is your boyfriend responsible for what went on at the compound?"

I wondered when he started following me, and I didn't want to be sent home until Snyder, whoever he was, had been captured. Somehow I needed to convince Kendall I was still valuable to his mission. "Kendall, I never told him I was in Sedona. I swear. He somehow tracked me down. But I did learn from him that Barton is really Rodney Kalstein. Have you heard that name before?"

"Yes. An arms smuggler. Is that why your boyfriend is in town?"

"As far as I know, Conner's family isn't into smuggling weapons."

"Things change."

"You could be right."

With his eyes boring into me, he said in an even tone. "I'm going to ask you one more time. No more. Sara, is your boyfriend responsible for what went down at the compound?"

I sat quietly staring at him, wanting to lie, but fearing the consequences if he somehow discovered the truth. "I don't know. Maybe. But I'm not positive."

"Can his actions be linked to you?" He asked as if I had answered "Yes" to his previous question.

"I doubt it, but if I quickly left town someone might put that together."

"Besides Blake, did anyone else see you at the compound?"

"A guard. I took care of him. But don't worry. It won't be traced to a Tegen since some of our spiders are loose there. Two people were bitten on the floor where Worthington's niece had a room. There might be more victims. I didn't have a chance to check the whole building." I waited for a response from Kendall. He continued glaring at me. Finally, I couldn't take it anymore and said, "Please don't send me home. I want to see this through. Conner is going to give me a list of the new residents. Blake wants me to call him…Oh, when Marge talked to him, did he reveal the name Snyder is using at the compound?"

"No," he said as his eyes remained fixed on me.

About a minute later, which seemed much longer than that, Kendall spoke again. "Sara, I don't give second chances. But since you didn't volunteer for this mission, I'm taking that into consideration. If you go to the compound again without Worthington or being invited by a resident, you will be sent home. As a member of my team, you *must* follow my orders. Do you understand?"

"Yes, Kendall. I promise." As he rose to his feet, I asked, "Is it okay if I call Blake?"

"Tomorrow, after work." He pulled a phone out of his pocket and handed it to me. "Use this. He doesn't know your true alias. Keep it that way." He lifted the corner of the drape and looked out. Then he opened the door and left.

19

A NEW PLAYER

With less than three hours of sleep, I trudged into the medical center and went to my nurse's station. I had just sat down when Libby came rushing down the hall. "Susan, you're wanted at the compound. Pronto. There's been some kind of shooting. The details are a little sketchy, but from what I've gathered, one of their residents went berserk."

"Anyone dead?"

"I don't know."

"Should I bring supplies?"

"Dr. Worthington didn't request any."

"Just in case, I'll gather up a few and then head out."

"I'll call the scheduled patients. That compound is going through some tough times—first a fire and now this." She shook her head as she walked away.

Going over the bridge leading to the compound, I meandered around two police cruisers. The guard next to the open gate was chatting with an officer. It almost appeared like they were enjoying themselves, joking and laughing. I caught the guard's attention, and he waved me into the compound. As I parked my car, I didn't see one police cruiser inside the fenced area and wondered how Barton managed to keep them out. Then I thought about Barton—would he even talk to them for fear of being recognized? He was probably keeping a low profile or hiding somewhere.

I left the medical supplies in the car in case Worthington didn't need them.

Hoffman stepped through the doorway and stood on the porch. "Susan, in here."

"What happened?" I asked, going into the house.

"Oh, terrible. Just terrible. One of our residents, Kyle Watford, had some kind of a complete mental breakdown and wildly started shooting. We have no idea where he got the gun. Besides our guards, no one has guns here. Kyle used to be such a nice young man, but then he changed," she said, walking down the hall next to me. "Poor Dr. Barton has had such a hard time controlling him. He thought he could straighten him out, but now look what's happened. One member is in the hospital fighting for his life and two others were injured. Dr. Barton is just sick about it. He's gone to the hospital."

"Is Kyle in police custody?"

"Oh, no. Before the police could get here, he ran off with his girlfriend, Ashley. The police are looking for them."

"Did you see the shooting?"

"Oh, no. Thank goodness."

I had to hand it to Barton. He was clever to pin the shooting on Kyle. Now the police were searching for the fugitive couple. Even if Kyle and Ashley told the truth about the compound, they'd have no proof. And those loyal to Barton, like Hoffman, would make Kyle out to be a troubled person, easily capable of shooting up the place, not caring about who might get hurt in the process.

When we reached the room at the end of the hall where Worthington was busy stitching up a woman's arm, Hoffman turned and went toward the front of the house.

"What would you like me to do?" I asked Worthington.

"Make sure the patients in the room across the hall are resting comfortably. When I finish with Alice, we'll go to the administration building."

I went into the other room to find two men, asleep. Including the man in the hospital, that made four gunshot patients. Strange. Hoffman mentioned three had been shot. Why didn't her count include all of them? I rejoined the doctor.

"Take one of these every four hours." Worthington handed Alice a pill bottle. "They should help with the pain and swelling."

"Thank you, Dr. Worthington." Alice moved slowly as she left.

I helped the doctor gather up the remaining supplies.

As soon as we stepped off the front porch and were alone, he grabbed my arm. "What went wrong getting Kyle and Ashley out of here. Did you give him a gun?"

"No. And Kyle was in no condition to shoot a gun. He had to be carried out of the makeshift jail."

"Who carried him?"

"Not me." Then, maintaining my FBI persona that Worthington believed, I said, "All I am at liberty to tell you is that Kyle and Ashley are out. They had nothing to do with the shooting, and neither did the FBI."

Worthington gave me a puzzled look. "Then who?"

I shrugged. "Maybe a disgruntled member? Someone else being held here against their will?"

"Is the FBI looking into it?"

"Sorry, I can't discuss the case."

"Earlier, a news crew was at the gate. They weren't allowed inside, but a compound member—I don't know who—went out and talked to them. Everyone here has been told that Kyle is responsible. That's probably what's going to be on the news. Can I tell my wife Kyle wasn't involved?"

I shook my head. "No. Not yet, but it won't be long."

Walking along the path, I noticed some vehicles with shattered windows and numerous bullet holes. As we got closer to the building, I saw a crew boarding up its windows. "Why are we going to the administration building?"

"To check on the injured."

"Mrs. Hoffman said only three had been shot and one of them is in the hospital. She forgot to count one of the patients you just saw. How many were really shot?"

"Seven."

"Why not tell the truth?"

"Had one man not been so badly injured that he needed to be taken to the hospital, Barton probably would've claimed no one was shot. Publicity isn't anything he wants."

"Any idea why they just didn't say only one guy got shot?"

"Someone most likely said two others were injured before Barton could silence him or her."

Worthington had complained earlier that Barton didn't allow ambulances into the compound. Those that became sick and should've gone to the hospital were kept at the compound. Why did Barton allow an ambulance into the compound to pick up that man? Was he in Barton's inner circle?

A tall, thin man stood on the front stoop. He opened the door and escorted us in. Going past an unmanned counter, I heard a man say, "...not at the trailer."

Another voice followed. "Keep looking."

A bald, beefy-looking man came rushing out of a doorway. I wondered if the "trailer" was the burnt one at the gun range.

Worthington walked into that room with me right behind him.

"Dr. Worthington," said the man sitting at a large oak desk. He had thick auburn hair, a ruddy completion, and appeared to be in his late forties.

Worthington opened his medical bag, pulled out a package, and laid it on the desk.

I assumed Barton was the man behind the desk, the same man Hoffman claimed had left to be with the hospitalized gunshot victim, but I had already figured he wouldn't venture away from the compound.

He looked at the package and gave a nod. "All finished?"

"Mrs. Hoffman mentioned a woman became very ill last night. Would you like me to see her after I check in on the injured?"

Without answering Worthington's question, he looked at me, stood up, and walked around his desk. "Is this your new nurse?"

"Yes. Susan Anderson."

"Susan, welcome to the Fellowship of the Good Earth," he said, eyeing me up and down.

"Thank you. This is such a lovely place," I said, and I meant it. The appearance of compound was nice, but the workings of the place didn't blend with it.

"I'd like to discuss a private matter with you. Would that be possible?"

"Yes," I said, wondering what he had in mind.

"Would you be available to come to the compound sometime Friday evening?"

Since he wasn't Snyder, I doubted I needed to be concerned,

unless Snyder had played a role in Barton's invitation. "I think I can arrange that."

He handed me a business card. "Call if you can't make it."

"I'll do that." I headed toward the door with Worthington.

Worthington stopped at the threshold and turned to Barton. "Do you want me to check on the sick woman?"

"No. She's much better today."

I tagged along with Worthington to check on the four patients he had stitched up earlier inside the building. We were escorted down the hall to a large open space with closed doors lining one side of it and a sitting area on the other side. Only one person occupied that area, a bearded man in his twenties. He sat on the couch, reading a newspaper. A table with a few chairs in front of it stood between two of the closed doors. When we had spread out medical supplies on the table, our escort opened one of the doors, stuck his head inside, and called out the first patient.

The man on the couch occasionally peered at us over the top of the newspaper. I speculated if he was just curious or if he had been instructed to keep track of us, but our escort never left our side. Wouldn't one pair of watchful eyes have been enough? I shuffled around the medical supplies, trying to look busy as Worthington checked the patients. Two had bandages wrapped around an arm, one had a bandaged head, and the last one was limping around with a bandaged foot. From the sawdust on their clothing, it appeared they had all been working on something in the adjacent room. The door to that room remained closed except when each man slipped out of it to see Worthington.

As I mulled over how the last guy ended up with a bullet wound in his foot, Worthington said softly, "Some flying debris went right through his shoe."

The four patients didn't have severe injuries, but they all had pale faces and tired-looking eyes. Leaving the building, I asked Worthington, "Shouldn't those men be taking it easy, at least for a day or two?"

"Yes, but I can't force them to rest."

"Who was the guy on the couch?"

"Nathan Milner. I've run into him a couple of times in Barton's office. Barton introduced us."

"He's not one of your patients?"

"No."

"Do you know if he's part of Barton's inner circle?"

"Alex Newark and Sean Lange seem to be. Outside those two, I don't know, but Milner does hang around the admin building, and I've never noticed him working on anything. He could be one of Barton's chosen few." Worthington walked me to my car. "Susan, Barton is a dangerous man. I realize in your position you want to learn everything you can about him, but do be careful if you come here Friday night."

"I'll have it covered."

Worthington patted me on the shoulder as he glanced around. "I have to decide if I'll ever return to this place. I don't need to protect Ashley anymore. The first thing I heard when I got here was that Kyle and Ashley had taken off." He inhaled deeply. "Ashley is free, and so am I. Take the rest of the day off, Susan. That's what I intend to do."

As I drove away from the compound, I thought about the man named Nathan Milner. Worthington had never seen him as a patient. Neither Newark nor Lange was the illusive Tegen. Milner appeared to be the right age to be a Tegen. Could he be Snyder? Thinking about the possibility, I checked my watch—11:59 a.m.—and then flipped on the radio to catch the news.

"….slowly emerging about the early morning shooting at the Fellowship of the Good Earth," a reporter announced. "What we've gathered so far is that one of the members went on a shooting spree. One victim is in critical condition at a Phoenix hospital. Two others have minor injuries. The police are searching for a person of interest, but they haven't released the name. Now to the national news..."

I pushed off the radio, feeling relieved that the local police hadn't given the press Kyle's name. The more I thought about the whole incident at the compound, the angrier I grew with Conner. I had asked him to create some commotion, not to shoot up the whole place. It was lucky no one was killed. Or were there fatalities? Would Barton even mention if someone had died? That would draw more unwanted attention to the compound. And what about the man and woman who had been bitten? Could the woman be the same one that Worthington had heard was sick? What happened to the bodies that Snyder either couldn't or didn't want to consume? One Tegen can only eat so much.

As more questions buzzed around in my head, I turned onto the street leading to my motel. Then I recalled the first conversation I overheard in the administration building—the man mentioning a trailer and Barton saying "keep looking." Could it have anything to do with Snyder? Instead of heading to my motel, I decided to take a little detour—to the gun range.

20

UNFORESEEN DEMAND

I parked on the shoulder of the road past the turn off to the gravel road leading to the gun range. I opened the trunk and pulled out my binoculars. Standing next to the fence and surveying the area, I couldn't see any vehicles or people at the range. I slipped on a black t-shirt over my white blouse and tied my hair back. Then my cell phone rang, and I pulled it out of my purse and looked at the screen.

"Hi, Alex," I answered.

"With the shooting at the compound, I can't make dinner tonight. How about tomorrow?"

"That works for me. I was there earlier with Worthington. I just don't understand how someone could do that."

"Kyle's been a problem for a while. We should've seen this coming."

"Have you heard how the guy in the hospital is doing?"

"His surgeon isn't giving him good odds."

"What a shame. I'll pray for him."

"He'd appreciate it."

After we said our goodbyes, I turned off my phone and dropped it in my purse.

Glancing at the passing cars and not wanting to draw any attention, I put on a cap and sunglasses instead of a ski mask.

With the binoculars dangling around my neck, I jogged along the gravel road for a few hundred feet. Then, I quickly climbed over the fence and ducked down between sagebrush. Peering through the binoculars, I checked out the area again. Still no sign of any vehicles. Remaining on high alert for cars turning onto the gravel road, I stood and ran toward the gun range. When I reached the gate, I saw it had been repaired with sturdy timber. I scurried over it and crept toward the storage shed. The place was completely deserted and the burnt trailer gone. A pile of ashes remained were it had once stood.

Any vehicle pulling onto the gravel road would stir up a cloud of dust. The driver could see a woman wandering around but wouldn't be able to make out my features. Knowing that, I strolled around the gun range with no idea what I was looking for. A piece of pipe lay next to the storage shed. I picked it up and combed through the ashes. Something shiny caught my attention. I bent down and lifted it up—a broken silver watchband—and examined it closely. There wasn't anything unusual about it. I went back to searching through the ashes. Nothing. I gazed at the shed, irritated with myself for not having any picks with me. Still, I tugged on the padlock. It remained tightly locked. I continued walking around the gun range as my eyes drifted over the ground. A small pile of ashes was next to the gate. Sweeping the pipe through them, I heard a clinking sound, like the pipe had struck a metal object. I spread out the ashes with the pipe. Not hearing the sound again or seeing anything, I bent down and ran my fingers through the disbursed ashes. I touched something hard. Guessing it might just be a rock, I wrapped my hand around it and pulled it up. Opening my palm, I stared at a mud-caked Tegen ring. I bit my lower lip, and my eyes moistened. Isaac's ring. He was the Tegen I never met who died at the hands of Snyder.

I raised the bottom of my t-shirt and rubbed the ring. As the clumps of dirt fell on the ground, I noticed its size. It seemed too small to fit a man's finger. In fact, it looked about the same size as my ring. To verify mine was still securely in place, I stuck my hand in my bra and inhaled deeply when I felt it. Was Isaac a small man, or did the ring belong to someone else? Putting it in my pocket, I wondered if it could be what Barton wanted his men to find.

After placing the pipe by the shed where I'd found it, I wiped off my fingerprints, and then headed back to my car.

Reaching my motel room, I used the cell phone Kendall had given me in the early hours of the morning to call Blake.

"Hello," he answered in a hesitant tone.

"Blake, it's Sara."

"Sara, did Kendall do all the shooting at the compound so you could get Ashley Phillips out of there?"

Since Ashley and Kyle had been talked about at the compound, I figured that was how he heard her name, but wanting verification, I asked, "How do you know the name of the woman I was with?"

"Kendall wouldn't send you here to break her out without a reason. She's been working on the spider project. And from what I hear, she was close to making a breakthrough."

"What are people saying at the compound about the gunfire?"

"That Kyle Watford, Ashley's boyfriend, started it. The higher-ups know better. They suspect it's connected to the rescue of Ashley and her boyfriend since they were the only two missing after the shooting. Someone thought Ashley's uncle might be behind it, but they've ruled him out. Now they're looking into Watford's family. Some of those folks have plenty of bucks. Where are you hiding her?"

"In a safe place." I doubted Blake was really on our side.

"You don't trust me. Do you?"

"Blake, I don't know you well enough to trust you."

"I didn't squeal on you last night. I'd never let Snyder hurt you. That's why I kept trying to call you, to warn you. You need to stay away from the old barn at the compound."

"Why?"

"Ted." He always referred to Snyder by that nickname. "He'll catch you for sure if you go in there. It's booby-trapped."

"Is that where he keeps his spiders?"

"Maybe. He's pretty secretive. He's not as chummy with me as he used to be. Don't know what's going on, but it's something to do with the spider project."

I feigned ignorance. "What's the spider project?"

"Kendall never told you?"

"Does he know?"

"Marge knows. She'd spill it to him."

"So what is it?"

"They're trying to turn some regular spiders into Tegen spiders."

"Did Snyder tell them about our spiders?"

"Yes, but he didn't tell them about Tegens."

"Why do they want spiders like ours?"

"Ted's being hush hush about it. Can't get a word out of him, but it has to be something big. He's become Barton's best buddy, and Barton's hired some scientists and chemists to work on the project."

"He won't tell you a thing?" I still doubted Blake was being truthful. "Do you think Snyder no longer trusts you?"

"Nah. He still trusts me, and he likes having a Tegen on his side. It's not exactly like he could recruit another Tegen. No one would even consider it. No matter what he promised them."

"Did he promise you something?"

"Sexy chicks and wealth. Never happened."

"What alias is Snyder using?"

"If I tell you, can you get the council to let me off the hook for escaping and for not squealing on Ted?"

"Blake, I don't have any pull with the council, but I will tell them how you helped us. I'm sure that will count for something."

"No. I need some kind of assurance," he said in a firm tone.

"Maybe Kendall can give that to you. Let me see what I can find out."

"Call me when you get it squared away." He disconnected.

Blake wanted assurance that I couldn't give him, and I doubted Kendall would even consider contacting the Council on Blake's behalf. Help in identifying Snyder wouldn't be forthcoming from Blake.

Conner promised to have a list compiled of the newer residents at the compound, those that had been there less than five months. Snyder's alias had to be on that list. It couldn't tell me who Snyder was, but at least it would narrow down the suspects. I put away the cell phone I had just used and went to the bureau to retrieve the one Andy had given me. It wasn't tucked underneath my sweater where I had left it earlier. I rummaged through all the drawers. It was gone. In desperation, I searched through my purse, hoping somehow I had dropped it in there. The only phone in it was the one Kendall had given me when I first arrived in Sedona, and I'd be going against his orders if I used it for personal calls. Knowing an intruder had been in my room, I hurried to the fridge and examined the milk bottles containing *venotrolia*. Their caps were still intact. Next, I pulled out the bureau and saw the dart gun tucked underneath it. It appeared nothing else had been snatched or disturbed. The missing cell phone only had one number in it—Conner's. Why would someone take it?

A knock came on my door.

Contemplating grabbing the dart gun, I peered through the peephole and saw a short woman in her early forties. I cracked the door open. "Yes."

"Dr. Alston wanted me to give you this," she said, handing me an envelope.

"Are you supposed to wait for a reply?"

"He instructed me to slip it under your door, but before I did, I wanted to make sure you weren't in. In case you want to talk to me after you read his note, I'll wait here."

I noticed the envelope was addressed to Susan Anderson, Red Hills Motel, Room #214. Inside was a handwritten letter. I recognized Father's writing.

Dear Sara,

After hearing about the shooting at the compound, I assumed Dr. Worthington might discover your lack of nursing skills if he hasn't already. Crystal Matthews, the woman who delivered this letter, is a registered nurse. Perhaps you could sway Dr. Worthington into allowing her to work by your side, and she could fill in for you if your mission requires your attention during work hours. She will be staying at the Hilton.

Please be careful.

Love, Father

I tucked the letter back into the envelope and opened the door for Crystal. "Please come in." After she entered and was settled in a chair by the table, I asked, "What did Dr. Alston tell you about my work assignment?"

"Well, he woke me up around 3:00 a.m. to ask if I would consider flying to Sedona, Arizona, to help out a woman who's on a special assignment and is pretending to be a nurse. I wasn't to ask her any questions about the assignment or tell anyone that she wasn't a trained nurse. In return, I'd be staying at the Hilton Sedona Resort, all expenses paid. When my services were no longer needed, Dr. Alston would fly out one of my friends to join me. Then we'd enjoy a two-week vacation, also all expenses paid, at the resort before flying back to North Dakota. I jumped at the chance, quickly packed, and took a 6:25 a.m. flight. Must admit, right now I feel pretty beat."

"He didn't tell you anything about the special assignment?"

"Not a word. I've worked for Dr. Alston for a while and I trust him, so I know it isn't anything shady."

"Can you give me your cell phone number?"

She nodded.

I tore a page out of a notepad and handed it to her. I waited while she wrote it down and then said, "I'll call you tomorrow morning after I figure out how this will work."

As soon as she left, I went into the bathroom and burned the letter from Father in the sink. Then I sat down on the couch and thought about the stolen cell phone. Suddenly it occurred to me that whoever had taken it might not have realized it only had one number in it. Guessing the culprit who stole it had some connection to Snyder, I worried that Conner might be in danger.

Snagging my purse, I headed out the door.

21

QUID PRO QUO AGREEMENT

Driving toward Conner's hotel, I kept my eyes peeled for possible followers. Even though I didn't see any, I still parked a block away. As I walked toward his hotel, I continued scanning the street and sidewalk for anyone following me. In front of the hotel, I noticed a limo with two men, dressed in suits, standing stiffly by it and looking around. From their demeanor, I figured they were bodyguards. When Conner traveled, he normally was driven around in a Cadillac Escalade, not a limo. I didn't see a limo in the parking lot last time I visited him. There was a possibility that the limo passengers had nothing to do with Conner, but I knew his other family members always used limos regardless of where they went. Since they all believed I was dead, I had to avoid running into any of them.

As a precaution, I walked to the back of the building. A few people milled about outside, making it impossible for me to climb up the structure without being observed. I continued along the walkway until I was right below Conner's suite and looked up. Seeing the drawn drapes and empty balcony, I had no clue if Conner had company. I noticed his balcony door stood ajar and walked through the rear building entrance and climbed the stairs to the second floor. I gazed toward the other end of the hallway and saw three suit-clad men standing outside Conner's suite. Bodyguards. But three seemed excessive. Had something happened? Maybe they weren't all employed by Conner.

I wanted to find out if he had a visitor and knocked on a door near to me, hoping that room was unoccupied. No one answered. I knocked again and intensely listened for movement. Nothing. I fished my picks out of my purse, and then dropped my purse. Pretending to be gathering up the spilled contents, I quickly picked the lock. Within a few seconds, I was inside. Personal items were lying around; someone was staying there. I slid open the balcony door and stepped out, closing it behind me. All the balconies on that side of the building were vacant. I slipped off my shoes and tucked them along with my purse behind a planter. Then I swiftly crawled on the roof to Conner's suite and eased down to his balcony. Sitting on the railing and prepared to scoot underneath the balcony if his door opened wider, I began to eavesdrop.

An unfamiliar male voice said, "...positive it's him."

"Senator, we've verified his fingerprints," Conner said. "And it will be handled like we discussed."

"No body," the unfamiliar voice said. "This has to be kept quiet. No one is to know what happened to Kalstein."

Kalstein? I actually believed Conner when he told me he didn't know anything about the man except what he heard on the news. Duped again. Had I led him to Kalstein? Or was he already homing in on him before I showed up in Sedona? And it sounded like a hit job. I didn't realize his family's business included doing murder-for-hire. Or was it a favor to a senator? The Crussetts, Conner's family, had a few politicians in their pockets. Maybe that was how they acquired them, by doing favors.

"You'll be informed when it's been taken care of."

Feet pounded across the carpet and then onto a tile floor. I assumed they were walking toward the door.

"Then I'll make sure the charges against your friend are dropped," said the unfamiliar voice.

"Nice doing business with you, Senator," Conner said as a door clicked open.

I continued to hear voices but couldn't make out what was being said. I hurried back to the balcony where I had left my purse and shoes. I looked through the glass door to check that the hotel guests hadn't returned. After putting my shoes back on, I intended to climb down the exterior of the building, but then voices drifted up from the patio below. I contemplated crawling along the roof until I found a place where I could go down unseen. Not sure if I would find such a place, I opened the balcony door, hurried across the room and peeked out into the hallway. To my relief, no one was nearby. I looked toward Conner's suite. Only one suit-clad man stood outside his door. I headed down the stairs to the first floor and went to the lobby. There, I used a house phone and called Conner's suite.

"Yes," he answered.

"It's me. I'm in the lobby."

"Susan, can you come up?"

I smiled, thinking he remembered to use my alias. "Yes, but I wanted to make sure you didn't have any visitors."

"No visitors. I've just been on the phone most of the day."

"I'll be right up."

Stepping out of the elevator, I was greeted by one of his bodyguards, who opened Conner's door for me.

Conner wrapped me in his arms. "You're off work early today. Did Worthington fire you?"

The corners of my mouth curved up. "No. He thinks I'm doing a great job."

He brushed his lips against mine and then led me to the couch. "Moving right up that professional medical ladder."

"Some people were injured at the compound…from the wee hours of this morning's excitement. Worthington had me go there to help him, and then he gave me the rest of the day off."

"Injured? What's the tally?"

"Eight total. That includes a guy who cut his foot on debris. Of the seven shot, one's in the hospital and the rest are at the compound."

"According to the news only three were shot. Kalstein most likely doesn't want the authorities to know the extent of the gunfire. Interesting that he pinned it on Kyle Watford."

"Can you do anything about that?"

"Already taken care of. When Watford no longer needs to stay in a safe location, he'll have an ironclad alibi that he left the compound the day before the shooting."

"How is he?"

"Not good, but he'll recover. Based on his injures, he wouldn't have survived the week without medical attention."

"And Ashley?"

"She doesn't have a scratch on her. She's diligently watching over Watford."

"Conner, when I asked you to create a diversion, I didn't intend for you to shoot up the place. It's just lucky that only one person needed to be hospitalized."

"Is that what Worthington believes?"

"Yes. Were there more hospitalized?"

"Not hospitalized. Dead."

"How many?"

"Four. Maybe more."

"Any children?"

"No." He gently raised my chin and gazed into my eyes. "Sara, we didn't start the shooting. The explosions were planted in the gulley by my men and timed to go off at various intervals. They were loud, but not intended to be destructive, similar to fireworks. My men only used weapons to defend themselves. Kalstein had a few people he wanted eliminated and took advantage of the commotion. The guy in the hospital, James Herman, is part of Kalstein's inner circle. One of the targeted fellowship members got off a shot before he died. The bullet struck Herman."

"How do you know that?"

A faint smile crossed Conner's lips, and he stroked my cheek. Without answering my question, he said, "The guy who survived the shooting at the gun range is starting to talk. He has described you in broad terms—slender, brown hair, five-foot-eight or nine, and you wore a cap, sunglasses. When he's moved out of the ICU, the cops intend to send a sketch artist to his hospital room."

"Any idea how soon that might be?"

"Three, four days."

"Here I came to warn you, and you're warning me."

"Is that the only reason you came here?" Conner kissed my neck and began unbuttoning my blouse.

"Well," I said, enjoying his attention, "I'm glad my date was postponed."

"Date?"

"Yes, with Gil Tunell, alias Alex Newark. Remember, I'm looking for the source of the spiders. He's my link to get close to Kalstein." I had the urge to tell him that Kalstein wanted to see me Friday night about a personal matter, but since he had plans for Kalstein, I decided against sharing that information.

His mouth smothered mine with a kiss as he continued unbuttoning my blouse. "Can you stay all night?"

"No. The team I'm working with might want to have a meeting." I ran my fingers through his hair. "But I'm not in a rush to leave."

Shortly before 11:00 p.m., I finally managed to pull myself away from Conner and dress, feeling blissfully rejuvenated. "I'll call you tomorrow. Oh, that's what I came to warn you about. The phone Andy gave me has been stolen. It was the only thing taken from my room."

"I have another one for you." He went and took a cell phone out of the drawer.

"Conner, your phone number was in it. Aren't you worried about that?"

"No. I'm the thief." He handed me a phone.

"Huh?"

"After the problem that occurred early this morning...the bug situation...my security expert had some concerns about that phone. The bug in your car could not have picked up my part of our conversation. This phone," he said, handing it to me, "has additional security features."

"When I finished talking to you, I told Ashley what type of vehicle we were looking for, and that conversation could've been overheard."

"Good point."

"You just rummaged through my drawers without even talking to me about it?"

"Sara, my security guy felt it needed to be handled quickly. You weren't at your place of employment, and I couldn't go out to the compound to discuss it with you. There was no option."

Here I had told him about going to the compound, and he knew all along. He was probably also aware of my trip to the gun range. Wondering if any of his men had observed me climbing to and from Conner's balcony door, I felt my stomach churning but forced myself not to show any signs of being worried. Would I have looked like a skilled climber or someone with unnatural abilities?

As I picked up my purse, Conner pulled me close to him and passionately kissed me. Then I realized even if he knew about me spying on him earlier, it wasn't a problem. Suddenly, the list popped into my head. "Oh, do you have the names of the compound's new residents?"

"Right here." He took a folder from the desk. Before he gave it to me, he caressed me again in his arms.

A tingling sensation ran through my body, and I wanted to return to his bed but lacked the time. Since I hadn't been in my motel room all day and with Snyder on the loose, Kendall or another member of the team was probably searching for me. "I need to go."

22

THE LIST

Climbing out of my car at the motel, I saw the blue truck two stalls away from me and caught a glimpse of the back of a man's head through the driver's window. I walked at a brisk pace to my room. Just like I expected, the door was unlocked. I figured Kendall was inside waiting for me.

As I pushed the door open, I saw Marge sitting on the couch and Kendall leaning over the desk, thumbing through a stack of papers.

Marge smiled. "How was your date?"

"Because of the early morning shooting at the compound, Newark postponed our date until tomorrow night."

"Then where have you been?" Marge seemed annoyed.

"With a friend." My eyes swept around the room. "Will Todd be joining us?"

"No," Kendall said.

"He's been busy working while you've been busy having fun." Marge made no attempt to hide her anger.

I eased down onto a chair. "Marge, I'm not supposed to contact Kendall unless it's an emergency. Outside that, I have no way of letting you or Kendall know my whereabouts. And if an emergency arose that I didn't know about, I assumed one of you would contact me. Has something happened?"

"No. We're here to discuss Blake," she said, and it surprised me that she appeared to be the spokesperson instead of Kendall. "Have you talked to him?"

"Yes, I called him earlier. He refuses to tell us the alias Snyder is using unless we can assure him that the Council will forgive him for escaping and his association with Snyder. He wants a complete pardon for his offenses."

"Not acceptable," Kendall said. "Can you get him away from the compound?"

"Maybe. I'll try. How can I contact you if I succeed?"

Kendall handed me a slip of paper. "Call this number."

"Which cell phone should I use?"

"Either. Refer to him as a package, no name."

"Blake mentioned I shouldn't go into the old barn at the compound. He claims it's booby-trapped."

"I've been in there," Marge said. "That's where Blake showed up and we talked. I didn't see any signs of it being booby-trapped. Some bales of hay were stacked near one wall, and a large pile of straw was in the corner. Snyder could be hiding his spiders behind the bales or in the straw. Blake might've said the barn was booby-trapped to keep you out of there. We're not convinced he isn't playing both sides."

"We've looked for the spiders in all the small structures at the compound," Kendall said. "The barn will be searched thoroughly tomorrow night when you're on your date."

"Newark won't be at the compound, but what about Snyder?" I asked.

"I'll be watching for anyone approaching the barn while Kendall is inside," Marge said.

I held up the folder Conner had given me. "Since Blake's help most likely won't be forthcoming, this might help us figure out who Snyder is. This file contains a list of the new residents at the Fellowship."

Kendall moved closer to me as I opened the folder. "How did you get the list?"

"From a friend." I placed the list on the coffee table.

We all hovered over the table and studied the thirty names on the list. Next to each name was the date the person moved to the compound. Handwritten notes next to some of the names indicated their occupation—chemist, scientist, engineer, and arms expert. Others had question marks next to them. As I looked closer, I detected it was a copy. Conner had kept the original. While I speculated about what Conner planned to do with the information, I scanned the names and immediately noticed Sean Lange and Nathan Milner on it. A question mark was written next to Lange's name and "arms expert" by Milner's. Both men had arrived at the compound almost five months ago, within two days of each other. I pointed to Milner's name. "I saw him at the compound today. He was in the same room where Worthington examined some of the injured from this morning's shootings."

"What was Milner doing?" Kendall asked.

"Reading a newspaper, but it seemed like he was keeping an eye on Worthington and me."

"Describe him," Marge said.

"Brown hair, in his twenties, and he had a beard. Beards of all sizes and shapes seem to be popular with the guys at the compound."

"How tall?" Kendall asked.

"He remained seated all the time we were there, but I'd guess around six feet. Worthington did say Milner hangs around the administration building and he's never seen him do any work."

"We can rule out women on the list and those that arrived within the last three months. That leaves seven." Kendall looked at me. "Any possibility this list isn't complete?"

I shrugged. "Right now, it's all we've got to go on."

Marge pulled a notepad and pen out of her purse. "I'll have someone research these people. Maybe we can narrow it down some more." She scribbled down names.

Kendall picked up the papers on the desk, the ones he had been thumbing through when I walked in. "I obtained copies of all compound purchases made during the last two months."

"How did you get those?"

Ignoring my question, he pulled out one of the documents. "Milner ordered some of the items, mainly different types of ammunition. Newark also ordered items along with a woman, Mrs. Hoffman. Besides those three and Barton, no other names appear on any of the purchase orders."

"Milner must be in Barton's inner circle," I said. "Hoffman is an elderly woman and runs the main house. She's loyal to Barton, but I assume he keeps her in the dark about lab business, especially anything of a criminal nature. Doubt she even knows that Barton is using an alias."

"Alias?" Marge said.

"Yes. He's Rodney Kalstein, an arms smuggler hiding from the Feds."

"Did your boyfriend tell you that?" Marge asked to my surprise.

I had no idea that she knew anything about Conner. Then I figured Kendall must've mentioned him. "Yes."

"Is that why he's in town?"

"I don't know."

"He hasn't told you why he's here?" Marge's tone conveyed doubt.

I wanted to shout, "He's in town to be with me!" Instead, I said, "Conner is secretive about his business." Wanting to get off the subject of Conner, I took the Tegen ring out of my pocket and placed it on the table. "I found this at the gun range today. Was Isaac a small man?"

"No." Kendall lifted up the ring and examined it.

"Snyder told you that he had eliminated another member of the team. This ring must've belonged to that person." I stared at Kendall. "Who else did you have working on this mission?"

"Why did you go to the gun range?" Kendall asked without answering my question.

"When I was at the compound today, I overheard Barton say 'trailer' and 'keep looking' to a guy. Then I thought about the burnt trailer. After Worthington finished up with the patients at the compound, he went home and gave me the rest of the day off. I headed to the gun range."

"You shouldn't have gone there without discussing it with me first." Kendall showed no emotion.

"I figured if something were there that Barton wanted, his employee would be heading to the gun range soon. He might find it before we had a chance to look. Hey, I'm not sure if the ring is even what Barton wanted the guy to find, but I didn't run across anything else, and without my picks, I couldn't get into the storage shed."

"If I get a chance, I'll check out the shed tomorrow," Marge said.

"This ring was in the trailer?" Kendall asked.

"No. The trailer is gone. The ring was in a pile of ashes near the gate."

Kendall pulled his cell phone out of his pocket and gazed at it. Since it hadn't made a sound, I assumed it was on vibrate. "What?"

Even though Kendall didn't put it on speaker, I still heard a male caller say, "There's been another fire at the compound. It was put out quickly. The side of another dorm building was scorched."

"So what's the problem?"

"A large van pulled in. Three guys are loading it with wrapped items from one of the small buildings, the one we call 'IB.' Kendall, I think it's bodies."

"How many?"

"Nine. I have to keep ducking behind a building, so it might be more than that. Do you want me to follow the van when it leaves?"

"Yes. Do any of the three guys fit Snyder's description?"

"Two seem to be about the right height and build, but I can't get close enough to make out any features. The third guy is shorter and heavyset. The van's taking off." He disconnected.

"I heard," Marge told Kendall. "Do you want me to take Todd's place at the compound?"

"No. I'll go." He lifted the corner of the drape and looked out. "Sara, drive around a block or two. See if you can draw away that blue truck."

"Any idea who's driving it?"

"No. It's registered to a corporation in Wisconsin. That's all we've got so far." Kendall dropped the ring into his pocket.

"Can I have the ring?"

"Why?"

"I might be able to use it to draw Blake away from the compound."

He handed it to me.

I put the ring in my purse, opened the door and walked out, closing the door behind me. I hurried down the stairs, climbed into my car, and drove around aimlessly while continually checking my mirrors. I never spotted the blue truck.

Twenty minutes later, I parked at the motel. The blue truck was nowhere in sight. I headed back to my room. Kendall and Marge were gone. After getting ready for bed, I peeked through the small opening between the drapes and saw the blue truck back in the same spot where it had been parked earlier.

Then I went through my nighttime routine: bolting door, removing ovoid container with my precious spiders from my purse, feeding and putting them in my nightstand drawer, and finally retrieving the hidden dart gun for better access beside the bed. Convinced I was prepared for any intruders, I slipped under the covers and fell asleep.

23

WANDERING ARACHNIDS

Sensing spiders crawling on me, my eyes snapped open as I wondered how they got out of their container. With the aid of my enhanced night vision, I saw the delicate creatures climbing up my arm and more on the blanket. My container only had six spiders in it, not hundreds. I sat up in bed. Most of the spiders fell off my arm and landed on the sheet. Picking one up, it didn't emanate the warmth of a Tegen spider. Then I lifted up another one and immediately felt the soothing sensation my spiders gave me. Upon closer examination, some of the arachnids were Tegen spiders, but, besides their color, the other spiders lacked any other similarities to Tegen spiders. I leaned over and opened the nightstand drawer to check my spiders in the cage. None of them were missing.

Staring at the little creatures moving over my bed and on the floor, I knew there were too many of them to have wandered into my room of their own accord. They had been planted, but why and by whom? I carefully climbed out of bed to avoid stepping on any of them and took my disk out of my purse. I got a plastic container out of the kitchen and then pushed the button on the disk and gathered up the Tegen spiders that came. Hoping there weren't any more among the other spiders, I closed the container lid. Skirting around the remaining crawling creatures, I verified the door bolt was still in place and searched for potential small openings. The bolt remained secure, but the bottom corner—less than an inch—of the door was missing. The edge next to it was rough, like it had recently been broken off. To funnel that many spiders through a tiny opening had to have been planned. But why?

As I wondered how to handle the other spiders and worried some Tegen spiders could have left my room the same way they entered, I glanced at the clock—6:45 a.m. My alarm would be going off in thirty minutes. Not coming up with any quick way to take care of the problem, I decided it fell under the emergency category, picked up my cell phone, and called Kendall.

"What's wrong?" he said in an even tone.

"Spiders. Over a hundred were planted in my room. Some are Tegen spiders. I think I've corralled all of them in a container, but there is a chance a few could've gone exploring. I don't know what to do about the other spiders, and I need to get ready for work. Should I call in sick and do a thorough search of the motel for Tegen spiders?"

"No. Go to work and…"

A loud scream echoed through my room.

"Someone screamed. I'm going to check."

"I'll be there soon."

I disconnected, slipped on my robe and slippers, stuck my disk in a pocket, and went out the door.

A few people peered out their doors, and two motel maids stood by my neighbor's open door.

"What happened?"

"We don't know," one maid said. "The manager is on his way."

Gazing into the room, I saw a man in pajamas stretched out on the floor as feet pounded on the walkway behind me. "I'm a nurse." I moved around them, knelt next to the man, and turned him over. His eyes were fixed open.

"Is he dead?" a shaky male voice asked.

I looked over my shoulder. A pale-looking, short man dressed in black slacks and a blue shirt with a name tag attached to the pocket stared at the guy on the floor.

"No. He's had a seizure. One of the motel guests has called 9-1-1," I lied, not wanting him to call anyone and knowing Kendall was on his way. "I'll watch over him until someone arrives."

"Is there anything I can do?"

"Just make sure the walkway is clear for the paramedics. That would help."

"I'll do that." He turned on his heel and walked out the door.

When he and the maids were out of sight, I stood, slightly pushed the door, leaving it ajar, and used my disk. Three Tegen spiders crawled up my leg. I cradled them in my palm.

A siren blared off in the distance and kept getting louder. Could Kendall have acquired an ambulance?

I went to the bathroom for tissues to wrap around the spiders, hiding them from anyone entering the room. The door was shut. As I began to turn the doorknob, I heard movement inside and stopped. Knocking on the door, I asked, "Anyone in there?"

An attractive, skimpily–clad woman with bright red hair inched the door open. "Are you the only one here?"

I moved my hand that held the spiders behind my back. "Yes. I'm waiting for the paramedics."

"I thought he was dead. Last month, a customer keeled over on me. Died right on the spot. Men. Some just aren't fit for having a good time." She tilted her head toward the man on the floor. "He's married. I need to get going." She grabbed her dress off the chair and wiggled into it. "His wife wouldn't understand me being here."

Doubting any wife would, I watched her slip on her heels.

"Don't tell anyone you saw me." She headed toward the door.

Before she could leave, the door flew open and Kendall entered, pulling a gurney while Todd pushed it. Both men wore green scrubs.

The hooker charged around them and out the door.

"We can handle it from here," Kendall said.

I figured that was my signal to leave. "The container I mentioned earlier is on my kitchen counter."

He nodded.

Still holding the spiders and hurrying toward my room, I glanced at the parking lot. An ambulance stood prominently next to the stairs. I went to the kitchen to place the Tegen spiders with the others in the plastic container. It was gone. I grabbed another container and put the three spiders in it.

Worried about the dart gun, I turned around and saw it wasn't by the bed. I bent down and checked underneath. Nothing. I headed to the fridge. The *venotrolia* hadn't been disturbed. Next, I looked through my drawers to see if anything else was missing. Nothing appeared to have been touched. Even my spiders were still secure in their ovoid container. My eyes swept around the room, and I saw the zipper on my duffle bag was open and rummaged through it. My knife and sheath were gone. Then, I searched through my purse. The lipstick that held the small darts hadn't been snatched. Except for it, I had no way to defend myself against Snyder, and without any manmade weapons, I'd have no choice but to use my poison if I had a confrontation with a mortal.

Mulling over the robbery, I showered and dressed while avoiding the non-Tegen spiders crawling on my bed and floor. I figured as soon as a maid entered my room and saw them, the manager would attempt to eradicate the spider infestation. I wanted the spiders to leave before that happened, so I left my door ajar. I put on my shoes, and then tucked my spider case, the list of newer compound residents, and the cell phone I had used to call Blake into my purse. I slung my duffle bag strap over my shoulder, picked up my purse, and walked out the door, closing it behind me.

The ambulance was nowhere in sight, but the blue truck sat in its usual spot.

When I reached my car, someone on the second floor yelled, "Spiders everywhere!"

The manager came running out of the office and up the stairs.

I dropped my duffle bag in the trunk and climbed into the driver's seat, hoping I had collected all the Tegen spiders. Sitting in my car, I watched people rushing toward the open door two rooms from mine. A man clearly shaken stood in the doorway, pointing behind him. Some spiders must have already migrated to his room. Maybe leaving my door open for a while hadn't been a good idea.

Another man upstairs shouted, "Call an exterminator!"

My spiders were safe with me. Knowing there was nothing I could do if another motel guest was bitten and Kendall already knew about the problem, I drove out of the parking lot. On the way to the medical center, I thought about the spider invasion. Not one logical reason came to mind why anyone would want to put them in my room. Most weren't poisonous, so had I been a mortal, I might've panicked but possibly emerged unscathed. If Snyder was behind the spider release, maybe it was to test whether or not I was a Tegen. Killing another mortal most likely wouldn't have bothered him. Since I had gathered up the Tegen spiders and left them contained on the counter, that would leave no doubt in any Tegen's mind that I was one of them. Or would it?

People who worked in the lab knew about the disk. Yet, it was unlikely a mortal, unless properly attired, could retrieve Tegen spiders without being bitten. But who's to say I didn't have on some protective clothing? Also, maybe that was how the intruder was dressed and their only purpose was to retrieve the Tegen spiders. In the process, he saw the dart gun and grabbed it and then searched for other weapons. Or could the spiders have been a diversion to get me out of the room in order to snatch the dart gun and darts? But how did anyone know I had those? Could Snyder have forced that information out of Isaac before he went up in flames?

Questions kept streaming through my mind as I worried my cover might've been blown. At any rate, had I been a mortal, I would've reacted differently to the spiders, like the man yelling upstairs. With that thought, I decided I needed to justify my lack of reaction to the spider incident during dinner with Newark, hoping it would get back to Snyder, whoever he was.

It was after 8:30 a.m. before I walked through the door at the clinic. While I looked over the daily list of Worthington's appointments, Libby, the receptionist, came into the nurse's station.

"Dr. Worthington won't be in until ten," she said. "I tried to reach his nine o'clock appointment. Her phone went to voicemail. I left a message, but she could show up. Do you want to take care of her if she does?"

"Yes," I said, feeling disappointed that I couldn't talk to Worthington about Crystal before patients started arriving.

Libby leaned closer to me. "Did you hear the news this morning?"

"No."

"The police are searching for Kyle Watford in connection with the shooting at the compound. His picture is all over the news. Worthington's niece used to date him. The police said Kyle took his girlfriend with him when he ran off, but they haven't given her name. When you were at the compound yesterday, did Worthington say anything to you about it?"

"You know more than I do. All I heard was that the shooter took off. No one even mentioned his name."

"Really?"

"The shooting happened when it was dark. Maybe the gunshot victims never got a good look at him, or the police might have told them to stay quiet about it."

"That's probably what happened. Yesterday, the police wouldn't give out any names. Maybe they had a lead on him and thought they could apprehend him. Will you let me know if Worthington says anything to you about his niece?"

"Will do."

Libby turned and headed toward the reception counter.

I looked at the nine o'clock patient's chart. She was coming in to have a cast removed from her arm. Not anything I knew how to handle. While I hoped she had listened to the message, I continued going over the list of appointments. Not seeing any familiar names, I turned my attention to checking the examination rooms to make sure they all had sufficient supplies.

At 9:10 a.m., the receptionist buzzed my phone and told me that Worthington's patient had arrived.

I headed to the lobby and went straight to the only person wearing a cast. "Mrs. Bensen, Dr. Worthington had an emergency, and he won't be in until ten. Would you like to wait for him or schedule another appointment?"

"Wait. I can't stand having this thing on my arm any longer."

"Do you want to wait here or in an examination room?"

"Here. I can watch TV."

"You'll be his first patient when he arrives."

Going back to my desk, I decided to give Blake a call before Worthington showed up. I fished the right cell phone out of my purse and clicked on his number.

After five rings, he finally answered. "Sara?"

"Yes. I have a couple of things I want to talk to you about, but I'd rather not do it over the phone. Can I meet you someplace?"

"Is Kendall with you?" he asked suspiciously.

"No. I'm at work at the medical center. He tends to keep track of me, but not when I'm at work. If you're worried about him, we could meet someplace for lunch or you could pick me up."

"I'll pick you up." His response was almost too quick. It put me on guard.

"Blake, you will be coming alone, won't you?"

"Sara, I already told you that I wouldn't let anyone hurt you. Trust me."

"Some of the patients that come to the clinic live at the

compound, so it might be better if you picked me up in the parking lot. Can you pull around behind the clinic and wait for me by the employee entrance? Say one o'clock? Do you know where the Sedona Medical Clinic is located?"

"I've gone by there before. See you at one."

After putting away that phone, I rummaged through my purse until I found the other one and the note with Kendall's phone number on it.

"T.M. Shipping," a female said, catching me by surprise. I had anticipated hearing Kendall on the other end of the line.

Guessing the voice belonged to Marge, I said, "The package will be arriving at my place of employment at one o'clock, but then I'll be going to lunch. It should be ready to be picked up around 2:00 p.m. near the employee entrance."

"We'll have a truck there ready to receive the package."

"Thank you." I disconnected.

I dreaded tricking Blake. He might be on our side and just wanted to regain his freedom and avoid being prosecuted when he returned to North Dakota.

Wondering how Kendall intended to get Blake to talk about Snyder's identity, only one thing came to mind—torture. I became distracted until Worthington, his face pale and his eyes pinched with worry, went past the nurse's station.

I hurried after him. "Dr. Worthington, are you okay?"

He unlocked his door, and I followed him inside. He closed the door behind me. "Barton sent some goons to my house while I was busy patching up his people at the compound."

"What did they do?"

"Terrified my wife. They had only been gone for a few minutes when I got home yesterday. Had I been there, I would've called the police, but Sheila was too worried about Ashley to do anything. They barged in, searched every room, and didn't even tell her what they wanted until they were leaving. I had to give her a sedative to calm her down. She was convinced they planned to kill Ashley and Kyle when they found them."

"What did you tell her?"

"Susan, I couldn't help it. I had to tell her Ashley and Kyle are in a safe place. The Feds had them. I'm sorry. She promised she wouldn't tell anyone. But seeing pictures of Kyle on the news and hearing the police are looking for him in connection with the shooting, she'll want to defend him. I doubt she's going to be able to keep that promise."

"We don't want to scare Barton into running before we're ready to move in," I said, going along with the FBI scenario. "Do you think you can keep her quiet for a couple of weeks?" Once Kendall learned Snyder's alias, I didn't think it would take that long to capture him and locate his spiders. But if word got out that the FBI was looking into the compound, the real FBI might show up to check it out. Snyder would pull another disappearing act. More lives would be lost before he could be tracked down again.

"I'll try. I didn't give her your name or anything like that, so your cover hasn't been compromised."

"That's good. How would you like to have a real nurse working by my side?"

He gave me a puzzled look. "Another FBI agent?"

"No…no. She doesn't know my true identity, but she does know that I'm using my position here as a cover. Since I lacked the skills expected that a nurse should possess, an acquaintance thought I might be struggling and sent her to help out. She's a genuine registered nurse."

"I sure could use her, but the clinic doesn't have the funds for me to have two nurses."

"You don't need to pay her anything. Her salary is all taken care of. To continue using my cover, I thought we could call her a student nurse. She's in her forties, but I'm sure she wouldn't mind. Would that work for the clinic?"

"We have had students here before, shadowing the nurses. I can make the necessary arrangements. How soon can she start?"

"Today or whenever you want her to start."

"Have her come in this afternoon. I'll have it set up by then."

"Now we better get to work. Are you up to seeing a patient? Mrs. Bensen has been here since 9:10, waiting to have her cast removed."

"Show her into one of the examination rooms."

Since Worthington came in late, his appointments quickly piled up. All four of his examination rooms had a continuous flow of patients. I took care of the easy ones—those that only needed a vaccine or a dressing changed—while he attended other patients.

It was almost eleven before I had a chance to call Crystal.

"Everything will be ready for you to come in this afternoon. Do you know where the clinic is?"

"Yes. Any specific time?"

"Make it at 2:30. We have lunch between one and two. Ask for me at the receptionist's desk. Oh, you're probably going to hate this, but you have to pretend you're a student nurse. Dr. Worthington, he's the doctor you'll be working for, doesn't have funds for two nurses. He knows you're a registered nurse. Dr. Alston is paying you a salary while you're here, isn't he?"

"Yes. In fact, he gave me a raise. I don't mind playing the role of student nurse."

"See you this afternoon." I hung up, feeling relieved that a skilled nurse would be working for Dr. Worthington and I could concentrate more on my mission.

At 12:45 p.m., I showed the last morning patient into an examination room. That patient needed to have some stitches removed, a procedure beyond my scope to handle. I stopped Worthington in the hall. "I have a lunch appointment. Is it okay if I leave now?"

"Yes, but some of yesterday's patients were moved to this afternoon, so try not to be late."

"Will do," I said. "And Crystal Matthews, the student nurse, will be here around 2:30."

Worthington smiled, and then I went to the nurse's station, grabbed my purse, and headed out the door.

Blake sat in the driver's seat of a white Chevy truck with the engine running. He didn't make any movement to get out of the truck while I moved around the hood and let myself in on the passenger side. "How's it going at the compound?"

"Most of the debris from the shooting is cleaned up, but a lot of holes on the buildings still need to be patched up. You want to go anywhere special?"

"No, but I need to be back in an hour. There's a pub close by. We could go there."

"I heard about a small Ma and Pa place not far from here. Their sandwiches are supposed to be pretty good."

"You're the driver."

Pulling out of the parking lot, Blake asked, "You have any nurse training before this job?"

"A little. So far I've managed to look like I know what I'm doing. Have you got a job at the compound?"

"Nope. Not a regular one. I have some carpentry experience. I've been helping fix the burnt building. Did you hear about that?"

"Yes. One of the doctors at the clinic went there to take care of the injured." I didn't want to admit I was using the alias Susan Anderson since I had lied to him when he caught me with Ashley.

"We had another fire there." He turned into a strip mall parking lot. "Not a big one, but it left more repair work."

Blake led me to a small restaurant at the corner of the strip mall. It was a seat yourself place. I started moving toward a booth by the window. "It's too bright there," Blake said, heading to a table at the rear of the establishment.

After we placed our orders, I pulled the Tegen ring out of my purse. "Do you know who this belongs to?"

"You?"

"No. Mine's in a safe place. I'm thinking Kendall had another woman working on this mission."

"Marge is."

"Yeah, I know her, but this isn't hers." I held up the ring. "Any idea?"

He shrugged. "Where did you find it?"

"In a pile of ashes at the gun range."

"Any bones?"

I shook my head. "Just ashes. Snyder called Kendall and told him that another member of his team had been eliminated. You know about Isaac, right?"

"Yeah. Nice guy. I didn't know anything about it until Ted started bragging that he'd never be caught. He intends to eliminate one member of the team at a time."

"Even if Kendall's team was all eliminated, does he believe Tegens will give up and not send another enforcer?"

"It's a game to him, and so far he's winning."

The conversation stopped as the waitress delivered our sandwich platters.

"Homemade bread." Blake took his first bite of the large sandwich loaded with sliced roast beef.

We ate in silence for several minutes. Then he said, "Was the ring what you wanted to talk to me about?"

"Well, that… and bodies."

Blake narrowed his eyes while he chewed. "Bodies?"

"Ashley mentioned there had been a lot of disappearances at the compound. Given the fact that Barton wouldn't let her leave, I figured people only left there in a body bag. Am I right? And is Snyder the killer?"

"Barton hasn't got a clue that Snyder has that type of ability. He has marksmen living there—his little band of soldiers. Ted isn't that good of a shot. If Barton wanted someone taken care of, it would be with a bullet."

"Then if those bodies were discovered, there wouldn't be anything to connect them to Tegens or our spiders?"

"Why are you concerned about that?"

"Blake, you know as well as I do, if someone has been killed by a Tegen, that body must be burned. Completely. I saw ashes at the gun range. Is Snyder responsible for those?"

"Yeah, I guess he is, but he does a good job. You don't need to worry about anyone running across remains of a poisoned victim."

Had that been true, Tegens never would've learned that Snyder was hiding out at the compound. It was a changed obituary from a poisonous spider bite to influenza that alerted Tegens to investigate further. But having lunch with Blake wasn't to discuss victims. It was to help Kendall snatch him in order to obtain Snyder's alias.

Blake took a big gulp of his beverage. "How's the pardon coming?"

"Kendall isn't too gung ho about obtaining you any assurance. I understand where you're coming from. You don't want to find yourself back in the Tegen brig. I've talked to my father about your request," I lied. "He's going to discuss it with some of the other Council members. So there's a chance something might be worked out."

"It needs to be soon. After the shooting at the compound and the recent fires, I'm not sure how much longer Ted is going to stick around. He doesn't like to be at places with problems."

I thought how ironic—Snyder was the chief problem maker. My eyes dropped to my watch—1:54 p.m. "Oh, I need to get going." I smiled. "My nursing career will go up in a puff of smoke if I get fired."

As Blake turned into the medical center parking lot, I scanned all the parked cars. I didn't see Kendall's Chevy anywhere, and I had no idea what type of car Todd or Marge were driving.

Blake stopped behind the building. "How about going to dinner one of these nights?"

"Maybe Saturday. Kendall keeps close tabs on me during the week, but he lets up a little over the weekends. If anything unusual happens at the compound, will you call me?"

"Sure," he said.

Climbing out of the truck, I wondered if Kendall would even show up. Had something else come up that required his attention? Heading to the entrance, I turned to give Blake a goodbye wave. That's when I saw it—a dart sticking into his neck.

24

INFORMATIVE DATE

Between patients, the receptionist called, "Crystal Matthews is here to see you."

I hurried to the lobby and saw Crystal, dressed in a nurse's uniform. After leading her to my nurse's station, I had Crystal put her purse in the cabinet next to mine. "Dr. Worthington has four examination rooms and a patient is in each one." I pointed out the rooms. He's with the patient in Room 2."

"Where would you like me to start?"

"The patient in Room 4 only needs to have some stitches removed in his foot. I've laid out all the necessary equipment."

I escorted Crystal into that room. "Mr. Simpson, this is Ms. Matthews, a student nurse. Dr. Worthington and I are very pleased that she'll be finishing her internship here. She'll be removing your stitches."

A worried looked crossed his face.

Crystal gently touched his arm. "Don't worry, Mr. Simpson, I'll take care of you." She smiled. "Removing stitches is one of my specialties."

Then I stood aside as Crystal tended to the patient.

Dr. Worthington stepped into the room and watched Crystal skillfully taking out the stitches. "I see our student nurse has this under control." He put his hand on the patient's shoulder. "Mr. Simpson, you no longer need to keep that area dry."

"Thanks, Doc, but I kinda liked havin' my wife wash my foot."

After that, I spent the rest of the day straightening up examination rooms, directing patients to them, and laying out equipment and supplies while Dr. Worthington and Crystal handled patients. Occasionally, I looked in on Crystal as if I were mentoring her.

Still, it ended up being a long afternoon. It was almost six before I was able to properly introduce Crystal to Worthington. Then I left the clinic and drove to the motel. My room reeked from the nauseous smell of pesticide. Sliding open all the windows, I noticed a letter from the management on the desk.

It read "Today we completed our semi-annual spraying to keep insects out of our guests' rooms. The smell associated with the chemicals used should dissipate sometime this evening. Sorry for any inconvenience. The Red Hills Motel Management."

I noted they used the term "insects" instead of "spiders," and it wasn't a routine spraying like they claimed. I'd stayed in other motels/hotels where they'd sprayed pesticide and always been offered an opportunity to move to another room. I figured Red Hills must not have any vacancies, so that option wasn't available.

Taking shallow breaths, I got ready for my date with Newark. When I slipped on my shoes, the phone Conner had given me rang.

"Hi," I answered.

"Just calling to see if Tunell, alias Newark, postponed your date again?"

"No, we're still on."

"Where is he taking you to dinner?"

"He never said. Why? Are you planning to join us?"

"Do you think he'd mind?"

"Don't know. Do you want me to ask if you can come along?"

A knock came at the door.

"I need to answer the door. Hurry, give me your answer."

"Have fun." The sarcasm was evident in his voice.

I disconnected. Most likely, he'd have someone following us and be informed of my whereabouts. That might be a good thing if Newark was in cahoots with Snyder.

I opened the door. Newark had on a pair of jeans and a short sleeve casual shirt. "I guess I over dressed." I wore a blue silk dress and stilettos.

His eyes roved over my body. "No. You look perfect."

"Would you like a glass of wine before we leave? Sorry, I don't have any beer," I said since that was the only beverage I had ever seen him drink.

"Better not. Our reservations are for 7:30, and I've been running a little late all day." He held my hand as we walked to his truck.

In my outfit, I found it to be a little challenging to get into the passenger seat in ladylike fashion. As Newark pulled out of the parking lot, I spotted the blue truck behind us. Newark drove along the highway and then turned onto a road abutting scenic red rock formations.

"This is beautiful."

"Exactly my sentiment. We should go climbing after the problems at the compound settle down."

"That would be fun. You said problems. Have there been more than that awful shooting this morning and the fire?"

"Flu outbreak."

"I saw a flu patient once when I was there with Dr. Worthington. How's he doing?"

"He's back to working in the garden."

"So now others have similar influenza?"

"Three more cases."

"Is Dr. Worthington treating them?"

"No. Drugs don't seem to help. The illness needs to run its course, but it sure makes a dent in the manpower."

If the flu was a cover up for people bitten, like it appeared on some death certificates, that dent in manpower would soon be permanent. I rubbed his arm. "You work too hard there. When everyone is well, you should think about taking a little holiday. You could stay at a hotel in town, and we could go rock climbing every day."

He smiled. "Sure could go for that, but what about your job?"

"Well, in a few weeks, I'll be gainfully unemployed. I could manage to take a little break before I start hunting for another job. Did you tell Dr. Barton I'd be looking for a job soon?"

His brow creased as he turned into a restaurant's parking lot. "We can talk about it when we get inside."

The maitre d' led us to a table next to a bank of floor-to-ceiling windows. The view was magnificent.

Newark ordered a bottle of wine without even asking for my

preference along with a platter of stuffed mushrooms.

While we waited for it, I said, "Oh, you won't believe what happened at the motel this morning."

He cocked his head. "Your motel?"

"Yes." I stopped when the waiter came with the wine and poured two glasses.

"Go on."

"Spiders. They must've come out of every crack and crevice. I've never seen that many in one place before."

"Spiders. In your room?"

I nodded. "Most were harmless southern house spiders, *Kukulcania Hibernalis*, but the guy in the next room got a little excited. He screamed."

He narrowed his eyes. "You know about spiders?"

"Yes. I worked for an arachnologist in his lab when I was in high school. He used to be a medical doctor, but then he got interested in spiders and changed his career."

"What's his name?" he asked in a suspicious tone.

"Drigson Aldo," I said, giving him the name of a man, one of my adoptive parents' colleagues, who died of a heart attack the first year I was in college. "Working in his lab sounds like I had some skill, but all I did was clean his equipment and straighten stuff up. Nothing that required any expertise, but he did teach me some interesting things about spiders. Some of the spiders that visited my room this morning, I didn't recognize. Curious about their species, I managed to put them into a container. I had intended to do some research about those spiders later, but someone took them. I thought my whole room had been vandalized, but nothing else seemed to be missing." I had no intention to tell him about the stolen dart gun or knife. "Can't figure out why anyone would go into my room just to snatch those spiders."

A puzzled expression flashed on his face. "Happened this morning?"

I nodded. "I didn't report it to the motel manager because nothing of value was taken."

"Are you sure?"

"I looked through my drawers. It didn't appear anything had been touched. It's partly my fault a stranger entered my room because I left my door unlocked when I went to see why the man was screaming."

With his head slightly bent, he stared at the table and appeared to be in deep thought. He was probably mulling over the spider episode.

I took a bite of a mushroom. "This is delicious."

Newark sat up straight. "My favorite appetizer." His eyes moved to my wine glass. "Do you like the wine?"

"Oh, yes." I raised my glass and sipped the Merlot.

The waiter came back and took our dinner orders.

"When you pulled into the parking lot, I asked if you told Dr. Barton that I'd be looking for a job soon. Did you?"

He gave me a mischievous smile. "I might've mentioned it."

"Is that why he wants to see me about what he called a 'personal matter' in front of Dr. Worthington?"

"It might be. It sure would be convenient to have a nurse at the compound." He reached across the table and placed his hand on top of mine. "Especially if you were that nurse."

"I'm going to see him Friday evening. Will you be at the compound?"

"No. Something's come up that I need to handle. I'll be out of town for a few days. I should…" He stopped while the waiter placed salads and rolls on the table and then went on. "Be back sometime on Saturday. Could you keep Saturday night open for me?"

My mouth slightly curved up. "I think that can be arranged." Earlier, I told Blake I might be able to have dinner with him on Saturday, but I figured after he had spent some time with Kendall, he wouldn't be too anxious to see me. "Have you got the list of compound rules for me? It might be good if I went over them before my meeting with Dr. Barton."

"Sorry, forgot it, but you won't need to know them for the meeting. I'll bring it on Saturday."

Two hours later, we climbed back into Newark's truck.

"I had planned we'd go do a little dancing, but I still have things to take care of at the compound before I leave tomorrow morning."

"If you're leaving early, I could drive you to the airport," I said, attempting to pry out information about his trip. Did it have anything to do with Snyder or the spider project?

"No need. We're driving."

And then I recalled, Newark was a wanted man—Gil Tunell. If at all possible, he'd avoid airport security. But who was the *we* he mentioned?

At my motel, Newark walked me to my room, and just like I had anticipated, he wrapped his arms around me and kissed me. Continuing in my role, I actively participated. When the kiss ended, his eyes glowed and he said, "I'm already looking forward to Saturday night." And then, he waited while I unlocked my door.

As I stepped inside, I wondered how soon Conner would hear about that kiss. Then as if he had read my mind, the cell phone Conner had given me rang.

"I'm glad you didn't invite him in." Those were the first words out of Conner's mouth.

"He needs to think I'm interested in him if I hope to complete my mission. Like you said, he's Kalstein's right-hand man."

"And I recently learned he's also Kalstein's nephew."

"Interesting." Prior to that revelation, I wondered why Kalstein had picked someone in his twenties to be his right-hand man. Now, it made sense.

"Your date ended early. Was he called back to the compound?"

"No," I said, speculating if one or more of Conner's men had been up to something there—maybe setting a trap for Kalstein, alias Barton. Then I stopped myself from telling Conner the reason our date had been cut short. Snyder might take off if another problem occurred at the compound. If Conner knew Newark along with others—probably some of Kalstein's loyal employees—would be away for a few days, he might decide that would be a good opportunity to move on Kalstein. "He's been busy at the compound and couldn't stay away long."

"He cut a date short with you, so he could hang out with the guys at the compound?" Conner said in a tone of disbelief.

"I guess he did, but I'll be seeing him again on Saturday night."

"So you're free for the rest of the night?"

"It appears I am."

"I'll be there in ten minutes."

"No. The spider team could show up. I'll come to you."

Before I left, I wanted Kendall to know that someone had taken the dart gun and Newark was going out of town with at least one other person in case it had a bearing on our mission. I placed a call to the non-emergency number Kendall had given me. No one answered. Hesitantly, I left a message. "Tomorrow some of my new friends will be going out of town for a few days, and I can't seem to locate an item you gave me along with its accessories." That was the only way I could think of to tell him about the dart gun. I hoped he would understand my message.

25

ASSIGNMENT

Conner and I never talked about the compound all night. Our time together ended too soon when I had to go back to my motel to get ready for work.

Stepping into my room, I expected to see Kendall or Marge sitting on the couch with scornful expressions on their faces. But my room appeared as though no late night visitors had entered. Nothing had been disturbed. I checked both cell phones Kendall had given me for messages. None.

Within thirty minutes, I drove away from the motel. I had the urge to go to the compound to see what I could find out about Newark's trip, but I had promised Kendall I'd stay away from there unless I went with Worthington or I had been invited. Sneaking around could get me sent home or worse.

Crystal was already at the clinic going over Worthington's appointments when I arrived. "Anyone needing just a vaccine or any simple procedure I can handle on the list?"

"Yes. His nine o'clock. A flu shot."

As I put away my purse, my cell phone rang. Not recognizing the caller's number, I said, "Hello."

"Sara, it's Marge. Are you in a place where you can talk?" Marge sounded anxious.

I strolled toward Worthington's office, guessing he wasn't in yet. "Yes."

"I'm at the compound and can't reach Kendall or Todd," she said, her voice just above a whisper. "Two men—one is Newark—just came out of the lab building. I've seen the other guy around, but I don't know his name. That guy is carrying a container that looks similar to the tightly-woven mesh cages we keep our spiders in when we're not traveling with them, but his cage is two or three times bigger. The man put it in the back of a van along with three duffle bags. It looks like they're taking spiders someplace. "

"Last night when I was out with Newark, he said something had come up and he'd be out of town for a few days. I called Kendall and left him a message about that. Are you going to follow the van when it leaves?"

"Kendall has given me orders to stay here and watch for Blake."

"Blake? Didn't Kendall get him yesterday?"

"Sara…Sara, three men are getting into the van. They're going to be leaving soon. Can you make an excuse at work and follow it?"

"But I'm not there. How will I know what direction it went?"

"I can make it to the road. If it doesn't head toward Sedona, I'll call you. It's a white Chevy van. The license plate number is…"

"Wait, let me get a pen." I grabbed a pen and a piece of paper off of the nearest unoccupied desk. "Ready."

She rattled it off while I scribbled it down.

"I'll be waiting by the highway for it." I clicked off and hurried back toward the nurse's station when I bumped into Worthington. "Something really important has come up. I need to leave."

"Go, go," he said. "Glad the student nurse is here."

Moving into my nurse's station, I said, "Sorry Crystal, I need to leave. Dr. Worthington already knows I'm going."

"Will you be back today?"

"No." I picked up my purse and walked at a brisk pace to the back door, and then sprinted to my car. Before climbing in, I opened the trunk and took out my baseball cap, a pair of oversized sunglasses, and a long-sleeve pink sweater.

Five minutes later, wearing the cap, sunglasses, and sweater, I parked alongside the highway, watching for the van when my phone rang.

Recognizing the phone number, I answered, "Don't tell me they went the other way."

"They sure did."

"I'll try to catch up with them." I hung up, pulled into traffic, and then made a left turn into a parking lot. From there, I inched into the traffic heading east. The car in front of me seemed to be moving at a snail's pace, but with the flow of traffic going the other direction, it made it impossible for me to pass. Finally, the car turned right. I wanted to floor the gas pedal, but at the same time, I didn't want to be stopped by the local police. Still, whenever the traffic thinned out, I went at least fifteen to twenty miles over the speed limit.

As I came closer to the interstate, it wouldn't be long before I had to make a decision to either go north or south. Newark had planned to be gone a couple of nights. Flagstaff was the first major city going north. He could've made a trip there back and forth in one day, but that might not be his destination. Phoenix and other major Arizona cities were south. If they intended to try to extort money by using the spiders—the plan behind the spider project—they'd probably head someplace that offered more opportunities. I doubted they had been able to duplicate our spiders. Maybe they had decided to use the Tegen spiders Snyder had given them for that purpose. Could Kalstein be running out of money? Or did he want a larger nest egg to establish himself in a new location? Or was this a trial run to see how their extortion plot worked out?

Reaching the intersection, I headed south on Interstate 17. Even if I were going the right direction, I guessed it would take me over an hour before I saw the van. I pressed on the gas until the speedometer registered eight miles over the speed limit, and then put on cruise control. Since Newark was a wanted man, I doubted he would push the speed limit. Then it occurred to me that he might not be the driver. With that thought, I went five miles faster and kept a watchful eye out for the highway patrol. A truck sped past me, and I decided to match its speed, staying approximately one hundred feet behind the vehicle.

While I continued toward Phoenix, I mulled over what Marge had said, or more accurately what she hadn't said. She was at the compound looking for Blake. How did Blake escape from Kendall? Kendall must not have been able to obtain Snyder's alias before Blake got away, or Marge wouldn't be staked out searching for him. Instead, she'd be searching for the alias. And why couldn't she reach Kendall or Todd on the phone? Had they tangled with Snyder? Or were they just someplace where they couldn't answer the phone?

More questions kept buzzing in my head. I wanted to call her for some answers, but it probably wasn't a good idea for her to be on the phone more than necessary while she crept around the compound. Also, I figured when Kendall heard about my recent activity, he'd be calling me, and he wouldn't be a happy camper. Marge seeking my help likely wouldn't make a difference.

A white van was several cars in front of me. I slowed down and moved into another lane to see the license plate. After catching the first two digits, I knew it was the wrong vehicle. I increased my speed and drove past it. Then I saw several white vans. Only one was a Chevy, and it had the wrong plate number. As I got closer to Phoenix, more white vans appeared on the road. Moving back and forth between the lanes so I could see the license plates, I worried that Newark might recognize my car, but then I dismissed that thought since there were hundreds of Toyota Corollas on the roads. My car wasn't unusual in any way. Plus, he had no reason to believe I was following him. One of the license plates had the right first two digits, but that was the end of the match. The traffic was getting heavier and my gas gauge was getting closer to empty. If they had headed south, I should've caught up to them by now. Maybe they had, but there were numerous places where they could've turned off. Doubting I could ever find them, I saw a sign for a gas station and took that exit.

After I filled up my gas tank, I pulled my car forward and parked while debating whether to drive back to Sedona or continue going south. It seemed hopeless. That van could be anywhere. Then suddenly, an idea popped into my head. I rummaged through my purse until I found the cell phone from Conner and then called him.

He answered on the third ring, "Sara, why aren't you at work?"

"You wore me out last night, so I thought I'd take the day off."

"And then you decided to take a road trip in your worn out condition?"

I should've known I'd have a tail. It just never entered my mind to even look for one. "I wish I was as good at following someone as your men are."

"You do realize, it's difficult to follow someone when you're sitting in a parked car at a gas station, don't you? Unless, of course, your target is inside the store."

He didn't only have someone following me; he was watching me through a camera.

"That's my problem. I can't find my target. Can someone be located through their cell phone number?" I asked, climbing out of the car and looking around. There wasn't another car in sight with one person sitting in it, and I didn't see any glare from a lens pointed at me. His men were impossible to spot. As I sank back down into the driver's seat, I noticed the cameras near the roof line of the store in front of me. Could he have tapped into that?

"Yes. Assuming their cell phone has GPS. Most cell phones do."

"If I give you a phone number, how long will it take?"

"Around thirty minutes, providing that person is someplace where they have cell phone coverage."

"Will you try to find someone for me?"

"If you'll tell me why it's important to locate that person."

"Spiders. He's taken some of the poisonous spiders from the compound. I have no idea what he intends to do with them, but I'm sure it isn't for any heroic undertaking." I didn't want to tell him there were three men. Unless one was Snyder, I could handle being outnumbered. And if one was Snyder, Conner's men would be defenseless against him.

"He'll be armed. Are you?"

"No."

After waiting impatiently for him to say something, I blurted out, "Please, Conner, help me on this."

"Where's the rest of the spider team?"

"Dealing with other problems."

"What's the number?"

"Let me look it up." I pulled another cell phone out of my purse and went to Newark's number. "Here it is," I said and gave him the number.

"Why don't you go inside the store you're parked in front of and get yourself something to eat while I have this researched?"

My stomach growled. I hadn't even felt hungry before Conner said that. "Okay. I'll do that."

Sitting in the car, eating a hotdog and drinking a diet soda, I kept scanning all the people filling their gas tanks and who went into the store, trying to figure out if any of them worked for Conner.

I jumped when my phone rang. With a mouth full of food, I answered, "Ha..lo."

"Enjoying that hotdog?"

I swallowed. "Yes. This place has pretty good hotdogs. Maybe we should come here and have dinner one night."

"Can't do it...no wine service. Your boy is driving toward Tucson."

"I'll head that direction. Can you let me know if he stops someplace, or if he continues past Tucson?"

"Yes. I'll update you if he leaves the interstate. Sara, remember my men are nearby, they can help you if you find yourself in a sticky situation. All you need to do is call me, or yell 'Help.' They'll be there in a flash."

"I know you have me well protected, but I am quite capable of taking care of myself. The man I'm following has a supply of deadly spiders, and I doubt your men are immune to the poisonous venom. I've heard the compound has protective gear to keep those working around the spiders safe."

"Bullets can pierce those outfits, and my men have blowtorches with them. They've been warned about the potential danger."

I cringed hearing the word "blowtorches." Fire was my enemy. It was the only thing that could destroy Tegens. Going without *venotrolia* or their rings could weaken Tegens to the point they might not be able to maintain their human form, but fire would kill a Tegen. Then I recalled the pile of ashes at the gun range that I suspected was all that remained of one Tegen. "I need to take off."

"Be careful, Sara."

"I will." I disconnected and made my way back to the interstate.

Almost an hour later, my cell phone rang. "What's the update?" I assumed Conner was on the other end of the line.

"He's stopped in a residential neighborhood in Tucson," a female voice said. "Would you like the address?"

"Could you text it to me?"

"Certainly."

"Tell Conner thanks."

"I'll give Mr. Crussett your message. Is there anything else I can help you with?"

"Could you let me know if he's on the move again?"

"Of course."

When I reached Tucson, I took the first exit and found a place to park. There, I brought up the text message and put the address into my car's navigation system. Once the map appeared on my screen, I followed the directions. I was led to a quiet street in an upper middle-class neighborhood. All the homes were at least 4000 square feet. A white van with colorful signs on both sides advertising "Tracy's Catering" was parked on a circular driveway in front of a two-story, red brick house. Was I at the right place? I compared the address against the one in the text Conner's employee had sent me. They agreed.

Assuming the van had been camouflaged in order to use it for a nefarious purpose that was not catering, I pulled over to the curb in front of a parked car three houses away. I climbed out, got my binoculars out of the trunk, and scanned the neighborhood. Not seeing anyone outside, I looked through the lenses to check the license plate. The number wasn't a match. Exactly what I expected. There'd be no reason to change the exterior appearance and keep the same license plate number. Still, there was a chance it was the wrong van. I raised the binoculars and stared through the windshield. It appeared no one was inside.

I walked at a brisk pace along the sidewalk until I reached a row of bushes that separated the red brick house from its neighbor. Staying on the neighbor's side, I cautiously moved closer. When I was near the corner of the house, I heard a car engine, and it sounded like it was heading my direction. I sank to the ground between the bushes to wait for it to go by, but then the engine became quieter as if it were slowing down to stop. I separated a few branches, peered through, and saw a black Mercedes pulling into the driveway. It parked behind the van. A well-dressed, middle-aged man climbed out and went inside the house.

Gazing at the house, I knew Newark and his comrades could leave at any time. I didn't have a clue why they were there but figured it wasn't to make friends. Were the spiders important to the visit? Wondering about that, I edged through the bushes and hurried to the gate at the side of the house. Peeking around the back corner of the house and seeing no one, I inched the gate open.

A door slammed at the front of the house.

I closed the gate and charged around the bushes, scraping a wrist in the process, but it would heal quickly. Hunkering down, I headed toward the front of the house.

"That was easy," a husky, unfamiliar voice said.

"Step one done," Newark said.

I found an opening between the bushes and watched Newark and a rugged-looking man with a full, thick beard climb into the van and drive away.

When the van was out of sight, I sprinted to my car. Sitting in the driver's seat, I picked up my phone, prepared to call Conner's number, and noticed a missed call and a message. I clicked to it, saw Conner's number, and listened to the message.

"The man is on the move," a woman said. "He's heading east. I'll text you his current coordinates."

I transferred text message information into the navigation system, and then flipped a U-ey and drove toward the van.

As I continued going east on that street for fifteen minutes, my cell chirped, indicating I had a new text message. I cut to the curb. The message read "He stopped at a Holiday Inn." And then the text went on to give me the location.

Within ten minutes, I saw the Holiday Inn. The van wasn't parked in front of the building. Wanting to know if the spiders were still in it, I pulled into the parking lot and drove slowly around the building. When I saw the rugged-looking man coming out of the building, I turned into a parking spot next to an oversized truck, out of the man's line of sight. I quietly moved out of my car, crept to the tailgate of the truck, and peered around it. The white Chevy, with the sliding side door open, stood in the far corner of the parking lot. It no longer had the advertisement on its sides, and the license plate number matched the number Marge had given me earlier.

The rugged-looking man stood near the back bumper, talking to someone inside. An arm appeared through the open door and handed the man two duffle bags, and then the person inside emerged. Without seeing his face, I knew it was Newark. He picked up a duffle bag, closed the side door, and locked the van.

"Tim," Newark said, "it doesn't take anyone that long."

"It took him longer," Tim said.

They both chuckled as they strode to the entrance and went inside.

Trying not to draw any unwanted attention, I walked at a normal pace to the van. In order to stay hidden from the motel's back entrance, I moved to the passenger side and attempted to look in through the heavily tinted windows. My night vision allowed me to see shadowy square forms, but I couldn't make out if one was a spider cage. With the potential of people coming and going from the Holiday Inn, I didn't dare risk being discovered breaking into the van. Knowing I'd be alerted if Newark left, I drove to a Hampton Inn I'd noticed a short distance away.

It was 5:45 p.m. when I checked in. The only credit card I had with me was in the name of my alias, Susan Anderson. Reluctantly, I used it. Before going to my room, I asked the motel clerk if there was a Walmart or Target close by. Following the map she had given me, I went to a Target and purchased an assortment of items I'd need for my stay in Tucson, including a pair of slacks and a blouse. On the way back to my motel, I stopped and bought a sandwich so I could stay in my room until Newark made a move.

Reaching the Hampton Inn, I opened the trunk and took out my duffle that held the dark clothing and items I might need if Newark ventured out at night. I pulled out the thermos I kept underneath the front seat, stuck it into the duffle bag, and put the bag's strap over my shoulder. Then I gathered up my packages and headed to the motel entrance.

As I walked through the lobby, the motel clerk said, "Ms. Anderson," and held up a package.

I went to the counter.

"This was delivered right after you left."

"Thanks." I took the package, figuring it had to be something Conner sent since he and his men were the only ones that knew my whereabouts. Or had someone else also been tailing me—like the driver of the blue truck?

With my hands full, I headed down the hallway to my room. Trying to balance everything, I slid the key card into the slot as my cell phone rang. I set the packages down on the floor and pulled out the ringing phone, anticipating it was Conner or his employee calling. But I soon discovered it was the other phone that was ringing. Recognizing the number, I decided not to answer Newark's call. I slid the key card into the slot again, pushed open the door, and moved my belongings inside. I quickly changed from my nurse's uniform to my black jogging suit. I doubted Newark and his comrades would venture out again while it was still light outside, but I wanted to be prepared just in case.

I examined the unknown package for anything that might indicate who had sent it. Nothing. The package showed nothing other than Susan Anderson—printed with a black marker. I cautiously removed the exterior wrapping and then saw a handwritten note on top of the box: "You might need this. Max Heller," Conner's alias.

Smiling to myself, I raised the lid. Inside was a Berretta, a silencer, and a box of 9mm bullets. Conner was right that I might need it, but not for the reason he believed. I was well equipped to handle Newark and his men, but the manmade weapon could help me to avoid using my Tegen poison. Death by a bullet was cleaner than a victim dying from venomous poison that could lead police to search for the source. It was my duty if at all possible to keep Tegen abilities a secret, or we might all be in danger.

I sat on the edge of the bed fabricating an excuse to give Newark if he asked me about my work day, and then picked up that cell phone and returned his call.

"Hey, Susan," he answered. "How are you feeling?"

"A little better...How did you know I went home sick?"

"I called the Doc to get a prescription refilled for one of his patients at the compound. I was routed to his nurse. The woman who picked up the call wasn't you. She told me you weren't feeling well and went home."

"I'm feeling so much better than I did earlier. I might've just caught the 24-hour bug."

"Hope that's what it is. Don't want you to cancel our date."

"Neither do I. And I don't want to miss my meeting with Dr. Barton."

"There's a chance I might be back in town late tomorrow. If you make it to the meeting and things go well, I could give you an evening tour of the compound."

"I've seen so little of it. I'd like to see more. Your out-of-town trip must be going well." My phone made a soft beeping sound for call waiting.

"So far everything is running ahead of schedule. I need to work on a few things tonight, but if it stays on track, I'll be out of here tomorrow. Drink plenty of fluids and get some rest."

"Yes, Dr. Newark, I'll follow your instructions."

As soon as I hung up, I clicked on missed call and saw Marge's phone number. I already intended to call her or Kendall after I figured out what Newark and the two men were up to. Until then, I had nothing to report.

Newark said he needed to do some things tonight. Getting text messages would help me find him if and when he left, but tailing him from the Holiday Inn would be better. I decided to wait to return Marge's call after I was parked closer to Newark's motel.

I took the thermos out of my duffle bag and drank the delicious *venotrolia*. I placed my new gifts in my duffle bag and carried it to the Corolla. The sun was setting when I parked in a good spot with a clear vision of the Holiday Inn entrance and the driveway leading to the parking lot. Then I called Marge.

"Sara, where are you?"

"In Tucson."

"You found the van?"

"Yes. Newark and his buddies are staying in a motel. I'm keeping track of the van. The spiders might still be in it, but I haven't been able to confirm that. Were you able to reach Kendall or Todd?"

"Kendall called around ten, but I couldn't answer my phone. He left a message saying he had to take care of an emergency and couldn't be contacted. He said he'd call sometime tonight."

"And Todd?"

"He's at the compound. We're both searching for Blake."

"Have you gone to the gun range?"

"Yes. A semi is parked there. Its trailer is empty. Todd and I have been speculating about that. All we've come up with so far is that Barton got spooked by the gunfire the other day and he's planning to clear out, taking all his guns, ammunition, and maybe the spiders with him. Have you got any different thoughts?"

"No. You're probably on the right track, but that will mean Snyder taking off too. He wouldn't stick around for new management, and since the spider project was his idea, he'd want his share of the profits."

The white van pulled out of the driveway and turned onto the street.

"They're leaving. Need to go." I disconnected and cut into the traffic, several car lengths behind the van.

My other cell phone rang.

I grabbed it and pushed the answer button.

"They're on the move, going toward the Interstate," a woman said.

"I'm behind them. Thanks. I'll call if I lose them."

Stopping at a red light, I saw the back of the white van turn left a block a head of me. A minute later, I followed yet couldn't see the van. I continued along the narrow street to the next intersection and looked in both directions, hoping to spot the van. Not seeing it, I proceeded onto the same street. At the next intersection, I again searched for the van. Irritated with myself for lacking the ability to properly tail someone, like Conner's men, I pulled over to the edge of the road. I took out my phone, prepared to call Conner's number, and then decided to check out the house where they had been earlier since I was already heading in that direction. I dropped the phone on the passenger seat and drove to the two-story red brick house.

26

CAPTIVES

The van, decked out again with the catering signs, and the black Mercedes were parked in the circular driveway. I stopped several houses away. After glancing around the neighborhood and not seeing anyone out in the dark, I grabbed my duffle bag from the back seat and, sitting in the driver's seat, dug out the gun and loaded it. I stuck it in my waist band and climbed out of the car. Following the same path I had taken earlier to the side gate of the red brick house, I kept an eye on the van in case someone was still in it.

Reaching the gate, I pulled a ski mask out of my duffle bag and tugged it on and then quietly opened the gate and crept into the backyard. My eyes drifted over the exterior of the house. I had hoped to see a balcony, but there wasn't one. No lights illuminated any of the windows on the second floor. One was ajar and, to my relief, didn't have a screen on it. I slipped off my shoes, dropped them in my bag, and scaled the back of the house to the window. Before entering, I listened intensely for any sound within the room. Satisfied, I raised the window and climbed in. With the aid of my night vision, I saw the pink bedspread, fluffy pink curtains, and posters of young, good-looking male singers pinned on the walls.

I put on my shoes and a pair of latex gloves as my eyes drifted between the three closed doors in the room. On one door, a badge with the name Carol on it hung from a chain. I wiped my fingerprints off the window and the ledge.

Assuming Newark and his buddies were in the house on business, and if one of them spotted me, I doubted they'd hesitate to shoot. At the same time, not wanting to use my poison, if I got a shot off first, I didn't want to alert the others of my presence. I pulled the gun out of my waist band, screwed the silencer on the barrel, and then put my ear against the door closest to the window. Not hearing any noise, I carefully opened it. On the other side was a bathroom. A closet with stacks of clothing scattered on the floor was behind the next door. The third door had to lead to the hallway. I gripped the doorknob, intending to ease it open.

A creaking sound came from the closet.

I moved to that door, guessing someone was hiding under the clothing and it wasn't Newark or his buddies. I inched open the door. "Whoever is hiding in here," I whispered, "I'm here to help you, not hurt you. I'll keep you safe."

In the back corner, two red, puffy eyes appeared.

I stepped into the closet. "Don't worry about my covered face. It's only so they won't recognize me." And then I realized she probably couldn't see me without any lights on. "Are you Carol?"

"Uh-huh. Mom...told me to hide," she snuffled. "Are Mom...and Dad okay?"

"I don't know. Besides your parents, are there other family members in the house?"

"No." She wiped her eyes with a piece of clothing lying on the floor. "But...but Helen...might still be here."

"Who's Helen?"

"She...cleans...every Thursday."

"Do you have a cell phone?"

She held it up while tears ran down her cheeks. "Battery's dead."

"Are there other cell phones upstairs?"

"Mom's maybe...only uses it...when she goes out."

"Where would it be?"

"On top...of her dresser."

"Where's her bedroom?"

"Across...across the hall."

"Stay hidden," I said, closing the door. Then I moved my duffle bag behind the other side of the bed, out of sight from anyone peeking into the room.

I listened at the hallway door and heard muffled voices coming from downstairs. I slowly opened the door and looked up and down the hallway. Seeing that it was clear, I stepped out and eased the door shut behind me. The bedroom door across the hall stood wide open. Trying not to make a sound, I crept into that bedroom and saw a dresser on the other side of the room but no cell phone. My eyes swept around the room, and I spotted one on the nightstand. I grabbed it and left the room.

"… not my money," a man yelled downstairs as I opened Carol's bedroom door.

I went into the closet and handed the phone to Carol. She immediately turned it on.

"Don't use it yet," I said softly, thinking sirens might cause Newark and his comrades to start shooting and then take off, leaving no survivors. And what about the spiders? But if she explained everything, the cops would approach the house without their sirens blaring. "Let me check on your parents first. Stay hidden in the corner like you were before. If I'm not back in half an hour, call 9-1-1."

She nodded as her lips trembled and tears continued to drizzle down her cheeks.

I watched her drape clothing over her head and then I closed the door.

Loud voices drifted up the stairwell as I stealthily moved down the hallway toward the stairs.

"Where is she?" Newark said in a harsh tone.

"I've already told you," a woman said, her voice shaky. I assumed she was Carol's mother. She went on. "She's at a tennis tournament and won't be home until Sunday."

"Why do you want my daughter?" The bass voice must have belonged to Carol's father.

"I'm ready for the transfer," a man with a husky voice said. I recognized it as Tim's.

I stopped at the top of the stairs with my back pressed against the wall while I contemplated how to break up the confrontation below without getting Carol's parents killed in the process.

"What's it going to be? The money or your wife?" Newark said.

"But it's not my money. It belongs to the foundation."

"I guess you've already forgotten what happened to Helen. Or do you still believe she might come around?"

"No...no...she's dead."

"These little creatures are nipping at a chance to show your wife a good time," Newark said. "See how they're crawling, anxious to get out?"

"Please, I'll give you everything I own. Just don't hurt my wife."

Wanting to know if Newark and his comrades had covered their faces, I bent down and took a quick peek through the stairwell railing. One man sat on a chair with a computer on his lap. His back faced me, but I clearly saw his medium-brown hair. Newark, no mask, stood in front of a woman tied to a chair. From my vantage point, I couldn't see the third man or Carol's father. Since at least two of the trio could be identified by the couple held captive, they had no intention of letting them survive. Neither Newark nor Tim wore any protective clothing to handle Tegen spiders. Did the third man wear any? Or could Tim or the third guy be Snyder?

"All you have to do is transfer the funds into our account," Newark said, "and then we'll be out of here, and your family will be safe and sound. If not, we'll even wait for your daughter to get home. These spiders like that smooth, young flesh. She'll probably be lucky enough to get a few bites before she ends up like Helen."

"William, please...please, give them what they want," Carol's mother pleaded.

"Sean, it appears Mr. Calder needs a little persuasion."

Lange? The third member of the extortion team? I knew Newark had a criminal record, but no one, not Kendall or Conner, had mentioned anything about Lange. Maybe he didn't have one, and this was the first time he was involved in criminal activity. Or maybe he had been involved in it for a while but had never been caught. He was in Kalstein's inner circle; Kalstein, a gun smuggler, was not exactly a law abiding citizen.

"No...no, please," Calder said.

Carol's mother screamed, "William."

I was just about to start shooting when Calder yelled, "No...no...I'll do it."

"Over here," Tim said.

No one spoke as clicks on a keyboard echoed up the stairs.

Feet pounded on the floor.

"All done," Tim said.

Sirens sounded off in the distance, and they continued getting louder. Carol had probably called 9-1-1.

"You think those sirens are for us?" Tim asked.

"Where's your daughter?" Newark snapped.

"I've told you," Carol's mother said. "Ouch."

The front door opened.

"Take care of them," Newark said. "I'll wait for you at the corner."

The door slammed shut.

Knowing Carol's parents were out of time, I charged down the stairs. Tim swung around with a gun outstretched in his hand, ready to fire. I shot first; the bullet penetrated his chest. His body hit the glass coffee table, sending shards of glass over the carpet. Lange was nowhere in sight. I figured he had left with Newark. Then I noticed Carol's mother, her eyes wide open, staring without seeing. She had been bitten. I was too late to save her.

My eyes moved to Carol's father, cupping his head in his hands, sitting on the couch. Poor man. Suddenly, he tumbled over and hit the floor. I knelt next to him, and to my horror, his eyes were wide open, and then a Tegen spider crawled up my arm. I carefully lifted it up and cradled it in my palm.

Figuring the police could show up any minute and there might be more spiders there, I securely held the spider, ran upstairs to Carol's room, grabbed my duffle bag, and ran back down the stairs. I pulled out my tightly-woven cage, a cage I sometimes used for my spiders—but my precious arachnids were safe in an ovoid container in my purse in the Corolla—and placed the spider in it. I fished out my disk, pushed the button on the black side, and waited. A spider came to me. I slipped it into the cage. Then I pushed the button again and walked around the room. No more spiders came. I assumed Newark and Lange only gave up two spiders, dropping one on each victim when they left. But then why did Newark ask Tim to take care of the Calders? Had I not shot him, he probably would've been the next one bitten.

There were no witnesses to what had happened, and I didn't want the police trying to identify the source of the unusual poisonous venom. To cover up the cause of the deaths, I reluctantly raised my pistol and shot Carol's parents and a woman, probably Helen, whose body was stretched out on the floor in the corner of the room.

I stuck the gun in my duffle bag and wanted to tell Carol she didn't need to hide any longer, but she needed someone to comfort her when she learned her parents were dead, and I couldn't be that person. Hopefully, a policeman could handle that job.

Then I started looking for the back door and heard noise outside. I hurried back up the stairs and looked out the window in Carol's room. Scanning the ground below me, I saw a policeman with his gun at the ready, peering in a window at the back of the house. I quietly scurried up to the roof.

I crouched down and cautiously crawled to the side of the house without the gate. Peeking over the edge, I saw some bushes against a fence, but no people. Guessing it wouldn't be long before cops swarmed all around the house, I hurried down and clambered over the bushes and fence. Yanking off my ski mask, I bent down and then removed the top of my black jogging suit and pulled a yellow t-shirt out of my duffle bag. When I had it on, I stuck the ski mask and black top in the duffle bag and placed the strap over my shoulder. I quickly went to the neighbor's front door and walked at a leisurely pace along a stone path that led to the sidewalk.

At least three unmarked police cars were parked along the curb. The turned-off row of lights inside the back windshield gave them away. Farther down the street, I saw two police cruisers with strobe lights flashing, blocking it off. I continued to my car, put the duffle bag in the back seat, and slid behind the steering wheel.

When I reached the cruisers, I had expected to be stopped by a policeman and asked a few questions—Did I live on the street? Who had I been visiting? Did I hear or see anything unusual?—but instead I was motioned to go around their vehicles.

I drove toward the Hampton Inn, feeling sad that I hadn't helped Carol's parents earlier. Risking getting them shot would've been better than being bitten by a Tegen spider. They might've survived a gunshot wound. No mortal survived the deadly venom.

Running over the events of the evening, trying to figure out how I could've handled it better, I climbed under the covers and stared at the ceiling.

A cell phone rang, not the one Conner had given me. Picking it up, I saw the caller was Kendall. I didn't feel up to talking to anyone and especially dreaded having to talk to him, but I couldn't ignore his call. "Hello."

"What went wrong?" he snapped.

"Aaah. What have you heard?"

"A member of the Fellowship was killed in Tucson."

"Wow. News travels fast. Did you also hear that a Fellowship trio extorted money from a man and killed him and his wife with Tegen spiders? And that happened after that man had been promised no harm would come to his family if he turned over the money. And now a teenage girl has been left orphaned. Did they tell you all that?" My voice became louder with each word.

I remained silent for a minute expecting Kendall to say something. "Kendall, did you hang up on me?"

"No. Were you there when it occurred?"

"Yes, but only within earshot. Had I realized they planned to use the spiders to kill them I would've acted more quickly. Two of the men left. The third guy had been instructed to take care of the couple. That's when I shot him to prevent him from blasting the couple, but it was too late. They were already dying from Tegen venom. To hide how the Calders were really killed, I shot them along with a woman who was a spider victim before I arrived at the house. Then, I gathered up two spiders—one to handle each of the last two victims—and took off."

"The teenager?"

"Hiding in a closet upstairs. Kendall, the two men who left had no intention of having their comrade, Tim, survive. The two remaining spiders would've gotten Tim; he wore no protective gear. He had been using a laptop computer to handle the money transfer with Calder. The computer was gone by the time I shot Tim. It had to have been taken by one of the other Fellowship members. Why not leave it for Tim to take if they intended for him to join them?"

"How did Calder acquire his money?"

"It wasn't his. From what I heard, the money belonged to a foundation, but he must've been the CFO or something like that."

"Could you identify the two Fellowship members?"

"Yes. Gil Tunell, alias Alex Newark, and Sean Lange….How did Blake escape?"

"Where did you get the gun?" He didn't answer my question, as usual.

"A friend gave it to me."

"Your boyfriend?"

Not wanting to discuss anything about Conner with Kendall, I said, "It came from a good friend worried about my well-being."

"Besides some Tegen spiders, what else was taken from your room yesterday?"

"The dart gun and darts." I didn't want to mention the knife and sheath since I never told him about that purchase.

"How soon can you be back here?"

"Sometime tomorrow morning."

Not hearing even the slightest sound at the other end of the line, I assumed Kendall had disconnected, but I still said, "Kendall?"

No response. I hung up.

27

GUNSHOT VICTIM

At 5:30 a.m., I left Tucson, hoping to be back in Sedona before Newark. In case he decided to call, it would be better if I were at the clinic performing my nursing duties. Thinking someone might be onto them, Kalstein and his guys could've already started to look for the person or persons responsible for shooting Tim. I didn't want to find myself on his suspect list. So far, it seemed like I wasn't even on his radar. But being out of town when the hit went down could change that.

As I drove along the highway, I sipped coffee and listened to the news on the radio about the murders at the Calder home. After the news reporter gave the names of three victims, he added, "The police haven't identified the fourth victim—a male in his mid-thirties." Then he asserted that more details about the tragedy were expected to be released later that day.

Listening to the brief news report, I wondered how long it would take the police detectives on the case to discover all the funds in the coffers of a foundation had been drained by Calder before his murder.

Shortly after 9:00 a.m., I pulled into the Red Hills Motel parking lot. To my relief, the blue truck was missing. Stepping into my room, I saw six milk bottles on the table and smiled. Kendall must've known that I'd be low after my trip. I took my thermos out of my duffle bag and filled it up. Then I sat down and devoured another bottle.

Feeling refreshed, I showered and dressed for work. Then I carried my duffle bag with the pistol still inside to the car and put it in the trunk and the thermos under the front seat. As I climbed into the driver's seat, I saw Nathan Milner, a member of Kalstein's inner circle, walking out of a room on the first floor. Was he here visiting someone? Or was he here because I was staying at the motel? Supposedly, he was an arms expert, or was that just a cover? Could he be Snyder?

I walked into the clinic around 11:00 a.m. as questions about Milner were still bouncing around in my head.

"Good morning, Susan," Crystal said, snapping me out of my reverie. "I didn't expect you to come in today."

"I had a late night, so I didn't wake up when the alarm went off."

"We've got a full schedule, and Dr. Worthington will be going to a place he refers to as the compound at three. Have you ever heard of it?"

"Yes. It's north of town. Members of the Fellowship of the Good Earth live there. Most of the residents don't like to venture away from the place, so Dr. Worthington sees them there."

"A religious group?"

"Yes. I've been going there with him."

"He intends to go alone today," Crystal said, her eyes fixed on the computer screen. "He mentioned earlier for me to check his late afternoon appointments, and those I couldn't take care of, he wants rescheduled. And then he asked me to pull some medical records for him to take."

The phone on the desk rang, and I immediately picked it up before Crystal had a chance. "Yes."

"Dr. Worthington's 11:15 is here."

"Be there in a minute." I disconnected and asked Crystal, "How did things go yesterday?"

"Not bad. It took me a little while to figure out the computer apps and where some items were kept, but Dr. Worthington and I worked well together. He is such a nice man. For today, do you want to escort the patients to the examination rooms, and then I'll take care of the ones that don't need Dr. Worthington's attention?"

"Aren't there any of the patients I could handle?"

She gave me a condescending look, but then smiled and said,

"There's one patient who's coming in for a pneumonia shot you could take care of. And two for physicals you could get them started."

Since I needed to appear that I was more skilled than the student nurse, I couldn't just sit at the desk when not leading anyone to an examination room or handling the easy part of two physicals. I ended up tagging after Crystal. I left her when I saw Worthington heading to his office.

Following him inside, I said, "You decided to remain the medical doctor for the compound?"

"Yes. I don't want Barton to think that I know anything about Ashley and Kyle's whereabouts since they're looking for them." He smiled at me. "Had you not told me they were in a safe place and I didn't know the Feds were going to be moving in on the compound soon, I'd think Barton and his band of thugs might find her and Kyle and drag them back. So I have to pretend I lack any knowledge about that. I'll be playing the role of a worried uncle and doing what Barton asks, like you're playing the role of a nurse. By the way, Crystal is wonderful. Just in one day, she really made my work day go smoothly. She took care of over half of the patients, so I only needed to visit with them for a few minutes. It left me more time to spend with the others."

"She told me you were going to the compound this afternoon. Can I come along?"

"I had planned to bring a nurse with me, but when you weren't here at nine, I assumed you wouldn't be coming in. I thought bringing Crystal could affect your cover."

"Thanks. You're probably right there. Did Barton want you to see a specific patient or more routine stuff?"

"He didn't want to go into details on the phone, but I'm having Crystal pull the medical records on the men that we saw on Tuesday. Might as well check on them when we're there if we have enough time. Barton has made it very clear that unless it's an emergency, he doesn't want me to be at the compound after five."

"Why?"

"Maybe that's when they gather to pray." His sarcastic tone surprised me. "Barton didn't give me any explanation."

Carrying a box of medical supplies, I walked out of the clinic with Dr. Worthington shortly past 3:00 p.m. Since Kendall had heard about the shooting in Tucson last night, I was curious if Worthington knew anything about it. On the way to the compound, I said, "There really needs to be some gun laws to keep weapons out of the wrong hands, but I guess it's hard to determine who those people are if they've never been arrested. Listening to the radio this morning, I heard a couple in Tucson was murdered in their home—shot to death—along with their housekeeper and another man."

"I saw something about that on the early morning news. Sheila and I talked about it during breakfast. Their daughter has now lost both her parents, just like Ashley did. Even if Ashley's parents weren't brutally killed and she was much younger, it was still a devastating loss. We feel for that poor teenage girl. Such a tragedy."

"I only heard part of the news. Did they mention if they have any leads?"

"No, but one victim hadn't been identified before the news report."

Worthington stopped at the gate and waited for the guard to open it. After he parked, we took the medical supplies out of the back seat and headed toward the house where Worthington normally saw patients.

When we reached the porch, a security guard approached us. "The patient is in another building. I'll take you there." He escorted us to a structure close to the administrative offices, one I had never been in before.

Stepping through the entrance, I was surprised by the foyer. It was spacious, tastefully furnished with two brown leather couches, matching chairs, and chrome and glass tables. Landscape paintings hung on the walls next to a huge flat-screen television. It was appreciably nicer than the building Ashley had lived in, and I guessed that the other buildings that housed the members of the fellowship looked more like Ashley's than the one I was standing in. Even the administration building lacked this kind of décor.

Our guide led us to a door off the lobby. When he opened it, I was awed with its appearance. It was designed like an upscale New York apartment with modern furniture and deep lush-brown carpet. At one side was a well-appointed kitchenette with stainless steel appliances and a granite countertop. The security guard gestured toward an open door. Moving toward it, I saw the corner of a bed and some of the furnishings. It was just as exquisitely decorated as the main room.

My eyes popped wide open when I saw Newark lying in bed with his arm wrapped in a towel, blood soaking through it.

I set down the box of supplies and hurried to the bed. "Alex, what happened?"

"I hoped you'd be coming with the doc." His pale face, etched with pain, alarmed me.

Had there been another problem at the compound? Or was he in an accident after he left Calders' house? Gazing at him, more questions kept streaming into my head.

Worthington slipped on a pair of gloves and stepped between me and Newark. He removed the towel and a tight bandage from Newark's arm. "Who wrapped your arm?"

"Sean."

"He did a good job. Stopped most of the bleeding."

Even though I wasn't a medical professional, I knew what a bullet wound looked like. Newark had been shot.

Worthington examined the wound. "When did this happen?"

"Last night."

"Why didn't Dr. Barton request me to come earlier?"

"It happened out of town. It took a while to get here."

I had also been in Tucson and knew it took less than four hours to get back to Sedona. With a gunshot wound, I couldn't imagine him sleeping comfortably at the Holiday Inn and not leaving there until today. Did he have to make a stop along the way? And more importantly, who shot him? Lange?

"You should've been taken to a hospital," Worthington said. "Are you in pain?"

"No. I've taken some morphine."

Worthington's brow creased. "Do you know the dosage?"

Newark's eyes moved to the guard standing in the doorway. "Travis, get the doc the prescription bottle."

"The bullet went right through your arm. It appears it missed your bone by only a few millimeters. I'll get you stitched up, but I'd like you to have someone take you to the clinic on Monday so I can have your arm x-rayed."

Travis came back with the bottle, and Worthington nodded as he looked at it. "Susan, we're going to need some towels."

"Where do you keep them?" I asked Newark.

"Bathroom cabinet."

I went into a spacious bathroom with marble on the floors and halfway up the walls. I took a stack of towels out of the cabinet. While Worthington filled a syringe, I placed Newark's arm on the towels. "Who shot you?"

"To tell you the truth, Susan, I haven't got a clue."

I squinted. "You were ambushed?"

"Something like that. I had just left a friend's house and heard a commotion inside. I started walking back to his door, and then out of nowhere, a bullet struck me. Neither Sean nor I could even figure out where the shooter was."

"Oh, that must've been terrible! Did you call the police?"

"Too much red tape. Who knows how long it would be before I could get back here."

Of course he wouldn't call the police. Gil Tunell was wanted in Florida. That's where he'd be shipped once his arm was patched up if the police had investigated.

I moved to the side and watched Worthington gently push the syringe needle into Newark's arm near the wound. I expected Newark to moan, but he didn't make a peep. Then I wondered how much morphine he had taken.

Playing my nurse's role, I asked Worthington, "Would you like me to check on the patients we saw on Tuesday?"

"No. We'll check on them next week."

"Susan, please stay while the doc works on my arm," Newark said, patting the other side of his king-sized bed.

Given where he was lying, there was plenty of room for me to sit there. I sat on the edge of the bed, slipped off my shoes, and scooted closer to him, and then held the hand of his uninjured arm. "This is what some refer to as a good bedside manner," I said with a forced smile crossing my lips.

"And yours is excellent." He squeezed my hand.

As Worthington tightened the tourniquet right above the wound on Newark's arm, I felt Newark's hand going limp and looked at his face. His eyes were closed. "He's asleep."

"Yes. He should stay that way for at least two hours. We'll be gone when he wakes up."

"Will he be in pain?" I asked.

"Yes, but I'll leave some pain medication for him along with a bottle of iron pills to help build up his blood. If he was in the hospital, he'd be given a pint."

While Worthington repaired the damage from the bullet, I ran last night's events through my head again. Newark had said they heard commotion inside. I had used a silencer and Tim hadn't fired one shot. The only commotion he could've heard was the glass table shattering. Could one of Conner's men have thought I was in trouble when Newark headed back to the door? Was that why he ended up with a bullet through his arm? If the shooter was one of Conner's men, he didn't intend to kill Newark or Newark would be dead. It must've been to prevent him from entering again. Was Newark carrying a gun that the shooter spotted? Then another thought occurred to me: Newark wouldn't consider entering the house if he knew spiders were loose inside. Did Lange leave them without Newark's knowledge?

As I considered the possibilities, my eyes swept around the room and stopped on the guard standing in the doorway. He had been keeping a watchful eye on Worthington and me since we arrived at the compound. I wondered if his job was to protect Newark or to make sure we didn't wander into a restricted area.

"Finished," Worthington announced. He removed the tourniquet. "Would you like me to apply the dressing?"

"Yes, and I'll get cleaned up. It's after five." Worthington headed into the bathroom to wash up.

Will we soon be physically escorted out? I thought as I took the needed supplies out of the box and began wrapping Newark's arm. When I finished, his arm was bandaged from his shoulder to his elbow, and I must say that I did a good job. It looked very professional.

While we climbed into Worthington's car, he said to the guard, "Have Dr. Barton call me if Mr. Newark experiences significant pain or becomes sick to his stomach."

The guard nodded. "I'll let Dr. Barton know."

When we reached the highway, I asked, "Besides the people you treated on Tuesday and Alex today, have you been called in to take care of other gunshot victims?"

"No. But once at the compound, Mrs. Hoffman told me that a young man accidently shot himself cleaning a rifle. Since he was the last scheduled patient for that day, I assumed his injury wasn't severe. After I finished with the other patients, Mrs. Hoffman said that the young man no longer required my services."

"What a strange way of wording it. Do you think the guy died?"

Worthington shrugged. "I don't know. A body wasn't delivered to the morgue. Do you still intend to see Dr. Barton this evening?"

"Yes. I need to elicit more information from him," I said, wondering if I could pry anything out of Kalstein during the meeting that would help shed some light on Snyder's identity.

28

THE MEETING

Dressing for my meeting with Kalstein, I considered taking a large purse with my gun concealed inside. But then figured Kalstein would be on high alert after the gunfire early Tuesday morning and Newark getting shot the night before. An oversized purse might draw Kalstein's attention. Not only could it hide a gun but other, more dangerous, weapons.

I called Conner and hoped I'd be talking to him and not his employee.

He answered, "I was just thinking about calling you."

"Thanks for the gun."

"Any reason you didn't already have one?"

"It wouldn't fit my nurse role. But after last night, this nurse needs to be armed. Did you hear about what went on?"

"Yes. A few things don't seem to add up."

"Like what?"

"All of the victims were shot with a 9mm, and Tim Wilder was packing a 45."

"Interesting. So you think I killed everyone in the room?"

"Maybe Wilder. Not the others. Care to explain?"

"Nope. Why did one of your men shoot one of the guys that left the house?" I asked though I wasn't certain who had shot Newark.

"He was heading back toward the house with his gun drawn and needed to be slowed down."

"How about the other guy? Wasn't he returning to the house?"

"He was. The first bullet hit him, but it didn't stop him."

"Huh? Where was he shot?"

"On the sidewalk."

"Conner, you know that's not what I meant."

"His leg. The bullet struck the side of his calf."

I wondered why Lange didn't have Worthington look at his wound. Maybe his wound wasn't very bad. The bullet probably just grazed him since he managed to get Newark back to the compound.

"Was that guy wearing any gear that could protect him from spiders?" I asked as a thought suddenly sprang into my head. Was it possible that the blood on the napkin I had tested didn't belong to Lange? Then I recalled Carol's mother saying "Ouch." She knew how dangerous the spiders were. She'd be more emotional if one had bitten her. Perhaps scream. Did Lange scratch her?

"I was told the bullet ripped a hole in his jeans. Not protective gear. I don't know what else he was wearing. Let me see what I can find out. Are you thinking he might be immune like you?"

"Possibly."

"So there were spiders in the house? Is that how some of the people died?"

It sure didn't take him long to put that together. "Conner I'm not going to discuss it."

"If I promise not to mention it again, can I visit you this evening, or would you like to come here?"

"I can't. I'm having a meeting with Kalstein tonight."

"Kalstein? How did you arrange that?"

"When I was at the compound on Tuesday with Worthington, Kalstein said he wanted to discuss a personal matter with me."

"Sara, you're not safe there."

"What makes you think so?"

"They know you didn't stay at your motel last night, but they have no idea where you were. You fit the description of the woman at the gun range the gunshot victim gave the cops. It might not take them long to put two and two together, especially since that guy died early this morning when you weren't in your room."

"How? Conner, you didn't…"

"No. But his death must have appeared suspicious. An autopsy was ordered. No results have been released yet."

I doubted he was being truthful about not being involved. The police intended to send a sketch artist to the guy's room. Conner would protect me from having my face appear on a wanted poster. Then I thought about Newark and Lange arriving much later in Sedona than I did, and Newark needed medical attention. Could there be a connection to the guy's death? But why would they want to silence an employee? That gunshot victim had guarded a Tegen with a dart gun. Did he know too much about Snyder?

"Conner, I still need to find out how Kalstein acquired the spiders. My mission here, remember? I have to go to the meeting. That's why I'm calling you."

"You want a bodyguard close by?"

"No. I want a sheath and a knife. Can you get that for me right away?"

"Yes. If you'll do something for me."

I softly laughed. "I thought I already did."

"True, but this is a business request, not personal."

"You want me to ask Kalstein who's handling his gun smuggling business now?"

"If you can find a way to work that into the conversation, I could put that information to good use."

"I'm sure you could. And while I'm at it, I could just ask him how he got the spiders."

"It certainly would save you some time, and then you wouldn't have to hang out with Gil Tunell."

"It's doubtful Kalstein would be open to that type of discussion, no matter how much charm I turn on. Okay, what do you really want?"

"For you to wear a bug and to leave one in Kalstein's office."

Since he came up with that request so quickly after I mentioned the evening meeting, I figured he already knew about it. "That's two things. Let's condense it into just one. I'll wear a bug and leave it in his office."

"You want two things—a sheath and a knife. It's only right we should make this even," he said in an amused tone. "Actually, that wouldn't make us even. There's still the tracking I did of Gil Tunell. I'm going to have to come up with a third thing you could do."

"How long have you known the phone number I gave you belonged to Gil Tunell?"

"When you said all the numbers."

"Do you have the phone numbers of everyone at the compound?"

"No. Only Kalstein and his inner circle."

The clock on the nightstand caught my attention. "It's after seven. I need to get going soon. If I leave a bug, will you give me a sheath and knife?"

"Two bugs. You wear one and leave one."

"Conner, I intend to visit with Alex—Gil Tunell—after I've seen Kalstein. I don't want you to overhear that conversation." The real reason was that I planned to check out some of the buildings, and then there was the possibility I might run into Kendall or another team member. I couldn't allow him to listen in on that conversation.

"Why are you going to see him?"

"We're dating. I need to maintain my role by pretending I'm interested in him."

"What you want will be delivered within the next half an hour," he said with an edge in his voice.

"Conner, my relationship with Gil Tunell is strictly business, nothing more. When I get back to my room if it's not too late, I'll call you."

"Sara, be careful."

"I always am," I said, but Tegens didn't need to be very careful, except around fire.

Almost thirty minutes later, someone knocked on my door. Opening it, I saw the motel clerk with a package in his hand.

"This just came for you. The man said it was urgent that you receive it immediately."

"Thanks." I took the package, assuming the clerk had been tipped well for his speedy delivery.

After opening the box, I secured the black sheath to my calf and slipped the knife inside, covered it with the bottom of my black silk slacks, and slipped on a pair of black stiletto heels. Then I attached one of the small bugs, less than half an inch in diameter, to my cuff, stuck the other one on my purse, and picked up a black sweater that I intended to wear over my low-cut, blue silk blouse when I left Kalstein.

Before I pulled out of the parking lot, I called Kalstein.

"Hello, Ms. Anderson." He sounded in good spirits, which struck me as odd given Newark's injury.

"I'm calling to let you know I'm on my way. I should be there in twenty minutes."

"I'm looking forward to seeing you."

As I drove along the curvy road, I thought about Blake. I hadn't cancelled my tentative date with him for Saturday night, but I planned to go out with Newark. Was there a possibility he didn't realize I had set him up for Kendall to capture him? With Newark laid up, I decided I'd call Blake tomorrow to confirm our date.

I stopped at the compound gate. The guard's lips twisted as if he were suppressing a smile. He opened the gate. Was I walking into a trap? Unlike mortals, I didn't have anything to worry about unless Snyder was involved and came at me with a blowtorch or knocked me out with a dart.

A guard inside directed me to park up by the administration building and followed my car along the path. I parked, pulled the bug out of my purse, and attached it to my dashboard.

After escorting me into the building, the guard stopped in the foyer and gestured toward my handbag. "Your purse, please."

I handed it over and watched him check the contents inside. He handed it back and finished escorting me to Kalstein's office.

"Good evening, Ms. Anderson." Kalstein gestured toward the couch where Milner sat. "Please have a seat."

I settled on the other side of the couch, and then Kalstein introduced me to the man I already knew, Nathan Milner.

"Pleased to meet you." I extended my hand toward him.

He briefly touched my hand and mumbled something that I took as a greeting.

I had the impression that Milner either didn't want to be here or he wanted to skip all formalities and get to the heart of the meeting.

"Ms. Anderson, you're probably wondering why I wanted this meeting."

"Please call me Susan, and yes, I had been wondering about the 'personal matter' you wanted to discuss with me."

"Well, I had intended to ask if you'd be interested in a nursing position at the compound, but then I learned about a problem."

"A problem?"

"Yes. Alex was told you weren't at work yesterday because you were ill, and you confirmed that when he spoke to you last night. He was concerned about your well-being and asked a member of the

Fellowship to check on you. That member discovered you weren't in your motel room. I have to be able to trust my employees. Can you explain why you lied to Alex?"

"It's rather personal, and I feel uncomfortable discussing it."

"Unless you can give me an explanation, I'm afraid I can't offer you a position."

"Aaah...Could I explain it to you in private?"

"Nate." Kalstein tilted his head toward the door.

Milner rose and trudged out of the room. Could the man walk any slower?

"Go on." Kalstein closed the door. "Tell me." He returned to his desk.

Intending to attach the bug on my sleeve to the back of the couch, I placed my sweater on the armrest, put my purse on top of it, and walked closer to Kalstein. "The first time I had a drink with Alex, I told him I had just broken up with a guy, a person that I wish I had never met. Yesterday, the old boyfriend called me at work. I didn't know he was in town. He was drunk, slurring his words, and said if I wouldn't come see him, he'd go to the clinic and talk to me there. How would that look, having a drunk ex-boyfriend show up where I worked? And I will need a good reference when I leave. I just couldn't risk it. So I agreed to go to his motel room and then told Dr. Worthington I wasn't feeling well.

"When I got to the ex-boyfriend's room, he was so smashed it took him a while to answer the door. A few minutes later, he became deathly ill. I ended up taking care of him. He finally fell asleep. I booked him a flight and planned to return in the morning to take him to the Flagstaff airport. He woke up as I opened the door to leave and staggered toward me. Then I told him I'd be back in the morning to take him to the airport. He grabbed a bottle, took a swig, and bumped into a chair and collapsed on the floor. I had heard he had a drinking problem, but it never seemed out of control when we were dating. I broke up with him for other reasons.

"I managed to get him back in bed, and then I dumped the rest of the booze down the sink. But knowing he could easily get more liquor, I wanted to make sure he didn't cause me any trouble while he was still in town. So I stayed in his room and slept in a chair. This morning, he seemed sober. I drove him to the airport and waited for the plane to take off. Then I called his sister and told her what had happened. She agreed to pick him up at the airport. Now you know why I didn't want to talk about it. Alex called while I was there, but I couldn't answer my phone. I called him back when the ex-boyfriend fell asleep, and I lied to him. Please, don't tell Alex the truth. I don't want him to know I spent the night with an ex-boyfriend."

"What motel?" he asked suspiciously.

"Casa Sedona Inn."

"His name?"

"I've told you why I lied to Alex. If you need more than that in order to offer me a position, then I'm afraid it's not going to work out." I swung around and went to the couch to gather my belongings. With my back to Kalstein, I quickly removed the bug from my sleeve, stuck it on the back of the couch, and picked up my purse. Then I turned back to Kalstein and said, "Is it okay if I see Alex before I leave?"

With a thoughtful expression on his face, Kalstein rubbed his chin. "Susan, would you still like a position at the compound?"

"Yes, but if you don't think I'm trustworthy, I can't work here."

"Alex speaks very highly of you, and I rely on his judgment." The corners of his mouth slightly curved up. "He's never steered me wrong. I'd like to offer you a position here."

"Are you sure?"

"Yes. There's a possibility that the Fellowship might move to another location. We need more space if we want to increase our harvest and expand the number of crops we plant. Are you free to relocate?"

"Absolutely. I don't have any ties in Sedona."

"I'll pay you double what you're making at the clinic, and you'll be provided an apartment similar to Alex's. Are those terms agreeable?"

"Oh, yes, but I can't start until Dr. Worthington's nurse returns. That should be in a couple of weeks," I said though I never intended to work for a man who extorted money and ordered innocent people beaten and killed.

His green eyes roved over me. "That will give us time to have the apartment ready for you. Call me when you're able to lock in a start date."

I forced a smile. "I will, and thank you. Is it okay if I go see Alex now?"

"Yes. He wanted you to stop by before you left."

Moving toward the door, I noticed, out of the corner of my eye, Kalstein nodding at the guard. That guard stayed a short distance behind me as I walked to Newark's apartment. His door stood ajar. I opened it a little wider, stuck my head in, and said loudly, "Alex, is it okay if I come in."

"I've been waiting for you." His voice came from the bedroom.

I stepped in and closed the door before the guard reached the doorway, thinking about how I could lose the guard after I visited with Newark.

As I entered his bedroom, he patted the other side of the bed. "Sit here."

I moved to that side, sat down, removed my heels, and slid closer to him. "How are you feeling?" I rubbed his arm.

"Much better."

"I have some good news." I grinned.

"Ka...Barton offered you a job?" he said, and I guessed he was about to say Kalstein.

"Sure did. And he's going to give me more money and an apartment like yours. I hope it's in this building."

"This is the only building that has apartments. You've got to keep that quiet from the other members of the Fellowship."

"Yeah, that could cause a problem." Then I recalled the door with Newark's name next to it in the dorm building where Ashley had stayed. That name plate was just a façade so the members wouldn't suspect the high echelon received special accommodations. That was the room where two bottles of *venotrolia* had been found, initially reassuring Kendall's team that Newark was Snyder. Anyone could've planted the bottles there without having to worry they'd be discovered by Newark.

He threaded his fingers through mine. "When do you start?"

"Not until Dr. Worthington's nurse returns from her trip."

"We'll have to go and celebrate."

"Not until Dr. Worthington says you're well enough to get out of bed. Besides you going to his office on Monday for an x-ray, he wants you to stay in bed for at least a week. You lost quite a bit of blood. Dr. Worthington left you some pills to help build it up. Did you take your medicine when you woke up?"

"Yes, Nurse Anderson." He pointed to the glass of water and the open pill containers on the nightstand.

"Does Dr. Barton live in this building?"

"He has an apartment upstairs but rarely uses it. He sleeps at the house. I think he likes Mrs. Hoffman catering to him, and she's a great cook. Sometimes I'm invited to dinner."

"Where do the other members of the Fellowship eat?"

"The last building up the lane on the right side contains a mess hall. The food is pretty good there, but it doesn't compare to the spread Mrs. Hoffman lays out."

"How many live in this building? Any couples?"

"No couples. Right now, just a bunch of guys. You'll be a big improvement."

"Any idea where my apartment would be?" I hoped he would divulge the names of the other residents.

"Sean has the apartment next to mine. Maybe I can talk him into moving into another one."

"How many are there?"

"Six, but only five, no, wait…just four are occupied including Barton's."

Tim Wilder must've had an apartment in this building, but the structure was much larger than six apartments the size of Newark's. Something else must be in here. Maybe guns? Whatever it was, I doubted it had anything to do with Snyder. I looked at the window and an idea popped into my head. "I love how lush and green everything is around here. Do you have a good view of the woods?"

He nodded toward the window. "Go look for yourself, and tell me what you think."

I slid off the bed and opened the drapes. Trees and foliage covered the landscape. No other buildings were visible from my angle of sight. The chain link fences encircling the compound disrupted the natural beauty of the woods. Newark's window was around eight feet above the ground. I put my hands on the sill and checked the lock. It was secured. Raising my hand while turning toward Newark, I quickly pushed the lever into the open position. "This is wonderful. No buildings block your view." I closed the drapes.

"The apartments across the hall only have a view of a building twenty feet away."

I gave him a big smile as I slid back onto the bed. "Well then, if you can't get Sean to move, I guess you'll have to move across the hall."

"You don't think you could just move in with me?"

"Maybe someday. Would that be breaking a rule?"

"Some rules are meant to be broken."

I shook my head. "And here I thought you were the one that enforced them."

"Some broken rules only become a problem if someone discovers you broke one."

"It's getting late, and you need your rest. I'd better get going."

"Can you come back tomorrow?"

"Yes. Would you like me to bring you anything?"

"Nothing I can think of," he said as his face twisted in pain.

"When was the last time you took your medicine?"

"Around seven."

I glanced at my watch. "That's over four hours ago. Time to take some pills." I edged to the side of the bed and slipped on my shoes.

"One of those pills wiped me out earlier for over two hours. I wanted to be awake while you were here."

"Well, I'm leaving now, so you should sleep." I handed him a pill from each container and a glass of water. After he swallowed the pills with a gulp of water, I placed the glass back on the nightstand and kissed his cheek.

He put his hand on the back of my head and attempted to kiss my lips, but the movement must've jarred his wounded arm. He moaned.

"Take it easy." I stroked his face. "You're not well enough for that, and I don't want you to pull out any of your stitches." I backed away from him and put on my sweater. "It's starting to get a little cold outside."

"You can always climb under the covers next to me. And in my condition, all we would do is sleep."

"I'll see you tomorrow." I walked to his door that led to the hallway and slowly opened it, expecting to see the guard on the other side, but he wasn't there. I looked up and down the hallway. No guard. I eased Newark's door shut behind me and then went to Lange's apartment and knocked. I listened for any movement coming from inside. Nothing.

Staying on high alert, I pulled my picks out of a hidden compartment in my purse and worked on the lock. Within a minute, that job had been tackled, and I was cautiously moving toward the bedroom to make sure Lange wasn't sleeping. After seeing the unoccupied bed, I unlocked the window and opened it a few inches in case I needed a quick escape route. Knowing he could show up at any minute, I searched for a pair of jeans with a hole in the leg. A hamper stood in his closet. The jeans were crumbled among the dirty clothing. Blood stains surrounded the hole. Blood that I intended to have tested. I headed to the window and peeked out. Not seeing anyone, I dropped the jeans to the ground. Then I went to his kitchen and opened the fridge. I smiled when I saw a white plastic half-n-half bottle, similar to my milk containers. But did it have *venotrolia* inside? As I picked it up, it felt almost empty. I removed the cap, took a sip, and briefly savored the taste of the red liquid.

The sound of footsteps and voices drifted through the door.

I quickly screwed the cap on and placed the container back in the fridge. I hurried to the bedroom window and took off my shoes. Holding them, I climbed out and closed the window. I scurried down the side of the building and then put on my shoes, pulled off my sweater, and wrapped the jeans in it.

"Stop right there." A raspy, male voice called out from behind me.

Turning around, I saw the guard who had followed me to Newark's apartment step out from behind an overgrown bush, gripping a pistol.

"I knew you were up to something. Let's pay a visit to Dr. Barton." He gestured with his gun for me to walk toward the administration building. "I'm sure he'd like to see you again."

I didn't budge while I tried to think of an acceptable explanation for sneaking around.

The guard jabbed the gun into my arm. "Get moving."

I had no option. I ejected my needles and, with one swift move, scraped the hand that held his weapon.

"What have you got?" He forced my fingers apart.

"Nothing. I was just walking around, enjoying the place. You know, I'm going to be living here soon."

"Not after Dr. Barton hears you've been snooping around." He gestured with his weapon again for me to move.

I stalled for time while waiting for the poison to take effect. "Can't we talk about this?"

"Nothing to talk about."

I moved in front of him and slowly began walking toward the

administration building. Hearing a thump behind me, I swung around and saw the large, muscular guard spread out on the ground. With the possibility some Tegen spiders could still be freely roaming around in the compound, would Barton and his cohorts believe the guard had been bitten by a poisonous spider? Then I looked at the scratch on the guard's hand. Snyder might suspect the guard was killed by a Tegen. I knew what had to be done, but I didn't want the guard's body found close to Newark's window. I tucked the blood-stained jeans under a bush and laid down my sweater and purse. Using all my strength, I tugged on the man's legs until he was around the corner of the building. There, I raised my pant leg, pulled out the knife, and stabbed him in the chest, making sure the splattered blood didn't land on me. I wiped the blade on his pants and slipped it back into its sheath.

Rushing back to my belongings, I heard voices coming from the direction where my car was parked. I removed my heels and picked them up along with my purse and sweater. Then I crawled up the side of the building to Newark's window and slowly opened it. Trying not to make any noise, I held the drape aside.

Newark was lying on his back with eyes closed. Hoping the pill had completely knocked him out, I eased into his room as the voices became louder. I shut and locked the window. Newark hadn't budged. I headed to his door that led to the hallway and locked it. I removed the sheath with the knife securely in it and wiped fingerprints off of it. Looking around for a spot to hide it, I ended up tucking the sheath between towels in Newark's linen closet, a place where I could easily retrieve it. Then I shucked my slacks but left my blouse on to conceal my special camisole and slid into Newark's bed. I inched closer to him and laid my arm over his stomach and my cheek against his shoulder. Wishing I were lying next to Conner instead of Newark, I closed my eyes.

29

STORAGE SHED

I awakened when someone kissed my lips. Conner had monopolized by dreams, and without opening my eyes, I automatically wrapped my arms around the man by my side.

"Aaah, easy." Newark stopped my hand from pressing against his wounded arm.

My eyes snapped open as the early morning sun filtered through the drapes.

"What a pleasant surprise," he said.

The night before sprang into my mind. "Well, you did say I could climb in bed with you." I gave him my best charming smile. "As soon as I reached the entrance, I decided to take you up on it. When I came back in here, you were zonked out. I hope you don't mind I'm here."

"Are you kidding?" He rubbed his bare legs against mine. "But how about taking this off?" he said, pulling at my blouse sleeve."

"I left it on, on purpose. You're supposed to be resting and taking it easy. I just wanted to lie next to you, but I didn't want to take a chance that staying with you could delay your healing. You're not up to that type of activity right now." I ran my fingers over his chest. "If you invite me again to climb into your bed when you're well, then it won't be just the blouse that comes off."

Pounding on his door echoed through his apartment.

"What the..."

"Sorry, I locked the door. I didn't want anyone to know I'd broken a rule before I even started to work for Dr. Barton."

"The closing of a door when a visitor is inside rule doesn't apply to this building."

"Then I'd better put on my slacks and answer your door," I said as the rapping continued.

He leaned over me with his good arm and lightly kissed my lips. "I'm not up to doing any work today. And I like having you next to me. Unless the place is on fire, they'll give up and go away."

My eyes popped wide open. "Fire?"

"Relax, I don't smell any smoke."

A loud thud came from the direction of the hallway. Shoes stamped across a floor. Two guards appeared in the bedroom door frame.

"What the hell do you guys think you're doing!" Newark snapped. With his good arm, he pointed toward them. "Get out of here, and get your walking papers."

The guards looked behind them and then moved aside. Barton walked between them and stepped into Newark's bedroom.

"What's this about, Sheldon?" Newark hissed.

Barton eyed me as he held up his hand in a stop motion. "Ms. Anderson's car was still parked by the administration building, and we were concerned."

Newark gritted his teeth. "So you barged in here because you were concerned?"

I rubbed Newark's shoulder. "Alex, relax. In your condition, it's not good for you to be upset. I should be going anyway. You need your sleep." I scooted away from him.

Newark wrapped his hand around my forearm. "No, stay." His eyes bored into Barton.

Barton cocked an eyebrow and gave me a suspicious look. "Has Ms. Anderson been here all night?"

"Yes," Newark said.

Barton's eyes remained fixed on me. Since I was wearing a blouse, I thought he needed a little reassurance that Newark was telling the truth. "It's time for your pills." I moved Newark's hand from my arm and slid out of bed. The bottom of my blouse hit right below my waist. As I rose to my feet, my lacy, bikini panties were clearly visible while I walked to the other side of the bed and took two pills out of the containers and handed them to Newark. I gave him the glass of water while I sensed the men in the doorway ogling my derriere.

Newark's eyes were also focused on that part of my body as he drank the water.

Thinking I had given them enough of a peep show, I climbed back under the covers and moved close to Newark.

Newark glared at Kalstein. "Now that you know Ms. Anderson's whereabouts, is there anything else you need?" Newark's anger was evident in his tone.

"We had a…" Barton began.

He stopped when someone in the hallway yelled, "In there."

Feet pounded on the carpet.

A few seconds later, Lange pushed one of the guards aside. "What happened?" He glanced at Barton then at Newark and me.

"Another guard was killed last night."

Playing my role, I creased my brow and tried to look scared. "Killed?" I whispered to Newark. "I'm glad I stayed with you."

He squeezed my hand. "So am I."

"Where?" Lange asked.

"Between the back entrance to this building and the fence."

"Shot?" Lange squinted.

"No. Stabbed." Barton's eyes moved back to Newark and me. "We'll leave you two alone." Then he said to Lange. "We'll discuss it in my office."

The four men turned and walked away.

After the hallway door closed, I stood. "I really should get going. You need to sleep, and I doubt that will happen while I'm here."

He glanced at the clock on his nightstand. "Breakfast will be here in about twenty minutes. I could call and have two orders brought in."

"No, thanks. A friend is coming into town, and I'm going to meet her for lunch." I climbed out of bed. "Is it okay if I freshen up in your bathroom?"

"Sure." He sounded groggy. The pills were working.

I grabbed my slacks and purse, went into the bathroom, and shut the door. I turned on the faucet, and then took the sheath out of the linen closet and strapped it onto my calf. After pulling on my slacks, I washed my face, combed my hair, and fixed my makeup.

Strolling out of the bathroom, I saw Newark's eyes were closed.

Still, I played my role and kissed him on the forehead. Then I gazed at the sleeping man. Why should he sleep peacefully when he had led the team that killed Carol's parents? I felt nothing but contempt for him. And then I wondered how I could love Conner, knowing he was also responsible for multiple killings. But my heart always outweighed any rational thoughts when it came to Conner, and I doubted he had ever ordered an innocent person killed.

Stepping away from the building, I wanted to retrieve the blood-stained pants hidden under a bush. As I tried to formulate a plan to do it without getting caught, I saw Barton heading toward me.

"Did you enjoy your visit with Alex last night?" He showed no emotion as he eyed me up and down.

"Yes. Very much. Is it okay if I visit him later today?" I asked, trying to portray the image of a soon-to-be compliant employee.

"Of course, but don't stay after dark," he said without giving me an explanation as to why.

"I won't."

He turned and went up the stairs to the building entrance. I guessed he intended to talk to Newark. Would it be about the shooting or about me?

As I drove out of the compound, I waved to the guard at the gate. I intended to call Blake when I reached my room. Maybe I could find a way to ask him how he escaped Kendall. Marge mentioned that someone had helped him. I figured it was Lange, but could someone else also be involved?

I glanced at my rear view mirror and saw a dark blue Ford truck like the one that seemed to be almost always parked at my motel, two cars behind me. The driver was probably tailing me, but I saw no point in trying to lose him since he'd show up at my motel anyway.

Fifteen minutes later, I opened the door to my room. Kendall sat on the couch, talking to someone on the phone. "She just walked in." He disconnected.

"Why did you spend the night with Gil Tunell?"

"How do you know that?"

"You were seen climbing in his window, and you didn't leave that building until this morning."

"Whoever saw me climb into his room must've seen what happened before then. Newark is laid up. He's not up to any action if that's what you're inferring."

"Todd saw you climbing in, but that was the first time he spotted you. Back to my question," he said in a demanding tone. "Why did you spend the night with Tunell?"

I proceeded to tell him about the jeans and the guard and then said, "Staying with Newark gave me a cover so no one would suspect I had stabbed the guard. And it worked perfectly. Newark said I had been with him all night, and that's what he believes. Besides the jeans in Lange's apartment, I also found *venotrolia* in his fridge, disguised in a white container similar to those you drop off. He sustained being shot in the leg without even limping. I doubt he has a mark there. I'm quite certain now that he is Snyder."

"What about the blood test?"

"Somehow he switched the blood-stained napkin."

"We found *venotrolia* in Tunell's room that's in another building. Whoever Snyder is, he could've planted *venotrolia* in several rooms to throw us off."

"Come on, Kendall. In a white container? No one would've put it in something like that unless they were a Tegen. Anyone visiting could've poured it into a glass. That certainly would have caused uproar at the compound.

"Kendall, I can't give you any proof, but every sense in my body tells me it's him. If you feel you need some additional verification, you can retrieve the jeans under the bush and have the blood on it tested, but you won't be able to get that done before I go back to the compound. With the shootings, Snyder might clear out soon. He won't stick around as more victims are added to the current police investigation. Is there any way you could capture him at the compound if I manage to get him alone?"

"Snyder said spiders would be released if he was captured. We haven't been able to determine what mechanism he has set up to make that happen."

"That could just be an idle threat to keep you working on that while he moves in for the kill. Blake mentioned that Snyder liked the game—seeing if he can capture the hunters before they capture him."

"He hid a supply of spiders in the barn. We managed to get those out. There were also seven preserved bodies in there. When we have Snyder in custody, someone might look for him in the barn. Those bodies have to be removed before they're discovered. Marge stayed there to watch for Blake or anyone else entering the barn, which could have been Snyder, while I obtained a trolley cart to haul out the bodies."

"Trolley cart? You intended to pull it out the gate?"

"No. It would be in the woods, on the other side of the fences. We intended to load up one body at a time."

"Intended to? Did you get any out?"

"No. Marge didn't answer her phone by the time I had the cart in place."

"Marge? Missing? What time was that?"

"When you were enjoying your night with Newark."

"Kendall, I wasn't enjoying myself."

"Around 2:00 a.m."

"It was around midnight when I was in Lange's room. I have no idea what time he returned or if he slept there at all. Did you have your phone on all the time?" I asked, recalling Marge couldn't reach him on Thursday.

"On vibrate."

"I turned mine off." I dug it out of my purse and pushed the on button, thinking Marge might've called me. Looking at the screen, there weren't any missed calls. "Let me check my other phones." I walked to the nightstand and pulled two cell phones out from underneath it. I also looked in the drawer to make sure my spiders were safe. They were crawling around in their case. Nothing had been disturbed. Then I clicked on the phone used to contact Blake. "Blake's called three times. He sent me one text." My eyes scanned it, and I sucked in a ragged breath and swallowed hard. "I'll read it to you. 'Sara, Snyder knows who you are. Marge blew your cover. Stay away from the compound.'" I raised my head and gazed at Kendall. "Do you think she's still alive?"

"Snyder would use her as bait. Marge wouldn't blow your cover, but Blake would do it to get back in the good graces of Snyder."

"But Blake doesn't know I'm using the alias Susan Anderson. He thinks I'm Lena something. And you don't think he was serious about wanting a pardon?"

"He could be playing both sides. See which one works out the best for him."

"I just don't think Blake is that dumb. He's got to know that someday Snyder will get caught, and he'll go down with him if they're bosom buddies."

Kendall didn't say a word while he gazed at the floor.

I turned on my other phone and saw two missed calls from Conner and one voice message. I glanced at Kendall. He still sat motionless as I listened to the message from Conner. "The man you're looking for is Theodore Snyder."

I shook my head, thinking, "Tell me something I don't know." Guessing he discovered that by listening to a conversation in Barton's office, I laid down the phone and fed my spiders. Since Kendall appeared to be in deep thought, I took a bottle of *venotrolia* out of the fridge and sipped it.

Kendall's cell phone rang, snapping him out of his deliberations. "Yeah," he answered. "No, Todd. When did he leave?...Blake...No...In an hour...Yes...Don't go in there." He disconnected and stared at me. "Blake knows your alias. In his room, Todd found a picture of you dressed in your nurse's uniform with the name Susan Anderson on the back. The semi that had been parked at the gun range pulled into the compound half an hour ago. The weapons and ammunition in the small structure are being loaded into it."

"In front of the residents?"

"Boxes are being put into it. The residents aren't aware of the contents."

"Yesterday, when Dr. Barton offered me a nursing position at the compound, he mentioned that they might be relocating...to a place where they could grow more crops. Besides the guard that I handled in the wee hours of the morning, there was at least one more recently killed because Barton said 'another guard was killed' when he referred to the one I stabbed. It could've been several guards, and he decided things were getting too hot for him there...time to clear out."

"It appears he already has."

"Huh?"

"He left the compound with Milner, an unidentified man, and two guards shortly after you did. The investigators we hired to keep track of Newark before we arrived never saw Barton leave, and neither did we. Given the fact that he's a wanted man and has enemies, his quick departure and the loading of the weapons signifies he has no intention of returning."

"What are we going to do if they start loading up everything in the lab?"

"There won't be enough room in that trailer."

"Even if one of those small buildings is stacked to the ceiling with weapons, it's not going to fill up a 50-foot trailer."

"More weapons are stored in the building where you spent the night."

"Unless some of those apartments in that building are bigger than Newark's, there's a lot of extra space in there for weapons."

"Correct. Guns, assault rifles, grenades, and various other kinds of weapons. If Barton intends to take all of them, one trailer won't be enough, but his arsenal isn't our concern. Todd is watching the lab. That's our concern."

"What about Marge? She might be held in the barn. Have you or Todd even looked for her?"

"She's not in the barn or at the gun range. We'll be searching the other buildings after nightfall."

"How did Blake escape you?"

Kendall frowned. "He was sedated, chained to a pole. Someone rescued him."

I had expected him to ignore that question like he always did. "Snyder?"

Kendall shrugged.

"I tentatively have a date with Blake for tonight. Since he left me a message, he must not be aware that I helped set him up for the capture. I'm going to give him a call. Maybe I can get some info from him. Unless there is something else you want me to do."

"No, but stay away from the compound today."

"I told Newark I'd see him this afternoon. Until Snyder is caught, I want to maintain my ability to come and go from there, and Newark is my ticket."

"Make an excuse for today. We'll have you covered tomorrow." Kendall stood and raised the corner of the drape. "Need you to draw that guy's attention away again."

I nodded and headed out the door.

The blue truck was parked in its usual slot. The driver's window was rolled down. I quickly glanced in that direction. All I saw was the back of a brown-haired man's head.

Opening my car door, I recalled attaching a bug and ran my fingers underneath the dashboard and felt it. I thought about removing it and then decided to leave it in place. With Marge missing and Snyder knowing my true identity, being able to immediately contact Conner might be useful. His men couldn't fight Snyder, but some gunshots might draw his attention.

After driving up and down the nearby streets for fifteen minutes, I returned to my room and opened the drapes to let the sun in and then placed a call to Blake. No answer. I left a message. "Blake, it's Sara. Do you still want to go out with me tonight? Give me a call."

Curious about how much Newark knew about Barton's swift departure and the semi-trailer being loaded, I picked up a cell phone and punched in his number.

"You missed a great breakfast. Mrs. Hoffman felt sorry for me. She brought over a stacked plate of her pancakes along with sausages, and a guy from the mess hall came over with a plate full of eggs, bacon, hash browns, and toast. I must've been starving. I ate all of it, except a piece of toast."

"Good. You'll have your strength back in no time. My friend called. She's running late. So there is a chance I might not make it back to see you today."

"Can't you come here after she leaves? It doesn't matter how late. Just call. I'll have two guards meet you at your car and escort you. "

"Dr. Barton didn't want me to be there after dark."

"He's not here. He had a family emergency and left for a few days. I'm in charge."

"But you're laid up."

"Sean acts as my eyes and ears around the compound. He keeps me informed. Before Sheldon left, he told me three guards were killed last night—two shot, one stabbed. That happened a day after I was shot."

Since Conner had plans for Kalstein, I wondered if he was responsible for the other deaths. "Do you think there's a connection?"

"Possibly. With a killer in our midst, you're not safe here without an escort. I'm keeping a pistol close by, and a guard is sitting in my living room."

One of my other cell phones rang. I immediately pushed it off. Hoping Newark didn't hear it, I continued to play the role of a woman interested in the wounded murderer. "Maybe you should get out of there."

"No. I'll be safe as long as I stay put. Wandering around the compound by myself could be a problem."

"How about the other residents?"

"As of right now, only guards have been killed. No members of the Fellowship."

"With everything going on, don't forget to take your medicine."

"I can't wait for you to spend a night with me when I'm in better shape, so I won't forget. The last time Sean came to see me, he mentioned he'd be happy to give you a tour of the compound. It might be a while before I'm up to the task."

"At night?"

"Depends on how late you get here, but you'd be safe with Sean."

That I didn't believe. Keeping me safe, I was sure, wasn't Lange's priority. Quite the contrary. But walking around with him in the dark might be what Kendall needed to make a move.

"Try to get some sleep. Talk to you later." I disconnected and then picked up another phone and saw Blake had returned my call. I tapped his name on speed dial.

"Sara, I didn't think we'd be going out. I heard you were pretty tight with Alex Newark."

"No. I've gone out with him a few times, but that's all." Now I knew that Blake had discovered my real alias, confirming what Kendall had said, and then doubted I had ever fooled him. "And would I be calling you if I wanted to be with him?"

"Yeah, for information."

"I do have a proposal regarding your request. I could just give it to you over the phone, but I'd like to see you in person. Are you interested in seeing me?"

"What guy wouldn't be?"

A banging sound came through the airwaves.

He continued, "I need to get back to work. Can I pick you up at seven?"

"Sounds good. See you then."

I stretched out on the bed and thought about Marge. I had a hard time envisioning her telling Snyder about me, but he could've tortured her to get the information. Blake's message probably held at least some truth—my cover had been blown. The question buzzing around in my head was who was the culprit who had told Snyder about me—Blake or Marge.

The answer to that question wouldn't be forthcoming with me

lying in bed. I sat up, trying to think of other places Snyder could've taken Marge. Kendall said they had looked for her at the gun range. Since I had been told to stay away from the compound, I decided to search the gun range again and not go the compound during daylight. Following Kendall's orders wasn't anything I intended to continue doing. I just had to make sure he didn't know that I purposely disobeyed them.

After showering, I lifted up my special camisole, ready to put it back on, and then figured I didn't need it anymore. Snyder knew I was a Tegen. There was no point in pretending any longer I wasn't one. Without the unusual fabric covering my upper arm, I could verify that Lange was a Tegen by rubbing my arm against his. Secreted pheromones never lied. They would either confirm his Tegen identity or prove I was wrong.

I pulled my Tegen ring out of the padded bra and stuck that garment along with the camisole in a drawer. I moved Conner's ring to my left hand and slipped on my Tegen ring. A soothing sensation surged through my body. I closed my eyes and enjoyed the feeling, like my whole body was awakening. I caressed the ring with my other hand and savored the sensation a little longer. The ring had touched my chest when I wore the padded bra, but that didn't compare to having it on my finger. Looking at my face in the mirror, I saw my cheeks becoming rosier, my eyes brighter, and my lips redder. I inhaled deeply. I hadn't realized how much my body had missed having the ring where it belonged—on my finger.

Invigorated, I dressed in a jogging outfit, tucked the pistol in my purse, and went to my car. As I drove toward the gun range, three black Escalades with heavily tinted windows passed me going the opposite direction. Could Conner be in one of them? I kept checking my mirrors to see if any of them made a U-ey. None did.

Like prior times, I parked near the gravel lane and used my binoculars to look for cars and people on the gun range. Not spotting any, I climbed over the fence abutting the lane and cautiously made my way through the sagebrush. Still not seeing anyone, I walked around the gun range and stopped at the storage shed. I pulled my picks out of my pocket and went to work on the padlock. Within a minute, it snapped open. I removed it and opened the door. I gasped and took a step backward. All the equipment, tools, and miscellaneous items inside were splattered with blood, and it was dripping onto the concrete floor. Fearing it had belonged to Marge, I pressed my lips together and stuck out a finger into the fresh blood and then raised my finger to my nose and smelled it. I sighed with relief when it lacked a pleasant scent like Tegen's blood. I gazed at the bloody mess, thinking that whoever lost all that blood was probably dead.

The sound of a diesel truck, wheels crunching the gravel lane, caught my attention. I quickly closed the shed door, attached the padlock and ducked behind it. I peeked around the corner and saw a cloud of dust surrounding a truck heading my direction. Remaining concealed by the shed, I hurried to the sagebrush a hundred feet away and dropped to the ground.

The dark gray truck stopped at the gate. A muscular-looking man got out, pushed the gate open, and put on a thick pair of black gloves that almost reached his elbows. He took a blowtorch out of the bed of the truck, and I cringed. He walked toward the shed. As he came closer, I recognized the man. I didn't know his name but knew he worked for Conner, or at least used to. About eight feet from the shed, he pointed the blowtorch at it and flipped a switch. Flames engulfed the structure. Smoke bellowed up in the air. Sparks from the burning wood flew around it.

The man turned off the blowtorch and watched the fire destroy the shed. Within thirty minutes, all that remained of the bloody scene were singed pieces of metal, sizzling charred wood, and ashes. He went to the truck, put the blowtorch in the bed, and lifted out a rake. He returned to the burnt debris and combed the rake through it. He bent down, picked something up, and combed through the debris again. Then he turned and went to the truck. He dropped the rake and the picked-up object into the truck bed and then removed the gloves and also put them in the truck bed. He pulled a cell phone out of his pants pocket and held it against his ear.

Looking through my binoculars, I saw his lips moving and wondered who was on the other end of the line.

After pushing the phone back into his pocket, he got a fire extinguisher out of the truck cab, walked back to the burnt debris and sprayed it, leaving a pile of white foam. He stuck the fire extinguisher back in the truck cab and then climbed in.

As he drove away, I thought about what Conner had said to the senator—he'd take care of Kalstein and no trace of him would ever be found. Did the blood belong to Kalstein? Conner had called and given me the information I wanted but not the alias I needed. I assumed he had overheard a conversation in Kalstein's office. Now I wondered if he had acquired it in another way. Had Conner's men snatched Kalstein shortly after he left the compound? If Conner got the information directly from Kalstein, did Kalstein say anything else about Snyder?

Wanting answers, I headed to Conner's hotel.

30

ENEMIES WITHIN

Before going to see Conner, I stopped by my motel room and changed out of my jogging suit and into a pair of jeans and a blouse. The blue truck pulled out of the parking lot right behind me. It went straight at the intersection where I turned left, but I figured someone might still be following me. In case that person was connected to the compound, I parked close to the same place I had parked before and walked while I kept a watchful eye out for potential followers.

Heading toward the hotel entrance, I noticed a limo in the parking lot. A man who appeared to be dressed in a chauffeur's uniform sat in the front seat. I wondered if the senator was visiting Conner again, and then I saw a freakishly tall man approaching the limo. Even though I stood over a hundred feet away, he was a man I'd never forget—Tyler, Conner's father's main bodyguard.

Since Conner had been using an alias at the hotel, I wondered how his father knew he was there and if his visit had anything to do with me. His father wanted me dead and believed he had succeeded. Then I spotted one of Conner's bodyguards near the entrance. Was he instructed to keep a lookout for me?

I went to the back of the hotel, making sure my face stayed hidden from the bodyguards and the limo driver. Close to the pool, I pulled out my cell phone and called Conner, curious about what he'd say.

"Hello, Susan," he answered in a formal tone.

"Hey. I'm not meeting the spider team until six," I lied since that was the time I'd be getting ready for my date with Blake. "So I thought I'd come see you."

"Now's not a good time."

"You don't want to see me?"

"That's not what I said. I'll call you later." He disconnected.

Still curious if the meeting with his father had anything to do with me, I moved along the side of the building and stopped under Conner's balcony. Using my purse like a sun visor, I looked up. No one was on the balcony, but a suit-clad man stood inside the glass doors. Then he turned, glanced out, and pulled the drapes shut. A window near his balcony door stood ajar, a window I had opened when I last visited Conner.

The drapes on the patio door underneath his balcony were closed and so were the ones on the abutting suite's patio doors. Most of the hotel guests probably were either sightseeing or enjoying the hotel's pool. I went to the closest patio, removed my shoes, and stuck them in my purse. Then I crawled up the exterior wall to Conner's suite and quietly sat on the railing, tight against the wall, so people looking up wouldn't see a woman clinging onto the building. And should the guard inside look out, he wouldn't be able to see me without opening the drapes.

I leaned toward the open window and perked up my ears to listen.

The first voice I picked up belonged to Conner's father, Cedric Crussett, "…see it…It's scorched and dented, but his initials RLK are clearly visible on the back. Do you intend to give this to the senator?"

"No. But it could come in useful sometime in the future. I'll get all the data together on the merchandise. This will be good for the family."

"Congressmen, senators, yes, but not the truckloads of arms. It's not part of our business," Cedric said in an angry tone.

"We'll make some customers very loyal. No distribution will be made until after I'm home. The family business has been changing. No more videos and we're still exceeding your financial expectations after I dropped that part of the business."

The videos featured child pornography. Buying and selling them had been part of his family's business. I smiled, believing Conner had eliminated the videos because he found them as disgusting as I did.

"We need to continue growing with the times," Conner said.

"These new deals are nothing you need to be concerned about. It's all covered."

"And the other problem?"

"It wasn't her. How could it be? Davidson's always been a strange guy. He's trying to stir up something. Just can't figure out what he hopes to get out of it."

That answered my question. I didn't need to hear more. I crawled down to the patio below, slipped on my shoes, and made my way to my car, staying out of view from the limo and the hotel entrance.

Sitting behind the steering wheel, I wondered who Davidson was and why he told Cedric Crussett he had seen me. If he wanted money, he should've gone to Conner. No, he couldn't have gone to Conner. He'd probably be dead if he did. Cedric would want proof. How could Davidson provide it? Pictures? Since they could be doctored, that wouldn't be enough. Would Davidson try to capture me with the intent to sell me to Cedric? Maybe that's what he hoped to get out of it. Unless a mortal knew my abilities and knew not to let me touch them, it would be impossible to capture me. Even if they knew, they might not survive the task.

I parked at the motel, ran the events of the past twenty-four hours through my head, and toyed with searching the compound for Marge during daylight. My cell phones had been turned off during my exploits. Before making a decision, I wanted to check them for messages. I dug the three phones out of my purse and then remembered the bug in my car.

As I headed toward my room, I saw a motel maid leaving it, but there wasn't a cleaning cart nearby. I cautiously opened the door. The fragrance of roses drifted through the air. A large bouquet stood on top of the table. Since no lilacs were mixed into the arrangement, I doubted Conner had sent them and pulled the card out of the small attached envelope addressed to Susan Anderson. It read "My dear beautiful Sara, We'll be together soon. Love always, Theodore."

I stared at his words of endearment on the card. Strange. It was probably part of his game to try to confuse someone pursuing him. I assumed the "together soon" meant it wouldn't be long before he made his move. Maybe the next time I visited Newark.

I sat down at the table and turned on my cell phones. Only one phone, the Blake phone, had a new voice message. He asked me to give him a call.

Blake answered on the second ring. "Sara, I have something I need to work on later at the compound. Could we move our date up to six?"

"Yeah, that's fine. See you then." I hung up, wondering what Blake could be working on. He said he had some carpenter skills. But would he do that at night? With the shootings the night before, Blake could've been enlisted to help stake out the compound to try to apprehend the perpetrator if he struck again. Had Barton requested something like that before he left? The blood—the blood that probably had belonged to Barton—flashed into my head. I didn't know his middle name but figured the initials RLK on the scorched item Conner's father mentioned stood for Rodney L. Kalstein. I doubted word of his untimely death had reached the compound. On that thought, I placed a call to Newark to see if by chance the news had leaked.

"Wow," he answered. "Two calls in one day from the gal I wished was still in bed with me. Are you heading here now?"

"No. My friend's on her way to Sedona and then we'll go out to dinner. With the compound becoming my home in the near future, I was thinking about the shootings. Do you think it's possible that the guy who shot some of the Fellowship members last week—the one in the news that ran off with his girlfriend and is still at large—could be responsible?"

"Mmm? Kyle Watford. Possible. Sean says the culprit has been caught, but then I heard him telling some of the members not to wander around the compound until we hire more guards. That doesn't make sense. You could be on the right track."

Newark was Kalstein's right hand man. He couldn't be clueless about the beatings Kyle had received before he escaped. Newark might've even given the orders. Kyle still remained bedridden, waiting for his body to heal.

"Maybe one killer was caught, but Sean thinks there might be more than one," I said. "Who was caught?"

"Don't know. The person isn't a member of the Fellowship. Sean's working on getting a name."

"What are the cops saying?"

"Barton doesn't like cops hanging around. Things become complicated. When Sean's convinced that person is guilty, he'll call the cops. Sean will have the name soon. He's good at getting what we need."

That I knew—he's good at threatening people with spiders, like Carol's parents.

After we said our goodbyes, I hung up, convinced he hadn't heard anything about Kalstein. And if Conner fulfilled his agreement with the senator, Newark would never learn what happened to Kalstein. The man would've disappeared without a trace.

I took a bottle of *venotrolia* out of the fridge and drank it as I pondered about what Blake would be working on later. Maybe watching over Marge while Lange dealt with the killing of the guards. Could Marge be the person Lange claims was the perpetrator? Then no one at the compound would question why she's being held there.

Planning to obtain information from Blake, I dressed to entice him in a pair of tight pants and a low cut red, sleeveless sweater, a top I couldn't wear with my special camisole.

Blake knocked on my door right at 6:00 p.m.

"Come on," I said, holding the door open. "And see what Theodore Snyder sent me." I closed the door and gestured toward the roses.

Blake's eyes narrowed. "Roses?"

"Yes. Does he send a dozen to all the Tegen women he expects to make his next victim?"

"No. He never sent roses to Sandy."

"Sandy? Who's Sandy? The ring. Was it hers?"

A sheepish look crossed his face. "Yes. I should've told you when you asked about the ring, but I didn't want Kendall to know I had read about her."

"Why? He knows you looked in the project folder at the Tegen administration building."

"Well…there were two folders. He thinks I only looked in one." He pressed his lips together. "Are you going to tell him?"

"No. He doesn't share very much information with me, so I'll keep a few things from him. What else was in the folder?" I felt irritated that I had shown the ring to Kendall and Marge, and they both acted like they had no idea who it could've belonged to.

"It was all about Sandy. She had become a member of the Fellowship and worked as a school teacher on the inside. Sandy had taught school before, so she didn't have to pretend."

"I think I could've pretended to be a teacher better than a nurse. Since Kendall had someone on the inside, do you know why he wanted me on the team?"

"Sandy couldn't attract any guy. You, on the other hand, almost had Sean and Alex fighting over you."

"How did Snyder discover Sandy was a Tegen?"

"He saw her talking to Kendall. After that, he managed to rub her arm, and the secreted pheromones confirmed she was a Tegen."

"She wasn't wearing anything on her arms to help conceal her identity?"

"Nope. And it wouldn't have made any difference when he homed in on her. He'd find a way to get to her bare arms."

"And her ring?"

"She kept it on a chain around her neck."

"What about *venotrolia*?"

Blake shrugged. "Don't know how she got it."

"So are you going to tell me what alias Snyder is using?"

"Maybe. But let's go to dinner first."

Walking toward the stairwell with Blake, I saw a black Escalade pulling into the parking slot by my car. Assuming Conner was inside the vehicle, I didn't want Blake to know anything about him. Hoping to stop Conner from approaching me, I took Blake's hand when we reached the bottom of the stairs.

As Blake led me to a white Chevy truck, I saw Conner climbing out of the back seat of the Escalade. He stood by it with his eyes fixed on me.

Blake drove out of the parking lot with the Escalade not far behind us. Did Conner intend to dine at the same restaurant where Blake was taking me? That question was quickly answered when Blake turned down a side street and stopped in front of a steak house. The Escalade drove past us as we got out of the truck. This time, Blake took my hand, and we headed to the entrance.

The place was buzzing with people. Blake had made a reservation, and we were shown to a table tucked in the corner.

"I requested this table so we could talk."

After the waiter delivered drinks and we placed our orders, I observed two suit-clad men being escorted to a table about ten feet from ours—two men that I recognized from visiting Conner's suite. I glanced around, wondering if he'd be joining them.

"Is everything okay?" Blake asked.

"Yes. Why?"

"You seem nervous."

"Blake, I've been nervous ever since I received those roses. Is Snyder somewhere in here?" I sipped my wine.

He shook his head. "No. Don't worry. He's at the compound. And I already told you that I won't let Ted hurt you."

I leaned closer to him. "I'd really like to believe you, but how can you prevent it?"

"Sara, I've got this. Why don't you tell me the proposal made regarding the pardon?"

We stopped talking as the waiter placed the food on the table.

Between bites, Blake said, "Now tell me about the proposal."

I began the lie. "Not all charges can be dropped, but over half of the Council members are close to limiting your punishment to just having you finish your house arrest, and then you'll be back in their good graces. This is contingent upon you helping us capture Snyder. Kendall doesn't know about this proposal. Can you keep it between us?"

He finished chewing the food in his mouth. "Your father is working on it?"

I nodded. "Yes. Are you willing to help us?"

"Can you stop Kendall from capturing me again?"

"Again?" I said, playing the naïve role as I cut into my steak.

"Yeah. Right after we went out to lunch."

I squinted. "Really?"

Blake nodded.

"Well, he obviously let you go, so why would he capture you again?"

"He didn't let me go. I escaped."

"Escaped from Kendall?"

He nodded. "Yep, with a little help from a friend."

"A friend? Snyder?"

"Nope." His eyes met mine, and his brow creased. "Todd."

"Todd? But he's a member of Kendall's team." It almost made sense that it could be a team member. Unless Snyder or one of his cohorts had been following us, how would he know Blake had even been captured? But Todd?

"We go way back. I had planned to break him out of the trailer, but you beat me to it."

"How often do you talk to Todd?"

"Almost daily."

Could Blake be telling the truth? Or was he just toying with me? "If you are such good friends with Todd, why did he agree to work with Kendall to capture Snyder?"

"Well, when he agreed, I was locked up in the brig. He didn't know I'd be part of the project."

"Do you pass everything on to Snyder?" I continued eating.

"No." He downed the rest of his beer. "And Todd doesn't tell me everything. Only stuff I need to know to avoid Kendall."

"Since Todd warns you, you don't need my help to stop Kendall from capturing you again."

"Kendall can be unpredictable."

"Blake, Kendall would only capture you to get information. If you tell us the alias Snyder is using, he'll leave you alone."

"No. He won't. I'm still a Tegen fugitive. He'll want to haul me back to Bismarck."

"Are you going to give me the name, or should I start guessing?"

He shrugged as he took another bite.

"Okay. I think it's Sean Lange. Am I right?"

"How could it be him? He came down with the flu this afternoon and can hardly get out of bed."

"It's not Sean?" I said, not able to think of anyone else at the compound that might be Snyder. "The flu is what people at the compound say someone has when they've been bitten. Was Sean bitten?"

"He'd be dead if he was. The way he looked, he might've preferred that. No, he wasn't bitten. He has the real flu."

Blake gestured to the waiter for another beer. "I'll accept the proposal, and I'll give you the name and help capture him after the proposal has been voted on by the Council."

"But Blake, then it could be too late. You even said when we had lunch that Snyder might be clearing out soon."

"Yeah, he might. So you better get your Father to call for a special meeting of the Council."

He rested his hand on the table, and I saw his Tegen ring clearly displayed on his finger. I reached over and laid my hand on top of his. "That still might take a few days. Can you help me at all?"

With his other hand he caressed my arm. "Sara, I'm already helping you by keeping you safe from Snyder."

"Even if you don't give me his name, can you tell me where he's holding Marge?"

Blake studied my face. "I can't. If I did, you'd head right to the building, and then I'd have a harder time keeping you safe."

"If I promise not to go there but just pass the information on to Kendall, would you tell me?"

"No." He patted my hand. "I've heard about your exploits. That's a promise you'd probably break."

Gazing at Blake, I realized he had been using a façade, playing the role of the not-so-bright Snyder sidekick. He was smarter than that, and I had underestimated him. Besides not giving me Snyder's alias, could he be a threat to the whole mission?

"And who has told you about my so-called exploits?"

He gave me a cocky smile. "Todd."

I didn't know Todd well enough to determine if he'd abandon his Tegen obligation to help a friend, even if that friend was his bosom buddy. Yet, I couldn't imagine any Tegen knowingly taking that risk. Was Blake trying to establish a lack of trust between Kendall's team members? Still, I needed to warn Kendall even if Blake was just feeding me a line about Todd. This dinner date certainly wasn't turning out the way I expected it would. I had hoped he'd confirm that Lange was Snyder, instead he confirmed he couldn't be. How could I have been that wrong?

The waiter cleared off our plates. "Would you care for any dessert?"

"No, thank you," I said.

Blake ordered a slice of a decadent chocolate cake.

Almost an hour later, Blake walked me to my door. "How about going out with me again on Monday night?"

"I'd like that," I said, knowing it would give me another opportunity to entice him into telling me more about Snyder.

Without warning, he grabbed me in his arms and planted a kiss on my lips. "I'll call you tomorrow." He turned and left.

Gripping the doorknob, prepared to turn it, I heard movement inside.

31

THE SUSPECT

Worried that Snyder, whoever he was, could be in my room, I dug in my purse for the unique lipstick containing hidden weapons. I pushed it into my bra and slowly opened the door.

I smiled when I saw Conner stretched out on my bed.

"How was your date?" he asked.

"Informative." I sat down on the bed. "I had intended to spend time with you this afternoon, but you weren't anxious to see me. I figured you were with another woman."

He pulled me down into his arms and passionately kissed me. "You know perfectly well I wasn't with another woman. Sneaking around my hotel like that could've gotten you in trouble. You're just lucky that my men made sure Cedric's men never saw you. But I must admit, had they not been on the lookout for you and not aware of your unusual climbing abilities, you probably never would've been spotted."

And here I thought I had gone unnoticed. I should've known with Conner's men that was almost an impossible task. "How do you know it was me?"

He lifted up his cell phone and clicked on it a few times. Without saying a word, he showed me the screen—a picture of me sitting on his balcony railing.

"That could've been photoshopped."

He leaned over me and kissed me again and then looked at the picture. "Point taken." He clicked on his cell phone again and showed it to me—a picture of me at the gun range. "You could've still been hanging around there."

Lying on the bed, I looked up at him. "Conner, exactly how many guys do you have tailing me?"

"Enough."

"And at the compound?"

"That sometimes creates a problem. But one of my men was impressed how well you handled the guard who caught you climbing out of Snyder's window."

"Snyder's window?"

"Alias Sean Lange."

"How do you know that?"

"You wanted the name of the person who had given Kalstein spiders. That was the first question he was asked. He said he bought them from Theodore Snyder. Since there was no one with that name at the compound, he was asked how he contacted Snyder. He said through Sean Lange. Background checks had already been completed on the members of Kalstein's inner circle, those that have apartments in the building where you spent last night. Lange's turned out sketchy, like the others who were using aliases. Fingerprints were acquired. Lange's background check was still sketchy, but his report contained numerous aliases. His real name couldn't be pinpointed. After the meeting with Kalstein," Conner said as if the *meeting* had been an agreed upon cordial gathering, "I looked at Lange's background check again. One of the aliases was Theodore Snyder. Or Theodore Snyder could be his real name."

Something was missing. It didn't add up. Lange couldn't be Snyder. He was sick and Tegens don't get sick, but I couldn't tell that to Conner. That alias was probably planted in Lange's background record to throw anyone searching for Snyder off his track.

"Who is this guy Davidson that told your father he saw me?"

"Saw you?"

"Conner, you know I heard you talking to your father. He mentioned a problem, and you said it wasn't her, how could it be, or something like that. Are you saying he wasn't talking about me?"

"It wasn't you."

Conner's father never said my name, but I wasn't buying that he was talking about someone else. "Well…if it wasn't about me, then who?"

"No one you need to be concerned about."

I stared at him. "Please tell me the truth. I need to know if this Davidson guy might be lurking someplace, ready to grab me to take me to your father." That wasn't how it would go down. Davidson wouldn't survive to take me anyplace. But Conner had to believe I was mortal, and a mortal woman would be worried.

He held me in his arms. "Sara, relax. Don't you think I would do anything in my power to keep you safe? My love for you never died, even when I believed you had. Davidson doesn't know anything about you, and he never will. He thought he saw a family member someplace she shouldn't be. That's all. Trust me. I would tell you if you were in danger." He raised my chin. "You are the only woman I have ever loved." He held me tighter and smothered my lips with his, sending a tingling sensation through my body.

Before I started peeling off my clothes, I was curious if one of Conner's men had also observed me on his balcony the day the senator visited, or had I gone unnoticed. Thinking it could be the later, I wanted to prove to him that sometimes I could escape his watchful guards. "So did you handle your agreement with the senator to his satisfaction?"

"Senator?"

"The prior person who visited you in a limo."

"When was that?"

"Tuesday."

Conner shook his head. "No senator stopped by my suite."

"You called him senator. Do you have a friend you refer to as senator—like a joke or something?"

"No," he said without the slightest hint he was lying. He held up his phone. "Do you have pictures? Maybe I could recognize him that way."

I rolled my eyes. "Conner, I didn't take any pictures. I guess I eavesdropped on the wrong suite. I hadn't realized that more than one suite on the second floor in your wing had bodyguards outside and a man inside with your same height and build and wearing an Armani suit, just like the one you wore that day." My eyes lit up, and I tilted my head. "I'll have to see if I can find that guy. It might be fun to spend a night with your twin."

He enveloped me in his arms and kissed the tip of my nose. "I have no idea what you're talking about, but I don't intend to share you. I almost had you hauled out of Tunell's room last night."

"That was completely innocent. One of your men shot Gil Tunell, remember. He wasn't up to anything, and he didn't even know I was lying next to him until he woke up this morning."

"I know."

"How?" I asked, thinking about the guards that barged into Newark's apartment right before Kalstein entered. Did one of them work for Conner?

A hint of a smile crossed his lips. "Let's go away together." He ignored my question, just like Kendall.

"I can't. I'm not finished with the project."

He planted kisses down my neck, and his hand moved down my body. "After you get all the spiders gathered up and shipped someplace or exterminated and Snyder has been handled, would you consider going with me to that island you love in the Pacific?"

"I don't know if I can, and I don't have a passport."

"Sara, a passport won't be a problem."

I stroked his face. "I might have to work on something else," I said, wondering if I'd have to appear before the Tegen Council in order to officially end my sentence.

"You'd rather not go with me?" Disappointment showed in his intense brown eyes.

I wrapped my arms around his neck. "No, Conner. I want to go with you, but I don't know if I can go right after the project here is finished."

"When will you know?"

"Not until my work here is done."

"I need to leave early tomorrow morning. If everything goes well, I should be back tomorrow night or Monday morning at the latest. Then I'll stay in Sedona until you have an answer."

"Good." I ran my fingers through his hair and kissed him.

He began to take off my sweater.

Suddenly, I remembered I had to warn Kendall. I caressed Conner's arm and pulled away from him. "Sorry, I have to make one quick call. I'll be right back."

"If it'll speed up your project, I can wait."

Doubting the call would have that type of impact, I grabbed a cell phone and hurried into the bathroom. I punched in Kendall's emergency number.

It only rang once when he picked up. "What?"

"I had dinner with Blake. He told me that Todd helped him escape when you had him in custody. He also said that Todd warns him about your moves so Blake can avoid being captured again. I don't know if Blake was lying about Todd or if it was true, but I thought you needed to know."

"Did he explain Todd's motive?"

"They're buddies and their friendship goes way back. Have you been able to find Marge?"

"Yes, but we can't get to her."

"Why?"

"The building is rigged. Anyone attempting to release her will also release hundreds of spiders at different locations. We're searching for all the spiders."

"Do you want my help?"

"Not tonight."

"Tomorrow?"

"Possibly." He disconnected.

I didn't feel like I was carrying my weight in capturing Snyder, but Kendall seemed almost bound not to let me do anything that had the slightest element of risk. Since he didn't want me at the compound, I intended to enjoy the night. I disrobed and freshened up, and then sauntered out of the bathroom, wearing only a seductive smile.

"Wow, you become more gorgeous each time I see you," he said, unbuttoning his shirt.

I strolled to him. "Let me do that." I took over undressing the man I loved.

32

CAPTURED TEGENS

After spending an ecstasy-filled night with Conner, my eyes fixed on the door he had just closed behind him. I found him to be intoxicating and always wanted more, but we could never really be a couple. He was a member of an organized crime family that he now ran, a crime family that believed I was dead, and if they spotted me, they'd be constantly trying to kill me again, and Conner couldn't prevent that. I wouldn't die, but how could I explain my continual survival? And I was a Tegen, a species mortals didn't know existed, and that secret had to be kept at all cost. Still, I did want to go away with him to our special island and shut out the world for a week or two. Then I wondered how long it would take to finish the project. Snyder's identity continued to elude me and the other members of Kendall's team.

A rap on my door snapped me out of my reverie.

Thinking Conner might've forgotten something, but in case it wasn't him, I climbed out of bed, slipped on my robe, and grabbed my special lipstick.

Peering out the peep hole, I saw Kendall and opened the door.

"Your boyfriend left early." Kendall walked in, carrying a sack.

"He had an out-of-town appointment. How did you know he was here?"

"The black Escalade parked outside with a couple of guys in it. They took turns walking around, always keeping an eye on your door.

From that and the way they were dressed, it was obvious they were your boyfriend's bodyguards. Does he ever go anywhere without them?"

"I don't know. Maybe you should ask him." I gave Kendall a minute to say something and then asked, "How long have you been waiting for him to leave?"

He handed me the sack. "A couple of hours."

I looked in the bag. It contained *venotrolia* concealed in milk bottles. "Can we talk after I make some coffee, or can't it wait?"

"It can wait."

"Do you want a cup or something else?" I headed to the kitchen area.

"Coffee."

While it brewed, I sat on the edge of the bed. "You came to the door without going to the bathroom window first. Isn't the blue truck out there?"

"It is, but your identity has already been compromised."

"How is the spider hunt coming?"

"Slow. We've retrieved five clusters. Snyder claims there are eleven."

"You talked to him?"

"Yes. He called after we found the first two."

"Voice?"

"Disguised, like always. He's using another untraceable burner phone."

I poured coffee. "What's the story with Todd?"

"Blake fed you a lie."

I handed a cup to Kendall. "I can't…" Suddenly, it dawned on me. "Lange is Snyder. Now it makes sense. Fran. Remember, I mentioned her?"

"Yeah."

"When I talked to Father on your phone, he told me that a Tegen would become deathly ill if they drank the blood of a Tegen-impregnated woman. No one can find Fran. That's got to be why Lange is sick."

"Lange's sick?"

"Yeah, Blake mentioned that at dinner. It made me think that I was wrong about Lange. And when I was in his apartment, there wasn't very much *venotrolia* left in his container. He had to replenish it."

"How about Milner?"

"But Todd told you that he left with Kalstein."

"He could've doubled back."

Kalstein was captured shortly after he left the compound. Had Milner been a Tegen, that never would've happened. "It's not him."

"How do you know?"

I couldn't tell him. "Okay. There's a chance, but I intend to verify Lange's status first. In his condition, he won't be a threat, and it would be my duty as a nurse to check on the sick at the compound. It won't be long before I'm a full-time employee there," I said with a smirk and then sipped coffee. "But that's not why you came here so early. Is there something you'd like me to do?"

"Todd. He went missing sometime last night."

"Captured?"

"Most likely, but he's not being held in the same building as Marge. It's possible a mortal captured him by using a dart gun."

"It never occurred to me that Snyder would solicit the help of mortals to capture us. He might be using the shootings at the compound, wanting anyone sneaking around or anyone found on the grounds who's not a member of the Fellowship to be darted and brought to him or put someplace for questioning. Newark told me that Lange was in charge of that. With Lange laid up, any idea who's taken on that role?"

"No. Blake's been hanging around the building where Marge is being held, but it doesn't appear he has any authority. One of the guards has been spouting out orders, like he's in charge."

"What do you want me to do?"

"Visit Newark. Find out how many dart guns are at the compound. Check on Sean Lange. See if you're right. Then call me."

"If dart guns aren't in the hands of mortals, Newark might not know about them. But I'll see what I can find out. A mortal couldn't survive one of those powerful darts. Are you going to be at the compound?"

"Yes." Kendall stood, sat down his empty coffee cup on the table, and walked out.

An hour later, I was ready to leave for the compound with the sheath strapped to my calf and the pistol in my purse. Before I headed out, I placed a call to Father.

"Project finished?" he asked after we greeted each other.

"No. We're still not sure what alias Snyder is using, and he has places rigged up to let spiders loose if we make a move on him. How's the search for Fran Michaels coming?"

"Nothing so far. The investigator is still working to locate her. Her parents have filed a missing person's report. Has Kendall found any preserved bodies?"

"Yes. I doubt he's identified any of them yet, but the man I suspect is Snyder became ill yesterday. He might've drunk the blood of a woman he impregnated. I suspect it was Fran. I intend to find out if he's the elusive Tegen."

"Call if you obtain any answers. Until we can determine Ms. Michaels has been poisoned, the investigation into her whereabouts will remain active since she could be carrying a Tegen's child."

"Father, when this project with Kendall ends, do I have to report to the Council in order for them to declare my sentence has ended?"

"No. Kendall will provide that proof."

I wanted to ask him what would happen if Kendall didn't survive, but then I'd be reinforcing how dangerous this mission was and he'd ask me again to come home.

"Kendall has a few jobs for me to do. I need to get going."

"I love you, Sara. Please be careful. Unless Snyder has become incapacitated, he is ruthless."

"I will. And I love you too, Father."

Strolling toward my car, I saw the blue truck prominently parked in its usual spot. I had the urge to go and tap on the driver's window, but if mortals were equipped with dart guns, I could be making a costly mistake.

Within twenty minutes, a guard at the gate waved me into the compound. I stopped next to the administration building, the same place I parked on Friday night. Climbing out of the car, I noticed the back of a man who had his arm in a sling walking beside a guard about thirty feet away. Newark?

As I hurried toward him, he turned around. "Alex, you should be in bed."

His face looked drawn and pale. His eyes were glassy and appeared unfocused.

"Can't. Sean is sick, and Sheldon and Nate aren't back yet. Wherever they are, they don't have cell coverage."

Thinking he had no idea how true that statement was, I said, "Dr. Worthington wouldn't approve of you wandering around. Are you in pain?"

"Just a little."

"You're not going any farther. You're going back to bed now." I looked at the guard. "Escort him back."

"Bossy. I didn't have a clue you could be like that," Newark said, pain racking his features from his forehead down to his close-clipped beard.

"To bed." I pointed to his building as I continued playing the role of a medical professional and his girlfriend. He didn't argue when I grasped onto his good arm and led him back with the guard walking on his other side.

As we entered the building, I saw two guards patrolling the hallway. When Newark was situated back in his bed, I gave him a pain pill and then asked, "Sean's sick?"

"Yeah. He has the flu or something. He's in worse shape than I am."

"I'll go check on him. If it's the flu, I have a prescription in the car that should help," I said, though there wasn't one pill in it.

"He's not big about seeing doctors or anyone like that. He didn't want me to call Dr. Worthington. Doubt Sean will even let you take his temperature."

"Maybe I can sweet talk him into it."

"That you can probably do…or bully him into it." Newark smiled, and I knew the medicine was already starting to relieve his pain.

In the hallway, one guard talked into his walkie-talkie. The other one approached me as I gripped Lange's doorknob. "Ms. Anderson, Mr. Lange has told us not to let anyone disturb him."

"But he needs medical attention which I intend to provide." I turned the doorknob and pushed the door open. The guard didn't make any attempt to stop me from entering Lange's apartment, probably because I was Alex Newark's girlfriend and he was the man currently in charge of the compound.

"Who's there?" Lange mumbled.

"It's Susan." My nose wrinkled from the stench permeating his apartment.

"Go away."

Reaching his doorway, I saw a thoroughly utilized garbage can next to his bed and a towel along with his beard saturated with vomit. If it weren't for the mission, I wouldn't have hesitated turning around and running out of there. I looked at the dark circles around his bloodshot eyes and his trembling hands.

"Get out."

"Oh, Sean, I had been told you had the flu." I forced myself to touch his matted, unkempt hair. "This is worse, but I need to do something." Since he was in no condition to protest, I bent down and rubbed my arm against his and felt the pheromones being secreted.

"No." He moaned and closed his eyes.

"Yes, Theodore Snyder, you've been found out."

He gasped for air. "It…wasn't me."

"What wasn't you?"

"I didn't…I didn't… kill John… or his helpers. We were…friends."

"Are you trying to make some kind of a deathbed innocent plea, hoping to confuse us? I've heard you like the game. Well, Snyder, checkmate. You've lost. This game is over."

"Not…me."

I wondered how he intended to get out of his predicament. "Who then?"

"Blake…he's…the one."

Blake was in the brig when Snyder moved to Arizona. He saw the project files in the Tegen administration building and knew what Tegens were going after Snyder in Sedona. If Blake was the guilty party, he would've made his move earlier to capture Kendall and his team…unless he had been using us in order to get back into the good graces of the Tegen Council. And then Snyder would've been a loose end. Did Blake plan to terminate Snyder? Send him up in flames? On the other hand, this could all be another game Snyder was playing. In his condition, he probably thought he'd be dying soon and wanted to take someone with him.

"What about the spiders, the ones you turned over to Barton?"

"I…did that. I met Milner…in Florida. He told…me about Barton…and the compound. I needed an in."

"Innocent people have died here."

"Couldn't…be helped. No Tegens."

"No Tegens? What about Isaac and Sandy?"

"Sandy who?"

"A Tegen that taught school in the compound."

"Don't...know her."

"And Isaac."

"Wasn't...me. How did Kendall...know who...I was?" Snyder gagged, leaned over the edge of the bed, and spewed into the garage can. He wiped his beard with the towel and laid his head back on the pillow.

"He didn't. I suspected, and now I know."

"But...he poisoned me."

"And who told you that?"

"Blake."

"Kendall didn't poison you. You did that to yourself."

"Huh?"

"Fran Michaels. Do you remember her?"

He nodded.

"Did you poison her?"

"She...she saw the bodies."

"When did you drink her blood?"

"Yester...day afternoon."

"She was pregnant with your child."

"No." He closed his eyes again.

"Are you saying it wasn't possible for her to be pregnant with your child?"

"No...it was...she never said."

"You're going to be sick for a while, and then it'll even be longer before your body will be able to tolerate good *venotrolia*. Fran's body will need to be burned. Where is it?"

"The barn...upstairs."

"How are the spiders rigged up to spread through the compound if you're captured?"

"Huh?"

"The spiders," I snapped. "We don't want any more innocent people being killed because of you."

"Not...me."

"Okay, okay. Whatever. Blake. What's the mechanism to release the spiders?"

He shook his head. "Don't...know."

Footsteps pounded toward us.

A guard appeared. "Ms. Anderson, Mr. Newark would like you to join him."

"Tell him, I'll be there in a minute."

I waited for the guard to leave and then asked Snyder, "Dart guns. How many do you have?"

"One…Blake…has it."

Figuring I couldn't get anything more out of him, and doubting Blake was the mastermind behind everything, I said, "Whether or not you're responsible for the deaths of the Tegens terminated in Florida, or if Blake is, it makes no difference. You have broken the prime Tegen rule—no killing for revenge or sport. Innocent people have died, people who couldn't have been a threat to you. You'll be taken back to North Dakota to be punished. There will be no trial."

"But…I didn't…"

I held up my hand in a stop motion. "Save it. The council has evidence."

After leaving his apartment and before I entered Newark's, I called Kendall. With the guards pacing the hallway and within earshot, as soon as Kendall answered, I said, "Lange is sick with the flu similar to the one Fran had."

"He's Snyder?"

"Yes. He thinks he caught it from his traveling friend."

"Blake?"

"Yes. He blames everything on him."

"Any dart guns?"

"One. He lent it to that friend. I'm going to go see Newark now. I hope he doesn't come down with the flu."

"Have you talked to Newark about dart guns?"

"Not yet." I disconnected and walked into Newark's apartment.

"How did it go with Sean?" Newark's eyes drooped.

"He's not able to keep anything down. Pills wouldn't help. It could be more than the flu, but I don't have anything with me to test that prognosis. I suggested a visit to the emergency room might be in order. Sean got angry and said he wouldn't go there. I didn't want to upset him any more than he already was, so I let it drop. It doesn't appear he's running a temperature. His forehead wasn't warm to the touch. I'm going to have Dr. Worthington look at him tomorrow."

"It sure came on quick. He was fine when I saw him yesterday morning, and then it hit sometime in the afternoon. Completely wiped him out."

"In case he's contagious, stay out of his room. Until your arm is much better, it could cause a setback if you came down with something."

"I was only in there for a minute. Don't worry, I won't be going back to his room until it's been sanitized."

That was exactly my sentiment, but I might not be able to avoid it. "He mumbled something about dart guns. Are you using tranquilizing darts to capture the perpetrator that killed some of the guards?"

"No. Dart guns? Don't have a clue what he's talking about. Maybe he's delirious."

"He seemed rational, but that doesn't mean he was. Do you have a dart board or anything like that here?"

Newark shook his head. "We play sometimes at a bar."

"He might've been thinking about that. Did you make arrangements to have someone else be your eyes and ears while you're laid up?"

"Phil, a guard, has been keeping me informed."

"Then why did you venture out?"

"The woman Sean caught was carrying on—demanding to talk to Barton. Thought I'd see what the fuss was all about."

"The suspected killer is a woman?"

"She didn't act alone. Last night a guy was seen sneaking around, but the guards weren't able to catch him."

"Did Sean get the woman's name?"

"Marge something. He didn't get a last name before he got sick."

"Is anyone else questioning her?"

"Phil tried to get information out of her, but she won't talk."

"Did you hear what she was carrying on about?"

"Something about bugs invading us. It didn't make any sense."

Interesting, that he referred to the spiders as bugs. And, I was sure he knew exactly what Marge was talking about. "Sometimes women disclose more when they're questioned by another woman. Would you like me to talk to her?"

"No. We'll wait for Sheldon and Nate to get back."

"Was Sean sure she was guilty?"

"Yeah. There could be more than her and the guy that was spotted. The guards are walking the perimeter in case he returns or another intruder shows up."

I caught a whiff of smoke. "What's burning?"

"Nothing I know of."

I looked out the window. About twenty feet away, I saw an unconscious guard being dragged into the bushes and assumed Kendall was the assailant. The smell of smoke lingered in the air, but I couldn't see the source. "There's a fire someplace."

"I don't hear anyone running around. It can't be close."

"I'm going outside to check. I want to make sure you're safe in here."

I hurried out of the building and saw puffs of smoke coming from the direction Newark was headed in earlier. As I walked up the path, a guard sprayed water near the building I believed housed the lab. Next to him, another guard held a blowtorch that wasn't in use. I guessed someone had spotted a spider, maybe more, and it had been swiftly handled.

Farther along the path, two guards with pistols at the ready were stationed in front of a small building.

Reaching them, I asked, "Is the prisoner inside?"

"Yes. Nurse Anderson," the taller one replied. He didn't appear familiar. I figured he probably saw me, dressed in my nurse's uniform, with Worthington.

"Is she injured?" I asked, though I knew if Marge had been, those injuries would've healed quickly.

"Mr. Lange wrapped her hands because they sustained some kind of injury."

"Then she needs some medical attention. Open the door."

"We've been ordered not let anyone see the prisoner without contacting Mr. Newark first."

"He sent me, and right now he's probably sound asleep. But if you feel it's important to obtain verification, by all means call him."

The other guard nudged him and whispered something.

"No. That won't be necessary," said the taller guard, unlocking the door.

My mouth fell open when I saw Marge. Her wrists were chained to the arms of a metal chair, her ankles to its legs, and her hands completely wrapped in a heavy black material. Marge's hair was dirty and matted, her eyes red, and her clothes were soiled. Near the chair stood a small table with a water bottle. A straw stuck out of it.

"Is Alex aware of these deplorable conditions the prisoner is being held under?"

"He hasn't been here. Mr. Lange set it all up."

"This is intolerable. There isn't even a toilet in here, and being bound like that, she couldn't use it if there was one. I know Alex wouldn't approve. Has she even had anything to eat since she's been here?"

"We've been told not to feed her," the tall guard said in a meek tone.

"Locking the door, don't you think that would be enough to keep her inside?"

Neither guard responded.

I pointed toward Marge. "I want those chains removed."

Neither guard budged.

"Now!" I hissed.

The shorter guard fumbled in his pocket for a key ring.

I grabbed it from him. "I'll do it." I marched into the small building and bent down, preparing to unlock the chains, and then whispered to Marge, "Are these chains hooked to anything where spiders will be set free if I unlock them?"

"No," she murmured.

As the unlocked chains dropped to the floor, I began unwrapping Marge's hands.

"What's going on here?" A muscular guard stood in the doorway, a man I hadn't seen before.

"This prisoner needs medical attention, and I intend to provide it."

"Call Mr. Newark," the muscular guard said to another guard as he drew a weapon and pointed at me.

"Phil, that's Ms. Anderson."

"Call him," Phil snapped. He stared at me without lowering his weapon.

I turned away from him and continued removing the black thick material around Marge's hand. I whispered, "I'm going to pretend I'm asking you questions. Just mumble anything." My questions didn't make sense and neither did her answers.

"Mr. Newark wants to talk to you." Phil held up a cell phone.

"Don't do anything until I get back," I whispered to Marge. Then I took the phone from Phil and walked outside.

"Alex, you won't believe the deplorable conditions inside the building where Marge is held."

"What are you up to?" He sounded angry.

"I'm trying to help. She already answered a lot of my questions. All it took was a little kindness. Her last name is Harper. Did you know that Sean hit her, pounded her in the stomach? Men aren't supposed to hit women. What's wrong with him?"

"Susan, you've overstepped your boundaries. Come here. We need to talk."

"Listen Alex, you need to get a hold of Dr. Barton. Marge Harper was employed by Nathan Milner, and she was hired to kill someone by the name of Kalstein. I've never heard that name. Is he a member of the Fellowship?"

The airwaves became silent.

Wondering how he'd respond to the name Kalstein being mentioned and the accusation of Milner, I waited for him to say something.

"Did she say anything else?" he asked, the anger in his tone replaced with concern.

"That she'd rather be in the pen then chained up any longer in that building, and Nathan Milner assured her if she was caught at the compound, he'd make sure she got away. She might've answered those questions because he lied to her. If the guard hadn't interrupted me, I think she would've talked more. Is there anything you want me to ask her?"

"Yes. Ask her how she contacts Nate and how many others were hired by him. I'll have other questions if you can get her to answer those. In the meantime, since Sheldon isn't answering his cell phone, I'll attempt to contact him through an acquaintance."

"Alex, she has been very poorly treated. I think she might be more willing to answer those questions and others if she could get cleaned up a little and have something to eat. Also, I'd like to check her stomach. She moaned when I started feeling around where she said Sean hit her numerous times. Is there someplace I could take her where she could have a shower? And get her something to eat? "

"The two-story building on the other side of the path, there's a communal shower on the main floor. I'll have two guards go with you in case she decides to run off. Someone from the mess hall will deliver food. Let me talk to Phil."

I moved the phone away from my ear and looked at the muscular guard. "He wants to talk to you."

After I handed him the phone, I went back into the small building. "Ms. Harper," I said and winked at Marge, "I've made arrangements for you to have a shower. Come with me."

Marge slowly rose to her feet.

"Can you walk okay with your painful stomach, or would you like one of these guards to carry you?"

Taking my cue, Marge wrapped her forearms over her stomach. "I think I can manage." She gasped for air.

When she reached the doorway, I held onto her elbow and led her to the building across the path and up the stairs to the main floor with two guards following us. The first door we saw inside the building had a sign on it—"Women."

I held it open for Marge and walked in behind her. A row of showers, separated by floor-to-ceiling partitions, were against one wall. Sinks and bathroom stalls were across from them. On the far side, a bank of drawers with a stack of towels on top stood below a window.

Marge immediately stripped off her clothing and stepped into a stall and drew the shower curtain closed.

Listening to the splashing water, I rummaged through the drawers and found a clean triple-X t-shirt and a holey pair of coveralls that appeared to be large enough to fit a stocky man. Outside that, there were a couple of hairdryers, ribbons, hair clips, soap, and several bottles of shampoo.

"Marge, do you need any soap or shampoo?"

"Shampoo."

I pushed a bottle through the side of the shower curtain.

"Thanks."

I looked out the window. A guard paced below it.

As Marge stepped out of the stall, I handed her a towel.

"Oh, it feels so good to be clean." Her eyes dropped to her dirty clothing. "I'd rather walk around here with only a towel wrapped around me than put those back on."

I lifted up the t-shirt and coveralls. "I found these. They're clean, but pretty big."

She grabbed them. "I'll make them work."

In no time, Marge had on the makeshift outfit. The coveralls were rolled up. The t-shirt hung over them and cinched at the waist with a tied ribbon. The combo didn't look all that bad. She slipped on her shoes and then gathered up her soiled clothing and stuffed them into a garbage can in the corner of the room. She ran her fingers through her hair, attempting to get out the tangles. "That will have to do. Now what?"

"Haven't formulated a plan yet. If I get a chance, I'll call Kendall. There's some *venotrolia* in my car. I'll figure a way to get it to you. Todd is missing. Kendall thinks he's being held somewhere in the compound. That's another thing to work on. How were you caught?"

"A dart. It struck me in the shoulder from behind. I swung around to pull it out, but the drug was already in my system. As I sank to the ground, I spotted a man dressed in a compound security guard uniform holding a dart gun. His features were a blur. Then I woke up chained to the chair where you found me."

Wondering if the guard was mortal or a Tegen, Snyder or Blake, wearing a uniform, I asked, "Did Blake come and see you while you were held prisoner?"

"He looked in once but didn't say anything."

"Some food should be delivered soon. With the threat of spiders being set loose, we have to play this very carefully. A lot of innocent people live here, and I don't want to see any of them getting hurt."

I went out into the hallway with Marge.

"This way," the guard standing next to the door said and then escorted us to a room at the other end of the hall.

Inside stood a large, oval table surrounded by ten chairs. A covered tray sat on the table.

"That must be for you," I said to Marge.

She sank down in a chair, pulled the tray closer to her, and raised the lid. A piece of meatloaf, green beans, mashed potatoes and gravy, and a roll and butter covered a plate.

"Oh, this looks so good." Marge dug in.

I turned to the guard standing inside the doorway. "Can you watch her while I get some medicine?"

He nodded.

Not wanting to leave Marge alone very long, I hurried out of the building and jogged to my car. I quickly pulled out the thermos from underneath the driver's seat. In order to have enough room in my purse to conceal it, I ended up taking out the pistol and hiding it under the driver's seat where I had previously stashed the thermos.

The muscular guard named Phil stopped me on my way back to Marge. "Mr. Newark wants to see you."

I raised my purse. "I have some medicine in here for Marge Harper. Can I take that to her first?"

His eyes fixed on me.

"Let me call him," I said, taking out my cell phone.

Phil didn't move while I clicked on Newark's number.

"Alex, is it okay if I drop off some medicine to Marge Harper before I come see you?"

"Yes, but make it quick."

"I will." I disconnected. "He says I can take this to her first." I stepped around him and headed to the building where Marge was enjoying her first meal after her prolonged confinement.

When I reached Marge, I saw she had finished every morsel on her plate and was devouring the roll.

"I prepared the medicine for you," I said to her in front of the guard as I took the thermos out of my purse. "Drink it slowly. It should help with the stomach cramping." I tilted my head toward the guard. "Is there someplace she could lie down while I talk to Mr. Newark?"

"Need to check." He clicked on his walkie-talkie.

While he talked, I said softly to Marge, "If I'm not back before dark, do whatever you need to do to escape from here. Stay away from Blake."

"Huh?" A puzzled expression came over her face.

The guard spoke. "There's a room she can use a few doors down the hall."

I watched Marge take a sip of the *venotrolia*, and knew it wouldn't be long before she had her strength back.

I looked at the guard. "Will you be stationed in the hall?"

"Yes."

After Marge's experience in the compound's prison, I doubted he'd still be stationed there when I returned.

33

FALSE ACCUSATIONS

Phil was waiting for me outside the building. Without saying a word, he walked behind me all the way to Newark's apartment door. Opening it, I wondered why Newark had ordered him to keep track of me.

"Sit." Newark's eyes bored into me. He gestured toward the chair next to his bed, a bed he currently occupied.

Phil stood in the bedroom doorway.

Something definitely was amiss. "Alex, what's wrong?"

"What were you arguing with Sean about?"

"Huh?"

"Sean…when you saw him earlier…what was the argument about?"

I squinted. "Nothing that should upset you."

"What…was…it…about?" He enunciated every syllable of every word.

"Okay. He refused to see Dr. Worthington, and according to Dr. Worthington, he previously refused to have flu shots. We have no medical records for Sean Lange. I asked him if he was seeing another doctor, thinking I might be able to have him request the medical records so I could check them over. His current illness could be something serious, but he has no medical records. The man is against seeing any doctors. He can't even remember going to one since he was ten years old. Yes, I got mad at him. Really mad. I told him he was going to see Dr. Worthington tomorrow, if he wanted to or not, even if I had to hold him down on the bed. I take my medical oath very seriously, and I won't stand by and watch someone's health deteriorate without stepping forward. What did he do...complain to you that I snapped at him? I'd do it again. I might have to tomorrow if he still refuses to see Dr. Worthington. Dr. Barton has hired me to take care of the medical needs of members of the Fellowship. I haven't started that job yet, but I'm still working for Dr. Worthington, and he's the doctor for the compound." I rose to my feet. "Alex, what are you going to do...tell Dr. Barton to fire me before I start, because I nag when someone neglects their health like you were doing this morning—wandering up the lane when you should've stayed in bed?"

A smile crossed Newark's face. "Calm down, Susan." He patted the side of his bed, motioning for me to sit there.

I sat down on the edge of his bed and moved closer to him.

He put his arm around my shoulder. "I'm seeing a whole different side of you today. Here I thought you were a little timid." He chuckled. "Sean probably climbed out the window after you scolded him."

I raised my head and turned toward Newark. "What are you talking about?"

"Sean's gone. The guards in the hallway never saw him leave. His bedroom window is wide open."

"You thought I threw him out?"

"No, but one of the guards heard you arguing with him. I needed to know if that argument played a role in his disappearance."

"Sean isn't well enough to be going anywhere. I can't imagine him getting in his car and taking off just so he wouldn't have to see a doctor."

"Neither can I." Newark nodded toward Phil. "Get a couple of guys to check the grounds. He couldn't have gone far."

Phil turned and walked away. Newark's apartment door clicked shut.

"Why would Sean run off?"

"Beats me. Did you get any more answers from Marge Harper?"

"I asked her how she contacts Nathan Milner. She said she calls him or he calls her. His number is in her cell phone. It was taken from her when she was caught. She doesn't have the number memorized. So either a guard or Sean has her cell phone.

"She knows Nathan hired at least two other people. She thought it could be more. I asked her how she'd be paid. All those he hired would each receive $20,000 when Kalstein is dead. The killer would get $50,000."

"That's quite an incentive."

"Then she mentioned something about guns and other weapons, like Kalstein had some kind of an arsenal that Nathan Milner plans to take. There isn't anything like that here at the compound, so I couldn't figure out what she was talking about." I leaned on my elbow and looked at him. "Does any of that make sense to you?"

"No." His lips twitched and his eyes narrowed.

Newark sure didn't know how to lie like Conner. Conner maintains a poker face, showing no emotion at all each time he lies to me, no matter how deeply I pry or what I've seen to the contrary. "Did you ever get hold of Dr. Barton?"

"No. I've left messages a few places."

"Is there anything else you want me to ask her?"

"In case someone else has been using Nate's name, see if she can recognize him." He moved his arm from around my shoulders and picked up his cell phone from the night stand. "I'm going to send you three pictures. Have her pick out her employer." He clicked numerous times on his phone. "Sent."

As he laid the phone down, I glanced at the silver inlayed initials—A.N.—on the back of it and then stroked Newark's face. "When was the last time you took your pills?"

"This morning when you gave me one."

"That was a while ago, and I only gave you a pain pill, not the other one." I slid off the bed, tapped a pill from each bottle into my hand, and handed them to him along with glass of water. After he swallowed them, I said, "You need to get some sleep. I'll go and talk to Marge Harper."

"Be careful. Make sure a guard is close by. Criminals often become aggressive."

I knew he was talking from firsthand experience. "I'll be fine."

Walking up the path, I heard singing—not just children's voices but also adults—coming from the direction of the small chapel. Then

I recalled today was Sunday and worried about the worshippers. Crime, killings, and deception ran rampant in this place; it no longer possessed the mission behind the Fellowship of The Good Earth. I wondered if it would ever return to the tranquil, happy existence it had under the former leader, a religious man who invited everyone to join—no fences, no guns.

I passed two guards with pistols secured in holsters clearly visible, snapping me out of my contemplations.

Up ahead was the old barn. Gazing at it, I decided to take a quick detour to look inside for Todd. The double doors were locked and voices came from inside. I ducked back and forth behind bushes and zigzagged my way to the back of the structure. While turning off my cell phone, I scanned the exterior wall. The hayloft door stood open and slightly vibrated in the soft breeze. I glanced around. Not seeing anyone, I slipped off my shoes and scurried up the side of the barn. Once inside, I spotted a blanket stretched over a lump near the wall and, from what Snyder had said, figured it covered the remains of Fran Michaels. The task of getting her body out needed to wait until Todd had been freed and Blake captured. Since Snyder was missing, I assumed Kendall already had him.

"…won't come," Todd's voice echoed through the barn.

I crawled to the loft's ledge and peered down between scattered piles of hay.

A rope hung from the rafters. Todd's hands were tied to it and stretched over his head; his feet dangled a foot or so above the floor. In the corner sat Blake, eating from a food tray in front of him. A dart gun lay on the floor near his feet. I saw the number 12 boldly printed on its side, identifying it as the dart gun Kendall had given me, the one stolen from my room. Was Blake the thief or was it Snyder? Or maybe someone hired by one of them?

"Todd, you know he'll come for you. I'm prepared for that. Don't even need to be here when he shows up. Haven't you enjoyed our talks?"

"Can't say I have. Why do you want Kendall?"

"He treated me like shit in the brig. He needs to suffer for it."

My eyes drifted over the space, looking for some kind of a trap that could be set off. Nothing struck me as a possibility, but there was a dark heap in the corner opposite Blake. Could it be the preserved bodies, or did it hide some kind of trap? From my vantage point, I couldn't see the front double doors. I crawled backwards and started to move toward the ledge closer to the door. Right before my hand touched it, I saw a painted, black line running from the ledge to the wall. As I wondered if it meant anything, I remembered Blake's words outside the Tegen administration building, "Don't cross the line."

I inched away from the line and headed to the loft door. After scaling down the exterior wall, I put on my shoes, stepped away from the building, and walked to the path. There, I pulled out my phone, turned it on, and called Blake.

Hearing the sound of a cell phone ringing on the other side of the doors, I moved farther away.

"Hi, Sara."

"Hey. I'm at the compound. I've been visiting Alex, but he's fallen sound asleep. I talked to my Father earlier. He gave me some good news about the deal you want. I know you're busy but wondered if we could chat in person for a few minutes."

"Not now. How long you going to be at the compound?"

"Not sure. Alex wants me to have dinner with him later, but I haven't decided if I want to stay."

"I could meet you in two hours."

"Okay. I'll stick around then." There was a chance he already knew Marge was no longer chained, but in case he didn't, I had no intention of informing him. "Maybe I'll go to the chapel and listen to the singing for a while. My car's parked by the administration building. Can we meet there?"

"Sure. See ya." He disconnected.

I called Kendall.

"What?"

"Are you at the compound?"

"No."

"I got Marge peacefully out of the small building. Everything is cool. She's resting now. Blake's holding Todd in the old barn. He's going to meet me in a couple of hours."

"Why's he meeting you?"

"He's been led to believe I'm working on his pardon. Anyway, I could keep him busy while you free Todd."

"Can Marge help?"

"Guards are still watching over her. She's no longer bound and could easily escape, but I'm hoping we can avoid any more trouble at the compound. I don't like the possibility that innocent people could end up in harm's way."

"I can make it there in time. It'll be dark then."

"Blake has the barn rigged. I climbed in through the hay loft door and crawled closer to the front of the building. Then I saw a black line. Somewhere on the other side of it might be something that triggers whatever he has set up. Also, he has a dart gun, the one stolen from me. And that's how Marge was caught, being shot with a dart. The shooter wore a security guard uniform."

"A mortal?"

"She couldn't make out the face."

"Todd might know. Did you ask Newark about dart guns?"

"Yes. He doesn't know anything about them."

"He could've been lying."

"From his reaction, I doubt it."

After putting away my phone, I went to see Marge. As soon as I reached that building, I sensed something was wrong. I looked around the entrance, the bushes next to it, and along the side of the building. No guards in sight.

Fearing the dart gun shooter might be nearby, I inched the door open and peeked in. The place was eerily quiet. Feeling uneasy, I slowly moved toward the room where Marge should be. I came to an abrupt stop when I spotted a small red splotch on the floor. I bent down, touched the tip of a finger to my tongue to make it moist, and then ran my fingertip over the splotch. Smelling it, I knew it was regular blood, not tainted by a Tegen. My eyes swept over the floor as I continued down the hall, but I didn't see any more red marks.

I listened at her door and heard nothing. Snyder's condition would make him harmless. Blake was busy with Todd. There was nothing for me to fear on the other side of the door unless someone had either tranquilizer darts prepared to launch from a dart gun or a blowtorch. Staying concealed by the door, I cautiously opened it.

"Ms. Anderson, is that you?" Marge said.

I swung around the edge of the door and closed it behind me.

Marge appeared to be relaxed, stretched out on the bed with two pillows behind her head and her hands folded in her lap.

"What's happened here?"

"The guards have all been shot and hauled away. Thought about leaving but decided to wait and see if you showed up before dark."

"Who shot them?"

"Beats me. One gunman had on a security guard uniform. The others wore black, almost like body suits. After all the commotion, it's been quite pleasant here."

"Come on, Marge, give me more than that."

She waved a hand. "Okay, I owe you. I took a little snooze and woke up to yelling, pounding, and banging noises. Then I worried about the dart gun and needed an escape route. I looked out the window to see how many guards were close by. Earlier, one had been stationed right below the window and a few others walked around. The guards were all gone, but there were a couple of guys, dressed in black, carrying pistols with silencers on them. So I figured whatever was going down, they didn't want to draw any attention. And given that we know Kalstein deals in arms, I doubted it had anything to do with our mission. No reason to get involved." She splayed her fingers. "With these, I could handle any trouble that came my way, except darts." She nodded toward the door. "A muscular guy wearing a security guard uniform opened the door, looked at me, and then said to a man in black. "It's not her." Behind him, I saw a guard being dragged out. No one else opened my door until you did. But when everything became quiet, I looked out the window again. Didn't see anyone outside. Then I peeked out the door. No guards in the hallway. No bullet shells. No blood. No bodies. It didn't look like a battle zone. The guys must've cleaned up after them. Very tidy. Their moms would be proud."

Wondering if any members of the Fellowship had been caught in the gunfire, I asked, "Any idea where the building residents are?"

"At the chapel. Overheard two guards talking about it while I was eating. There's supposed to be some kind of a party in the mess hall after the services." She sat up and rubbed her forehead. "Newark, Tunell's alias, will probably think I played a role in the guards disappearing."

"Probably. To throw him off our mission, I told him you had been hired by Nathan Milner to kill Kalstein. He doesn't think I know Kalstein is Barton."

"I've never seen Nathan Milner."

"Newark doubts Milner has gone rogue but sent me three pictures. I'm supposed to have you identify which guy hired you.

Now it's a moot point since the guards have been killed, you won't be sticking around to have anyone question you."

"In case I get caught by a trigger happy dart gun enthusiast before I leave the compound, show me the pictures so I can reinforce your story."

I clicked on Newark's text message, brought up the first picture, and showed Marge the screen.

She squinted. "Blake?"

"He's new at the compound. Maybe that's why Newark thinks he hired you." I clicked to the next picture. "This is Milner. He's about six feet tall and a little on the thin side."

After Marge studied the picture, I clicked to the third one, curious if it was someone I knew at the compound. Seeing it, my eyes popped wide open, and I felt blood draining from my face.

"Who is it?" Marge asked, looking over my shoulder.

"Conner."

"Oh, he's dreamy. No wonder you don't want to give him up."

I had believed Newark bought all my lies. Now, I wasn't sure. How did he get Conner's picture? Did someone take it when Conner left my motel room? Does Newark know Conner's name? Questions kept buzzing through my head as I stared at the picture.

"Have you talked to Kendall about me?"

I glanced at my watch. "In about an hour, I'll be meeting Blake." Then I told her about the plan to free Todd.

"I'm going to the old barn. Maybe I can find what's rigged in there before Kendall shows up. He might need my help."

"Wish I had a cell phone to give you, but I only brought one with me."

"I know where Kendall enters the compound. I'll find him after I've searched the loft."

34

NO TRACES LEFT

Wanting to find out how much Newark knew about Conner, I headed toward his apartment. The path seemed deserted. No guards roamed around. Singing continued coming from the direction of the chapel. I figured some of the guards were hanging around there. I still couldn't get over how some Fellowship members thought the compound was a wonderful place to live—like Beth—while others found it to be a prison—like Ashley and Kyle. I knew they wouldn't be enjoying the singing or the party planned in the mess hall. They'd probably be dead if they hadn't escaped.

Rustling of leaves in the windless day and pounding of feet on the hard ground caught my attention. I glanced over my shoulder. No one was behind me. My eyes swept around. I spotted a man moving between the buildings a distance from me. Wondering why he hadn't taken the path, I ducked behind some bushes, hidden from the man's line of sight. As he came closer to the building that housed Newark's apartment, I saw it was Blake and watched him enter the building. Maybe he didn't know Snyder wasn't in his room and intended to visit him. Or had he just heard that Snyder was missing and planned to talk to Newark about it. With the guards patrolling the hallway, would they let him in Newark's apartment? If what Snyder had told me was true about Blake, the only way Blake could keep the Tegen

Council believing Snyder had committed all the crimes would be to silence him. He had to burn him in order to make that happen. Maybe Blake was worried. Snyder going missing could quash his plan.

Mulling that over in my head, I continued toward the main entrance.

The front of the building seemed deserted, like the path. Not one guard was within eyesight. I slowly opened the door and listened for voices and movement. Silence reigned inside. Remaining shielded by the door in case Blake was armed with the dart gun, I peered into the empty hallway. Prepared to enter, I suddenly heard running footsteps and closed the door. I leapt from the porch, dashed behind a bush, and waited, expecting someone to come charging out.

Five minutes later, I emerged and made my way to Newark's window. It stood ajar. I scaled the wall and looked in. The bed had been stripped down to the mattress. Trying to figure out what was going on, I pushed the window up and climbed in. I glanced around the room, looking for signs of a struggle. Everything seemed orderly, but the bedding was nowhere in sight. I went to his closet to check the hamper. All his clothing was gone. I searched through his drawers. Empty. I wandered through his apartment. The place was completely devoid of any of his personal belongings, and it appeared everything had been cleaned. Had Newark learned about Kalstein's untimely death and taken off? Or had the men in black, the ones Marge saw, played a role in Newark's disappearance like what happened to the guards stationed to keep track of her? If that was the case, I suspected Conner was involved, especially since Newark had a picture of him.

I edged open the door that led to the hallway. Not seeing anyone, I hurried to Snyder's apartment. His bed had also been stripped. His clothing and personal items gone. His fridge empty. But the apartment wasn't left in the same pristine condition as Newark's. I figured Kendall had removed everything that could possibly have a trace of Tegen blood or venom on it.

I went upstairs to check out Kalstein's apartment. There were three apartments on that floor. They all looked ready for new occupants. No personal items were in any of them. I glanced at my watch. Seeing it was almost time to meet Blake, I rushed down the stairs, out the back door, and walked at a brisk pace away from the building. Then I headed to the pathway and strode toward the meeting spot.

Blake was leaning against my car. "Where have you been?" he asked in a suspicious tone.

"Visiting Marge. She's being held in the building across from the place where I found her shackled."

"Is she chained to anything?"

"No," I said and then began my lies with a little truth blended in. "She's resting comfortably on a bed. They've feed her, but she's still weak and needs *venotrolia*. I'll bring her some tomorrow."

"Why hasn't she escaped?"

"We're thinking that Snyder, whoever he is, might try to get to her. Kendall's keeping track outside. Since you won't tell us who he is, it's the best we can do for now."

"Did she mention me?"

"Yeah. She said you saw her in the makeshift prison but didn't say anything."

"I intended to do something after I got the okay from the council on the pardon."

"Father has another council member lined up to vote 'Yes' on it. He still needs to talk to your father. Do you think he would object?"

"No. No. He'll easily go for it."

"I don't know when the council is going to meet about it, but I'll give you a call when I hear. Have you got any idea where Snyder is holding Todd?"

"Yes, but I'm not saying anything until that pardon is finalized."

The acrid smell of smoke floated through the air. An alarm blared.

I turned around and saw a black cloud of smoke coming down the path. I ran toward it with Blake right next to me.

When I came closer to the barn, I saw flames shooting out of its roof. A crowd had gathered, and men were running around with hoses, spraying water.

Thinking Blake had rigged up the place to burn if an intruder entered, I yelled at him. "You…you…you're burning them! What Snyder told me about you is true!"

He grabbed my arm. "You know what I've done. Wanting to meet with me was just to get me away. Let's see if you burn as easily as Darwin." He pulled me toward the flames.

I scratched and kicked him.

A shot rang out. People screamed and hurried into a nearby

building.

Blood oozed from Blake's shoulder, but he continued yanking me toward the barn.

Then suddenly he released his hold and snatched a dart protruding from his other arm. Worried I might be the next dart victim, I ran away from Blake.

"Sara," a female voice shouted.

I looked over my shoulder and saw Marge, carrying a dart gun, sprinting after me. I stopped and waited for her to catch up. "Are Kendall and Todd okay?"

"Yes. Kendall started the fire."

"Why?"

"When he cut the rope holding Todd, spiders emerged from every corner. Only Kendall had a disk. No way we could gather them all up before some got out. There was no other option."

"Where are Kendall and Todd now?"

She closed her eyes and lowered her head.

"Are they in the barn?"

Marge raised her chin and hesitantly said, "No, but we can't save the rest of the spiders here."

"Marge, what's wrong?" Then I saw Kendall, carrying a blowtorch, on the other side of the fence and pointing the flame toward the compound, engulfing the back of a building.

"He can't burn down this place. People live here. Innocent people." I moved toward a hose wrapped around a fire hydrant.

Marge gripped my wrist. "Stop, Sara. There's no other choice. After he got the fire going in the barn, Kendall took off to see if other clusters of spiders had been let loose—like Snyder had warned—but now we know it was Blake. Kendall found some near the back entrance of that building," she said, nodding toward the burning building. "And some crawling out of the lab building."

I swung around to look at the lab building. Flames were shooting out the door. Then I looked at the building where the people had gone. It was intact, and I doubted they knew about the other fires. "I need to warn the residents," I said as the small structure next to me ignited in flames.

"Sara, there are probably spiders loose in that building too."

"Even if there are, some might not have been bitten yet. Come on, help me get them out." I charged down the path toward the building where the residents had gone.

I pushed the door open and yelled, "Three buildings are burning. Get out of the compound!"

The adults sat at rows of tables; some held crying babies. Children played on the other side of the room. None of the adults budged.

I gestured toward the door. "Go, go, before the flames and smoke make it impossible."

A woman near me said, "We've had fires here before. Some of our members are trained to put them out. It's better if we stay here—out of their way."

"This isn't like the other fires. Three, now maybe four, buildings are burning. Hurry, you all need to go."

Still, no one budged.

I stepped out to see if more buildings were enflamed. Black smoke and flying ashes drifted through the air. Flames were shooting out of the backs of more buildings, and a dark, murky haze began to enclose the path. I went back inside the building and grabbed the spokesperson's arm. "Come see. This is worse. You're going to burn in here if you don't get out now."

As I began pulling her, two men rose from the table and came to her aid.

"Ms. Anderson," one said. He had a bandaged head and I recognized him as a patient of Worthington's. "I know you mean well, but we've been instructed to remain inside if a fire should break out in another building. Dr. Barton or Mr. Newark will send someone if we need to leave this building."

"But Dr. Barton isn't at the compound, and Mr. Newark is laid up from a bad shoulder injury." I didn't want to tell him that Newark had disappeared. "There isn't anyone to warn you but me."

"Don't worry, Mr. Newark will still send someone even if he can't warn us personally." He motioned toward an empty chair. "Please join us." He looked at a man standing next to him. "Mark, why don't you lead us in some songs while we wait for the all clear alarm?"

"But you'll die here." Frustrated, I said, "Let me at least get the children out of here."

"We'll all be fine." He gave me a warm smile.

Feeling helpless and not knowing what else to say to the devoted followers, I headed out the door. As I walked through the smoke, I heard singing, and then footsteps trailed behind me.

"Susan," a woman yelled.

I turned and saw Beth, carrying an infant, hurrying toward me. "We'll go with you."

I hugged her and the baby as I wondered about her boyfriend. "What can I say to the rest to get them to leave?"

"Nothing. You said all you could."

"Your baby?"

"No. Vivian, a member, wanted me to get Lucy out. Viv won't leave her husband."

"Did you see any spiders in the mess hall?"

"No. No. And don't mention spiders. That's all Josh talks about. He believes they're going to make him rich. Whoever heard of anything so silly? I couldn't take it any longer, and we broke up."

"Did Josh stay in the mess hall?"

"No. He went with Dr. Barton someplace. I hope I never see him again."

Since he was with Kalstein, he probably ended up with the same fate. I figured Beth would get her wish—he'd never be seen again.

We continued down the path with flames beginning to devour the buildings on both sides. The front of the structures still looked intact while smoke rose from the windows. I didn't see anyone trying to put out the fire.

Beth pointed behind us. "Here come some more."

I looked and saw over a handful of people—three children, two women, one holding a baby, and one man. Even if I couldn't save everyone, at least these people might survive.

The ash and soot became thicker, and the crackling sounds of buildings caving in grew louder. The smoke began to irritate my eyes and lungs. "We need to hurry." I lifted up the bottom of my blouse and covered my nose and mouth. The others did the same. I took the hand of a child while her mother held the baby tighter, shielding him from the smoke.

We all picked up the pace.

The sound of a roaring engine came through the billowing smoke. A second later, I saw a black Escalade. The driver's door flew open. Andy stepped out. "Get in," he said to everyone as he opened all the car doors.

We piled in.

With no place to turn around, Andy backed down the path at a fast speed. The black, dense smoke didn't seem to be a problem for him.

As he went past my car, I saw flames approaching it. Explosions echoed around us. The babies cried, and the children hugged their parents. Sirens screeched.

When we reached the parking lot, the Escalade was doused with a blanket of running water. Firemen stood at each side, spraying it. Then they moved away and directed their nozzles toward the burning compound. Fire engines and emergency vehicles were spread around us.

Two other firemen opened the doors. Everyone climbed out of the car and stared at the spiraling fire, flames spiking high in the air and smoke spreading for miles. One of the firemen bombarded us with questions about the people still inside—How many? Is there another way out? Any protective underground shelter?

As he spouted out questions, I wanted to make sure no spiders had made it through the smoke with us and pulled my disk out of my purse. Holding it against my side, out of view, I pushed down the black button and looked for spiders.

I continued pushing down the button, but no spiders appeared. Some medical personnel came over and started checking everyone. When the babies, children, their mothers, and Beth were loaded into ambulances, and I felt confident no one had accidently carried out a spider—either in their clothing or hair, I put away the disk.

Watching the ambulances drive away, I thought about the small flock, nine people, I had talked into leaving and wondered how many of their loved ones had perished. Anger surged through me, knowing Kendall had done nothing to rescue the people before sending the compound up in flames. And neither Marge nor Todd did anything that would've saved some lives.

I felt sad and disgusted. The Tegens I had spent so much time with over the past few weeks, whom I trusted, lacked any true humanity. Tears drizzled down my cheeks. Precious innocent lives had been lost here, and I couldn't think of anything I could've done to prevent it.

Wiping away the tears, I went over to Andy and asked, "Can you take me to my motel?"

He looked at me. "Yes, Ms. Jones." He opened the passenger door, and I slid in.

As he drove around the emergency vehicles, I stared at the burning compound. "Besides the group you picked up, do you know if others made it out?"

"A few in the main house. Outside that, unless people climbed over the fence, no one else escaped the fire."

I didn't want to see or talk to Kendall or the other team members. There was nothing they could say that justified their indifference to the people who had lived at the compound. When Andy pulled into the motel parking lot, I asked, "Can you wait here while I get my things and then take me to Conner's hotel?"

"Yes."

Getting out of the vehicle, I automatically looked at the spot where the blue truck usually parked. It was empty.

Within fifteen minutes, I had gathered up all my belongings, including the *venotrolia* in the fridge and my spiders. I stepped outside and closed the door to my motel room for the last time.

At the Amara, Conner's hotel, Andy carried my suitcase and escorted me to Conner's suite. To my surprise, two bodyguards stood by it. Did that mean he was already back from his business trip?

A guard opened the door for me, and I went inside. I looked around and felt disappointed that I didn't see Conner. Hoping he'd be here sometime during the night, I wanted to wash away the smell of smoke that clung to every inch of me.

Before I showered, I sat down at the desk in the suite and called Father. When he answered, I said, "It's over. Snyder was a killer, but Blake was the one that murdered the Tegens in Florida."

"Kendall called earlier. We know about Blake. Snyder has been punished there. Blake will be handled here. You've completed your sentence."

"The fugitive Tegens were caught, but this didn't go down well. I'm angry and enraged with Kendall. A lot of innocent people lost their lives."

"What happened?" he asked with concern evident in his voice.

"I'm not up to talking about it yet. I'll tell you when I see you."

"When are you coming home?"

"Well...Conner wants me to go on a trip with him. I want to do that."

"Then, my darling girl, you should."

"I love you, Father."

"I love you too, Sara. Don't ever forget that."

"I won't."

As I disconnected, I noticed the corner of a cell phone sticking out from underneath a notepad. Conner never went anywhere without his phone. I pulled it out, and my eyes fixed on the engraved, silver initials—A.N. Since Conner had Newark's phone, there was no doubt left in my mind that the man in charge of the team that killed Carol's parents was dead. He had joined Kalstein, and he'd never be seen again.

After putting the phone back where I found it, I looked at the soot on my clothing and the vision of all the innocent people sitting around tables at the compound flashed into my head. The innocent people I couldn't motivate to leave. A dreadful sadness rolled over me for the lost lives while anger toward Kendall and his team still churned inside me.

Hoping to calm my emotions, I headed to the bathroom, stripped, and stepped into the shower. The water cascaded down my body. I closed my eyes, tilted my head, and felt the warm water running over my face. The shower door creaked open and then arms wrapped around me. I swung around and buried my face in Conner's chest. He held me tighter and stroked my hair.

"A bad night?"

"The worst." I looked up and gazed into Conner's eyes. "I want to go away with you."

"Can you?"

"Yes. We can leave whenever you're ready."

He smothered my lips with his as the water washed away the horrors of the day. "You are the love of my life, Sara."

Even though I possessed Tegen abilities, I felt safe and secure in Conner's mortal arms, and at that moment, all I wanted was to forget everything else and just be with him. "I love you." I pulled his head closer and kissed him.

ABOUT THE AUTHOR

Inge-Lise Goss, an award-winning author, was born in Denmark, raised in Utah, and now lives in the foothills of Red Rock Canyon with her husband and their dog, Bran. She spends most of her time in her den writing stories. There, with her muse by her side, her imagination has no boundaries, and her dreams come alive. When she's not pounding away on the keyboard, she can be found reading, rowing, or trying to perfect her golf game, which she fears is a lost cause.

www.Inge-LiseGoss.com

www.ingramcontent.com/pod-product-compliance
Lightning Source LLC
Chambersburg PA
CBHW071118170626
46809CB00002B/412